THE ~~DEARING DO OUTS~~

*Volume One*

*Also by David Wake*

**NOVELS**
I, Phone

**NOVELLAS**
The Other Christmas Carol

**ONE-ACT PLAYS**
Hen and Fox
Down the Hole
Flowers
Stockholm
Groom

## THE DERRING-DO CLUB

*and the*

# Empire of the Dead

## David Wake

**WATLEDGE BOOKS**

First published in Great Britain by
**Watledge Books**
Copyright © 2013 David Wake

This paperback edition 2013
1

ISBN-10: 1492727040
ISBN-13: 978-1492727040

Cover art by Smuzz
www.smuzz.org.uk

*For*
*ArmadaCon*

This adventure of the Deering-Dolittle sisters takes place after they have been sent to the Eden College for Young Ladies, which is in Switzerland near the Austro-Hungarian border.

# CHAPTER I

## <u>Miss Deering-Dolittle</u>

It was during Latin that the Austro-Hungarians arrived with their dogs and zombies to kill everyone at the Eden College for Young Ladies. As the lesson started with the conjugation of 'amo', Miss Earnestine Deering-Dolittle lifted her skirts and crossed the threshold into the East Wing. This forbidden zone was protected by a thick rope spanning the wide corridor, an 'Out Of Bounds' sign and - strongest of all - Miss Hardcastle's long lecture during assembly about expulsion: the shame such a punishment would inflict upon their families and the commensurate decline in the marriage prospects of the disgraced young lady.

"And, girls, I have turned off the heating."

Earnestine's breath condensed in the still air. She longed to be expelled: she could bear the shame and didn't give two hoots for marriage; after all, she'd read Mary Wollstonecraft's *A Vindication of the Rights of Woman*. However, she would never be able to bring herself to explain such appalling disobedience to her two younger sisters, Georgina and Charlotte. Indeed, that very morning she had given her two siblings a very stern lecture about the necessity of controlling their curiosity: they were here to study and not to go exploring.

It had been Earnestine's burden as the eldest sister to cut the trail for them to follow. She knew she was well suited with her sharp, angular features and her pragmatic common sense. Georgina was the beautiful one, with a lovely round face that far was too trusting, and Charlotte was simply pretty and frivolous. They were both so naïve: their looks, or others' reactions to their looks, insulated them from the ways of the world.

So, she had raised her finger and had said, clearly and firmly: "No more adventures!"

It was dark and mysterious in the East Wing, but Earnestine had come prepared with both a dark lantern and her trusty Misell Electric Device. The latter was known as a 'flashlight', which was both its name and its instructions. She flicked it on for a moment, and then let the yellow light go out. To keep it lit continuously would be to drain the battery. Her father had bought the almost magical object back from a visit to New York, where all the policemen had been given one by the American Electrical Novelty and Manufacturing Company.

Once she felt she was deep enough in the forbidden zone, Earnestine used a Bryant and May safety match to light the dark lantern. As soon as it had flared into life, she slid the shutter down to create a narrow beam of illumination. Even so, she kept her lamp as carefully shielded as she could, so as not to be seen, but her hand could not contain the light any more than her mind could grasp her reasons for this reconnoitre.

She was not, under any circumstances, going 'up the river', but her thoughts meandered, which would not do at all. Put simply, she was a Prefect investigating an incident before reporting it, that was all, and it mattered not a jot that it involved the new Gardener's Hand, a mere youth, who would insist upon greeting her every morning as she crossed the quad.

"Good morning, Miss Earnestine," he said in his thick Germanic accent.

It was intolerable. For goodness sake: she was the eldest, so the proper greeting was 'Miss Deering-Dolittle'.

And he was only a gardener, less than a proper gardener, and also a presumptuous oik. She wouldn't even have known he'd been bundled towards the East Wing by his fellow gardeners, if she hadn't been looking out for him. There seemed to have been a lot of gardeners hired recently. Hopefully, they'd give him the good thrashing he deserved for his attempts to consort with the girls; rightly so, for how irritatingly he murdered his vowels, how jolly grating was his endearing smile, how sparkling his bright blue eyes, how tousled his dark hair, how tall he stood and-

Earnestine stopped still and, in a heartbeat, determined to do the right thing and go straight back to the Prefect's Room.

As Earnestine crept on, shafts of flickering yellow from her lamp played across the moulded plaster ceiling and along the oak panelling, chasing shadows as she went deeper into the maze of the East Wing.

Her trail followed a sound long before Earnestine realised there was anything to hear. It was hard to make out: a distant choir perhaps, fractured and disjointed, sometimes silent, and beguiling. The damp brickwork funnelled the echoes up through the chimneys and dumbwaiters from below. She stopped and listened, heard nothing more; she shook her head to clear it of any wild imaginings.

This was stupid: Miss Hardcastle would give her lines if she found out. *I must not explore*, a thousand times. *I must not explore*, she repeated to herself, a thousand times, *I must not explore*. It was a mantra now, something that had lost all meaning, for her footsteps took her further along the passageway to the stone steps that led to the basement as if drawn down by distant baritone sirens. She knew her way around the East Wing having explored (not 'explored', 'wandered', that was a better word)... wandered through every nook and cranny when she first arrived at the Eden College for Young Ladies. It had always been dark, even when the summer meant it was 'in bounds'.

Except there had been lights the other night as there had been for over a week at least, so the Family Curse had reared its head and up the river she went... no, no! She was stronger than that.

*I must not explore, I must not explore.*

She swapped the lamp to her left hand as her right cramped. Having exhausted the delights of English, French and Latin, she'd have to scrawl the repetitions in Greek next.

At least Georgina and Charlotte weren't affected. Earnestine was thankful for that. If she could keep them safe from the wanderlust, then she would consider she had done her job. Let Miss Hardcastle catch her, let her have five hundred lines - a thousand - just so long as her sisters didn't find out. Any penance was worth that. She'd give herself lines when she returned to the school proper.

*Keep them safe,* mother had said, *no exploring, no trouble, no adventures.*

Voices, without question: still distorted by the echoes and full of hard, sharp consonants. There were Slavic, German or one of those other harsh Latin-less languages that grated as much as romantic French poetry when droned by girls who didn't know the meaning of the stanzas.

Earnestine froze: aware of her lamp swinging vast shadows across the wall and sending its beam forward.

Closer now, she could distinguish more than one voice, each heavy, deep and jolly definitely male.

"Es ist kalt."

"Ja."

Eden College for Young Ladies boasted three male members of staff: a Mathematics Professor, a Caretaker and a Gardener, but none of those doddery old gentlemen ever had a stamp as heavy or a voice as deep. They must be those extra Gardeners, all gathered together in the forbidden East Wing.

*I must not explore,* thought Earnestine, craning her head around the corner.

The room beyond had been emptied of all its academic trumpery and instead a card table and some chairs had been set up. Three men gathered around.

The one facing her had buck teeth and his colleague was a small man, probably smaller than Earnestine herself. A third man, bulkily built and wearing a hat indoors, paced, stamping his feet again to keep his circulation going. For all the world, they looked like giant toy soldiers having a tea party while they waited for their tale of adventure to begin, and it reminded Earnestine of *Alice's Adventures in Wonderland*: the March Hare, the Dormouse and the pacing Mad Hatter, except that instead of cucumber sandwiches, the table was covered in discarded playing cards from an abandoned hand of whist or bridge... or one of those salacious gambling games.

Behind her: a cough.

Earnestine spun round - a fourth man was so close that she had to step back. Chairs scrapped loudly as the other men stood.

This new man in front of her was young, perhaps in his mid-twenties, with the beginnings of black stubble that shadowed his features and made his bright eyes sparkle. It was the Gardener's Hand, cutting a dashing figure in a bizarre uniform.

"Wer sind Sie?"

"Was ist das?"

"Mühe!"

"Excuse me," said Earnestine, "but I think you should explain yourselves - at once!"

She stood her ground, chin up, shoulders back, defiant.

"Es ist ein der Mädchen."

"I would trouble you not to speak in that appalling... whatever it is, and answer me directly."

"Was machen wir?"

"Do any of you speak English?" Earnestine rounded on the company, taking them all in. "Do you speak English, Eng-*lish!* Parlez-vous français? Operor vos narro Latin?"

"I speak the English," said the Gardener's Hand.

Earnestine turned on him. He smiled - damned impertinence - and Earnestine felt her resolve softening inexplicably. Not that she intended to show that, of course: "Would you care to explain yourself, Sir."

"My... friends and I are playing a little card game to pass the time."

"I can see that! And clearly you thought dressing up in military costume was part of card playing. Perhaps I didn't make myself clear: what are you *men* doing in my *girls'* school?"

They honestly looked crestfallen.

"You may well be the March Hare, Mad Hatter, Dormouse and the..." Earnestine ran out of characters around the table at the Tea Party and looked to the young man's amused smile for inspiration: "Cheshire Cat, but-"

Gunshots sounded from above, accompanied by barking dogs.

"Was ist das?"

"Ich erklärte Ihnen, dass ich etwas gehört habe."

"Wo ist Hans?"

"English and answer the question."

The March Hare went over to the corner and pulled out some rifles wrapped in rags, which he handed to the others.

"Haben Sie Ihren Revolver?"

"Ja!" said the Gardener's Hand. He took out a revolver from a holster hidden beneath his coat, flipped it open to check it was loaded, and then tucked it back beneath his layers.

"Ich sollte das überprüfen."

"Konnten Sie gesehen werden?"

"All this show... excuse me, I am speaking!"

"Nein, aber wir müssen gehen."

"Und die Kinder?"

"Wir können nichts anders; die Zukunft von Europa ist in Frage."

The Gardener's Hand pointed at the glaring Earnestine: "Und sie?"

"Was!?"

"Wir nehmen sie mit uns."

"Wir können das nicht."

"Wir lassen sie nicht," said the Gardener's Hand standing directly in front of the tallest.

"Wir können sie nicht mitnehmen. Gehen wir."

"Wir können sie nicht verlassen."

There was a stand-off now between the Gardener's Hand and the others: the Cheshire Cat looking up to the bigger, older and well-built Mad Hatter, but the Cheshire Cat dominated.

"This is all jolly fascinating, I'm sure, but-"

"You are coming with us," said the Gardener's Hand.

"I most certainly am not," Earnestine said.

"I am afraid you must."

"Who are you to be giving orders?"

"I am..." He looked at the others briefly. "Pieter."

"Well, Mister, I don't care if you are Peter the Great, I am not-"

He looked over her shoulder: "Metz."

Earnestine was seized from behind, a greatcoat thrown over her, and they bundled her backwards. As she struggled defiantly, she lost her footing and dropped the lantern; it clattered away, its light useless in the enforced, suffocating darkness. Her boots struck it a few times. Her hand found her flashlight, which she held like a baton, but her arms were pinned so it too slipped from her fingers. She kicked out, some of her attacks found their mark, but the thick material was smothering, overpowering, all encompassing...

...*I must not explore, I must not explore...*

# Miss Georgina

Georgina could see distant figures moving towards the college in an arrow formation. They were dark shapes against the virgin snow like a daguerreotype negative of Miss Price's screeched chalk didactics on the blackboard. She longed to be out there, or indeed anywhere, instead of being trapped in the airless sepia dungeon of Classroom 5.

"Again!"

Georgina joined in the monotone: "Amo, amas, amat, amamus, amatis, amant..."

It was a lovely day, or had been before the grey clouds rolled over the distant mountains, and the time should have been spent striking out amongst the peaks and valleys on a long, bracing walk, but the School Rules were very clear on the matter: girls were not to exert themselves. They had to stay indoors in an ever diminishing Bastille as the Principal, Miss Hardcastle, strove to save on heating. Everyone knew that Miss Hardcastle would rather squirrel away their fees in a local bank than stock up the coal bunker. Classes were now forced to cram together in one half of the sprawling building as the entire East Wing had been abandoned early.

Through the ice crystal-etched window and across the quad, Georgina saw the supposedly dark windows of the forbidden wing. There had been a light, she was sure of it, just before that huge shadow had travelled over the school accompanied by the whirring sound of... who knew what? Certainly something like a firefly had flitted from window to window on the ground floor. The East Wing was occupied; she was sure of it. Before first bell, she and her sisters had gathered in the ski locker room and Georgina had told the others of her observations: the lights, the smoke and the ice melting from the eaves - all sure signs of occupation. All the girls had been in class, she'd pointed out, and all the teachers never left the roaring fire in the staff room.

But Earnestine had told her not to be silly: Oh Georgina, how foolish, the caretaker must check for leaks in the roof and needs a light to see his way; he must check the chimneys, hence the smoke, and, finally, did she not realise that the sun does melt ice. The East Wing was 'Out of Bounds' and that's all there was to it.

Georgina had looked to Charlotte for support.

Charlotte had beamed with pleasure at being included in the discussion and had said: "Do you think soldiers polish their buttons every day?"

Charlotte - oh, honestly.

If only she could get out, Georgina thought: somewhere else, anywhere else, anywhere at all.

Outside, the men were closer, tearing up the white landscape as if scrawling black marks across an empty page. They reached the border of the college and filed through the stone archway into the quad. Behind them, shambling through the snow, were numerous other figures like an approaching army.

Miss Price thwacked Georgina on the back of her hand to snap her attention back to the lesson. The other girls giggled until Miss Price's angry scowl raked the classroom.

"Miss Georgina," Miss Price said, "do pay attention."

"Miss?"

"And?"

Georgina panicked: "And, Miss?"

"The third person second participle?"

"The third person... of..."

"Amo?"

"Oh, yes, Miss, am, er...um?"

Miss Price sucked on her teeth and then tutted, an angry explosive sound that was her habit.

"Am*erum*, a novel conjugation, certainly," said Miss Price. The rest of the class giggled at their teacher's wit. "Honestly, Georgina, you are an utter disappointment. Your mind wanders like the tributaries of... what was that river your father and mother went up: the Nile, the Amazon?"

"Miss, it was-"

"I wish..." Miss Price searched her mind for the most cutting remark possible and, with an unerring accuracy, she found the most apposite phrase: "...you were more like your sister?"

Georgina's face burned more than the back of her hand. She wanted to see Miss Price dead. She knew to which sister the Latin harridan was referring and it wasn't Charlotte. Charlotte was silly, Charlotte was foolish, Charlotte was... never even expected to emulate the oh-so-wonderful eldest. Everything Georgina did was measured against the yardstick of the perfect Miss Deering-Dolittle, Earnestine, who never did anything wrong; whereas Georgina was always considered lacking.

"Julietta."

"Amazo, *amazon*... sorry Miss - I was a little lost. I mean, amo, amas, amat, amamus, amatis, amant."

"Very good, Julietta."

Julietta beamed a smile just for Georgina.

It was so unfair, because it had been Charlotte whose action had led to their incarceration in this Swiss-bordered prison, and yet somehow it was Georgina's fault for not keeping an eye on the wayward child. The responsibility was surely the faultless Miss Deering-Dolittle's: after all, it had been her idea to delegate. But the blame had landed on Georgina, who was such a disappointment: the older Earnestine had even gained credit for having the fortitude to bear the indignities heaped upon her by her younger sisters.

The problem was that no-one understood how much worse life was for the middle sister of three: Earnestine had that bearing and deportment that came naturally to one with such a regal, elegant appearance, and Charlotte had blonde prettiness on her side, but Georgina knew that she was dumpy with a round, blank face. She was the one who would be passed over when it came to marriage.

Miss Price marched between the desks to the front and began stabbing the Latin word for 'love' with her long rule.

A pellet of paper struck Georgina from behind and when she turned round, several of the other girls were pulling faces. Georgina ignored them and tried to concentrate on the board instead, but her gaze was drawn back to virgin snow before Miss Price reached the first person plural.

When the first group reached the College buildings, men split off to go left and right around the building. Georgina continued to watch as the distant majority, a mass that lurched forward with a strange mix of marching and stumbling, negotiated the stone archway into the grounds. There were dogs too, great barking beasts that strained at their leashes with a wild ferocity.

In the first group, the lead figure, striding ahead, looked by his bearing like an officer. He pulled off his leather gloves, gathered them together and then slapped his palm before glancing up: Georgina caught sight of his aquiline features, dark moustache and saturnine beard. She jerked back like any guilty schoolgirl and when she leant forward again, her breath freezing on the pane and creating a complex craquelure of ice, he had vanished from view.

"...amant," said Miss Price.

Somewhere in the distance, a bell jangled for attention and Georgina heard barking and male voices.

Glancing across to the East Wing, Georgina saw that light again and this time it was joined by another.

There was pounding on the front door and she heard the Caretaker's voice, shouting and then subdued. It couldn't have been the Caretaker in the East Wing then, Georgina realised, could it, because he couldn't be in two places at once? She'd tell Earnestine and that would show her, the pompous-

There was a sharp crack, like a distant shot.

"Georgina!"

Georgina snapped her head round to study the conjugation of 'amo'.

"The third person second participle is?"

Georgina was saved by a commotion outside the room.

"Wait here, page fifty two onwards," said Miss Price. She went outside, ready to vent her spleen at the girls responsible for the noise; however, she returned forthwith. "Girls, we're wanted downstairs. Girls!"

The class rose quickly, eager to be away from Latin, and began filing out.

"Leave that!" Miss Price commanded: "Hurry along now!"

At the top of the stairs, Georgina saw the other classes gathered below in the hallway with a group of officers. There was a barking dog and some strange shambling men. Miss Hardcastle was arguing with them, but they seemed adamant. Charlotte would probably be able to identify them as Dragoons or Fusiliers or-

Oh my giddy aunt!

Charlotte was not with her class. The stupid girl had wandered off - just typical, absolutely typical. Didn't the silly thing hear any of the taunts and jibes from the other girls? Earnestine wasn't there either. She was probably searching for Georgina, armed with disapproving looks, to ask why Georgina had lost Charlotte - again.

The man-in-charge was shouting: "All of you in the library! All, I say!"

Georgina tarried, knowing just where to slip out of line and down a side corridor to the back stairs.

A voice shouted after her, mocking: "Off exploring!" It was Julietta, smiling in that sweet and irksome manner.

The others joined in: "Amazo, Amazon, I'm-a-spot, am-as-gone, am-as-lost, as-an-ant?"

Georgina turned back: "Don't be so childish."

"Derring-do, derring-do…"

"Drop dead."

"Oooh…" but one of the teachers shuffled the line along and Georgina slipped away.

The back stairs had been the servants' stairs before Miss Hardcastle had taken over the building. Down Georgina went and then along to the Geography Room. This was where Charlotte would be, daydreaming about soldiers no doubt.

Except, she wasn't.

Nor was she in the next classroom, History, reading about famous battles.

"Georgina!" It was Miss Trenchard. Georgina was in trouble now, but at least it wasn't Earnestine scolding her. "What are you doing here, girl?"

"Miss, I'm trying to find Charlotte."

"Are you lost, Georgina? Going off to search for another family member?"

Georgina's face burned: it was awful getting these comments from her school 'chums', but utterly unbearable for the teachers to be joining in.

"I'm sure she can find herself," Miss Trenchard continued. She tapped her yardstick on the floor impatiently. "Come along, you are wanted in the Library."

"Why, Miss?"

"Don't be impertinent, girl."

Miss Trenchard ushered her into the corridor and propelled her along towards the library. When Georgina glanced back, the teacher was just going into the Geography Room, presumably to check for other errant pupils.

Georgina's head stopped first, her feet a moment later, so that she was left leaning backwards, sniffing. The smell was off-putting and it took her a moment to fail to recognise it. What was that?

At the far end, a group of men shambled towards her. Perhaps they would know, she wondered, but something was wrong, very wrong. They moved awkwardly like puppets, as if they weren't put together properly, and a low moaning issuing from their throats. Their clothes were old, worn and filthy, and their skin was yellow. On the side of each of their heads was a brass box that - Georgina saw with wide eyes - was nailed into their skulls! A spark, like miniature lightning, played inside the metal casing, and the creatures jerked and straightened up.

"Ach," said a smart officer standing behind the monsters, "do you like my little pets?"

He held up a device, wooden with brass fittings, and pressed a switch. The boxes attached to the men sparked again and the creatures shuffled towards her.

Georgina turned and fled.

A cry came up behind her: "Achtung!"

The moaning increased and she could hear the sounds of pursuit.

Georgina sprinted back the way she had come, paying little heed to the risk that the polished parquet represented. She had to get away: Earnestine, she needed Earnestine. Her sister would know what to do.

"Don't run in the corridor!" Miss Trenchard shouted after her. "Girls should not exert themselves."

Where would her sister be?

Georgina was panicking as she skidded to a halt by the entrance to the East Wing. Earnestine would not have crossed the 'Out of Bounds' sign, so where else could she be?

Behind her, Miss Trenchard screamed like a frightened child, a high-pitched and harrowing trill. Georgina looked back and wished she hadn't. The teacher defended herself, her yardstick striking at the brute, but to no avail. Georgina ran away in the only direction left to her, fear driving her onward, and, without having a plan, she found herself in the ski locker room.

Get help, she thought, outside help.

Everything was locked away.

She'd need something to keep warm outside, but there was no time; perhaps she could keep warm by running. Running did seem like a good idea.

She pulled open the outer door and plunged into the whiteness. Gunshots sounded and an angry bee zipped past her left ear, but she didn't look behind her. Instead, she kept going, aiming for the small stone archway that was her escape route from the grounds. It was close, closer, and she was there. The stonework shattered, spreading shrapnel in her path: she held her hand out to ward it off as she sprang through, and sharp stabs of pain peppered her palm.

Above, a terrifying black shape dominated a worsening sky as a massive, ominous lump hung impossibly in the air. Huge propellers whined and complained as they manoeuvred the bulk above her. The turbulence picked up the snow falling and whipped it into huge spirals. This was the incredible object that had cast a shadow across the school earlier.

There were distant shouts behind her: "Lassen Sie die Hunde los!" and the mad barking of the dogs changed pitch suddenly.

Beyond the arch was an open area, hidden by the wall, and then there was the treeline.

Her boots disappeared into the drift with each step to slip and stumble on who knew what. The hem of her long dress became soaked, the heavy snow leaching into her petticoats and pulling her down. Cold water reached her toes and it seemed that icy fingers rose up her stockings. She went downhill and suddenly a huge white arena opened up as she reached the frozen river. Slipping at first, she found a gait that worked and began running across the wide open space.

She heard snarling and risked glancing back: huge dogs smashed through the undergrowth towards her. The three mastiffs slid around too, but their four legs were more stable, and so they pounded onwards getting closer all the time.

Georgina ran, her lungs aching from forcing the cold air in and out.

The middle of the frozen river was marked by a cut where the water flowed still. To her right, the river narrowed to stepping stones and to her left, someway off, was the waterfall leading down to the valley. Which way?

The dogs were nearly upon her.

Georgina turned to run along the irregular channel, but her speed was too great. She slipped, fell and hurtled towards the churning water, scrabbling as she slid to slow herself.

Her hunters realised the danger too. One squealed as its paws came from under it and it crashed into Georgina. Animal and human went into the water.

The air slammed out of Georgina as the cold shocked her. The water frothed as the dog thrashed about. The other dogs tried to reach Georgina as she grasped the edge of the ice sheet, her hands blue, and she tried to pull herself up towards the snapping, biting jaws. She knew that she had to get out of the freezing water, had to.

But she couldn't and slid back, pulled by the current under the ice.

Deep breath!

Above her, the two dogs clawed and attacked the thin transparent sheet that protected her as she slipped away underneath.

## Miss Charlotte

As for the youngest of the Deering-Dolittle sisters: Charlotte knew that Georgina would murder her and, far worse, Earnestine would disapprove - for Charlotte was on the Zeppelin when it took off.

# CHAPTER II

## Miss Deering-Dolittle

For the men kidnapping Earnestine, it had gone badly. In an undignified rush they had bundled the struggling young lady along a corridor, up some stairs and then towards the stables. Earnestine had not been worried or afraid, because she was so thoroughly vexed with a kind of spitting rage that her usual refined and controlled demeanour did not know one end of from the other. For her part, she had lashed out at the March Hare, Mad Hatter and the Dormouse with her sharp pointed Baker Street boots whenever the opportunity had presented itself, and was rewarded as often as not with a yelp and a Germanic curse. Nevertheless, the indignities had continued and the Cheshire Cat, that irritatingly handsome Gardener's Hand, had eluded her.

The cold air on her ankles - oh, her dress must be riding up... it was mortifying!

They were outside and barely across the snow covered croquet lawn when Earnestine found herself pitched into the air and slung across the back of a horse. The beast's haunches forced the wind out of her lungs, blowing up the disgusting great coat that still imprisoned her like a bag. Her feet, stuck out of the coat, froze, and yet, struggling inside the thick material, she was too hot. Someone, she was fairly sure it was that upstart oik, mounted the saddle to her right and took control of the reins.

A man's hand slapped her derriere and they set off at a mad dash.

It was clear that the rider was deliberately choosing the most uneven ground as Earnestine was thrown about, bounced and bucked. She felt utterly sick, bruised and battered despite the armour of her corset, and then suddenly it was over. Hands grabbed her and manhandled her down like a package. She tipped alarmingly to one side as she slid from the horse's neck. Even dazed and confused she managed to kick out, unsure whether her frozen toes would know it if she did find a target.

"Hellcat!"

Luckily, she landed on her feet and she stood upright before, to her embarrassment, she dropped into a sitting position, hurting her pummelled and bruised dignity. When finally, by sheer pertinacity, she freed herself, the shock of cold air was stupefying. She sat, panting, almost retching as her internal organs shifted back into place.

The four ruffians had gathered around each other, speaking German.

"Excuse-" she managed.

"Sorry, we must get the horses inside," said... well, Earnestine didn't know, because they were just dark shapes in the swirling snow.

"Excuse me?"

They ignored her.

This would have made Earnestine apoplectic had her frame known how to generate such a state, and a barrage of 'excuse me's did not disturb them from their worried sounding Germanic mumbling.

Their attention was focused with quick glances up the road.

It was intolerable, utterly intolerable: "Excuse me!!!"

"Shhh, Fräulein, please."

This Gardener's Hand, even dressed up in some pseudo uniform, had the utter temerity to tell her what to do. *Her!*

"We must go back for the others," the Gardener's Hand said in English.

"Isn't one enough," the March Hare replied. He limped - *ha!*

"Excuse me!"

The March Hare raised an insistent finger: "Fräulein, quiet."

"I will not."

"You will," he said.

"We are responsible," said the Gardener's Hand, coming over to Earnestine.

"Pieter, we must get the horses inside," the Mad Hatter repeated.

The Gardener's Hand reached down and kindly helped Earnestine to her feet. She hit him, and then she ran off away from the looming building and into the white nothingness.

"Ach!" The man gave chase, slipping and stumbling after her. "Earnestine, Earnestine, we must get indoors."

"Get away from me!"

"Earnestine."

"Go to hell!"

She'd sworn!

Hopefully the wind had carried her words away and he wouldn't have heard. She glanced back: he wasn't far behind and she recognised the building now as the inn in the village down the valley. It was, as Miss Hardcastle had often pointed out, absolutely out of bounds: under no circumstances, girls, are you to go down to the village. Earnestine had tried so hard to be responsible, only to be thwarted by the Family Curse: *I must not explore.*

Pieter was a few paces away.

Earnestine forced her cold fingers into a fist. He stopped, scared, and finally Earnestine felt she was gaining control of the situation.

"Now, Pieter," she said, "you are to apologise, take me back to the college immediately and explain to the Principal. Do you hear? Do you hear?"

He hadn't - he was looking over her shoulder.

"Listen to me!"

"Earnestine-"

"Miss Deering-Dolittle to you."

"Miss, you must come with me now."

She wasn't going to look, she wasn't going to give him the satisfaction, but, of course, she did.

Behind a flickering curtain of falling snow that sparkled where the gaslight from the inn caught the swirling flakes, the road led up into the stygian night. In the distance were other lights, eerie and fizzing like lightning. She saw figures marching towards them in an uneven line, their distorted faces illuminated by the sparks in their... helmets? Their clothes were rags and yet they moved with complete disregard for the icy storm.

"Come with me or we will die," Pieter repeated, his hand touching hers gently.

She snatched her hand away: "I will die then."

"I'm not leaving you."

"I am not going on an adventure."

Pieter put his hands together as if he was praying and then touched his lips in thought.

He began carefully: "My colleagues, Herr Metzger, Hauptmann Schneider and Oberst Kroll, and I will protect you."

Earnestine followed his indication from the March Hare to the Dormouse and finally resting upon the solid frame of the Mad Hatter: Metzger, Schneider and Kroll... and Pieter: names to remember to tell the Head Mistress.

"We need to go to the inn."

"The inn?"

"It is a strong building and... they are nearly upon us."

"Oh, very well."

He marched towards the inn and Earnestine had to run to keep up.

Inside it was warm; the lights cast a red glow over the furnishings and a fire burned in the hearth. A woman, the Innkeeper's wife, bustled about, making everyone welcome.

"Barricade the doors," Pieter said.

The other gardeners had already selected the heaviest furniture.

The Innkeeper's wife started to protest and her clientele stood to assist. About twenty villagers, arranged around small tables, scraped their chairs back as they stood. The gardeners ignored them until one burly giant of a man grabbed the bench he was moving. They exchanged angry words in different languages.

"Achtung!"

Pieter stood on a table.

Earnestine was embarrassed: "Get down."

"We are about to be attacked and we must defend ourselves. Everyone!"

He repeated it in French and then German.

The pause that followed was long, and then someone said something that made the villagers laugh.

A crash!

The Innkeeper's wife screamed.

Kroll shouted: "Achtung! Achtung!"

Everyone mobilised, grabbing stools and fire irons in the rush. One of the gardeners, Schneider, took out a pistol and fired at the door. He took two strides forward, right up to the threshold, and discharged another three shots. They got the door closed. A bench was quickly jammed into position. Metzger unbuckled his belt and dumped his sword on a chair, so he could help pile more furniture against the entrance.

From outside, hands slapped against the windows and then faces, distorted by the old glass and insane expressions, pushed against the front. They were everywhere. A woman screamed.

"This is an adventure," said Earnestine to herself.

She was a calm pivot around which the villagers rushed: tables brought forward, a shotgun found and other men went to the back of the building.

"Why do you not want an adventure?" Pieter asked.

"Mother gave explicit instructions: no exploring, no trouble, no adventures."

"Go upstairs and look!" someone shouted.

One of the gardeners sprinted to the staircase taking the steps two at a time.

"I would like to know what's going on," Earnestine demanded.

"We are being attacked," Pieter replied. He checked his pistol.

"I fathomed that!"

Shouts at the back of the building intensified. Somewhere in the back room or beyond, Earnestine wasn't sure of the size of the inn, a skirmish was escalating. A man's scream, high pitched and utterly shocking, pierced the racket.

"They are inside," said Metzger.

Schneider came far enough downstairs to lean over the banister: "They are everywhere."

Someone shouted: "Ghuls, ghuls."

"Are we surrounded?" Kroll asked.

"Ja."

"Can't run, can't fight, can't..."

Dread moans issued at the rear of the inn, finally overcoming the shouts and screams. The battle tumbled into the passageway outside the main room. Earnestine became mesmerised by Metzger's discarded belt, the curved sword tucked safely in the leather protection of a scabbard. She took hold of the hilt and slid the cutlass out.

"Fräulein," said Metzger, "do you know how to use that?"

"Of course not."

"Best if you stab at arm's length and-"

Earnestine slashed sideways and cut through the 'ghoul' as he lumbered into the room: once, twice. The man kept going. Pieter grabbed her free arm and pulled her towards the staircase. Out of the lounge and in the hallway, it became obvious that the rear of the house had been breached. The ghouls fell upon the villagers; bodies lay strewn about, twitching, as the assailants bent down to bite and tear at the flesh.

Earnestine hacked at the one chasing them again, and when they reached the bottom step Kroll emptied two rounds into its chest. It lurched back, almost toppling, but then came forward again.

"Mein Gott!"

Earnestine felt like she was falling upwards, such was the force as Pieter pushed and Kroll pulled. Metzger flung a chair over them. They reached the landing and stumbled on.

Kroll stood his ground on the top step, aimed carefully and fired at almost point blank range at the next attacker. After the roar of the explosion, a small black dot appeared in the ragged landscape of the man's forehead, and the back of his head burst in a shower of red and black. The metal box attached to his head sparked and exploded. The corpse dropped like a stone.

"Now we know how to kill them," said Metzger.

"Ja," Kroll agreed. "Pity that was my last round."

"A soldier shouldn't run out of bullets," Earnestine chided.

At the end of the landing was a ladder leading upwards into a loft. Pieter went first, pulling Earnestine after him, and Metzger followed with Kroll standing guard with his useless gun. Kroll climbed then, slowly for his bulk, and then they pulled the ladder up after them and dropped the hatch.

"Where's Schneider?" Pieter asked.

"Hush..." said Kroll.

Below they could hear the sounds of struggle and that peculiar shambling gait these ghouls used. They huddled into the darkness, slowly going cold, feeling utterly useless. When it had been quiet for a long, long time, Earnestine asked: "What is-"

"Shhh..." Kroll answered and his tone brooked no argument.

Earnestine shivered.

"Here," Pieter whispered, almost inaudibly. He wrapped a great coat around her - it was the one she'd been kidnapped in - and, although it was thick and insulated, she could not stop trembling. It was the cold and not the fear, and most certainly not because of his proximity.

## Miss Georgina

The river was wide and tumbled down the rocks, the ice broken like panes of glass, and Georgina struggled to her feet. Her petticoats froze; a frost shimmered over her and turned her white as if forming a deathly bridal gown. She waded to the shore. Snow caked around her feet and ankles, and her long dress, soaked from the water, became hard and brittle.

Black shapes, thin and skeletal, jerked out of the blizzard; trees stripped of their needles by the wintery gales stood like sentries.

Perhaps she could just sit down for a moment, rest and then move on with her strength restored. Perhaps...

But she couldn't. She'd die. She'd become like Hideous Helga, whom the girls talked about in whispers. That poor lost soul had gone out in a storm to meet her lover only to be abandoned. Her flesh had been frozen off her features and her tormented ghost haunted the hills and mountains searching for her lost beau, and with every passing storm the wraith screeched and rattled at the windows.

A sound like an engine moved overhead and then, as she craned her neck to look, she saw a dark, ominous shape, whirring and phutting above, until it was lost in the blustering Alpine flurries.

Georgina's limbs were no longer cold, just numb; wooden as if they belonged to someone else.

She stumbled, saw her own hands in front of her, but she could feel nothing.

She tried standing, but her dress seemed made of card, stiff and unforgiving.

She crawled: her progress measured in yards, then feet and finally inches.

Three trees loomed over her, their branches leaning down to pluck her up; no, it was a bear with gigantic looming eyes, each reflecting a strange tormented face. She saw a pair of Hideous Helgas, but they were her own pitiful self, already as pale and insubstantial as a ghost reflected in the monster's eyes. Great arms reached down and huge hands swept her up from the snow.

The creature spoke: "I say," it said.

## Miss Charlotte

Charlotte worried about what her sisters would say with the same gut-wrenching feeling she had when she looked down. The ground was so far away now: it made her dizzy and excited. And it was a Zeppelin, they'd understand, surely? She'd put her thick blue coat on before going outside, like they kept telling her to, and she hadn't left the school grounds... as such, until the airship had taken off and flown east.

It had just landed at the back of the school, with airmen in dashing uniforms tying it to trees with thick ropes, and she'd only gone for a closer look, a teensy peek, and then, well, no-one had been watching, so she'd not exactly sneaked on board, but rather she'd gone to have a look inside. It had been floating off the ground, so she'd had to climb the ladder, hadn't she? Only a few rungs, no more than fourteen, and once she reached the top, she thought she'd just take a couple of steps inside.

When the rotors had fired up to speed giving her such a fright, she'd instinctively hidden in one of the cabins, but that was only so she wouldn't be caught. Earnestine would not want her to be caught, so she had done the right thing and Earnestine would be proud, and not cross as she usually was, wouldn't she?

But what did any of that matter: Charlotte was flying!!!

She'd hidden in a cabin and, opposite the wooden door made of the lightest wood, was a single small porthole. With her face pressed against the glass, she'd seen the trees zoom away and the school itself shrink to a doll's house, and then smaller still and the sky had become huge. There was no sense of movement, no buffeting like a carriage or a train, or a swaying of deck on a boat, just a gentle change of angle and a surge of engine noise. It had rained briefly, but then she realised that they had risen through the clouds. Above the dreadful weather, it was a bright, dazzling sunny day and the crisp Swiss air allowed a view of the entire world!

And there were mountains *below her.*

What was the point of hacking through a jungle or riding a camel, when you could simply soar above the unknown?

Charlotte looked up: a huge whale of darkness blotted out half the blue sky. The black skin of the beast was stretched over the visible ribs of a steel skeleton. The thrumming noise was not in her head but from the huge propellers that were turning lazily on outstretched beams.

It was magnificent.

Perhaps a little look round before she thought about how to get back to needlework class.

Charlotte returned to the corridor on tiptoe.

The propellers were strung out on wings halfway along, so perhaps the engine room was not at the stern. Instead there were signs for 'Damen' and 'Herren'. The doors to the cabins on either side were all identical, each with two numbers. The room she'd come out of had been '19/20'. The doors weren't numbered like a street, but rather clockwise starting, and ending, at the front with '1/2 3/4' on her right and '13/14 11/12' on her left. Wait, it was an air*ship*, so the big numbers were on the 'port' side. These end cabins were obviously quadruples. The door towards the 'bow' - see, she wasn't glocky - was blank.

Charlotte could hear voices from the room beyond. There were several men talking; the walls, thin presumably to save weight, let through every word. Unfortunately they were speaking in a Germanic language.

Well, she thought, what to do?

She'd have to wait until they descended and then sneak off while they were tying up. It wouldn't do to have 'stowaway' added to her school report, which was already going to rack up another 'absent' to its collection.

There was another noise, this one from cabin '1/2 3/4' - someone was inside. If she wasn't careful, she'd be outflanked.

She put her ear to the panel and heard a girlish whimpering, so it was unlikely to be Earnestine or Georgina. It was possibly another girl from the school, although her classmates had been singularly reluctant to climb out of the dormitory window when she'd suggested it.

Charlotte tried the handle: it turned and the door clicked open, but then jammed on a bolt. Strange that it was locked from the outside. Charlotte unlocked it and looked inside.

The cabin beyond was more opulent than the one she'd first hidden in, with a fine table and four chairs commanding the centre. There were bunk beds on either side, enough for four people, with the walls striped in blue and ochre with gold patterns matched by the curtain drawn across the window. Charlotte could not tell where the murmuring was coming from, until she stepped inside and looked over one of the expensive travelling cases.

It was another girl, not one from the school, who was backed into the gap between the table and the bunk bed, her legs and arms rigid like spears, and she gripped a butter knife in her hand. Her expression was a mix of terror and grim determination.

"Shhh, shhh," said Charlotte closing the door behind her. "I'm Charlotte, Lottie... Lottie."

"Lottie?"

"Yes, Lottie," said Charlotte. "And you?"

"No-one!"

Charlotte smiled: "I can't call you no-one. How should I address you?"

"Your... nothing. Just Fräulein..."

"Just Fräulein?"

There was no sense of movement and the whirr of the propellers was distant. They could be two girls hiding in a cabin anywhere and not, as they were, flying.

The other girl relaxed a little.

"I'm to... it's worse than death."

"Is it?"

Charlotte had heard the phrase 'worse than death' before. Miss Jones had used it in one of her tirades when she'd warned the girls against going down to the village where there might be boys. Charlotte suspected that this was going to turn out to be one of those foolish things that adults kept from children, men kept from women, and everyone kept from Charlotte. Considering Miss Jones's, and now this Fräulein's, reaction, it was most likely to be more important than, say, brandy or cigars, but in her bones, Charlotte suspected it would turn out to be something dreary like a lecture on workhouses or sewerage. For her own good, apparently, Charlotte had had to sit through visiting speakers droning on about solving poverty, supplying clean water and building sewers. Old men, bearded and reeking of brandy fumes and cigar smoke, seemed to be inordinately interested in sewers. Charlotte never wanted to go anywhere near sewers, but she knew far more about the passages under London than she did about interesting subjects like Fusiliers, Cavalry Officers and... and... flying airships.

"Gott... what to do?" the Fräulein said.

"I can't... perhaps."

Charlotte was simply stringing words together, hoping that her gentle tone would keep the other girl talking. Perhaps she would know how to escape from a Zeppelin and get back to school.

"My parents promised me to..." And then, like the students running down corridors after the break time bell, the words tumbled out in a rush: "I'm betrothed. A political alliance. Once I'm there, my life will be over. I love Franz."

"Franz?"

"He's an Alferes."

"Ah, the uniforms."

"Ja." The girl laughed, joining in with Charlotte's giggle.

Charlotte had an idea: "Uniforms..."

"Uniforms?"

"What if we were to change clothing? They can't marry me off, can they? If it comes to the 'just cause' moment, then I'll just admit who I am. They won't marry me because they want an alliance. And you? Well, there's a chance that wherever we're going, you can escape if you tell them you are of royal blood."

"How did you know I was a Princess?"

Charlotte just smirked.

"It does not sound like a good plan," said the Princess.

"No, I suppose not."

"It is better than doing nothing."

"That's the spirit."

Charlotte jumped up and took off her dark blue coat. The Princess realised and began to take off her clothes, turning away, and then asking Charlotte for help. Clearly Her Royal Highness was not used to dressing unaided. Charlotte handed over the patched blouse that Earnestine had discarded when it was torn, the petticoats that had been Georgina's, and Earnestine's before that, and the second-hand corset. In return, she put on the Princess's fine silk dress. Soon they were fussing over each other: the Princess inexpertly put Charlotte's hair up with a jewel encrusted diadem.

"You're English," said Charlotte, tugging down the Princess's hair.

"Nein."

"No, I mean you are English now."

"Ja."

"Yes."

"Yesss. And you are Bavarian."

"Ach, mein Gott, bratwurst, yawol."

"Perhaps it would be better if you kept quiet."

Charlotte was none too pleased by this comment: "We can't be found together."

"Nein, where were you?"

"I was in the... back at the stern. Cabin nineteen and twenty."

"Ja."

They went to the door and the Princess peeked out: "At the stern, you say?"

"Yes... I mean, Ja."

"Ja," the Princess corrected.

"I said 'Ja'."

The Princess closed the door behind her leaving Charlotte alone.

"You're as bad as Ness," Charlotte said to the teak panel.

The bolt clicked back across locking her in.

Charlotte tried the handle.

"Shhh..." said the Princess, "they will be suspicious if it is unlocked."

"But Fräulein," Charlotte hissed back, "Fräulein... your Highness... oi!"

Silence: except for the rotors of the Zeppelin and distant creaking of metal fuselage.

Around her, large trunks were flipped on their ends and opened at their hinges. Inside them, Charlotte found fine clothes, silk handkerchiefs and ribbons arranged in shelves and integral drawers. There was a dressing table with a mirror. Charlotte saw how badly her hair was arranged, so she sat down, the light wicker chair creaking under her, to fix it. Eventually she had to take it all down, brush it and start over.

If only Earnestine and Georgina could see her now, all smart and grown up and sensible. How clever she had been to come up with the idea, all by herself, of swapping clothes: how stuffy they both were with their talk of 'responsibility' and 'duty' and 'thou shalt not blah-blah'. From now on, Charlotte resolved, she would be her own person, so she stood and twirled around, admiring her reflection and imagining herself as the Princess. This was something she could choose for herself and not something imposed by her bossy sisters.

What was she now? An Acting Princess certainly, and she had the little crown to prove it. It was surely better than being a stowaway, and certainly better than being the little sister; whereas Earnestine was only a mere Prefect and Georgina was... nothing, so they'd both have to bow and scrape and show respect all the time, and then perhaps they'd understand what it was like to be the youngest and never allowed to have any fun. She would have pudding without finishing her vegetables, and she would talk all the time and they'd have to listen for once.

But not until after a snooze, she thought, because it had been such an exciting day.

# CHAPTER III

## Miss Deering-Dolittle

Earnestine felt warm, cosy and safe. A heart beat strong and steady nearby, its deep resonance comforting, and her body gently rocked by waves of breathing: in, out, in, out...

And then she became sharply aware of her dreadful situation. She was snuggled up with a man, her face against his chest and his arms actually around her. She jerked up and scuttled away leaving a trail in the dust across the floorboards.

"It's all right, Fräulein, they've gone."

Gone! But they were still here: Kroll, Metzger and that wretched Pieter, particularly Pieter, whose comforting embrace was now safely well over on the other side of the loft space.

"Oh!" she realised what he meant, what he thought she was afraid of, and then she realised that she was afraid. That shivering last night had been terror, pure and simple, and clearly something to get under control. Five hundred lines: *I must not be afraid,* in Greek; that ought to do it.

Pieter glanced at the loft hatch: "We hope."

"Where's the March Hare?" Earnestine asked.

"Schneider is guarding below," said Kroll.

Pieter corrected him: "We don't know."

The loft was dark, but light shone in sharp pencil beams from a variety of holes in the roof. The floorboards were sound and there were crates arranged neatly. The inn used this space for storage.

Earnestine idly cut a vertical line into the floorboard with her nail, two peaks next and then a 'V' for a 'U'. She stopped herself: no time to do lines. *I must not do lines.*

"What were those things?" she asked. "Ghouls?"

The men exchanged glances, clearly not wanting to explain. Eventually Kroll told her.

"Die Untoten."

"Untoten?"

"Not alive."

"Undead," said Pieter.

"This is the age of enlightenment," Earnestine said. "Steam trains, clockwork machines, science... not a time of superstition and demons."

Pieter nodded: "Precisely."

"We have to go," said Kroll.

No-one replied: they all just looked at the closed hatch.

"The Oberst is right," said Pieter. "Those creatures can't reason like we can, but their masters will work it out sooner or later."

He reached for the handle, but Metzger beat him to it.

"I'll go," Metzger said. He opened the hatch and ducked his head through the floor to look around. "Clear."

They took the ladder, fed it down through the opening and then Metzger disappeared.

"We'll stay together," said Pieter.

"Metzger can scout ahead," said Kroll.

"We stay together," Pieter insisted.

Earnestine was last to leave their sanctuary.

The inn was different now, ominous. There were signs of battle, broken chairs, discarded weapons, splatters of dark stains that could be spilt claret, but Earnestine knew that they weren't. Downstairs in the lounge it was the same, although the barricades had been pushed aside.

"No bodies," Metzger said.

"The stables were round the back," Kroll said.

The rear room, another area for people to drink, was covered in broken glass. Some doors with windows in the French style leading to a terrace were smashed. It would have been lovely in summer. This was why the untoten had breached the defences here; the opening had been too wide to barricade.

The chill air outside was clean, invigorating and fresh. Earnestine closed her eyes and let it fill her lungs for a few deep breaths before she followed the others to the stable.

"Mein Gott!" Metzger exclaimed. "The horses..."

The nearest horse appeared to be asleep, lying snugly on the hay with steam rising from its flank, but the steam buzzed and hovered like...

The air outside was still as clean, invigorating and fresh as before but Earnestine felt herself choking. She closed her eyes, desperate to deny what she'd seen as she tried to keep herself from retching. Even so, her mind's eye was fixated on an image of horses torn apart.

The others had a quiet discussion in German, all hushed urgency and pointing. Pieter broke away to come over to Earnestine as the other two went back to the inn.

"Fräulein, we have-"

"They ate the horses!"

"Come now."

"They ate the horses!!"

"They killed the villagers and Schneider. I've known Schneider from when I was a boy. All these deaths, but you, the Great British, don't care. After all, we're only foreigners. But a horse gets served up on a plate with garlic and your whole nation goes insane - questions in Parliament, letters to the Times - you make me sick."

Kroll and Metzger returned with supplies and the three men set off down the road into some woods.

The penny slowly dropped. That - words failed her - had just insulted the British. Of all the utterly dastardly foreign tricks. She'd have given him a piece of her mind if he hadn't just walked away.

Earnestine was alone in the courtyard.

She wanted to go home: to read by the fire in their house in Kensington with Mama and Papa poring over their map collection, Georgina doing needlework and silly Charlotte re-enacting Rorke's Drift with her dolls. They'd have a pot of Earl Grey and sandwiches with the crusts cut off, and later hot Cadbury's cocoa essence while Uncle Jeremiah read them a story.

That was it: she would give him a piece of her mind right now and put him straight by explaining that, untoten or no untoten, he could not simply kidnap a British subject without so much as a 'by your leave'.

She caught up with them: "Excuse me!?"

They carried on walking.

"Stop! At once!"

"We need to keep moving," Pieter said.

He had actually contradicted her. He seemed to understand English and yet, with all the perversity possible, he refused to agree with her. Despite his sparkling blue eyes, this was intolerable, and she had to tell him so, at length; and if this didn't elicit the correct response, she would repeat her points, enumerated, loud and clear with such careful pronunciation that even a boot boy would be able to follow them.

"Perhaps you have forgotten that you kidnapped me, and I..."

Instead of stopping, the men continued to walk away from her, gesticulating to each other and pointing down the snow covered valley. Earnestine didn't know where they were going, and indeed she did not care.

She stamped her foot.

The Gardener's Hand deigned to look at her: "You are marvellous," he said.

"I beg your pardon."

"When you are angry."

"I am not angry! I am British, I am never angry."

"If you say so."

"Look," she said, adopting her patient tone - again. "I am a British Subject. You," she pointed so that he wouldn't confuse himself with someone else, "must take me to the British Embassy."

"I cannot take you to an embassy."

"Or Consulate. A Consulate would be quite acceptable in the circumstances."

"Neither. I cannot take you to a Consulate either."

"That's almost a double negative. Look, I can see you're not following me."

One of his compatriots shouted from ahead: "Ach, she is English, there is no arguing with them."

It was infuriating. The others knew English well enough when it suited them.

"English, yes. So an English Embassy or Consulate would be acceptable. English and British, it's the same thing," she said, biting her lip because she knew that it absolutely wasn't. No, it was no use, they'd never learn if someone didn't try to educate them. "In fact, it's not the same thing, England is part of Britain, but again, in the circumstances, I'm prepared to overlook such... Excuse me!"

She was suddenly in the air, hoist like the crossbar of a letter 'T' across the shoulder of one of them. It was Kroll, who was big and broad, and carried her like she was a rag doll. She couldn't see properly, her corsetry making twisting or bending impossible, but she felt keenly the indignity of having her bustle thrust into the air.

"Put me down! Down! Now! This instant."

The path through the woods bounced around beneath her, swinging from side to side. They were somewhere in the valley now going along a dirt road. There were coach tracks frozen in the hard mud like dirty glacial crevasses.

"Put her down," said the Gardener's Hand.

"Sire-"

"Now."

The man did so.

Earnestine brushed at the creases in her dress and fumed, so angry with herself that her face felt red. It was bad enough to be kidnapped, but this embarrassment was too much to bear.

"I can stand it no longer," said Pieter and he pointed. "England is that way."

He marched off and the others fell into step.

"It jolly well isn't," said Earnestine to their retreating backs. She gesticulated to the sky and the woods. "The sun is there, the moss is on that side of the tree, any fool can see that's south east, you're going north, England is-"

"What did you say?" the Gardener's Hand demanded.

Earnestine took a deep breath, finally: "I am a British Subject and you need to take me to-"

"About the direction?"

"Yes, direction. To a British Consulate."

"About moss and the sun?"

"Pardon?"

"You said we're going north."

"Yes, moss grows on the north side of a tree in the Northern Hemisphere and the sun, particularly at this time of year, is also to the south. At this time of the morning, it's to the south-east, so..."

"Mein Gott, we're going the wrong way."

He signalled to the others and they began marching back the way they had come.

"Very well, it's clear to me that you don't know where the British Consulate is, so I'm willing to compromise and agree that you can take me back to Eden College for Young Ladies."

"We cannot go back."

"The College has a telephone apparatus and the authorities need to be informed about the untoten uprising."

"I cannot go back."

"Look, I'm sure if you apologise and throw yourself on Miss Hardcastle's mercy, she will overlook..."

This was nonsense, and Earnestine knew it. Miss Hardcastle, mercy - they didn't really go together. Hopefully the old Gardener himself would give this underling a good thrashing. Earnestine knew that she would relent; she didn't really want him to be beaten, but she did want to relish the idea for a while longer.

They'd left her - again.

"Excuse me?"

She could escape, but to where? They were going south-west, so she could go north, but was that a sensible direction?

"Excuse me."

She set off south-west after them, nearly tripping over a rut in the frozen earth in her haste to catch up.

At the end of the road, and Earnestine missed its arrival because she was desperately trying to avoid turning her ankle, there was a coach and horses waiting. Other riders hung around tending to their mounts. Their saddles and equipment were - Charlotte would know - cavalry, fusiliers, mounted military of some sort. They all snapped to attention when the Gardener's Hand and his friends rounded the bend.

Pieter went up to one of the men, a functionary, and they began arguing in German. Or Austrian. Or Hungarian. Or some other harsh tongue.

She snapped: "English!"

"Sorry," said the Functionary in English, "I meant no disrespect."

The Gardener's Hand was smirking! This outrage was never ending.

The soldiers came towards her, saviours all of them until they raised their rifles.

"Excuse me, but... this is intolerable."

"Achtung!"

Earnestine's attention snapped from the officer to the clutch of Germans. Pieter, or whatever his name was, looked resigned.

"Mein Prince," said the officer.

"Otto."

"Schweinehund, ich..."

"English," said Pieter, "we have a lady present."

"Ach, Mein Royal Highness, you have led us a merry chase, but now, alas, it is time to fulfil your responsibilities. Ja?"

"Ja."

Pieter led the way and his colleagues fell in behind, despondently. One of the soldiers shoved Earnestine roughly with the butt of his rifle causing her to stumble forward.

"Otto!" Pieter's anger was all too obvious.

"Ach, shall we have your parole, Ja?"

"Ja."

"You have your duty," said Otto as he reached for the coach door. "I have my orders."

Absolutely, thought Earnestine. He must take her back to the school, apologise for the outrageous behaviour he displayed to one of the young ladies of the College, vis-à-vis herself, and jolly well sort out the lawn borders. Hopefully, Miss Hardcastle would take the unctuous youth down a peg or two.

The man had opened the door: "Your Royal Highness."

There, that would put him in his place and make the oik think twice about-

"Excuse me!" Earnestine demanded. "Could someone please explain what you are talking about?"

The functionary tried: "His Royal Highness is being taken back to his family castle and you are coming too. In!"

"I don't take orders from... whoever it is you are."

"In or I'll have Franz carry you in."

This was intolerable, but she didn't want to be carried again like some baggage.

"Very well, but under protest."

"Noted."

"Aren't you going to write it down then?"

"Nein, get in."

Refusing the functionary's hand, Earnestine climbed in and flomped down in the rear facing seat. Sitting directly in front of her was the Gardener's Hand, looking very handsome and refined.

"Your Royal Highness?" she asked.

He bowed and clicked his heels together despite being seated.

"It was a question."

"I am Prince Pieter."

So, Earnestine thought, a rough uncouth workman and liar to boot.

"And gardening is an essential skill for royalty in these parts?"

"It is an education."

"Because I was wondering when you were going to rescue the school's roses."

"I have already rescued an English Rose."

"You really aren't a gardener, are you? If you were, then you'd know that that Miss Hardcastle's roses are Rosa Moyesii, a variety that originates in the Orient."

The carriage jerked forward throwing Earnestine towards the so-called Prince. She put her hands up to stop herself and for a moment they embraced. Earnestine fumbled him away and sat back. After another less violent movement, the carriage began to move along the road, throwing them side-to-side as it crunched over the frozen tracks. Not before time, the wheels found the 'rails' left by previous standard sized axles and they proceeded much like a tram.

"I was being hidden at the school in order to escape certain forces intent on persuading me to certain actions," Pieter explained. "You understand?"

"I hadn't asked."

"And the gardening because I was bored. I prefer action."

"I hadn't asked."

Earnestine let the awkward silence fill the plush interior, pleased to see the three men, the Gardener's Hand and his valets, sit more upright and rigid. She was angry: after all, she'd been kidnapped and manhandled and taken on an adventure, so she was going to ignore them and instead stare out of the window at the passing trees. Even if her eyes kept wanting to gaze into his face, she was made of stern stuff and wouldn't even glance, not once, and it was easy, despite his sparkling blue eyes, for she'd noticed his wry smile mocking her.

"Did you want to ask something?" he said.

"No."

"Only you keep looking at me."

"I do not. I simply wanted to know why we're not going to the school."

"We're going to Ravensbruck."

"And what, pray, is at Ravensbruck?"

"Fresh horses."

"That is not really an answer."

"From there we will go to the Eagle's Claw."

Earnestine was appalled: "Is that a public house?"

"Hardly," the man smiled, so pleasingly. "It is my family home, a castle."

"Really? Will we have tea and scones while you introduce me to your Mama and Papa?"

"My mother is dead and my father, the Crown Prince, is... indisposed," said Pieter. "As for the rest of my family, you don't want to meet the dowager Gräfin."

"Why ever not?"

"You and she are too much alike."

# Miss Georgina

Her first sensations were of varying heat: her head was warm, her body hot and her toes numb, but in between, around her ankles, she was cold. Her internal organs and the very marrow of her bones felt painfully icy. Her ears burned: she heard voices, clear, concise, the clipped retorts of military speech.

"What was she doing out there?"

"She's not a peasant girl, that's for sure."

"Why do you say that?"

"Her hands, smooth and delicate."

"Merryweather!"

"They are... and she's c- c- conscious."

Georgina kept jolly still.

"You're wrong, she's still out."

"Her b- breathing has changed."

Georgina became aware she wasn't breathing. She was holding her breath as she tried to work out what breathing was supposed to be like when one was asleep. She gasped when her hands were suddenly enveloped by another, a strong warm palm.

"M- M- Mademoiselle?"

Georgina shifted round, her eyes still tight shut.

"Do you speak English?" he said.

She blinked and then saw the most handsome brown eyes staring back at her, and then, unbidden, she heard her own thoughts articulated aloud.

"You have beautiful eyes," he said with his deep voice, his male voice, his voice about her, caressing her, "Mademoiselle."

"Monsieur," Georgina managed.

"I don't know why you are telling her that," said another voice further away. Georgina would have looked, but she couldn't tear herself away.

He had a nice, caring smile under his neat horseshoe moustache: "Parlez-vous français?"

"Merryweather, no point asking her that."

"Why not?" said the handsome man... Merryweather.

"Because you can't speak the lingo," the other man said. "Once she's said 'oui', your conversation is over. We'll be in the other room."

Merryweather looked in the direction of the kerfuffling and chair scraping. He waited until a door shut before turning his attention back to the still rapt Georgina.

"I know you can't understand me," he said. "But you are simply the most beautiful girl I've ever clapped eyes on. I can't usually talk to women, typical really, but knowing that you don't understand a word means that I can somehow... you are beautiful, I've said that, with a lovely countenance."

He smiled, dimples appeared in his cheeks, and he brushed a blond lock of hair away from his forehead.

"I feel like I want to spend the rest of my life with you."

"Are you proposing?" Georgina asked politely.

Merryweather leapt to his feet, yanking his hand away from hers as if she was a hot pan and in his haste he tumbled backwards onto the floor.

The door burst open and two other men came in: "Merry?"

"I... I... I..."

"Ah, she's come round," said the shorter, before looking across in Georgina's direction.

"Eng... English," Merryweather said.

"English?"

"Yes, I am," Georgina said.

"It... it..."

"That's right Merry, up you get," said the taller man as he hauled Merryweather to his feet.

"I'll... I'll..."

"Fetch the brandy, excellent."

Merryweather shuffled off in the wrong direction at first and then found the door to another room.

The tall man thrust his hand forward: "Caruthers, chap here is McKendry."

"Mac," said the shorter man.

Georgina shook both the proffered hands, each a firm, solid grip.

"And you've met Merry, Captain Arthur Merryweather," Caruthers continued. "You had a close call. Miss?"

"Georgina, Georgina Deering-Dolittle."

"Pleased to meet you Miss Deering-Dolittle. Surrey's a lovely county."

"I'm not one of the Surrey Deering-Dolittles."

"Oh... Ah!" said Caruthers, and he smoothed his chevron moustache to hide his embarrassment. "Kent is nice too."

"What's the matter with... Arthur?" Georgina asked, pointing at the door through which Merryweather had exited.

"Merry, can't talk when there's a Memsahib present."

"I see."

"Mac?"

McKendry brought over a white metal mug held in his mittens: "Miss? It's an old Southern recipe. Use the cloth, it'll be hot."

Georgina accepted the proffered cloth and then took hold of the mug.

Merryweather reappeared with a bottle of brandy.

"Ah, yes..." he said and poured a generous measure into the cup with a shaking grip.

At first Georgina felt nothing until her fingers warmed up enough for their nerves to start working. They tingled, a sensation not unlike looking into Merryweather's eyes. She breathed on the surface and the rising steam seemed to thaw her face.

"Thank you," she said.

"Don't thank me yet," said McKendry. "It's an evil brew, but it'll get some strength into you."

Georgina took a sip, scalding her mouth and throat, but it was a welcome feeling.

"Which part of the Home Counties is this from?"

"Not Southern England, Miss. It's an old Mississippi recipe with just a nip of brandy to get the circulation going," McKendry explained, pulling lightly on the black chin puff beard beneath his handlebar moustache.

"So how come you were out in the cold?" Caruthers asked.

"Oh!"

Merryweather took the cup from her, although whether he was catching it or whether he'd sensed the imminent risk of it tumbling to the floor, she didn't know.

She stared wild-eyed at Caruthers, Merryweather and McKendry as if to assign a specific responsibility to each in turn.

"Men! Guns... Creatures."

She was on her feet, or rather her legs gave way beneath her and she had to grab hold of Merryweather.

"We must go back," Georgina said. "My sisters... the school."

"There's a school nearby?" Caruthers asked.

"Yes, a prison of a place, but still... we were attacked."

"What h- happened?" Merryweather asked.

"Some foreigners attacked it, soldiers with peasant creatures. I did say."

The three men sat at the table, Caruthers pulling his chair back so that he could see Georgina. They looked serious, but none of them moved towards the door.

"Now!" Georgina insisted.

The men exchanged a glance and Caruthers gave the slightest of head shakes.

"You can't just sit there," Georgina insisted, "you have to-"

"Miss!" Caruthers leant forward holding up his hands placating. "It's night and there's a blizzard."

"It's not a blizzard," Georgina interrupted.

"I grant you it isn't, technically, merely snow, but enough to make us walk round in circles, particularly as we don't know where we're going. We wait until first light and see if the conditions have improved."

"What do you mean first light?"

"It's n- n- night," said Merryweather. "You've been asleep a n- night and a day."

"No, I can't have been. We have to go. Now."

Gently, Merryweather put his hand on her shoulder, only to be snubbed when Georgina wrenched herself away.

"Well, if you won't, then I will," said Georgina, standing with the full intention of shaming these cowards into action. Caruthers just sat back and folded his arms, the others followed suit.

"We admire your spunk," he said, "we really do, but you need to warm up and get some of Mac's soup down you. No-one's going anywhere until we know what we're getting into."

The others nodded and exchanged glances.

"This is only a holiday, after all," said McKendry.

Georgina drew breath to scream at them, but Merryweather put a kindly hand back on her shoulder.

"T- t- tell us."

## Miss Charlotte

There was a sharp knock at the door, three taps, precisely spaced.

Charlotte jerked awake not knowing where she was: a cabin, an airship.

"Come in," she said.

No, wait, she wasn't sure who she was supposed to be, but she knew she was supposed to be Bavarian. Or was it Belgian?

The door was unlocked and a tall man dressed smartly in military uniform clicked his heels and bowed in the doorway. He had a fine black moustache and pointed beard, strong and full, and he looked jolly important.

"Your Royal Highness, you speak English?"

"I do," said Charlotte. Wasn't a Belgian accent sort of French? "Oui."

"Your English is very good," he said.

Charlotte reddened: "Thank vous."

"Excellent, I am Graf Zala at your service."

Charlotte liked that: "My service," she repeated, trying to sound formal: her personal reaction to the man, this imposing man, was one of admiration. He did know how to wear a military uniform. However, she wasn't sure how Princess Wotnot would behave in the circumstances.

"Ja. I hope the delay was not overly troublesome."

"Not at all, Herr Graf."

"Is everything to your satisfaction?"

"Why was the door locked?"

"For your safety during landing and take-off."

"Oh yes."

"We made a short stop, but now we are properly en route I wondered if you would care to join us on the bridge?"

"Ooh, gosh, yes please."

It was best to play along, she thought, and she might learn something of use and also the bridge sounded jolly exciting.

"I also thought you may consider changing into a more suitable outfit for flying."

This just got better and better, she thought.

He clicked his heels and bowed before indicating to his left. An attendant in a white uniform quickly entered and deposited a neat stack of clothing on the bed. The subordinate kept his head down throughout and made no eye contact at all. Charlotte found herself revelling in the sense of importance that came from her new status.

"When you are ready, simply follow the gangway thus," said the Graf and he indicated towards the bow of the vessel. He bowed again and closed the door. It was not relocked.

Charlotte wondered if she should take advantage of this liberty, but obviously there was no way off the Zeppelin at this altitude, and so she turned to examine the clothes. They made up a uniform, somewhat imaginative in its design. Whereas, the army and the navy had long traditions to maintain, the new flying service displayed both innovation and practicality in their outfits. This one was made of a thick material, plain without any of the frippery sometimes associated with the military. Charlotte liked all the braid and brass, but somehow this seemed more appropriate particularly when weight was an issue. It was buff and-

Trousers!

And boots!

Charlotte fumbled with the buttons in her rush to change and even decided to divest herself of her corset.

This was heaven; she was literally flying through heaven.

The trousers felt strange and it took her a few moments to get the flares to stick out properly. Her boots were loose. She admired herself in the mirror, pulling the buttoned up tunic down a few times to make it straight. Her stupid chest stuck out in a most non-regulation manner, but even so she liked the final effect. She tried a variety of stances, one hand behind her back, both, arms folded, attention.

This was the future: soon the British would have a Flying Corps and Her Majesty's Aerial Ships would patrol the skies. With the Suffragette movement, perhaps... yes, Charlotte imagined herself as the Captain of such a ship. HMAS Dreadnought, an ironclad airsteamer, protecting the Empire in far-flung places under the direction of the First Sky Lord. Hands behind back, feet apart, head up - definitely.

The corridor was uphill, the Zeppelin was climbing, but there were thick ropes on either side to act as handrails.

With the tiniest of coughs, Charlotte ventured onto the flight deck. Graf Zala turned and nodded appreciatively as he took in her buff-coloured uniform, its front button smartly to one side, the trousers flared at her thighs and her calf length boots black and polished, one solidly on the wooden deck and the other hitched up on its toe.

"Smart," he said.

Charlotte reddened slightly.

"Come, come," Zala said waving her in. "This is where we control the Zeppelin."

Charlotte trod firmly into the room and took in the polished brass fittings and controls. It was modelled on a ship, a naval tradition transformed for the modern age, streamlined and new. Charlotte was drawn to the huge wheel, a wooden set of spokes that dominated the centre of the flight deck.

The Graf sent the Ensign away with an imperious gesture and held the wheel in his gloved hand.

"Here," Zala said, "take the wheel."

Charlotte stepped up: "May I?"

"Of course."

Charlotte's fingers wrapped around the wooden handles as Zala stepped behind her, wrapping his body around her. His hands over hers were still very much in control.

"Take the strain," he said.

Charlotte's knuckles stood proud as the Graf let go. For such a solid man, his hands hovered like butterflies over hers until he was satisfied. He stepped back leaving Charlotte in control of the 128 metre leviathan and she could feel the massive length of the machine at her fingertips.

"Turn to starboard," said the Graf.

Charlotte glanced at the compass joggling in position as the vast vehicle succumbed to the whims of the air currents.

"Turn to starboard," the Graf repeated. "Right hand down."

Charlotte pulled; it stuck and then gave with a lurch. The central handle leant and a moment later the horizon pitched.

The Graf was delighted: "That's it!"

Somewhere far back the rudder flexed and changed the airflow, the big lazy propellers whined in protest and long cables zinged. The airship turned.

Charlotte laughed aloud.

"Too much," said the Graf.

As the airship turned sharply back to port, a nervous ensign took a few steps to steady himself. Charlotte threw her head back, her blonde hair flying away from its moorings, as she began to master the beast.

"You are a natural," said the Graf.

"Sir."

"Now trim-"

"Yes," Charlotte already held the lever. She pulled it causing the cabin to tilt upwards. "How high can we go?"

The Graf laughed, deep and hearty: "All the way to the stars."

# CHAPTER IV

## Miss Deering-Dolittle

The coach brattled over the medieval bridge into Ravensbruck, and when they finally came to a halt, Otto directed Prince Pieter, Kroll, Metzger and Earnestine towards a large timber-framed building. Soldiers were already commandeering the inn, rudely hustling guests into the street, who had no choice but to join the clutch of braver villagers gathering to watch from a distance.

Earnestine decided to give the functionary an explanation of where he was going wrong: "Otto, is it? When the British Consulate finds out how you have treated a subject of Her Majesty the Queen, you-"

The man pushed her forward and she stumbled on the uneven road surface.

Pieter stepped towards them, but he was stopped by Kroll's heavy hand on his shoulder.

"Perhaps," Earnestine said, "you could persuade these people to take me back to the school."

"That wouldn't be wise," said Prince Pieter.

"No," said Kroll, "they'll have killed everyone at the school."

"Kroll!"

"Yes, don't interrupt," Earnestine agreed. "I don't think you... excuse me?"

"The untoten that attacked us came from the school," Kroll explained. "Then they came after us. They will have killed everyone at the school."

"Everyone?"

"We don't know that," said Pieter.

"But my sisters?"

"I'm sorry."

Earnestine's rising anger was extinguished by a cold feeling of dread. Her ears buzzed, but she ignored it: *stiff upper lip*.

"No, that can't be right," Earnestine chided. "Mother gave me strict instructions to look after them: no exploring, no trouble, no adventures. So, you see, Mister Kroll, you must be mistaken..."

The buzzing noise increased. A shadow fell across Earnestine's face. It seemed unreal. She couldn't take it in. He was lying. He didn't understand English. That must be it.

"We must go back for them," she insisted, trying to make herself clear over the increasing noise.

"Nein!" Kroll was adamant.

"Now!" Earnestine screeched and grabbed for his jacket, all reason lost.

A shout: "Zeppelin!"

"What?" Earnestine looked about and then, seeing the pointing hands, she looked up. The beautiful blue sky, complete with scudding white clouds, was blemished by an immense black shape as an airship thudded overhead. Shielding her eyes from the bright sun, Earnestine could make out the gondola section below the rigid frame.

"Zala?" Pieter said.

"Zeppelin," Earnestine replied, correcting him.

"Nummer Drei," said Kroll. "Ja, Graf Zala."

"Strange that he was here," Pieter said.

Metzger glanced at Earnestine: "He was bringing your... verlobte."

"Strange route then," Pieter said.

The dark shape moved up the valley, turning until it presented its cruciform fins and delicate looking propellers.

When it was a speck, the soldiers seemed to come back to life. They jostled Earnestine and the others up the steps and into the inn.

"Careful," Prince Pieter said.

"Mein-"

"English."

"We are under orders."

"Only to escort."

"Ja."

Inside the inn's hallway, it was dark, almost black before Earnestine's eyes adjusted from gazing into the bright clear sky. Out of the gloom, an old man with grey hair and a drooping moustache limped from a back room complaining.

"Achtung!" Two soldiers unslung their rifles and pointed them at the man. There was shouting, two sides locked in an escalating conflict until Prince Pieter stepped between them.

"I believe we should sign in," he announced. "Do you have your visitor's book to hand?"

The landlord blustered until Pieter repeated what he'd said in German. The book was produced and the Prince made a show of finding the right page and signing with a flourish. He passed the pen over to Kroll, who snorted and signed too. Metzger was next. He handed the pen back to Pieter.

"And I'll sign for the Fräulein," he said, scribbling.

Earnestine interrupted: "Excuse me."

"Yes?"

"I'm quite capable of signing for myself."

With a smile, the Prince passed the pen. Earnestine went to the leather bound volume of lines and writing. Pieter had signed his name neatly and added 'Prince' in the second column. Kroll was 'Oberst' and Metzger was 'Advisor'. Although Pieter had left the name in the next row blank, he had written 'Maid' in the second column.

He leaned against the reception top casually and whispered: "I think your presence needs an explanation."

"I am well aware of why I am here," Earnestine replied.

The landlord said something to her in German.

"He wants to carry your bags," Pieter said.

Angrily, Earnestine wafted her hand to indicate the empty floor around her feet.

The landlord tutted, took the Prince's bag and led the way to the stairs. He took each step one at a time and the Royal party bunched up behind him. Eventually they reached the landing.

As the old man led the way along the corridor, he pointed out various items in German, but with such a mumble that no-one could understand the importance of the pipe spigot in the wall, the heritage of a faded watercolour, the design of a blue chair or why a perfectly blank plastered wall should be of interest. Finally, he reached a door and ushered Kroll and Metzger inside. Further along was another room and he held the door open.

Pieter ducked his head under and Earnestine followed.

The landlord pointed to various items in what was clearly his best room. It boasted a wash basin, a writing desk and chair, an extraordinary view of the white peaked mountains and the large, robust four-poster that dominated the space.

Pieter tipped him a coin.

The man nodded, smiled and chuckled before leaving, closing the door behind him. Pieter and Earnestine were left standing next to the comfortable and inviting bed.

Earnestine coughed politely.

Pieter undid the top button of his jacket.

Earnestine blinked at him.

Pieter smiled, continued unbuttoning and the dark material teased open to reveal the white frills of his shirt.

Earnestine tapped the heel of her shoe on the floorboard.

Pieter took off his jacket.

Earnestine folded her arms and glowered.

Pieter placed the jacket over the back of the chair.

Earnestine pointed at the bed.

Pieter pretended not to understand.

Earnestine lips narrowed into a fine line.

Pieter held up his hands in surrender: "I'll sleep on the floor."

"Yes," Earnestine said sharply, and then when he didn't take the hint, she added: "In another room."

Pieter looked round as if somehow he could examine the entire inn: "I doubt there is another free room."

"I have a reputation."

"So do I."

"Exactly."

"No-one will know."

"I will know!"

"I don't see any alternative."

"Herr Cheshire Cat can sleep with the Hatter and the Dormouse!"

"I doubt there's enough space."

"That is hardly my concern!"

Earnestine snatched Pieter's jacket off the chair and handed it to him. The Prince contrived to hold Earnestine's hands as he took it back, but Earnestine jerked away.

"Out!" she commanded.

Pieter paused in the doorway to click his heels and bow: "Jawohl, mein Fräulein."

"I am not your Fräulein."

"But Liebchen, I-"

"Liebchen!"

Earnestine slammed the door, bolted it, pulled the chair in the way and then decided that the writing desk would be better, so she heaved the mahogany weight across. Once she'd finished, there was a knock on the door.

"Yes?"

"Sleep well."

Earnestine entertained a few choice retorts, but they all involved the B-word and so she held her tongue.

## Miss Georgina

Quickly and breathlessly with leaps back and forth, Georgina told the three British men about the Austro-Hungarian soldiers' arrival through the snow, Miss Trenchard being attacked, the dogs, the shooting and the urgency of rescuing her sisters. When she'd finished, Caruthers had forced her to sit down and go through it all again from the beginning.

The three of them then went into the other room to discuss the matter privately. Georgina sat and fidgeted. When they came back in, Caruthers simply nodded.

"B- but you have to stay here," said Merryweather.

Georgina let out a strangled screech: "You don't know the way."

"She is right," Caruthers agreed.

"B- but..." Merryweather flapped his arms in exasperation. "Ah! She has n- nothing to wear."

"That's true," Caruthers said, "doesn't Mac have some spare cold weather gear."

McKendry got to his feet: "Aye."

Merryweather turned to the others: "That wasn't what I meant."

Georgina was amused that Merryweather was still trying to think of an objection, or at least that's what she assumed the procession of expressions across his face meant - it was endearing.

McKendry came back in with a variety of bulky outfits and dumped them onto the table.

"We'll get changed in there," said Caruthers and the three departed.

The jumble sale of kit was extensive, but Georgina soon realised that she had to choose from the smaller outfits. Some of the overcoats were more like tents beside her frame. She selected a few, knowing that she needed layers, changed out of her petticoats and bustle and struggled into some heavy trousers and shirts. When she turned to pick up a windcheater, she saw Merryweather standing in the doorway. His horseshoe moustache extenuated his adorable hang-dog expression. They considered each other for a moment, Georgina trying to work out how long he had been there.

"I, er... d- d- didn't see... if that's what you were... Miss."

Outside it was crisp, the sunlight having that brightness that only seemed to exist with snow on the ground. Georgina, impatient, had to admit that Caruthers had been right last night. Even in the daylight, she had little idea which way to go to the school. The blizzard had covered all trace of any paths.

"Up or down?" Caruthers asked.

"I beg your pardon."

"Did you go uphill or down?"

After a brief reflection: "The lake... downhill... downstream."

"That figures. People being chased tend to go downhill."

They set off trudging upwards and after a while the landscape started to make more sense. Stuck in the College for Young Ladies, Georgina had spent a lot of time staring out of the window, so she knew the surrounding mountains from a particular angle. She pointed out the peaks and, down the valley, the small village with an inn which was just visible.

She strode ahead, the three men following in her footsteps. Eventually the gothic architecture of the building came into view as a brick edifice sandwiched between the snow on the ground and the snow on its roof. Georgina took them through the arch in the wall at the back of the building. She showed them the stonework.

"Fresh," said McKendry, when he examined the pock marks made by the bullets. "Eight millimetre, Ruck-Zucks."

The men exchanged looks. They hadn't exactly disbelieved Georgina, but now they clearly took her story far more seriously, and Georgina found herself affected by the new professional air they had about them.

The door to the equipment room was ajar, a horror that Miss Hardcastle would never have countenanced: her precious heating, what little she allowed of it, escaping into foreign climes. The door to the corridor was closed and once inside each of them dropped their voices to a hushed reverence. Somehow the vastness of the building sounded empty.

"It's freezing in here," said Caruthers.

"Is it?"

"Can't you feel it?"

"It's always like this. Miss Hardcastle doesn't agree with heating, she says it makes one indolent."

"Sounds like my boarding school days," said Caruthers.

Further in, Georgina hesitated: "It was down there, Miss Trenchard..."

"Don't worry," Merryweather patted her gently: "We'll look."

The three explorers went down the corridor.

"There!" Georgina directed. "Just to your right."

"Mac?" Caruthers said and his colleague crouched down to examine the floor. He rubbed wood and brought his fingers to his nose.

"Blood," he said, standing. "The evidence fits the lass's story."

Georgina could stand it no longer: "What is it?"

"We've found the place your teacher was attacked... no body."

"My sisters," Georgina said impotently, when she joined them. "We have to find them."

"We could split up," McKendry suggested, "cover more ground."

Georgina glanced at the floor, the dark patch stained the wood's varnish.

"I d- don't think so," Merryweather said quickly.

Caruthers was in charge: "I agree."

They started off in a clump, but Caruthers edged in front and McKendry dropped back while Merryweather stayed with Georgina.

"How many girls were here?" Caruthers asked. His voice, all their voices sounded loud in the hard library silence of the empty college.

"I don't know - fifty... and half a dozen... no, a dozen staff if you count the servants."

"Servants?"

"Maids, cooks."

"Any men?"

"Certainly not, well..."

"Well?"

"Doctor Mott, he taught Mathematics, and the caretaker, both rather old - sweet - and recently Pieter, the Gardener's Boy, and the other Gardener's hands."

"And the Gardener?"

"Oh, yes, sorry... he was old too. Miss Hardcastle didn't approve of young men."

They reached the trophy case outside the hallway.

"Merryweather!"

"Caruthers?"

"Keep the lass back."

Merryweather blocked Georgina's view of the... whatever it was that was in the hallway. She tried sidestepping, but Merryweather was too quick for her.

"M- M- Miss," he said. She could tell that he was torn between curiosity and concern for her wellbeing. His hand was raised, not threateningly, but simply as a gesture of friendship, but it hovered above her shoulder like a hummingbird considering whether to dip down for nectar. He was tall and strong and his presence was reassuring in a very strange, novel way. She wanted him to put his hand on her shoulder and make it all right, whatever 'it' was.

Caruthers and McKendry, who had knelt down to examine something, stood and backed away.

Caruthers didn't look across to her: "The caretaker was old, you say?"

"Yes," Georgina replied.

"Put up a hell of a fight," said McKendry, mostly to himself. If the school had been cold before, it felt freezing now.

Caruthers cast a pointing finger about the room. The others went to the various doors that led off: the Headmistress's office, the Staff Room, the Library...

"Bodies, I'd say," McKendry replied, his eyes tracking across the rucked carpet, "dragged... here or... oh damn!"

Merryweather's hand was now on Georgina shoulder.

"My sisters?" she asked.

"Keep her back," said Caruthers. "For God's sake, keep her back."

Merryweather was a brick wall.

Caruthers disappeared into the library. He was gone so long that Georgina's fingers felt raw as they squeezed Merryweather's coat. When he returned, Caruthers looked ashen - not white and clean like the snow outside, but grey and dirtied.

"My sisters?" Georgina said.

In a voice that sounded drained, Caruthers said: "They're all dead... murdered."

"I must know."

"No."

"My sisters, I must know."

Caruthers shook his head.

Georgina shoved Merryweather to force him to look at her. Her eyes moistened, her vision blurred as a deluge of tears threatened. She stepped back, smartly, sniffed, wiped her nose on her sleeve in a very unladylike manner, and took control of herself. When she spoke to the three men, it was in a tone that brooked no argument.

"I must know."

"You'd have to look at the bodies," Caruthers said.

Merryweather held her hand.

A few steps along and Georgina reached where the caretaker had put up a fight: there were stains everywhere, something had torn him apart. Georgina couldn't look and instead turned her attention to the library. Inside, arranged neatly, were piles of clothes with tiny feet sticking out foolishly, human-sized dolls discarded, shapes and forms that made no sense, because Georgina's head did not want to believe, did not want to take it in, did not want to see.

They'd killed all the girls, dragged their bodies to the library and piled them high. The teachers were to one side by the reference books and their charges were dumped by fiction and biography. So many lives cut short beneath tales of longer lives.

McKendry steeled himself and moved the bodies one by one, showing each face to Georgina.

"Beatrice," she said. "Dolly, Maud, Tilly, my roommate, Smithie, I don't know."

Georgina cried when she saw the girl she didn't know. For some reason being unable to acknowledge that she ever existed seemed too harsh.

"Do you want to stop?" Merryweather asked, his voice far away and soft.

"No."

"This one?" McKendry said.

It was a girl who wouldn't smile again: "Julietta... I hated her, she was a bully, but..."

"No-one deserved this."

"I told her to go to drop dead."

"It's not your fault."

"Amazo, Amazon, I'm a spot, am as gone, am as lost..."

"I'm sorry?"

"Nothing."

Caruthers bent to assist McKendry, so the process went quicker. After a while, Georgina's words became monosyllables. When they reached the Life and Times of Wellington, there were none left to consider.

"They're not here," Georgina said.

"Are you sure?" Caruthers asked.

"They're not here."

Georgina turned her attention to the teachers. They weren't laid on top of one another, so she could scan down the line by herself.

"I think all the tutors are here," Georgina mumbled, "except for old Motty."

Most had been shot, but some had been bitten, torn and ripped.

"Who could do this?" Merryweather asked.

"They had dogs, I heard them," said Georgina.

"I've never seen a dog do this," McKendry said.

"Miss Price was my Latin teacher, she was teaching me when... I wished her dead."

"Come away," Merryweather said.

"Gardener's Hand... unless they are elsewhere with Lottie and Ness... oh, help."

A darkness leapt up to take Georgina and Merryweather's arms were there to catch her as she toppled.


## Miss Charlotte

The magnificent airship turned as it dropped through the clouds. The castle below was rugged, constructed from large blocks of local stone, so it looked like it had been carved out of the mountain itself. Most of the towers ended with an elongated roof like a witch's hat, but one had been converted into a lighthouse. Its beam sliced across the valley to guide airships away from the rocks.

A loud boom reverberated.

"Oh," said Charlotte, "they're firing a... one gun salute."

"Nein," the Graf replied. "It is the battery signalling our return - see!"

Below the castle at the end of a zigzag path was a small building. A cannon was fired again.

The Graf laughed: "A two gun salute."

"One each."

"Ja."

The Zeppelin was close now as it bore down upon a platform of metal gantries that poked outwards and upwards. The wind gusted, so they had to manoeuvre to approach upwind. The motors strained as the giant behemoth narrowed the gap to yards and then inches as the crew called out in metres. The nose caught the gantry and a shudder coursed through the metal skeleton, a deep cavernous sound echoing the thrill that Charlotte felt.

Once the two cables from the nose had been secured, they grappled other lines and dragged the Zeppelin around. It trembled as the wind began to press against its side, but eventually it was tied off with the cabin section over another platform. As Charlotte waited by the exit with Graf Zala, ground crew jostled a large wooden staircase into position.

Graf Zala disembarked first.

"Careful, my Princess," he said.

Although the gap was only a foot or so, it was nerve-racking to step across, but Charlotte made sure the Graf saw how brave she was. He held the railing and she held his hand as they descended. When his boot hit the stone flags, those waiting dropped to one knee, bowing.

"Vögte?"

"Graf, willkommen in-"

"In English, Vögte, in honour of our Royal guest," said Zala, holding Charlotte's hand high as if presenting her at court.

"Es tut... Apologies, welcome home, Graf, and welcome, Your Royal Highness," the Vögte said. He was thin, gaunt, with his oiled hair slicked back and despite being clean-shaven, he didn't look like a boy. His starched collar meant he couldn't turn his head, which was funny.

Charlotte bowed in thanks: she was having such a good time.

The Graf turned to her: "You are tired. The Vögte will see to your needs."

"I'm not at all tired."

The Graf laughed: "I'm sure not, but I must leave you, duties you understand. I must see my father, the Crown Prince, and the dowager Gräfin. Tell her the good news."

"I'd like to see around the castle."

"Later, I will show you." He stood to attention, clicked his heels and bowed. "The Vögte will see to your needs."

Charlotte did the same in reply as she was still wearing the fabulous uniform with its trousers. The Graf strode away, every inch the leader of men. The Vögte, whatever that meant, was a subservient, bent figure, weighed down by his robes rather than augmented by them. He led a different way to a stone spiral staircase that descended seemingly into the bowels of the Earth, although each window afforded a spectacular view of the surrounding mountains. Finally, the dizzying rotation came to an end and a long landing stretched in a straight line to another wing of the castle. Everything was bare stone with the occasional hanging tapestry depicting mythical beasts or battles between knights in armour. It was all too thrilling.

Her quarters were spacious, furnished by big solid pieces of oak that were islands in the expanse.

The Vögte pointed out a few things without speaking: the four poster bed, the chest with linen and towels, and a water jug. He clapped his hands and a flurry of servants swept in and out depositing the luggage she'd last seen in the cabin of the Zeppelin. The view from her window didn't include the Zeppelin and its moorings; instead, there were mountains, a tower on a projecting section of the castle itself, and below a compound with large stone buildings that belched smoke.

"Mister Vögte, what's that?"

The Vögte came over: "They are factories, Your Highness. We are not so backward in this part of the world as people believe. The revolution in Britain has found its way to our little retreat. We have machines of all kinds in our Vulcan's forge."

"Yes?"

"Yes."

"And up there?"

"That is the research tower."

"What's there?"

"It is forbidden. There are experiments."

"Experiments?"

"Chemistry and gal-"

"And the flying machine is there," Charlotte interrupted, pointing in the direction she thought the airship was positioned.

"We have many airships."

Charlotte's eyes sparkled with delight.

A clutch of maids arrived to unpack her luggage. For a moment Charlotte wondered what they were doing, but then she realised that this luggage was hers on loan. She took to indicating where she wanted items placed, but she was only guessing. Her own battered suitcase always went under the bed.

"Hello," she said to one.

The maid looked away hiding her eyes. They all did, these identical maids, as if to look upon royalty would turn them to stone. Briefly, when the Vögte was engrossed in triple-checking the Princess's belongings were unpacked correctly, one of the maids made eye contact. Suddenly, the woman gripped Charlotte's hand and whispered, almost like a prayer: "Sie sind so mutig."

The moment passed as suddenly as it had arrived and soon everything was stored away. The maids stopped in a line, heads down and hands clasped in front of them.

With an imperative 'shoo', the Vögte ejected the women and turned to Charlotte, bowing in an altogether ingratiating way.

"I will leave you now, Your Royal Highness."

"Mister Vögte, what does 'Zee zint zo mootig' mean?"

The man raised an eyebrow: "You are so brave."

"Thank you," Charlotte said, pleased that she was a magnanimous ruler.

Once she was alone, all that remained for to do was to whoop, throw herself backwards onto the immense bed and grin foolishly.

She could go and have a little explore too, she thought. Except that a key turned in the lock. She ran over, banged on the thick oak and bent two hatpins beyond rescue in the lock before she admitted defeat, flopped down on the bed and went to sleep.

# CHAPTER V

## Miss Deering-Dolittle

It was a while before Earnestine realised that the tapping was real. It was dark, pitch black, and quiet except for the *tap-tap*. She got up, her bare feet protruding from the chemise she was using as a nightdress. The wooden floor was cold.

"Yes?"

"Fräulein?"

"Yes."

She kicked a chair as she felt her way to the door.

"I have food and currency."

It was one of the Austro-Hungarians: perhaps the small one.

Earnestine shifted the desk and opened the door, blinking against tiredness as well as the dark. It was Metzger, bent low, as if he was hiding, and more like a dormouse than ever. He had a basket of food and a shoulder bag.

"If you go down the valley, there is a road, twenty kilometres, no more."

"You can't possibly be asking a young lady like myself to travel alone."

"But Fräulein-"

"Fräulein nothing."

He glanced left and right: "May I come in to discuss this."

"I beg your pardon!"

Her loud voice made him start and check the corridor again.

"I leave them here," he said, and he put them down on a cupboard opposite the door before he stole away.

Ridiculous, Earnestine thought, that one of her kidnappers would bring an escape kit. Fleeing was obviously not something she could contemplate and any attempt had barely crossed her mind. It made her quite cross, so much so that it took her three attempts to strike the match that she'd palmed from the hotel's reception. The candle took, casting its light over the room. She dressed quickly, double knotting the laces of her boots, and then slipped out. She bent low and checked the corridor and then straightened when she realised she was copying Metzger's furtive movements. She added his bread, beef, knackwursts and cheese to the bag supplementing the rolls and the apple she'd purloined from dinner.

Down the corridor she went.

She hazarded that the reception was most likely guarded by the old hotelier and the Austro-Hungarian soldiers, so she'd already singled out a window with a balcony at the far end as the most promising exit.

It was locked.

The fish knife that she'd wiped on her napkin before tucking into her boot was just the thing to jimmy it open.

The air outside was fresh and cold. Distant mountains, darker against the dark sky, were visible, but everything was lit by moonlight rather than a hint of an approaching dawn. Earnestine took the few steps across the balcony to the railing.

Ah, the hotel was built on a slope and this had added an extra storey to the drop at the back.

"Are you going to fly?"

Earnestine stiffened and turned.

Kroll was standing in the doorway. He opened his dark lantern's hinged door and threw a band of light across Earnestine's face. She was forced to squint and look away.

"You shouldn't survive that."

"It's 'couldn't survive that'," Earnestine corrected.

"Ja."

"Would you like some sausage?" she said holding out her basket.

"I shall wait for breakfast."

"Very wise. I'll bid you goodnight then."

"Goodnight."

She went past the big man and then down the corridor again. When she reached her door, another opened suddenly. She and Pieter were only a few yards apart, he in his loose shirt and britches and she in her tidy clothes.

"Good night," she said.

"Good night," he replied.

Before she closed her door, she saw another shadow, low and creeping at the far end of the corridor, move.

She leant against the door listening, but there were too many good-nights in German for her to hazard another attempt tonight. Best thing to do, she thought, was get a good night's sleep.

## Miss Georgina

The bedroom that Georgina had slept in for the whole term seemed an alien place and it was no longer a blessed peace to find herself alone there. Her room-mates, formerly so irritating, were keenly absent. The other beds in the shared room were empty, because the occupants were downstairs in the library as if asleep together.

She packed her things, although it took a long time because she kept pausing at each keepsake. She found a photograph of the family. It had been taken before their mother had gone up the river. There was Earnestine looking regal and little Charlotte smiling foolishly. Their mother seemed maternal, but now Georgina looked at her, she seemed different, haunted, and Georgina knew how their father's absence had drained her. The arrangement of woman and girls was lopsided, the man's place was a gap on the left and there was almost a space to pour his presence into if... when he returned. Georgina knew he would return, but their mother had not been able to wait.

And now Earnestine and Charlotte were gone too.

Georgina foresaw further daguerreotypes containing just her own lonely figure pushed against one side of an otherwise empty frame. No, she thought, she would find them and then there would be pictures of all of them, new pictures, coloured with dyes, framed and covering every wall in their house back in Kensington.

There was a knock at the door.

"M- M- Miss."

"Merry?"

"We've looked, everywhere, n- nothing, sorry."

"That you didn't find their bodies?"

"N- no, I mean... I'm just... sorry."

"Packing!" said Georgina.

"I b- b- beg your-"

Georgina went to Charlotte's room, Merryweather trailing after her. There were six sets of beds, chests of drawers and small wardrobes. She knew which one was Charlotte's, the untidiest.

Inside Charlotte's wardrobe, Georgina found a spare school uniform and that silly summer dress, but there were three empty hangers. She'd be wearing her dress and a blouse, but where was her coat? Her blue coat should have been there. Miss Hardcastle did not allow the girl to wear their coats indoors, so the conclusion was obvious.

"The silly girl went out," Georgina said.

"That's good," Merryweather replied. "Is... Isn't it?"

"No, she'd have got in trouble and Earnestine would tell me off."

"B- But she could be still alive."

"Or... outside."

"I'll get Caruthers and McKendry to do a sweep."

"Thank you."

"What colour is the coat?"

"Charlotte's is dark blue."

Merryweather nodded and slipped out onto the landing.

Georgina checked Charlotte's chest of drawers. Under her handkerchiefs was the old cigar box that Uncle Jeremiah had given her for all her keepsakes. Georgina opened it, feeling guilty but at the same time permitted. It was full of buttons and insignia from cadets, tokens that *those* boys had given her. It was these that had been discovered and it had led directly to their incarceration in this hell hole.

A sudden thought drove Georgina out of the room and along the corridor. At the far end she raised her hand to knock, felt foolish and then went into Earnestine's room. As a Prefect, this small cubby hole had been an extra privilege. She looked in the wardrobe: Earnestine's dark red coat hung there along with her spare school uniform and a sensible formal dress. It meant something, Georgina knew, and Earnestine would 'tut' and tell Georgina to pull herself together: it was obvious.

Georgina slapped her forehead: come on, come on.

Charlotte's coat was missing so she had gone outside. Earnestine's was in her wardrobe, so she was inside the building. Earnestine's bedside cabinet had a top drawer and her sister's belongings were neat and organised: a place for everything and everything in its place; except that there was a place with nothing in it. A long and narrow gap for something long and narrow like... what? Georgina sat on the bed and tried to imagine the long and narrow object in her hand. A box maybe, or a set of ribbons... Georgina started sobbing, quietly but uncontrollably. Earnestine would know what to do, but Georgina did not.

"Georgina! Georgina!"

Georgina grabbed one of Earnestine's handkerchiefs and wiped her eyes.

"Here," she shouted. "Here."

Merryweather's cries increased and Georgina went to the door to shout along the corridor.

"There you are," Merryweather exclaimed, and then more softly, "you worried me."

"I was looking in my sister's room for clues."

Merryweather nodded, agreeing, the colour coming back to his cheeks. He reached out, hesitantly, and Georgina found she was doing the same. Their fingers almost touched, but Earnestine's handkerchief came between them and the moment passed.

"What is it?" Georgina asked.

"Mac's found something interesting in the East Wing."

Georgina felt aggrieved: they must search the grounds, not the East Wing: "We weren't allowed in the East Wing."

"Perhaps they went exploring," Merryweather suggested.

"Exploring!" Georgina practically shouted at him. "Earnestine wouldn't allow that."

"Let's s- s- see."

At the entrance to the East Wing, Georgina hesitated at the rope barrier and the 'Out of Bounds' sign. She could hear Miss Hardcastle's shrill tones and feared the woman's wrath, even though she knew that the Principal was lying in the library. Perhaps the woman would rise from the dead and haunt her, just like Hideous Helga, for trespassing. It took all her courage to step over into the forbidden realm.

"What is it?" Caruthers was asking when they arrived.

McKendry was crouched down again: "Austrian brand," he explained. "Both the cigarettes and the clothes. Austro-Hungary or thereabouts, I'd say."

"How many?"

"No more than a half a dozen. There was a struggle here."

Caruthers turned, smoothed his moustache and looked at Georgina questioningly.

"Not the people who attacked. I saw them arrive and there were three or four dozen at least."

"There's a mystery here," Caruthers muttered.

McKendry picked up a Two of Diamonds. Other cards, a mix of face down and face up, lay across the slate flagstones. McKendry turned over a Jack, just like he'd turned the young girls' faces upwards for scrutiny. Georgina looked away, putting her hand to her face.

"The young lady's sister, her coat is m- m- missing," Merryweather spoke in hushed tones. He was trying to be kind, Georgina knew, but it gave the cellar the air of a mausoleum. "She might be outside..."

Dead: that seemed to be the unspoken word. Charlotte, little Charlotte, must have met the attackers outside and Earnestine, of course, the eldest sister would have been protecting her, while useless Georgina was saving her own worthless skin.

Caruthers smoothed his moustache in thought, and then said, "The answer isn't here."

"I guess we won't be the first to climb that mountain," McKendry joked.

"I'm sure the peak won't be going anywhere," Caruthers replied. "We should go into town and let the Bürgermeister know."

"So much for avoiding entanglements."

They carried on talking, planning, and discussing the alternatives: the Bürgermeister, going it alone, contacting someone called Major Dan, but Georgina wasn't taking it in. She felt wooden and useless, a spare part and... strangely, she had been staring at it for such a long time without realising what she was actually seeing. Leaning against the upturned card table, where it had rolled, was a long and narrow object, a cream tube: Earnestine's-

She cried out: "Flashlight!"

That's what it had been.

The others looked round as she sprang forward and grabbed hold of it. She held it aloft for them like a trophy.

"It's Earnestine's flashlight."

Caruthers didn't know the term: "Flashlight?"

McKendry did: "It's a torch, Yank word. That's a Misell Electric."

"Father gave it to Earnestine when he came back from New York. The American policemen use them. I got a ribbon. Charlotte got lead figures."

She pressed the button and shone the yellowish light over their faces illuminating them, flicking it on and off as their father had explained.

"It was her prize possession," claimed Georgina. "She wouldn't forget it or lose it unless... there was a struggle here, you said."

"They kidnapped her and killed the others," said Caruthers, mulling it over.

"She didn't use it for everyday use, the batteries don't last, she only used it when she went exploring."

As soon as she'd said it, Georgina thought how wrong it sounded: *no exploring, no trouble, no adventures*; that was Earnestine's mantra.

"She found something then," said Caruthers "before..."

"They're alive," Georgina insisted.

"I hope so," Merryweather said. "I'm sure they are."

"Let's operate on that assumption," Caruthers said. "We'll go to town and send a coded telegram to Major Dan and-"

Georgina butted in: "Excuse me, but you're military men, aren't you?"

"Yes, Miss," Caruthers replied and the three men stood taller.

"Why aren't you with your regiment?"

"We're here to-"

"You're spies."

"Oh no, Miss, we're not spies, we're more... er..."

"Gentlemen adventurers," McKendry said.

"Gentlemen, yes," Caruthers agreed.

"Yes," Merryweather said, "spies have to have p- p- permission from M-"

"Yes! Merry! Whereas we are simply on holiday."

"To climb a mountain?" Georgina added.

"Yes, absolutely."

"To look at the view."

"Excellent views from the top of mountains."

"To spy on the land."

"Indeed, in a sightseeing manner, but tonight I think we'll be staying here," Caruthers announced firmly.

"Is that wise?" Merryweather asked.

"Probably not, but as I see it whoever did all this has left. They are unlikely to return, whereas if we go blundering about in the dark, we might run into them, as it were, and that would be unfortunate."

"Perhaps we should return to the hut?" McKendry said.

"Hardly a place for the young lady," Merryweather argued.

"I'm sure we'll find suitable accommodation where the teachers slept and so forth."

"I'm sleeping in my dormitory!"

Georgina was surprised by her own outburst and rather embarrassed to be the centre of attention suddenly.

"Well, I'm sure we could organise a... sort of..." Caruthers trailed off. "This is quite delicate."

Caruthers shuffled slightly, rubbed his moustache; McKendry adjusted his handlebar and tugged his chin puff, and Merryweather stared out ahead.

"There are other dormitories off the same corridor," Georgina said.

They nodded in agreement.

Back at Georgina's dormitory corridor, she indicated various options. The men selected a dormitory closer to the landing tacitly deciding to put themselves between the sleeping young lady and anything that might come up the stairs.

"There might be... you know," McKendry was saying as he and Caruthers went to inspect their bunks.

"I'm sure a medal winner like yourself can cope with ladies undergarments," Caruthers boomed from inside.

Georgina found their difficulties amusing. She smiled for the first time in an age, but that suddenly seemed wrong. She shouldn't ever be happy again, because... but best not to think about that. She found herself standing with Merryweather just inside her room, which was somewhat improper, but these were extraordinary circumstances and the door was open.

"D- d- do you have everything you need?" asked Merryweather.

"It is my usual room."

"Yes, of course... sorry."

"Do you have a medal?"

"I have a couple."

"What for?"

"India."

"You must show it to Charlotte when we find her."

"Yes."

"She likes that sort of thing."

Georgina was conscious of how small her room was. It had appeared spacious for the three roommates, but now this man seemed a giant in a doll's house. His presence was awkward and embarrassing. She quite liked being with this man, but... oh dear.

"You can't be in here with me alone," she said.

"N- n- no?"

"It isn't seemly."

"No, no, of course n- n- not. Sorry. So sorry, sorry, I apologise, of course."

Merryweather hesitated on the threshold clearly torn between competing aspects of proper gentlemanly conduct.

"You'll have to go."

"Of course."

Georgina, for her part, knew the other side of the coin. She wanted him to stay, to protect her, but it was impossible. Alone with a man in her bedroom at night was simply unthinkable, extraordinary circumstances or no extraordinary circumstances. He must go: she wanted him to stay. Perhaps there were good reasons for him to do so. For a start, there were the villains who had murdered everyone in the school. It simply wasn't safe for any of them. The idea of staying the night here was a risk, she knew that, so she probably did need a guardian close by. However, that wasn't entirely the truth. She wanted Merryweather to remain to protect her and she wanted Merryweather to remain because he was Merryweather. The thought shocked her.

"I'll say goodnight then, M- M- Miss Georgina."

"Very well, Mister Merryweather."

"Goodnight then."

"Goodnight."

"I'll be going."

"Yes."

"I'll just be down the corridor, if..."

"Of course."

"Goodnight."

"Goodnight."

The door closed.

She was alone in the room, he was outside.

Lucky escape there, she thought, as she took off her boots, removed her outer garments and slipped into her bunk in her chemise to hunker down under her blankets. She kept her hand on Earnestine's flashlight hidden under her pillow.

It was quiet, the silence was like a dough rising to fill the bread tin, heavy and full of meaning. She was conscious of her own breathing and then of distant male voices, Merryweather, Caruthers and McKendry, moving about in the next room and then that too ceased. She'd get some sleep, that would be best, she thought, and at least tonight Tilly wouldn't disturb everyone with her homesickness.

Suddenly, Georgina felt like crying, but she wouldn't.
She'd sleep.

If only she could sleep, but that comfort eluded her.

"Georgina?"

"Tilly! Is that you?"

"Why did you leave us?"

"I didn't."

"Amazo, amazo, amazo..."

"Please, don't."

"Amazon, I'm-a-spot, am-as-gone-"

Hands suddenly tore the blankets off, cold, gnarled hands with long clawed fingers, grasping, pulling, tearing. Tilly and Julietta, with ruined, smiling faces and metal boxes sparking with unnatural energies, bore down on her, their eyes yellow and watery, and red mouths, rotting teeth, biting, gnawing, ripping her skin from her face until-

Until she was sitting up on the bed, alone, shivering in a cold sweat and very aware that it was the middle of the night. As her rapid breathing slowed, the quiet descended again. Her feet were cold, she could see her toes in the pale moonlight.

Nobody came to her rescue.

She hadn't cried out. She hadn't been a baby. She didn't want Merryweather to think of her as a baby.

She got back under the covers, shivering. She thought about getting up and finding some milk, but the idea of wandering through the dark passages of the college did not appeal. She resolved not to sleep a wink, because she knew any sleep would be full of horrors.

## Miss Charlotte

The Vögte brought a tray of food: rye bread, bratwurst and salami, sliced ham, cuts of chicken breast, strips of duck and zungenwurst, with German mustard, pickle and horseradish along with a half bottle of wine. Wine! And it wasn't even Christmas.

Charlotte tucked in and found herself giggling at her good fortune even before the wine was finished. The heavy silver knife slipped easily between the old door jamb to jigger the lock. Tee hee, a little look round, Charlotte thought.

It was night, but Charlotte didn't feel at all tired. She had slept soundly all afternoon, the excitement of piloting an airship had quite worn her out, but now, refreshed by sleep, food and wine, she was ready for anything.

The stone corridor was quiet and dark, but there was enough moonlight coming through the windows for her to find her way if she was careful. At the window, she looked out through the diamond leading, and saw the valley below, beautiful and serene in the blue light. Vertically down a group of soldiers were berating a young woman: someone was in trouble, Charlotte sniggered: although, it would be best to be careful that they didn't catch her.

Where to go, she wondered. There were the factories below, which sounded unpleasant and dirty, or there was the laboratory, which also sounded boring. It was bound to have a blackboard and complicated nonsense that had to be learned by rote; however, it was forbidden, which made it exciting.

She made her way along the corridor to another spiral staircase that signified that she'd reached the far tower. Up she went, round and round, until she reached a landing. There were rooms off in various directions, but one had a thick door. Underneath light flickered like Earnestine's magic flashlight. Charlotte went over and bent down to peer through the keyhole. There were marvels frustratingly beyond the tiny frame.

Someone coughed behind her.

He was a tall young man, elegant, and dressed in a formal grey lounge suit, almost Beau Brummell in its cut and style.

"Good evening or is it good morning," he smirked. "Or are you going to be some bore who doesn't understand the language of Shakespeare, Byron and Shelley."

He turned his head slightly showing off his good side. He was handsome, attractive, clean shaven except for some fine sideburns that framed his beautiful features. He affected a silk handkerchief in his top pocket and a flower, purple with sharp edged leaves, from some alpine thistle. His face, when he gazed back at Charlotte, was open, honest and full of life. His bright eyes sparked in the candlelight.

Charlotte was having none of it: "Perhaps good night," she said.

"You do speak English? How wonderfully marvellous."

"Yes, I was educated in... Oxford," Charlotte replied.

"You won't believe how tedious it has been without anyone to converse with. Mater only speaks Latin."

"Latin?" Charlotte had a sinking feeling that she had not escaped school after all.

"The names of chemicals and other paraphernalia."

"Chemistry?" The curriculum was building up.

"Alchemy, medicine, galvanism," he continued.

Charlotte felt her shoulders slump: next he'd be offering to teach her golf or cricket or some other activity that could only be explained by the man putting his arms around the girl. It might be shooting, but he didn't look the shooting type.

"I prefer poetry myself," he said.

Even the humanities: yuck.

"I'm Leslie," he held out a hand, long and elegant, "Leslie Mordant."

Charlotte hesitated, quite unsure what the correct answer was in the circumstances: "Yes."

"I know all about you," he smiled. "Your Royal Highness. The castle has been in quite an uproar waiting for your arrival. People running hither and thither, so tedious. The research has been held back, quite interrupted, and Mater says it's intolerable."

"I'm sure she would."

"And now you are here."

"Research?"

"Oh, all very boring, I assure you. I sometimes have to watch the bottles and chemicals and wotnot boiling or percolating or whatever. It's such a tedium, honestly."

"I imagine, I'm not keen on cooking."

He chortled: "I'm sure not."

"What exactly is going on?"

"Oh, it's Doctor Mordant this and Doctor Mordant that and Doctor Mordant the other."

"You're never a Doctor!"

"And why not?" he teased. "No, I'm much too young and my talent lies in the finer things of life."

"Your father then?"

"Ha-ha, it is going to be such fun to have someone to talk to at last. This beastly castle has been a positive dungeon."

"It probably has a dungeon," Charlotte added.

"Ahem, yes, full of pretenders no doubt."

"Pretenders?"

"The Prisoner of Zenda," he said as if it was obvious. He must have seen her expression. "Anthony Hope, published recently."

"I've not read it."

He leaned forward, "Come with me, I can read you some verse of my own."

"Lovely," Charlotte lied.

Leslie led the way along the landing. At one point they came out across some battlements where they were assaulted by the chill air. Leslie returned fire with "oh the moon, oh moon, oh moon" before they were once again protected from poetry by the thick walls. Finally, they reached the far end and Leslie opened a door to reveal a small bedroom strewn with silk scarves and frilly shirts. Books lay about where they had been discarded, some open, and all with bookmarks jutting from their pages. It really was going to be nothing but poetry.

"Come in," Leslie gestured.

"Ah, I can't," Charlotte said. "You see... that's a bedroom, a man's bedroom, and I'm not chaperoned."

Leslie looked crestfallen.

"The laboratory looks interesting and I'm sure that you could show me in there as it's not a bedroom."

"My mother might be there."

"She could chaperone."

"Can I bring my Shelley?"

"Of course."

Back they went - "oh moon, oh moon" - and Leslie let them into the laboratory. It was a large room, possibly a converted dining room that was full of scientific equipment laid out on tables. The smells of acid and caustic properties were vile and stung Charlotte's nose, so she couldn't resist having a closer look.

"Shall I pick a poem?" Leslie mused. "Something romantic."

"Lovely," Charlotte murmured. This wasn't Chemistry and Biology, she realised, as in the mixing of potassium permanganate to turn water purple or to add yeast to flour to make bread; this, with its burners, smells, sudden sparks and frogs dissected on the table, was far more revolting and therefore considerably more thrilling.

The real question was what needed to be played with first. She reached out for an electrode...

"Don't touch that!"

Charlotte leapt back as if she had received a shock: "I was only looking."

The owner of the commanding voice was a woman, stern and foreboding with long red hair pinned back so that the shape of her skull was revealed: "And who might you be?!"

She had a long black dress, stylish, with a bustle, but draped across her front was a long white apron with vivid stains pockmarking the cotton. Tools and equipment poked out of the many pockets and she wore a necklace of steel and rubber.

"Mater," said Leslie. "May I present Her Royal Highness, Princess..." He waved his silk handkerchief in her general direction and his announcement trailed off as if he'd become bored of the whole business and Charlotte realised that he didn't know her name either.

"I don't have time for this," Leslie's mother said. "I was given assurances that I was not to be disturbed and now you bring me this..."

The necklace was a stethoscope: "You're a Doctor," Charlotte said.

Doctor Mordant gave Charlotte a long stare through the lenses of her glasses. Her eyes seemed to expand as the thick glass magnified Charlotte for closer scrutiny.

"Indeed, I am Doctor Mordant." There was a Scottish burr to her voice, an educated accent, Edinburgh. "Is there a problem?"

"Of course not," Charlotte replied. "Why can't a woman be a doctor or a lawyer or whatever she pleases?"

Or an officer in the cavalry, thought Charlotte, with braid and buttons and men of many ranks ready to take orders. While Charlotte was playing with this dream, Doctor Mordant considered the girl afresh, but with that expression that adults reserve for when they suspect they are being gulled.

"Your son tells me you are doing experiments," Charlotte said.

"Indeed."

Charlotte realised that this woman would not suffer fools gladly and nor would she be impressed by flattery. She was dedicated to her work.

"Important experiments, I hope."

"The most important."

"Oh, Mater, I found her," Leslie whined.

"Be quiet," Doctor Mordant snapped. "They are the most important experiments, young lady, of medical science and all the work of a woman."

Leslie snorted: "Based on that Genevese scientist-"

"I said be quiet!"

"As all medical science is based upon the work of Hypocrites," said Charlotte.

Doctor Mordant corrected her: "Hippocrates."

"Hippocrates..."

"Although perhaps you were right first time: the medical establishment are all hypocrites."

"And they forget that the importance of nursing, good health, clean practices and hygienic principles, were all the work of a woman, Florence Nightingale," said Charlotte; not to mention the gorgeous uniforms of the light brigade, she thought.

Doctor Mordant beamed, the skin of her face, pulled back by her hair, was unused to such an expression and her teeth were bared, but nonetheless Charlotte knew she had passed a test.

"Do you want to see?" Doctor Mordant asked.

Charlotte considered the vile smelling chemicals and the ugly stains across the Doctor's apron, and all the inevitable Greek and Latin that went with the complexities of Chemistry as well as the repulsive practices with dissection, but she knew the correct answer: "Oh yes, please."

Doctor Mordant waved away one entire bench, dismissing it as irrelevant, and led the way further into the laboratory.

"I'm going to read Shelley," Leslie called out.

Both Charlotte and Doctor Mordant spoke together: "I Imm..."

They passed a table connected to the ceiling by chains and pulleys. These led high up to a skylight through which the moon disappeared behind the clouds. Its light had long been surpassed by the lightning trapped in glass bulbs that were fixed to the walls in place of gas sconces. Doctor Mordant reached a bench filled with beakers, glass tubes and chemicals bubbling over gas.

"This is the important ingredient, the galvanic energy is mere fireworks, the spark if you like... you know about galvanism?"

"Oh yes, light bulbs and frog's legs jumping. My sister has a flashlight."

"Indeed, you know much."

"My parents were progressive, I had a governess and various private educations."

"Of course, even so the male of the household would have had all the advantages."

"Alas, only sisters."

"You are fortunate."

"You've not met my sisters."

"Sisters... I thought your family tree was-"

"The secret chemicals? They sound ever so interesting."

Doctor Mordant grimaced her smile again and turned to the bench. Lucky escape, Charlotte thought, clearly the Princess's family was well known by all but herself.

On the bench a multitude of pipes, flasks and condensation chambers bubbled and spat, powered by a gas burner set at a low rate. There were gauges of brass, thermometers and an open book like a ledger full of figures.

"Patching bodies is straightforward anatomy and considerably easier than surgery on the living. There's no blood being pumped around the arteries and veins. Once you've dismantled enough bodies, it's clear how they work. Which is precisely why those pompous cretins in Edinburgh are so precious about their dissection classes, they didn't want their secrets to be known. It's all handshakes and code words, boy's games. As if there weren't enough cadavers to go around. Edinburgh's

Kirkyards are full of them, the poor drop like flies simply because the grand men of medicine refuse to listen to the ideas of a mere woman like Nightingale."

"She saved so many brave men in the Crimea," Charlotte added.

"Indeed. And this is where we shall save so many more men and women."

"Will we?"

Charlotte felt quite caught up in the woman's severe excitement, her enthusiasm and commitment infecting her like tuberculosis as if she had not washed her hands.

Doctor Mordant took Charlotte around the galvanic engines, the distillation apparatus and the mobile surgical trolley. The Doctor explained everything to the young girl, her plans, the ambitions of the Graf and all the secrets. She gloated about how they would change the world.

Charlotte put on her most attentive expression and thought about airships. They were really exciting and if she asked nicely she was sure that the Graf would let her wear the uniform again with its trousers and-

"Are you listening?"

"Yes Miss."

"He may well have discovered the principle, but I have applied it on an industrial scale."

"Who?"

"The doctor I told you about."

Charlotte racked her brains: "Vincent-"

"Victor!"

"Yes, of course, please continue."

"This may be the veritable Age of Steam, but soon, very soon, will dawn the Galvanic Era. See this spark leaping from contact to contact, this is lightning that burns the very ether itself, harnessed and contained, flickering like a child's toy. What is iron and steel, what is coal and steam, when put against flesh, the very power of the Creator of the world? We can choose who we bring back and who we let lie in the silence of the grave. We will defeat that awful spectre, Death himself. Science, the application of Apothecary and Galvanism, will unleash our true potential: and I, a mere woman, will show those Neanderthals at the General Council of Medical Education and Registration of the United Kingdom of Great Britain, India and its Colonies."

There were lines of batteries on the bench in front of them all ready for the clever boxes that Doctor Mordant had carefully explained after she'd talked about the wotnot and the doo dah.

Doctor Mordant laughed: "Imagine if Burke and Hare had bought one of their finds in, fresh from the grave, and what if Sir Robert Knox himself had seen it risen before him in the anatomy room. That's only fifty years ago."

Charlotte sniggered too, trying to imagine the look on Sir Robert Whatever's face.

"These Austro-Hungarians have had this science for ninety years - nearly a century - and none of them could apply the principle in practice. They had all the equipment: the galvanisers, batteries and his chemicals, and the man's notes, for heaven's sake."

"Oh yes," Charlotte agreed.

"Admittedly his handwriting was appalling, but what do you expect from a male doctor."

Charlotte remembered something that Miss Hardcastle had once told her: "Good handwriting is so important."

"There will be a war, a war to end all wars, and once the old ways are swept away, those here want this new order to be ruled by the Austro-Hungarian Empire, the so called Kingdoms and Lands Represented in the Imperial Council and the Lands of the Holy Hungarian Crown of Saint Stephen. These men love their titles and uniforms."

Charlotte rather liked the uniforms, so she said nothing.

"But it will be the dawning of science, reason and common sense. In the future people will be rewarded for their merit."

"I agree."

"You know nothing of merit," Doctor Mordant replied, "you were born with a crown ready for your pretty little head."

"Which I would gladly give up to be measured according to my merits, my proper merits," Charlotte insisted. "I'm always being told what is proper and right, what to do, or more often to do nothing, when I should be striving to make my mark upon the world."

"I wish, Your Royal Highness, that you had been my daughter, but instead the Almighty blessed me with a wastrel son. The words of dead poets mean nothing: all spirits are enslaved that serve things evil. Oh, pleasant enough, but the witterings of a vegetarian. Now, the thoughts of great scientists, their equations and formulae, are what will change the world. Steam pressure, lift ratios or, to use my own research as the example, galvanic voltages, currents, anatomy, enzymatic properties and so forth."

Doctor Mordant looked to Charlotte for a comment. Hadn't Doctor Mordant said something about the future, Charlotte thought, so she said, "It is the future."

"Yes, why should the Fabians, the Speculative Society and the Elect pretend - Chronological Committee indeed - when we can create the future in the present?" Doctor Mordant rewarded her with another unpleasant smile: "It is good that you, from such an aristocratic background, can see the sense in what I say."

"It's self-evident," Charlotte said.

"Indeed. And society will be ordered along rational lines with three pillars - education, medicine and eugenics, and we will see the human animal rise in mind, body and blood."

Charlotte raised her hands in front of her: "I should applaud," she announced, clapping a few times.

"Women will lead the way."

"I have seen examples myself already," she said thinking of the control she'd had over the airship.

"Enzymes leaven the decaying flesh and reverse the tide of corruption until the spark of life, galvanism that leaps from the storm to strike the ground resurrects the body: life is not a soul, it's not divine, it's not the breath of a quaint deity; but rather, it is a process, a complex and understandable mechanism that replicates itself: life recreating life, life feeding off old life, and new life being created from the raw materials."

Doctor Mordant's own face crawled with a seeming life of its own as the flickering light of the galvanic engine sparked, a thread of energetic corona jumping up the apparatus burning its glow onto the back of Charlotte's eyes just as the scientist's own vision branded itself onto the young girl's mind.

The air between them buzzed with vitality.

# CHAPTER VI

## Miss Deering-Dolittle

There was someone in her room.

"Excuse me!" Earnestine said.

"Fräulein," came a voice, "I am sorry."

A hand pulled her bedding away while the other grabbed at her, holding her down. Earnestine fought back. Lying on her back meant she had all four limbs at her disposal against her assailant's arms. She kicked. The man stumbled back, falling.

"The Prince is too good for you."

It was Metzger!

"But you are not too good for me," he said as he pushed her back onto the bed.

"Excuse me."

"I know that you want it," Metzger growled, "your sort always do."

Earnestine pushed him away and kicked, her bare foot going between his legs and having a quite unexpected result. Metzger doubled up, coughing, but when he looked up, his rage was murderous. He shoved Earnestine back again, grabbed her hair and yanked back her head. He pushed his mouth towards her, closer, remorselessly, his breath playing across her tightly closed lips. Wriggle as she might, she was trapped, unable to grip anything, the sheets constraining her, everything she did creating a burning pain where her hair tugged. There was a fireside set nearby: a brush, dustpan, tongs and a poker. If she could just reach... she tried, her stretched finger nearly... but it was no use.

"Achtung!"

Earnestine was mortified to see Prince Pieter standing in the doorway. Irrationally, she didn't feel relief at her rescue but rather shame at being found in this compromising fashion.

Metzger jumped back, yanking a handful of hair out of Earnestine's scalp.

"Metzger!"

"Sire, she... tried to seduce me."

"I blo- bal- jolly well did not."

Prince Pieter looked at the two of them with revulsion. Carefully, slowly, deliberately, he took out his glove and cast it upon the ground. Metzger stared at the finely stitched grey leather with disbelief.

Pieter shouted loudly.

Metzger didn't move, couldn't move.

Finally, Pieter picked the glove up, thrust it into Metzger's hand and used the man's own hand to strike himself across the cheek. Metzger let out a strangled cry as if he had been the one struck.

They left, and by the time Earnestine had made herself decent, put on her boots and grabbed a few things, there was an angry gathering downstairs in the hallway. The Innkeeper complained in loud tones until Prince Pieter hollered at him. A soldier ran up with a long fancy case and Pieter opened it to reveal a pair of matched sabres.

The Prince grabbed one and Metzger, when offered the case, took the other out of its felt depression.

Soldiers parted as Kroll came striding up to the Prince: "Warum?"

"English!"

"Why?"

The Prince pointed at Metzger: "Der Hund versuchte, das Mädchen zu entehren!"

"Is this true?" Kroll said, turning to Earnestine as the Prince stripped off his jacket and started exercising his right shoulder.

"I don't speak German," Earnestine said.

"He said that Herr Metzger tried to dishonour you."

"He tried."

Kroll was aghast, his eyes wide with a moment of disbelief: "Metzger?"

"Yes."

"Outside!" Pieter commanded.

"We should wait until dawn," Kroll announced.

"It's dawn now."

"Not yet."

"Fetch lanterns then."

It was cold outside and dark, the Innkeeper himself came out with three great lanterns and handed one to each of the opponents. The Prince and Metzger held them by their hooks so that they swung about. The light, though weak, caused great shadows to leap and loom.

Kroll was shouting in German. Despite not knowing the language, Earnestine knew he was demanding to know what was going on: why, why? Or pleading for common sense, perhaps.

Everyone gathered in a wide circle, a distorted oval, on the rough ground outside. The two men circled until neither had the advantage of the gentle slope.

"Erstes blut?" Metzger asked.

"Death!"

Pieter and Metzger squared off about three yards apart, came to attention and flicked their swords in front of their faces.

"En garde," Pieter said.

He attacked.

Metzger parried.

"Fight me!" Pieter commanded, striking his subordinate with his lantern. Metzger's face was bloodied, a dark shadow on his right side that did not change when the lanterns moved.

The two men went at it again, steel striking steel with their lanterns acting as makeshift shields. Again and again they moved forward or were beaten back. The wall of people shifted aside too as the struggle moved downhill. The crowd followed, forming around them again.

Earnestine's hands tensed into fists and she realised she was holding something in her right hand. It was the poker from the bedroom fireside set. She didn't remember picking it up, let alone carrying it downstairs and outside. It was like a sword.

Prince Pieter bled from a cut across his face now.

This made no sense.

She must stop it.

Earnestine stepped forward bringing the poker up, but a hand caught her arm.

"You have done enough, Fräulein," Kroll said.

The two fighters came together, their sabres clashed, the sharp edges scraping down together until their hilts locked. Both struck with their lanterns causing a sudden shower of sparks. The Prince's was torn from his hand and fell; Metzger's went out and the man turned his face from the light to look at it. Pieter jabbed forward and the point of his sword punctured the other man's jacket up to the hilt. Pieter twisted and pulled his sword out.

Metzger dropped to his knees, spat blood and began to topple forward.

Pieter leapt to his aid, flinging his sword aside: "Metzger!"

The Prince caught his falling comrade and cradled him in his arms: "Why, why?" and then "Get a Doctor! Holen sie einen Arzt!"

"I saw the way you looked at her," Metzger coughed: "Such risk, I could not allow. You've never been one for the camp followers, you would have given her your heart."

"Metzger... you fool."

"She's a commoner..." Metzger swallowed hard, blood was filling his mouth making it difficult for him to speak.

"Metzger... Where is that Doctor!?"

"Promise me..."

But the man was dead. Prince Pieter's face was speckled with scarlet splatter; his uniform stained, but despite the cut across his face most of the blood had been Metzger's.

When everyone had left, when they'd carried the body into the inn with the Prince holding his friend's cold hand, and she was alone, Earnestine could taste ash in her mouth. Both lanterns were out now having cast the last of their sparks into the air. She dropped the poker into the dust and pushed it with her toe. It was light now, dawn, and the men were getting the horses ready, saddling some, attaching others to the coaches and all the activity was churning up the blood stained earth.

"Fräulein?" The heavy-set Oberst stood over her.

"Kroll?"

"A good man has died for you today," said the big man. "I suspect he will not be your last."


## Miss Georgina

In the morning, they dressed and saw to their ablutions. None of them suggested breakfast, and for that Georgina was glad, as the smell of death had gathered like dark clouds within the college. They trudged away through the snow down the road towards the distant village.

It was a long walk.

Georgina glanced from side to side, trying to catch sight of a dark blue coat, pleased to have not seen one, but on edge because they had discovered nothing about the fate of her sisters. There was only Earnestine's flashlight. Georgina found herself touching it to make sure it was real.

The sun was squintingly bright.

By the time they reached the village, the snow was turning to slush in places and clear bright water trickled into rivulets.

"Quiet," said McKendry.

Georgina caught up with the others and took in the picture postcard beauty of the alpine community. It was a like a painting, motionless and still. There was no smoke from any chimney, no-one stirring, the curtains were drawn everywhere and none tweaked to allow an occupant to spy on the four travellers.

"Perhaps they're still in bed?" Georgina regretted speaking immediately; it was such a stupid, facetious thing to say.

"Merry, stay with..." Caruthers ordered.

"Yes, sir."

"Best foot forward."

Caruthers and McKendry set off, and when they were a good twenty yards in front, Merryweather and Georgina followed.

Caruthers and McKendry stopped to confer and then McKendry went to the left and Caruthers moved towards the inn. The tall man went up the wooden steps and reached the door. When he opened it, it came off its hinges and crashed to the ground. The clatter brought McKendry running.

Caruthers stepped inside and jerked back suddenly.

He took a handkerchief out and covered his mouth and nose before re-entering the dark interior. McKendry adjusted his scarf and followed. The inn seemed to be getting smaller before Georgina realised that Merryweather had put his hand under her elbow to guide her away. For a moment, she resented being treated like a child, but she was glad he was protecting her.

"M- Miss Georgina?"

"Yes."

A few conflicting expressions seemed to register on Merryweather's features in a fleeting manner, then he seemed inordinately interested in the distant mountain peaks.

Finally: "Tell me about your sisters." He wanted to talk about something else, Georgina inferred, but what?

"The eldest is Earnestine. She's tall, dark red hair," Georgina began waving her gloved hand to indicate hair from her head to her shoulder. "She's very intelligent and beautiful, statuesque. Very attractive."

Merryweather raised an eyebrow.

"So I'm told, but she is."

"And then?"

"There's me and finally little Lottie. She's blonde, very pretty, although she can be... well, you know what little girls can be like."

"Not entirely," Merryweather admitted: "And how do you fit into the Deering-Dolittle family?"

"I'm the middle one, neither one thing or the other, and a little dumpy."

"I don't think you're d- d- dumpy."

Georgina had to turn away such was the heat she felt in her burning face.

The two of them stood quietly for a long time. Georgina didn't know what to say. This was all very strange. Was this... but it couldn't be, because that sort of thing, whatever that sort of thing was, happened at dances or dinner parties when some friend of the family introduced you to some dependable chap who came from a good background. Georgina didn't know anything about this 'Merry'. There was so much that a young lady ought to be informed about: his school, for example.

Caruthers and McKendry returned and shook their heads to Merryweather's questioning gaze.

"Perhaps we should..." Caruthers suggested indicating to one side.

"It can't be worse than the school," Georgina said.

Caruthers nodded: "It's the same. They're all dead. It looks like there was a fight, the inn has been barricaded in places, some gunfire, blood... I'm sorry."

"Go on," Georgina said.

"Blood stains and the like," Caruthers finished. "The strange thing is that all the bodies have been piled up in the yard behind the tavern."

"My sisters?"

"They're all villagers, we've no doubt about that, but only the women. There aren't any men."

"It's strange," McKendry added.

"What do we do now?" Merryweather asked.

Georgina put her hand out and gripped the toggle of his duffle coat, wanting his support because she felt faint. He put his hand over hers, and she was confused for a moment until she realised that he'd taken off his glove to do so.

"We can't inform the Bürgermeister if he isn't here," Caruthers said.

"There are tracks?" McKendry added.

"Where do they go?" Merryweather asked.

"A lot of tracks go north, the ground is really churned up, like an army passed through, but there are some tracks that go south: four people."

"And?"

McKendry paused; Georgina could feel him looking at her: "Four, three men and a woman."

"One of my sisters!"

"Perhaps we shouldn't get our hopes up, but..." McKendry said.

"But?"

"They aren't village shoes, they're heeled like... yours."

Everyone glanced down at Georgina's dolly boots.

"What were your sisters' names again?" Caruthers asked.

"Earnestine and Charlotte."

He nodded, then led them all down into the village and out again following the tracks south. Georgina glanced over her shoulder, she couldn't help herself, and saw the pretty town with the college visible in the distance framed by the majestic mountains. It was all so beautiful and she wondered if the whole world had been struck down by the horror here. Perhaps everywhere there were now piles of dead women and missing men.

## Miss Charlotte

Charlotte had a lovely lie-in snuggled between Egyptian cotton sheets. When she woke, there was a bowl of water for washing, which was actually warm, and set of clothes had been put out for her. After a moment's pique, when she realised that it wasn't going to be an airship flying day full of uniform and trousers, she dressed. A maid, who either spoke no English or didn't speak at all, helped her with her corset. Charlotte found some pearls that complemented the fine blue dress. The finished result made her look just as Earnestine and Georgina always tried to make her appear.

Finally, she was whisked along the corridors to another suite. Whereas her bedroom was lovingly furnished, these rooms were decidedly spartan. The maid did not come in with her.

As her eyes adjusted to the gloom, Charlotte became aware of a presence. The figure in the shadows spoke in German, a cracked voice of old age, but nonetheless strong and certain.

"I'm sorry I don't understand German," said Charlotte.

"It is not necessary to understand our language, so long as you understand your duties," the woman said, articulating each syllable carefully.

"And who might you be, may I ask?"

"I am the dowager Gräfin."

Charlotte did a tiny curtsey. She wasn't entirely sure of the etiquette. She was a Princess and the woman was only a Gräfin; however, it seemed wise to keep on the right side of this tall, imposing figure. She was aquiline in all her features, a sharp nose accentuated by fine, angled brows, and her hair was pulled back. Her words were clear, accented, and gave the impression that her tongue could become sharp at any moment.

"Do you know what a Griffin is?" she asked.

"It's the same as a Countess, isn't it?"

"Griffin, Griff-*in.*"

"Sorry, a Griffin is a mythical being, half lion, half eagle."

"Ja, the English lion and the German eagle combined into the one creature," she said. "To conjoin these two empires, you and I are to be the allies."

"Yes, Gräfin."

"The eagle at the head."

"Yes."

"Duty is everything."

"That is what I've been taught."

"Duty to your rank, duty to your new country, duty to your elders and betters."

"Yes, Gräfin."

"Duty to me."

Charlotte felt the Gräfin's gaze. "Of course," she said.

"I will die one day."

"Surely not," said Charlotte.

"Ach, I will... one day, and then all this will be yours."

"The castle and the land?"

"Nein, that yes, but more, much more: the endeavour."

The Gräfin came over to her and despite stepping back Charlotte was seized in a vice-like grip, almost lifted from the granite floor.

"The English Victoria reigns over an empire, but she is German, the puppet of the Saxe-Coburg. Through her their progeny have infected the royal houses of most of Europe. The Saxe-Coburg, where they lost in battle, they win in the boudoir."

"The bedroom?"

"The battlefield of the feminine," said the Gräfin, putting Charlotte back on her feet and flattening the creases with a flick of her fingers. "Women are limited by men. In the German lands even a woman of royal blood cannot inherit a throne. Queen Victoria was entitled to the throne of Hanover, but Salic Law prevents a woman from inheriting that title, so she had to make do with the British Empire."

"The British Empire is quite big."

"The men wish to fight wars, a great war is planned, one that will encompass the whole globe."

"You're talking about soldiers in uniforms."

"Ja, but their plans mean nothing if a ruler cannot be found to occupy all the thrones of Europe. That is our task, the Great Plan."

The Great Plan: it sounded jolly exciting and important to Charlotte. She smiled and tried to look attentive.

"It is my legacy to the world, to you," the Gräfin continued. "We must marry and breed, and then marry our progeny to the advantage."

"I don't understand."

"Royal houses marry royal houses, the seed is concentrated, the inheritances combined: soon, very soon, an heir to every throne of Europe will be born. If this king dies first, perhaps with a little push, and that marriage produces children of the right sex, and so on. If our King- Ach, Crown Prince lives a few more years and we can marry him wisely, then we - you, my little flower - will inherit Europe and whoever controls the thrones of Europe will control the world."

She seemed mad: surely the British Empire, which already covered three quarters of the globe would simply and inexorably expand as more of the world was civilised by all those handsome officers in their smart, red uniforms, but, as the brave lads used their Lee-Enfield rifles against the savages, this cunning woman was subverting everything that was right and proper. Were those of royal blood simply pawns to be played with, Charlotte thought, and then she realised that she too was a piece in the game.

"It's a game," she said.

"Exactly!"

"And my part?"

"You will marry my nephew, Prince Pieter. He will be pleased you have grown to be pretty, you are a brat in the picture we have. With him, you will produce a son, then a daughter and then a son. They will marry, and marry well, and then your grandson will rule all. Think of it, a plan that has been enacted for thirty eight generations. Does it not give you a thrill to know that we are only two generations away from complete success?"

"Spiffing."

"Your generation and your children's. And then, when all the blood lines have intersected, you and I will sit at your son's shoulder and direct his thinking."

There seemed only one correct answer: "Yes, Gräfin."

"Reports have reached us: your Prince comes here tonight."

"Is he handsome?"

The Gräfin considered this novel question: "Ja, he is handsome, kind and intelligent, but more importantly, he has the right blood."

"Does he wear a uniform?"

"Here everyone wears a uniform."

"I don't."

"That dress is very becoming."

"I like... you know, in their uniforms," Charlotte said. "If he is as nice as your say, then I think I might like very much to be engaged."

"That is good." The Gräfin swept out, but just before she left, she added: "Although your like and dislike will have nothing to do with it."

# CHAPTER VII

## Miss Deering-Dolittle

Prince Pieter flicked at his smart, although ostentatious, uniform to remove more non-existent fluff. It was the third time he had done so in the last two minutes at least.

"Yes?" Earnestine asked.

Pieter's eyes looked very blue.

"Fräulein Earnestine."

"Yes?"

"You will have to be my maid."

"Maid?"

"If they discover you came from the school then... things may not go well."

"I'm not a maid."

"Those that cause offence tend to be thrown off the battlements."

"How utterly barbaric."

"And you're too young to be a governess."

"Nonsense."

"I cannot have a governess who is younger than I am," Pieter said, not unreasonably. "Beside no-one will question your presence as a maid."

"I'm not being a domestic of any kind."

"Look-"

The carriage rattled suddenly, throwing them from side to side. The noise of the wheels changed abruptly from hard stone to an echoing wooden noise, and metal jangling on either side. Through the windows, Earnestine saw heavy chains hanging loosely. Upwards, briefly, there was an imposing view of granite walls complete with jutting gargoyles before they were through the outer wall and into the castle itself. The chains juttered as they were cranked back and the heavy drawbridge hoicked upwards in jolts until it blotted out the bright daylight.

There was more mechanical activity before the carriage jerked forward and turned before stopping. Boys in uniform sprinted forward, one opened the door and two others quickly positioned a small set of steps. Pieter disembarked first, causing the boys to snap to attention. The Prince accepted their salutes and then held his hand out for Earnestine. She took his hand and descended into the circular courtyard that seemed very like the bottom of a well, such was the height of the surrounding walls.

A man dressed in smart civilian clothing, with a high starched collar and oiled hair, rushed up.

"This is the Vögte," Pieter hissed in Earnestine's ear: "Careful."

"Welcome home, Your Highness," said the Vögte. He didn't, or couldn't, turn his head, which was unsettling.

"It is good to be home," Pieter replied, his voice pitched loud to be heard by everyone in the courtyard, and he turned like a performer accepting applause. This was for show, Earnestine realised.

"I see Oberst Kroll."

The bear-like Kroll had disembarked from the far side of the carriage and had now come around to face the welcoming party.

"Hauptmann Schneider and Herr Metzger were unavoidably detained," said Kroll.

The Vögte clapped his hands: "Ah ha!"

"They're dead," Prince Pieter said.

"Ah..."

There was a silence, while they all stood like actors on a stage waiting for someone to speak first. It was as if one of them had forgotten their cue. Earnestine wondered if it was herself, but she decided to keep quiet, and it turned out that she was the subject of the next line.

"And who is this?" The Vögte's gaze was intense, examining and quite rude, so Earnestine stood stock still, steeling herself not to flinch.

Pieter answered: "This is-"

"I am His Royal Highness's Secretary," Earnestine said.

"A *female* secretary?" the Vögte replied.

Earnestine felt herself bristling at the way the man twisted the word for her sex.

"Yes," she said. "I am proficient with the Malling-Hansen Writing Ball."

"Ah, we have a Sholes and Glidden Type-Writer."

"Slower though, isn't it," Earnestine countered, "with the keys not being in an optimum arrangement?"

"Slower perhaps, but you can see what you have written, whereas with a Malling-Hansen you cannot correct any mistakes."

"I don't make mistakes."

The Vögte snorted, turned and indicated that they should now go inside. Earnestine caught a glimpse of a huge grin plastered over the Prince's face before he regained his composure. The Prince and his party followed with Earnestine tagging along on the Prince's left. They strode through cold corridors made of large granite blocks and up seemingly endless stone spiral staircases before arriving at the Prince's quarters. Earnestine quite lost her sense of direction and the view from the window was of anonymous snow covered mountain peaks.

"These are the Prince's rooms," the Vögte told Earnestine, "his drawing room, his study, his bedroom."

"I see," Earnestine said, stopping at the threshold of that final room.

"Your room is through here and this connecting door," the Vögte informed her.

Reluctantly, Earnestine went through the male preserve with its Spartan bed and table. Finally, she reached another bedroom, functional, but perfectly adequate; indeed, it was luxurious in comparison to the dormitories of the Eden College for Young Ladies.

"There's only one door," she said, "without a lock."

"So that you are at the Prince's beck and call at any time of the day... or night."

"I see."

The Vögte sneered: "For *dictation*."

"I'm not sure I like your tone."

Unfortunately, the Vögte had withdrawn to the Prince's bedroom to whisper to his Master. Earnestine checked the bed, dressing table and chair to see if any of these would be suitable for barricading the door, but they were clearly wanting in this regard.

This fussing meant that Earnestine missed the arrival of another man, taller than Pieter, who filled the door to the corridor with his wide frame. Earnestine was startled by the man's appearance, his dark moustache and pointed beard.

"Pieter," he said.

"Gustav!"

"Sie sind zurückgekommen."

"Yes, brother, I'm back - I managed somehow."

"English, how quaint, we are all speaking English these days."

"Practice makes perfect."

"So, you agree with the plan."

"I do-"

The tall man, Gustav, barged past and stood as if he owned the room. Despite his uniform having all the usual frippery of medals and a sash, Earnestine had the impression that he had military experience: his boots were functional.

Earnestine stepped back in deference and found herself standing next to the Vögte, who diminished himself by bending his spine. She could smell his cologne.

"No more running away," Gustav said.

"I was on holiday," Pieter replied.

"And now you are unpacking your belongings, I see," Gustav said, lingering for a moment on Earnestine as he surveyed the temporary clutter. "And you have brought back a souvenir."

Earnestine blinked rapidly: yes, he had implied she was a 'belonging'. She wasn't going to stand for that and opened her mouth to-

"Any news!?" Pieter interrupted.

"Our plans proceed to schedule: don't they, Vögte?"

"Ja, mein Graf."

"And the Great Plan?" Pieter asked.

"Oh yes, brother, your destiny is here."

"My destiny?"

"Ja... and she is blonde."

When the two brothers squared up to each other, their profiles looked alike. They were from the same design, but where Pieter was elegant and chiselled, Gustav was coarse and constructed somehow. There was clearly no love lost between the two: she was pleased to think that she had kept a tight rein on her sisters and that there were no arguments amongst the Deering-Dolittles.

Gustav laughed, a deep amused chuckle: "I almost envy you," he said. "She has spirit for you to tame. Or perhaps she will domesticate you."

If Pieter had a reply, he missed his opportunity as Gustav marched out, his stride thumping down the stone corridor outside. He was long gone before anyone moved again. The Vögte slowly straightening his posture to raise himself to Prince Pieter's level and Earnestine shuffling away from both of the men.

"I'd like to meet her," Pieter said to the Vögte.

I bet you would, Earnestine thought, angry without understanding why.

"It is not wise for his Royal Highness to see his fiancée before the wedding," the Vögte said. "Bad luck."

"May I send her a message - a greeting, perhaps a declaration of love?"

The Vögte's eyes narrowed as he weighed up the Prince's intentions: "Very well, send it with your Secretary. I can show him.... *her* the way."

"Very well, Vögte, would you wait outside while I compose a letter."

"I have the confidence of the Graf and Gräfin."

"Vögte, wait outside."

"As you wish."

The Vögte bowed obsequiously and taking his time about it, and then he sidled out.

Earnestine and Pieter were left alone.

"What is-"

The Prince silenced Earnestine with a gesture, his finger to his lip. Earnestine was about to object when she realised that the Prince was listening at the door. She waited until he had checked outside.

"Clear," he said, closing the door gently.

"What is going on?" Earnestine asked. "What does he mean by 'your destiny'?"

"I am to marry a Princess."

Blinking, Earnestine said: "I see."

"It is-"

"Congratulations, I'm sure you'll be very happy."

"I have no feelings for her."

"Then why marry her?"

"To join our family in alliance with another and to produce an heir to two thrones. It's the Gräfin's Great Plan."

"Surely you have a say in this?"

"If I do not, then the Saxe-Coburg will win."

"Will win what?"

"The world."

"A nice wedding present."

"My Aunt has seen to it that I am to be married to a Princess, someone of the right connections and royal blood. It's all part of the 'Great Plan' - I could show you the plan: it's in another part of the castle."

He seated himself by his writing desk, hurriedly gathering various implements together, but he was flustered and dropped a pen on the floor. Earnestine bent down and retrieved it.

"Perhaps, as your secretary, I should do that."

"Good idea."

He vacated the chair and held it back for Earnestine. She sat, jigged it forward and then efficiently organised the desk for dictation. When she was ready, she looked at him expectantly.

"My dear... Your Royal Highness... My dear... I'm not sure how to start."

"Perhaps where you left off," Earnestine said. "What did you talk about last time you met?"

"We have never met."

"I see."

"What do you think I should write?"

Her pen hovered over the parchment, ready, the nib at the correct angle for her finest calligraphy, but she was conscious of the blankness and size of the page as well as the pregnancy and length of the silence.

"What do you want to say?" Earnestine asked finally.

The Prince sat on the bed and wrung his hands.

"Do you want me to be honest?"

"Honesty is the best policy."

"Are you sure?"

Earnestine was emphatic: "Yes."

"What I would like to write is... erm," said the Prince: "Your Royal Highness, thank you for the honour you are prepared to give to myself and my family - I'm not going too fast am I?"

"Not at all."

"...myself and my family. Regretfully I must decline."

Earnestine scratched across the parchment.

Pieter leant forward trying to look: "Is it?"

"It's fine."

"Where was I?"

"Declining."

"The truth is that I have fallen in love with an English girl, she is nothing... not even from Surrey - ha, but she has captivated me from the first moment I saw her: by her beauty, by her strength of character and by her honesty. I know that duty is important, but in this matter I must follow my heart. I intend to propose and marry her and... you've stopped writing."

"I thought it wise."

Sitting upright on the chair, Earnestine was higher than the Prince, who was still sitting on the bed, his hands together as if in prayer or to beg as he leant forward eagerly. She had read the works of Jane Austen: *Pride and Prejudice*, and other, vanity-published, three-volume novels. She thought it foolish when they described how men constantly dropped to one knee to propose. Girls in the Common Room, common girls, even boasted of the number of times some gentleman, if that was the correct word, had popped the question. She thought it akin to cricket statistics: so many proposals per marriage, the number of catches and bowlings over. She had always thought it was empty boasting, as made up as Austen's novels, but here she was, a mere three days out in the field, and here was no less than a Prince with his knee at the crease.

The Prince motioned at the letter.

What now, Earnestine wondered?

"Did you get as far my proposing?" he asked.

Earnestine glanced at the letter: "I didn't get as far as falling in love."

"Would you perhaps reach that far?"

"I am hardly a free woman."

"You are spoken for!? I apologise, I had no idea."

"Free as in 'not kidnapped'."

"Ah, yes, I had forgotten."

"I have not."

"But if you were free?"

"Would it be a condition of my release?"

The Prince stood and paced. A few times he paused as if to ask another question or make a debating point. Earnestine watched him, alternately amused and exasperated. Finally, he stopped.

"Perhaps this letter is a mistake," he said.

Earnestine put the pen back in its holder and crumpled the paper into nothing. Meanwhile, the Prince went to the door for her.

"Please convey my feelings to Her Royal Highness, the Princess," he said. "And find out what you can."

"What feelings are those?"

"Whatever feelings you deem appropriate," Pieter said. "My own are not wanted."

"If that is your wish?"

Prince Pieter did not reply, but instead showed her into the corridor and signalled to the Vögte, who was waiting at the far end by the leaded windows.

The Vögte, whom Earnestine saw more and more as some fawning troll, changed his posture as soon as the door closed behind her. Whereas he had bowed and scraped to the Graf, and showed a reluctant deference to the Prince, he was now erect and arrogant. Clearly, he held mere secretaries, even secretaries to royal personages, with contempt.

"You took your time," he sneered.

"His Royal Highness, Prince Pieter, wished to compose his letter carefully," she replied, enjoying the sound of his title and name as she said it.

The man's gaze raked downwards to fix upon Earnestine's empty hands.

"I am to convey his feelings in person," Earnestine explained.

"His Royal Highness's future consort is this way."

They started off down the various corridors, Earnestine making a careful note of every turn and making sure she glanced down the side passages as they went. She counted steps too, hoping that it would not be complicated and that she would be able to draw a good map while the memory was still fresh. She knew she would be capable of the task so long as she was not distracted.

"The Princess is very pretty," the Vögte said.

Pretty, indeed.

Earnestine remained concentrated on her task: thirty two, thirty three...

"No more than fifteen or sixteen," the Vögte continued.

...thirty four, thirty fifteen or thirty sixteen - honestly.

The Prince needed someone he could turn to. The offices of state clearly needed a confidante, someone trustworthy, to hear his thoughts and assess them objectively and truthfully. If he was surrounded by these fawning Jawohl-men, then he would lose touch with reality. What he really needed was someone firm, but honest; someone who understood duty, someone like... well, someone like herself.

She gasped.

The Vögte turned indignantly: "Did you say something?"

"Oh nothing, just a slight cough."

She looked behind her and realised that she had no idea where she was in this stone maze.

"Forgotten something?"

"Not at all," she said firmly. "Shall we continue?"

By the time they reached the landing and the Vögte came to a halt, Earnestine was sure they were at the far end of the world. The Vögte lowered his voice: "Remember to speak only when spoken to."

"I will."

"Remember, the Princess is your better."

"Of course, I know my place."

The Vögte rapped on the door three times.

A voice answered from within: "Come!"

The Vögte signalled Earnestine to wait outside before he opened the door, bowed low and entered.

Earnestine could not help herself leaning forward to listen.

"Ah, Vögte, come in."

"Your Royal Highness, I have a messenger from His Royal Highness, Prince Pieter."

"Not the Prince himself."

"Alas no, custom here says that it is bad luck to see your betrothed before your wedding."

"Surely that's only on the day of the wedding."

"Here it only allowed during a short betrothal ceremony, Your Highness, but you are permitted to exchange tokens and letters; hence, this messenger."

"Very well, show him in."

Earnestine snapped upright just in time as the Vögte reappeared. He gestured impatiently and then held the door open for her to enter. As she passed him, he hissed: "curtsey."

Earnestine curtseyed, formally, and as she rose she admired the fine blue dress of the Princess, its embroidery and lace work, the tight waist signifying the very best of whalebone corsetry, the bare, elegant neck replete with pearls and finally the noble brow and regal countenance of...

It was Charlotte.

## Miss Georgina

Caruthers was talking: "Nothing at Ingolstadt and nothing in his Geneva home, which leaves us with one choice."

McKendry's drawl answered him: "So you reckon it's the Austro-Hungarians?"

"Zeppelin sightings and a lot of supplies have been taken to their Eagle's Claw stronghold."

"They built that railhead. If nothing else we ought to find out what they're up to there."

The train clattered on, the scenery rushed past. As the line curved, Georgina, with her face against the window, could see along the carriages to the engine steaming away in front. Her face felt frozen to the glass, but she didn't dare move. She'd been pretending to be asleep for what felt like hours and only now had the three Gentlemen Adventurers relaxed enough to start talking as if she wasn't there.

"They're... men?" Caruthers said. "Controlled in some way?"

"Draugar," said Merry. "It's Norse mythology for golems, but they are made of clay."

McKendry took up the theme: "In Haiti, there are stories of 'Zombi'. It's a tradition in 'Vodou' of raising the dead to do your command. It's false though, the witch doctors use drugs to convince someone that they've died and been brought to life. They use other drugs to weaken their spirit and make them suggestible."

"That's all superstition," Caruthers said, and then he lowered his voice further. "Miss Georgina talked about control boxes, which suggests a scientific explanation."

"Which will be at the Eagle's Claw."

"We can't go there with..." Merryweather said. There was a pause and Georgina felt her face flush as she knew that they were all looking at her.

"We can't very well leave her here," Caruthers said.

"Perhaps we could split up, one of us looks after the girl and the others do the reconnoitring," Merryweather suggested.

"Who would look after the girl?" McKendry asked. "Should we draw lots or ask for a volunteer, Merry?"

Caruthers snorted and McKendry coughed as if they were sharing some joke: Merryweather was utterly silent.

"The idea has merit," Caruthers admitted.

There was some rustling and Georgina resisted the impulse to look. Presently the three men were talking and pointing at possibilities on a map: this connection here, that train there, let me check the timetable. The train clattered on, making its appointed stops according to the said timetable. The condensation on the windows formed droplets which cried down the glass.

Eventually Caruthers decided that they'd change at Innsbruck. After taking another journey, he and McKendry would follow a mountain trail to observe the Eagle's Claw, while Merryweather would set up 'camp one' at another station and collect supplies.

The idea of spending time at some hotel with Merryweather filled Georgina with conflicting emotions, although she couldn't quite put her finger on what those feelings were. She tried listing them: anxious, safe, apprehensive, excited...

Miss Georgina, they observed, could help him prepare the sandwiches.

Ah yes, at last, she thought: valued.

## Miss Charlotte

The sisters stood two sword lengths apart.

Earnestine took a deep breath: "I-"

"Speak only when spoken to," the Vögte commanded, before he spoke to Charlotte: "This is His Royal Highness, Prince Pieter's Secretary."

"Secretary?" repeated Charlotte.

"Yes," Earnestine said, "it's a fine profession and I am employed by a true Gentleman. And you?"

Charlotte beamed: "I'm a Princess!"

Earnestine's lips narrowed to a horizontal slit, which was so typical of Earnestine when she was angry, and she said nothing, which wasn't.

"So you say to me, 'Your Royal Highness'," Charlotte reminded her.

Earnestine gritted her teeth: "Your Royal Highness."

"You may go, er..."

"Vögte."

"Yes, leave us."

"Your Royal Highness," said the Vögte. He bowed low, but also somehow managed to sneer at Earnestine, which was funny.

Earnestine and Charlotte were alone.

Charlotte had been naughty, she knew that, but her only real infraction had been getting on the Zeppelin. After that, everything else had followed from her genuine desire not to make the situation worse. Earnestine would understand that, surely? And getting into a Zeppelin had been curiosity, nothing more... and she'd helped the real Princess, hadn't she? She'd helped her, she'd done what a real Royal Personage had asked her to do. That was a good thing, a jolly good thing, so really Earnestine should offer praise and thanks. And congratulations over her engagement!

"Lottie!" Despite Earnestine's low volume she managed to pack a lot of indignation into the two syllables.

"Ness?"

"I think we should have a talk."

Charlotte fidgeted: the last thing she wanted was for Earnestine to give another of her lectures and ruin all the fun. Earnestine had put her hands together as if praying for the right words, a prayer that Charlotte knew was always answered, because Earnestine was never short of words for Charlotte.

"I simply don't know where to begin," her sister began, as she always began: what she really meant was that she didn't know when to stop.

So, before Earnestine got started, Charlotte decided her best plan was to change the subject: "I'm engaged."

Earnestine looked appalled.

"You can congratulate me," Charlotte suggested.

"Engaged!!? You are the youngest sister. Before you can get engaged, there's Georgina and before her, myself."

"But I'm a Princess."

"That may be what people here believe you to be, but you are really a thoughtless and disrespectful child. What of us? If people discover you're engaged, then they'll naturally assume that there's something wrong with Gina and myself. We'll be on the shelf. I don't mind for myself, but it will break poor Gina's heart."

"Well, she's not here and I'm a Princess, so I can do what I like and you can't stop me."

"Charlotte Deering-Dolittle, you are-"

But Charlotte was holding up her finger to her sister: "You can only talk to me when spoken too."

"You spoke first."

"I did not."

"You most certainly did."

"Did not."

"Princess or no Princess, I am still the eldest and I can still send you straight to your room."

"I'm in my room. This is my room. It's a Royal Suite."

"So it is."

"Because I'm royal."

"Why? How? Everyone thinks you are a Princess. Charlotte what have you done?"

"I didn't do anything, she... the real Princess wanted to swap clothes-"

"You stole her clothes!?"

"I didn't! I... did as I was told."

"Did you?"

"Like a good girl."

Earnestine snorted derisively: "Why are you not in school?"

"Why aren't you?"

Earnestine gave her a sharp look.

"Ness," Charlotte whined. "I wanted to see the airship and the Graf-"

"Graf?"

"Graf Zala, lovely uniform and so manly and tall. He showed me round and let me fly the Zeppelin. You should have seen me, Ness, flying the Zeppelin, turning it and going up and down and everything. And he talked about the future, airships, aerial navies, glorious battles, military plans and... I wore trousers - imagine that, trousers."

"Women wearing trousers is bloomerism."

"It's-"

"Tell me, Charlotte, what was the one instruction you were given?"

"One instruction - what are you talking about?"

"The one instruction."

"I've had a thousand instructions."

"The important one."

"They're all important according to you."

"No exploring, no trouble and no-"

"That's two instructions."

Earnestine raised her hand and Charlotte cowered, she couldn't help herself. She wanted to be brave and assertive, and stand up to her eldest sister, but Earnestine was such a cow.

"Adventures!"

"My fiancé won't allow you to punish me," Charlotte wailed.

"Your fiancé will thank me... oh, Pieter!"

The blood drained from Earnestine's face: she looked genuinely shocked. Charlotte had only ever seen that expression when news of Papa had reached them, and then of Mama...

"You're engaged to Pieter," said Earnestine. She'd turned to look at the door, her hand now a fist and she was breathing short and sharp breaths.

"Have you seen this Prince Peter?"

"Pieter! Yes, I have seen His Royal Highness Prince Pieter."

"Is he very handsome? Does he wear a uniform..? Oh, Ness, don't be angry. You must tell me, you must tell me everything."

Charlotte took her sister's arm and led her to the bed and they sat next to each other, Lottie and Ness, Ness and Lottie, just like old times: Charlotte remembered all the evenings that Earnestine had read to her and Gina. She'd taken them through the looking glass, to Treasure Island and from pride to prejudice, and although Charlotte had discovered later that her sister had often skipped certain sections of certain books, they were happy memories. And now they were having their own adventure together and wouldn't Gina be cross to have missed all the fun. Charlotte bounced up and down on the bed.

"Tell me everything about him," she said.

Earnestine began composing herself: "Well, he is handsome, tall, and he does wear a uniform."

"Good, good, go on, go on."

"Looks are not everything, Charlotte, nor the cut of his cloth, nor money, nor anything else, except that which is in his character. Does he marry with the best of intentions or does he intend to run off with one of his staff?"

"Oh, I'm sure he won't."

"So am I."

"Do you have something in your eye?"

"Of course not, don't be silly, Lottie!"

"Sorry, Ness."

Charlotte had come a long way from Kensington and she wondered if this was the dreaded 'growing up' she'd been threatened with. Many, many times she'd been told what 'little girls' don't do: these rules, never written down she'd noted, tended to ban activities that ripped dresses and scraped knees like climbing and scrumping and fighting. There had been other rules too, those for the 'big girls', which involved avoiding boys of any size. This was why they'd been incarcerated in Switzerland.

Somehow the natural order of things had flipped over. The three sisters - little girl, big girl and young lady - had somehow exchanged roles. Whereas Charlotte knew the regulations for little girls and for big girls, she had not as yet heard about how a 'young lady' should behave. Indeed, the very mention of whatever that behaviour might be was forbidden to 'little girls'.

Charlotte thought she should probably ask.

"When we're alone, Prince Pieter... and I, should I call him 'Pete'?"

"You will absolutely not."

"Do you think he'll call me Lottie in private?"

"I imagine he'll call you by whatever name you've stolen."

"Oh yes, silly me."

"Charlotte, you don't seem to realise that you are going to be found out."

"You don't value anything I do."

"You don't do anything of value."

"The real Princess didn't want to be a Princess."

"Why ever not?"

"She didn't want to be bound by duty, because she wanted to run off with a Hauptmann."

"Hauptmann? Who's he?"

"A Hauptmann is a German Captain, they have three pips on their epaulettes and-"

"Charlotte!"

"She said it was going to be a fate worse than death."

"Which is now your fate."

"Oh, I hadn't thought of it like that."

The castle seemed dark and forbidding for a moment, the stone walls impenetrable and cold, and yet the room had such lovely decorations and beautiful furniture and gilded mirrors with all her wonderful luggage stacked neatly and her pretty dresses hanging in the wardrobe.

"No, Lottie," said Earnestine, "you don't think at all, do you?"

# CHAPTER VIII

## Miss Deering-Dolittle

"What is she like?"

Earnestine stood with her hands folded neatly on her lap and considered Prince Pieter's question. Her Royal Highness, Princess... Charlotte was the most difficult and impossible trouble-maker imaginable: one who had no concept of responsible behaviour, who smiled as she heaped misfortune upon others as if this was acceptable behaviour - which it was not! Who spent her entire life dedicated to making Earnestine's existence as difficult as possible. Earnestine had liked living in Kensington, but Charlotte's unruliness meant that their legal guardian, Uncle Jeremiah, had packed all three of them off to boarding school. Earnestine herself had adapted well to the regime and had even made friends, but then Charlotte's activities with the Boy's School cadets had meant such disgrace that all three had been sentenced to the Eden College for Young Ladies. In Switzerland. Even then, Earnestine had made the best of it, even becoming a Prefect, and she could see the value of the education that-

"The Princess," Pieter repeated: "What's she like?"

She's Charlotte: a silly, silly girl, who had contrived somehow to come between herself and the man in whom she would not be concerned about at all, ever, under any circumstances whatsoever.

"She's... young," said Earnestine.

"Pretty?"

Earnestine felt the pain of her back teeth biting the inside of her cheek: "...yes, I suppose."

"Intelligent?"

"No."

Maybe, Earnestine thought, she could just do nothing. She liked this idea, even as she knew that she could not as she was cursed with being the responsible Deering-Dolittle, but even so it had a certain charm. This kidnapper (let's not forget) would be saddled with her silly sister and Earnestine would have the pleasure every Christmas and birthday of seeing him suffer from her impossible scatter-brained schemes, which would serve him right for not having the courage to propose, albeit pointlessly and fruitlessly, to her. Equally delicious was the thought that her foolish sister would be taken in hand, bundled about in great coats and subjected to the horrors of random untoten attacks.

"I suppose I do not deserve both beauty and wits."

"And I suppose she does not deserve kindness and consideration."

Pieter was dour: "Do you understand about duty?"

What a stupid question: of course she understood duty; wasn't she the responsible adult with two young girls to see safely through a world full of violence and men and fates worse than death?

"Let me show you my duty," he said.

Pieter led her from his suite and down through various rooms. They were empty, opulent to a fault, but sterile and spoke only of former glories now faded. Portraits of harsh men and sullen women cluttered the walls as Pieter's ancestors jostled for position.

As if to forestall any questions: "Our family was once prosperous. Austro-Hungary had an empire, but now there's another family on the throne. We are whittled down to these storerooms of our past."

Finally, they reached an unassuming passageway. He had a key on his chain and opened an arched door.

"This is the command centre," Pieter said, "with the map of the war."

Pieter flicked a brass switch by the door: the bulbs buzzed and flickered, one popped and went out, but the rest shone on with a yellow light.

Earnestine gasped and felt foolish: although her family home in Kensington used gas lighting, she had lived in London and so she'd seen galvanic lighting.

The room was small in comparison to others in the castle with an oval table, teak, and matching chairs rather like a dining room. There was enough space to move around the table, but not enough for servants to hover unobtrusively. This was a private room. The decor was fine, dark red with gold filigree on three of the walls, a small, bedroom-sized fireplace on the far side. Electric light bulbs appeared at intervals and the chandelier had been converted too.

It was the end wall that was different: black. Close inspection revealed the same filigree swirls in relief, so the wallpaper itself had been sacrificed. It was covered in framed and unframed pictures, small portraits, some no more that postcards, arranged with apparent abandon and no regard for a proper pattern or balance. Notes with names and dates in tiny writing were pinned to each, and string, white against the black, had been attached linking picture to picture.

Earnestine saw Queen Victoria's image in one of the larger frames, her stern countenance with more string attached than any other picture. Below her was her Prince Edward, the Prince of Wales, and Victoria, her daughter, now the German Empress since her marriage to Kaiser Wilhelm II.

"It's a family tree," she said.

Pieter clicked his heels: "Excellent."

He moved closer like a professor about to deliver a lecture, and the wall took on the aspect of a blackboard. He waved his hand over the left side to include Queen Victoria and her offspring.

"This," he explained, "is the territory of the Saxe-Coburg and Gotha. Here, is the realm of Bernadotte, Norway and Sweden under Oscar II."

He had to stretch up to indicate a bearded man in a military uniform.

"Territory?"

"And down here."

Pieter moved his finger to the centre of the wall and pointed to a small, unassuming likeness set below waist height. Earnestine leant forward and saw what she expected: "Pieter."

"You have found me."

His picture was from a modern daguerreotype that had been cut from a group. A shoulder loomed next to him. The rest of this truncated image was in its own frame, his brother, Graf Gustav Zala, and above, joined by a thread, were other pieces of this jigsaw, a gallant man and a proud woman together in one frame and another woman fixed to one side.

"My mother and my... father, the Crown Prince."

A smear of glue discoloured the Crown Prince's image where something had been stuck on and then peeled away.

"This is my step-mother," Pieter added. "Another alliance after my mother passed on."

"I'm sorry."

"I was young."

"I don't see how this is a map of territory," Earnestine admitted.

"In Europe, there are two ways territory changes hands: by warfare and by marriage. One country may invade another, annex part of a state, to gain territory."

"And the other state loses it."

"Indeed. Also a state may lose territory by rebellion. This is warfare."

"And by marriage?"

"See the offspring of Queen Victoria, the grandmother of Europe, connecting with the progeny of King Oscar, the grandfather of Europe: their blood being distilled together like schnapps. A marriage alliance between two states can produce an heir to both thrones, so when a child grows up, then he ascends both thrones and two nations become one."

Pieter brought his hands together, locking his fingers to represent these peoples joined together.

"Not always the case, of course. Inheritance doesn't always follow the male line. For instance, your Queen Victoria inherited the British Empire, its lands and colonies abroad, but she did not inherit Hanover as she was not a male issue. So that land passed to Prince... King Ernest Augustus I and the House of Hanover."

Pieter paused to show that line: King George V, then King Ernest Augustus II.

Earnestine pointed at the corresponding label.

"Annexed by Prussia."

"Of course."

"These two lands could have been one, the British Empire would have territories in the very heart of Europe. Alas, Queen Victoria was a woman."

Earnestine bristled: "Alas."

"Also, a nation may not accept a foreign ruler."

"I can't see why any nation would."

"Your people, the Great British, have accepted a monarch, your Queen Victoria, who is German. Her mother tongue is German. I believe she can speak English, but only as a foreigner. Her own daughter, who became the German Empress and Queen of Prussia, spoke English and, I believe, educated her son, the current German Emperor, Wilhelm II, in English. They speak German as foreigners."

"That seems foolish now it's pointed out."

"All royal families are trying to gain alliances, combine thrones, and unite Europe."

The arrangement of portraits took on a different meaning. There was a match between these frames and the borders of nations, and the offspring could be seen as their troops, with white supply lines stretching hither and thither. Pieter was then a soldier ready to be sent into battle.

"I am a pawn," he said. "This is a chess game and one must make sacrifices."

"I see, so our Queen is like the queen in chess."

"Yes, and here is the King."

Pieter pointed to another portrait high on the wall. Earnestine came forward and stood on her toes, but even so...

"He is Ernst I, the man behind so many Saxe-Coburg successes: they say the Saxe-Coburg have lost on the battlefield, but won in the bedroom."

"I beg your pardon!?"

"My apologies, it is what they say."

She blinked, it must have been the awkward light: "I see."

"Ernst was the great manipulator linking so many crowns together."

Earnestine saw the tiny cross: "He's dead."

"But he sowed the seeds of the Saxe-Coburg success: see Ernst II, then it would have been Prince Albert, the Consort of Queen Victoria bringing the British throne and the Duchies of Saxe-Coburg and Gotha back together. The law did not allow this, so the Duchies went to Prince Albert's brother, Alfred. When he committed suicide, it went to the Duke of Albany, son of Queen Victoria's son, Leopold."

"A lot of Royals with the same names."

"They are all named after ancestors and to curry favour with other Royal Houses."

"And your House?"

"Here!" The Prince moved to the centre of the wall. "This is the dowager Gräfin. It is she who dictates our strategy, our Grandmistress if you like. She sits here often, as her mother and her mother's mother, and her mother's mother's mother and so on, did before her, and here she considers moves and counter moves."

"She looks nice."

"This was painted a long time ago."

"You said we were similar."

Pieter said nothing as Earnestine considered this novel approach to conquest. Queen Victoria gazed down from a few feet away, giving nothing away. Her countenance did resemble that of a studious chess player. The idea made sense; more than that, it was a game that had been played. To devote an entire room to this single endeavour indicated the seriousness with which they considered their strategy.

"And your move?" she asked.

Pieter traced a line up across to a pretty girl, who looked nothing like Charlotte even when she was that young: "The Princess who waits above."

"Hmmm."

"It is not my choice."

"No."

"My brother, Graf Zala, is destined to Russia. The Tsar Nicholas II has daughters; we have sons. The aim is to bring the Russian throne back into contention."

The light flickered: "I see."

Earnestine felt heavy, the room with its dark walls and eerie artificial light was oppressive. The pictures of Olga, Tatiana and Maria were those of babies, dressed in Christening robes or, Earnestine thought with a shudder, virginal bridal gowns.

"They're babies," she said.

"The only pictures we have, but yes, Gustav will have to wait."

Earnestine studied the pictures again. She felt a certain sympathy for Olga having to grow up with two younger sisters.

Earnestine's own picture was very much not on this wall; indeed, the Deering-Dolittles of Surrey were featured on more hypothetical walls than Earnestine, Georgina and Charlotte of the Kent Deering-Dolittles. Despite their education at the Eden College for Young Ladies, and Miss Hardcastle's insistence that it improved their prospects, their portraits would never feature on the wall of a drawing room in the Home Counties, let alone that of a royal command chamber.

"It is not my choice," Pieter repeated.

"We all have choices."

"Perhaps, but our choice is between my brother and I. I subscribe to the Great Plan, this strategy here, whereas my brother dreams of a Great War, victory and glory. Each method is made up of engagements."

"Not likely in this age of Pax Britannica."

Pieter shuffled uncomfortably.

"Why were you hiding in the school?" Earnestine asked.

"I thought that if I was absent, then my brother would have to marry here," he pointed at the wall, "or here. With the arms of a beautiful girl around his neck he would be less likely to complete his plans."

"Plans?"

"Nothing of note," said Pieter, but Earnestine was learning his ways all the time and recognised a lie.

"There's more to it than these arranged marriages then?" she asked.

"I have said too much."

Earnestine realised that she had overstretched her forces in the game that they had been playing. She took a moment to examine the wall, tracing the strings and thus all the connections in blood between families. She noticed again the picture of a Princess who looked nothing like Charlotte. This real Royal was a severe looking child, angry and plump, whereas Charlotte's visage would brighten up this dark wall.

"One day I will have to marry," said Pieter. "Mix my blue blood with the blue blood of another royal family."

Earnestine felt a sudden irrational loathing all Princesses.

"You'll need a couple of new pins and another piece of string," she said.

"It does not mean that you and I can't be together. It is common practice when marrying for duty to love another."

"I'm sorry?"

"I can keep some apartments in Vienna or Paris."

"I see," said Earnestine: "Would that be alternating with the Princess? Would you take Sunday off? Or perhaps I should ask my sister, Georgina, to fill in on the Holy Day and then you could have the full set."

"Are you feeling all right?" the Prince asked.

"Yes."

"Perhaps it's the modern lighting?"

"I'm fine."

"Let me get you a glass of brandy."

Pieter fetched a glass and bottle, pouring a generous measure: "Here."

When he passed the glass to her, he used his left hand, but Earnestine was having none of that coded nonsense and so took it with her right hand. Even so, their fingers touched as she took the offering.

The liquid was fiery, it burnt her inside as she swallowed, and was much like other fiery, burning sensations that coursed in the very red blood of her veins.

## Miss Georgina

Caruthers and McKendry had alighted at a railway station to catch a local connection. Once they had reached their starting position, they would await Merryweather's telegraph. Merryweather and Georgina continued on, arriving at the station below the Eagle's Claw. Merryweather was tasked with moving supplies along a mountain route and leaving them in a suitable hiding place. He would wire the instructions to Caruthers and McKendry so that they could approach the fortress from above without needing to carry too much equipment. It was a good plan.

Merryweather bought equipment and Georgina did make sandwiches.

"Merry, it's foolish."

"I don't mind making two trips."

"Yes, but I can carry a rucksack."

"I d- don't-"

"That's settled then."

She added climbing boots and a tweed mountain dress to the shopping list.

Her rucksack was considerably lighter than Merryweather's and he hired a trap to take them part of the way.

"We should leave the supplies here," Merryweather suggested.

"Nonsense, Merry," Georgina replied, "a little further."

They moved along the path at the base of the cliff, working towards the ascent route that Merryweather had chosen, until at times they could spy the castle itself, high and foreboding, ahead.

"This will suit the others well," Merryweather said.

"Perhaps a little further."

They had a light lunch in a small bothy. Georgina fussed, making house as if this was their country cottage and not a shelter for climbers.

"I can hide the supplies here," said Merryweather.

"What an excellent thought," Georgina agreed, "and the rest further up the path."

"B- b- but..."

It was bracing during the afternoon.

"M- Miss," Merryweather said, "this really is far enough. We must be underneath the castle by now."

The castle was indeed above them and she had taken advantage of his sweet nature for too long.

"We'll find a suitable marker," she said.

Merryweather looked utterly relieved.

They glanced around, and moved further along the path looking for some distinctive spot to hide the equipment. The mountain, close to, had an unfinished quality as if constructed by misshapen slabs of stone that didn't fit, such were the cracks and crevices. The path had deposits of droppings from goats, although why any creature would try to live here was beyond Georgina. Everything was grim and grey, except for some dark blue heap ahead and some quite beautiful flowers that somehow eked out an existence in this godforsaken place; they were quite gorgeous, tiny and coloured in purples, reds, yellows and vivid white.

She bent to pick a tiny flower, plucking it from its two neighbours.

"Merry," she said, "look at this, isn't it beau-"

"Stay back!"

Georgina felt a chill of fear: "What is it?"

"Keep back, please my dear."

Merryweather bent down over something dark blue, something that looked like material, something that, when she took a few steps closer, looked amusingly like a giant rag doll as the blue was a coat and underneath was a girl's dress and-

Merryweather stood in front of her holding her back. She fruitlessly stuck his chest with her fists and tried to sidestep around him. He held her until her energy waned.

"Is it?" she asked.

"She's... it's not a pretty sight."

"Her coat will have a name badge sewn into it... at the back."

"Wait here. Will you wait here?"

"Yes."

Merryweather was a long time as he carefully, ever so gently, examined the body, shifting the coat, bending closer to read. When he came back, he looked ashen.

Georgina knew. She'd known as soon as she'd seen the dark blue coat, just as she'd known ever since she'd sat in her sister's bedroom... but she waited for Merryweather to confirm the inevitable.

"Yes," he said simply. "It says C. Deering-Dolittle."

"Charl... oh god, Lottie, our little Lottie."

The wind stung her eyes.

After a long time, Merryweather went back to 'make her comfortable'. He piled loose rocks on top and Georgina went to help him once he'd covered her ruined face. When she went to collect a suitable rock, she saw that she had crushed the pretty mountain flower in her hand. She cried then, feeling that it was such a shame that something so fragile had been destroyed, because she simply couldn't bring herself to cope with the bigger trauma.

When they'd finished, they stood quietly side-by-side, neither speaking. The pile of rocks was so very obviously a grave.

"I'm sorry."

"It's not your fault," Georgina said, and thought that 'Merry' was not the word to use, so instead, she added: "Arthur."

"Even so, I'm sorry. We'll go back."

"No... there's still Earnestine to account for."

She glanced around at all the jumbled rocks and boulders with so many nooks and crannies that could all hide a body.

Merryweather then put his hand on her shoulder: "You're very brave," he said, but Georgina didn't feel brave; she just felt empty. Presently, on feet that were numb, they carried on along the path and left the pretty flowers behind.

# Miss Charlotte

"The flowers are dead."

The poor woman looked ill, her eyes sunken and her skin pale. Charlotte, in her role as a Princess, had so far been introduced to one future in-law, the dowager Gräfin, now she had been taken to the Queen. The King was not available.

Charlotte curtseyed: "Your Majesty."

The woman did not reply and Charlotte felt uncomfortable: perhaps she should say something, but there was a rule about only speaking when spoken to, or something. The woman had dark eyes, deep red lips and her hair, despite being streaked with silver, still retained rich black tones.

"You're the Queen," she blurted.

"I am not a real Queen," the woman replied, haltingly. Charlotte wondered if she should admit that she wasn't a real Princess, but the woman continued: "I am a Contessa."

"Your husband is the King."

"He is a Crown Prince, if that; they call him a King, but that is ambition."

"I'm a Princess."

"You are to marry Gustav or Pieter?"

"Pieter, Prince Pieter."

"You are lucky, he takes after my predecessor's side of the family."

"I've not met him yet."

The Queen looked out of the window: "We have no choice."

"Exciting though."

"So I thought, but here everything is death," the Queen said, and she pointed at the flowers to emphasise her point: the vase was full of wilting and brown stems. "I long now to see vineyards and wheat fields. Across the river. Here everything is death."

Charlotte could see only mountains, but she realised that this smaller window faced south and beyond there were probably vineyards, wheat fields and rivers. She remembered from school that the major imports and exports of Austro-Hungary were very tedious and boring.

"Will you sit and have a drink with me?"

"If you wish," said Charlotte, sitting opposite.

"Thank you."

"What's this?" Charlotte reached forward to pick up the woman's glass. She intended to sniff the mixture, expecting it to be some vile concoction, but the woman slapped her hand knocking the glass across the room.

It smashed into sharp fragments against a sideboard.

"No! It is a concoction of my Doctor's for my..." The Queen fanned her face with her hand to indicate an illness.

"I'm sorry."

"So am I. Please, fetch the sangria... no, there is only schnapps."

Charlotte nodded and searched the room finding a low teak cabinet full of bottles, each vying to be more ostentatious than the others with eagles, crests and coats of arms. Finally, she found one that appeared to say schnapps and picked two small glasses.

"May I have a larger glass?" the Contessa asked.

Charlotte nodded and returned with two larger glasses. The Queen had struggled with the bottle.

"Please, pour in the smaller glasses."

Charlotte did so.

"A generous measure," the Queen said. "My cup overflows."

Charlotte picked one and sniffed, it smelt oily and pungent. The Queen was pointing at a bag and Charlotte took the hint. There was another bottle there, the sort that pharmacists used. Charlotte poured this into the Queen's larger glass under the woman's hovering direction. She herself topped it up with her schnapps.

Charlotte went to put the tonic back in the woman's bag.

"Keep it," the Contessa said. "I have no more need of it."

"Isn't it your tonic?"

"It is yours now, drink it when you need it. Only then."

"Does it taste nice?"

"I imagine it tastes bitter."

"I... thank you."

"The dowager wanted another son in the family portfolio."

Charlotte didn't know what to say, so she mumbled: "That's nice."

The Queen raised her glass: "Salud!"

"Your health."

The Queen laughed and choked, holding her hand up to ward off Charlotte's help, and then she drank, a long careful draught draining her glass completely. Charlotte knocked hers back, becoming utterly startled as the liquid burnt the inside of her mouth and set fire to her throat. She tried to say something but only managed a half strangled squeak. It seemed incredible that people would drink schnapps for pleasure.

The Queen slumped, utterly finished: her glass fell from her hand.

Charlotte rushed around the table to her side catching her before she pitched off the back of the divan. The woman face was ashen, her lips blue even beneath the thick red lipstick, and her breathing was laboured.

"Oh! I'll get help."

"No, please, hide the bottle."

Charlotte saw the tonic on the table and understood: it was poison.

"You... killed yourself?"

"There are fates worse than death."

"I'll get help."

"No, let me rot."

Charlotte eased her down into a lying position, and then ran to the door. Outside there were a few maids chatting.

"Get help!" she shouted.

The women pretended not to understand.

"Help! The Queen has taken ill. Now!"

The women beetled away.

Back in the room, the Queen was much worse, her life ebbing away. Charlotte held her hand, an icy collection of bones now.

"Don't..."

"Quiet now, Contessa, save your strength."

The Queen grabbed at Charlotte's hair, feebly pulling her closer. Charlotte smelt the schnapps on her breath and something else.

"Don't let... Mordant, keep... Doctor Death from... me."

The door opened behind her, but Charlotte couldn't pull her head away to look.

"I see vineyards and wheat..."

The Queen's eyes stopped moving and any sparkle was merely the reflection of the candles. Her gaze had ended at the south window with its view of harsh rock walls.

Charlotte was pulled roughly away and the Vögte leant over the Queen, his hand going to her throat to feel for a pulse.

"She is dead," he said.

"There are fates worse..." Charlotte whispered to herself.

"What was that?" the Vögte demanded.

"Something she said."

Charlotte couldn't drag her attention away from the tonic bottle that was still on the table. It appeared so harmless next to the tall majestic German schnapps, and yet so deadly. As others arrived, Charlotte was pushed aside and ended up by the window.

The Graf was shouting: "Where's Mordant!"

Prince Pieter was there and so was his Secretary, Earnestine, who stayed by the door. She looked angry, her face betraying her assumption that this was all Charlotte's fault, which this time it absolutely was not.

Finally, Doctor Mordant arrived and shouldered her way to the front. She examined the body and then almost psychically went to the bottle of tonic. She sniffed it.

"Dead," she said finally.

Pieter's voice cracked: "Mother! Do something!"

"Get her to my laboratory, there's time and I've galvanic charge."

A few soldiers came forward to cradle the corpse in their arms.

"No," Pieter cried out, trying to stop them: "Not that."

"Brother, she has her duty."

"She's not your mother."

"She's not yours either. Our real mother knew her duty."

Held back by Graf Gustav, Pieter could do nothing to stop the stretcher bearers gathering up the dead woman.

"Let her rest in peace," Pieter pleaded.

"Halt!" The Dowager stood by the threshold, stick in hand. "Leave her. She is dead. We can turn this to our advantage."

"Now is not the time for the Great Plan," Pieter said.

"Now is exactly the time."

The Dowager glanced around and Earnestine found a chair for her. She sat; even lowered she dominated the room with her presence.

"With the Contessa dead, the King is free to marry again," the crone said. "This leaves a piece to gain a connection with the House of Holstein-Gottorp-Romanov."

"My father cannot travel to Moscow," Pieter protested.

"Not him, you Pieter."

"But…"

"Nicholas has three daughters: Olga, Tatiana and Maria, if you-"

Pieter went over to the dowager: "They are babies."

"Olga is five, you can be betrothed and wait a few years, six or seven at the most."

Pieter open his mouth to object again, but the dowager gripped his jacket and pushed her face against his, so close that he tried to squirm away from her breath.

"Patience, Pieter, patience - this is the long game, the Great Game, and I have waited so long, so very long, and given up so much: children of my own, who would have weakened our line and spread our influence too thin. No, you, my godson, will join our house with that of the Great Russian Empire. The world, Pieter, the world will be ours."

Pieter swallowed and gestured towards Charlotte: "What of her House? We need that connection too."

"Not as much, and we can still keep her in the family."

"How?"

"She can marry your father."

Pieter jerked back, a full stride, enough to rip his uniform from the old woman's grip. The gold aiguillettes came loose and hung down forlorn, dangling like untied cords.

He looked at Charlotte for the first time.

"She's too... innocent."

"She is Royalty, she will have to adapt."

"It's too cruel."

"Nothing is too cruel."

The old woman moved towards Charlotte like some harbinger, her bony hands folding in front of her like the wings of a bat.

"My dear," she said, "you are not to marry this Prince, but the Crown Prince, the King himself."

"Is he important?" Charlotte asked.

"The most important man in this whole country."

"Is he handsome?"

"He was once described as the most athletic and vital man in the whole of Christendom."

"Does he wear a uniform?"

"The finest."

"Oh good."

"But that will weaken us, spread the inheritances to others," the Graf said.

"You fool!" The dowager struggled to turn on him, with her stick in her right hand, she waved away assistance with the other. "The solution is simply: this Princess marries our King, binding that throne to us as required, but she bears only girls, freeing us to marry you, Gustav, and Pieter in a wider circle."

"No!" Pieter protested: "She's so young."

"It matters not."

The dowager left, her stick clicking across the stone. The others waited and then processed out, leaving only Charlotte and Earnestine. The dead Queen, utterly abandoned by her family, stared up accusingly, her eyes seemed to follow Charlotte as she moved to Earnestine.

"She killed herself," Charlotte said. "I poured the drinks and the tonic... she called it a tonic."

Earnestine ignored her and went over to the Queen's body. Charlotte steeled herself as she watched her sister bend over and close the Queen's eyes before finding a shawl to put over her face.

"I wonder why she killed herself," Earnestine mused.

"She said that some fates are worse than death."

"Are you happy now?"

"It wasn't my fault."

"It's never your fault, is it, Lottie?"

"I'm going to be a Queen."

"Congratulations on your promotion, Your Majesty."

Earnestine was such a cow, a horrible, unkind, cow, who didn't appreciate Charlotte no matter what she did: Princess, soon to be a Queen, but Charlotte was still treated like a little girl. Earnestine hated her because

Charlotte knew how to have fun and Earnestine was just a spoil sport.

"You're only jealous because I've been proposed to by two Princes... and now a King, and you're an old maid."

"Charlotte, it's not a competition," Earnestine replied sternly. "The Crown Prince can't have proposed if he's not met you."

"Just because you haven't had a proposal."

"As a matter of fact, I have... a fine gentleman... and it's none of your business."

"What did you say?"

"It didn't happen."

"He wasn't good enough for you, I suppose."

"Have you met their King?"

"No," Charlotte sniffed, "but I'm sure he's nice and much better than your stupid 'fine gentleman'."

They sat for a long time pointedly staring away from each other. A chill settled; the room wasn't heated, the sisters were not speaking and there was a body in the room. Charlotte decided she was going to be regal, practice made perfect after all and she must get used to being superior to everyone, although mostly she did this to irritate Earnestine. Or maybe Earnestine was now waiting to be spoken to before speaking. Well, as far as Charlotte was concerned, she could wait in silence forever.

"You should be happy for me," Charlotte said.

"You must accept the consequences of your actions," Earnestine replied. "The woman here talked about a fate worse than death."

"I'm sure that's just to keep people in line and it doesn't apply to royalty."

"Some people need to be kept in line."

"Will you be my maid of honour?"

"No."

"I'll send for Georgina then," said Charlotte.

"I don't think that would be wise," Earnestine said. "There's something going on here and I intend to find out what."

"That sounds like an adventure."

"Don't be impertinent."

"You can't talk to me like that anymore, I'm royalty."

"Not yet."

The door opened, held ajar to allow the dowager Gräfin to enter.

"My dear," she said "we must prepare you to meet your future husband."

Charlotte stood, smoothed her dress in front of her and dutifully went over. The old crone gripped her shoulder using her as a support. Charlotte winced, but kept quiet and allowed herself to be drawn out into the corridor.

Earnestine counted to ten and then followed.

The Gräfin held up an imperious finger: "Not you!"

Earnestine stopped and bowed to both the dowager Gräfin and Charlotte.

"Family only," said the Gräfin, putting her arm around Charlotte and leading her away.

# CHAPTER IX

## Miss Deering-Dolittle

For the first time since she had arrived at the castle, Earnestine was alone. She had seen the war room of the Great Plan, Pieter's task, and so there must be an equivalent room for the Graf Gustav Zala's machinations for his Great War. All the family would be off to see Charlotte's future husband, the Crown Prince, and so there was an opportunity to seize.

She pushed her head up, chin out, shoulders back, and strode into the corridor. There were soldiers on guard, who started to snap to attention until they realised her lowly status.

"I'm on an errand for the Prince," she announced.

"Ich spreche kein Englisch."

"I'm on an... OUT OF MY WAY!"

As the two confused soldiers snapped to attention, Earnestine strode imperiously past them and down the corridor. Prince Pieter's rooms were behind her, so ahead must be the answers she sought. Around the corner, there was a window that afforded a view of the north side of the castle. Below, perched on a plateau, were factories. She knew what they were because she had seen paintings of such buildings at the National Gallery on Trafalgar Square. The chimneys belched smoke and men, like tiny ants, scurried about. Leaning against the cold glass, she could hear clanging: blacksmiths perhaps, or machines.

Right, she thought, obtain some evidence, escape and inform the nearest consulate of the situation. The Ambassador would then have words with the Austro-Hungarian authorities - they wouldn't want him to have to inform Her Britannic Majesty, would they? - and all this would go away. Charlotte would be sent home, Earnestine would have a proper talk with her, and then she'd have words with Georgina for letting the silly girl get into such mischief.

Below the castle, there were carts and a railway station of sorts: transport.

At the end of this corridor, a spiral staircase led down, but it was full of soldiers, the spikes of their helmets stabbing up and down foolishly as they traipsed up and down the stairs. Those going up were laden with canisters. These were a variety of shapes and sizes: some with fins, others with nozzles, and identified by a stencilled letters and numbers in one of four colours: yellow, blue, red or black. It was as if there were two long lines of ants, one carrying their eggs upwards and the other returning for duty. Up and down, round and round, busier and busier, and blocking Earnestine's way.

Going down the stairs, passing every soldier by yelling 'out of my way' was bound to attract attention and she needed to slip away without being noticed. She'd need time before anyone realised she was missing to make good her escape.

But how?

Just as she was beginning to despair, two men dropped a canister. It clattered to the floor and burst, showering everyone with its contents. Clearly the canisters, or at least the one dropped, were pressurised.

The men panicked, swore and fled, only to be beaten back by another, a sergeant of some kind. Earnestine couldn't follow the rapid shouting, but she understood the meaning well enough: the sergeant, or whatever he was, was berating the useless men for carelessness and endangering everyone. Earnestine got the distinct impression from the terror, and the evident relief that followed, that they had been lucky - very lucky.

The sergeant finished his reprimand and sent the men away. This was their mess and they would have to clear it up.

The landing was empty, briefly. Earnestine seized her chance and crossed, but curiosity got the better of her. The canister was labelled in blue, 'TZ-146', with a nozzle attachment and the substance that leaked from its cracked casing was a yellowish grey powder made up of granules.

She made it across the landing before the next group of soldiers ambled down the spiral staircase.

There was a small window that afforded a view into the valley below. She could see where they were unloading the canisters from crates. They were taking them up and presumably placing them in one of those new-fangled airships. All this activity must be for some purpose. Graf Zala was planning a military campaign.

To the north there was Germany ruled by the Queen's grandson, Kaiser Wilhelm II. Going round clockwise, there was Russia ruled by the Tsar Nicholas II, who was married to the Queen's grand-daughter. These two countries were effectively family and so no threat to the British Empire. Romania, Serbia and the Ottoman Empire, and Montenegro had a border to the south. She remembered the map in her father's study, and that left Italy and Switzerland to the West. Of course with airships, Zala might be considering an attack further afield, jumping over territories as if he was playing draughts: Sweden, Norway, Denmark, Greece or France perhaps? Could a Zeppelin cross the English Channel?

The Austro-Hungarians had already occupied Bosnia and Herzegovina, so Archduke Karl Ludwig was a war monger. Graf Zala could be trying to curry favour with a military success and so raise the position of his minor Royal House. To make their Crown Prince into a real King would require other machinations to replace the Archduke: these foreigners seemed to get into a terrible muddle with their titles.

She was missing something with her political analysis.

It didn't matter, she realised, whatever he was up to, it was bound to be destabilising and the British Empire wouldn't stand for it. Therefore, the sooner Westminster and Whitehall were told, the better.

She took out an envelope from her shoulder bag and when the next gap in the line appeared, she nipped back to the canister and scooped a sample of the spilt contents: evidence.

Now all she had to do was get away.

Realising that the factories were going to be teeming with people, she glanced around for an alternative. To one side, east, there was a zigzag path leading down to a small building. Squinting, she could see canons on either side. It hardly seemed a defensive position, but perhaps there was a way down from there into the valley below. It was worth a try.

But how?

She'd be very exposed walking back and forth under the castle walls.

Of course, half-inch a coat and borrow one of those spiked helmets: at a distance, in a coat and pickelhaube, no-one would be able to tell her apart from a genuine soldier. She'd tuck her red hair under the steel helmet and brazen it out.

As she scanned around, she saw the floor marked with boot prints: if soldiers came in, muddy from the rough tracks, then they would go... ah ha, along this corridor. There was a small room, a hallway to the outside, packed with equipment: coats hung from hooks, there were strange masks with huge bug eyes and snow shoes stacked to one side.

There was plenty of choice, except that there were no boots. Clearly the men kept their personal equipment with them, so her Oxford folly boots were going to take a hammering going down the mountainside.

She was about to get dressed, when she heard voices: Pieter and... Gustav, she thought. She wasn't as familiar with Pieter's brother. Really it was none of her business and she ought to take the opportunity to make good her escape, but a little peek wasn't-

No, she'd get away! Sensible Earnestine, well done: *I must not explore.*

The voices came from further down the corridor and there was a wooden door set in an alcove. It was old with a large key hole and there wasn't anyone inside. The catch made an appallingly loud click as it opened and the hinges squeaked.

It was dark: if only she hadn't lost her flashlight.

She saw an oil lamp and matches set to one side. As she adjusted the flame, she was able to see the room clearly.

A large tapestry hung against one wall, a magnificent example of needlework depicting a battle, horses and cavalry rallying against the odds. Earnestine thought about all those poor women slaving away day after day to produce this monstrosity.

Opposite was a collection of weapons and armour attached to the wall for display. The family crest was painted on a shield and appeared as a banner in the tapestry.

Underneath was a desk full of papers: something, anything, but it was German and full of figures. They were... yes, manifests, stock ledgers and so on, all neatly tabulated in neither German nor English, but the international and impenetrable language of abbreviation: '147 TZ', '98 MU', '304 IB'. Clearly they had an awful lot of whatever they were manufacturing and loading onto the Zeppelin.

She didn't think this was their actual war room, but there might be a clue, so Earnestine set about examining each document. Entranced by the puzzle of it, she failed to hear footsteps behind her.

There was a cough: "Fräulein."

She stood bolt upright, hands held in front of her.

It was Prince Pieter.

"What are you doing?" he asked.

"Paperwork... I'm your Secretary, or have you forgotten?"

"This area is off limits."

"Really, there's no sign."

"There is a sign."

Earnestine looked at the door, perhaps she could make a run for it. The corridor to the storeroom was only a short distance, but it was impossible.

"Oh," she said. "Is that what those German words mean?"

"Verboten."

"Now you pronounce it, it does seem obvious."

"Perhaps you should return to our rooms."

"Our rooms?"

"Ja, that would be best."

That would be best: indeed it would, and having had this reconnoitre it would be straightforward enough to make her escape later tonight. Hopefully Pieter was a heavy sleeper and she would be able to slip out.

"What are all those canisters?" she asked. Always the Family Curse: curiosity led to exploring, exploring led to adventures, adventures led to further adventures until one disappeared up a river.

"You have seen them?"

"Hard to miss."

Pieter flinched: "That is unfortunate," he said.

"What is this all about?"

"There is war always, even during this age of Pax Britannica, so perhaps a war to end all wars would be a good thing. One ruler, one government, one people: if rigorously applied it would bring about peace in our time and for all time."

Pieter did not look or sound convinced himself.

"How?"

Heavy boots stomped towards the room: "Pieter!!!"

"Gustav!"

Pieter pushed Earnestine back and stood between her and the doorway. In the jiffy she had, Earnestine hid behind the tapestry.

"Graf," Pieter said.

"Mein Bruder."

Earnestine held her breath and desperately wracked her brains for the identity of this man. 'Bruder', of course, he must be the Graf, Pieter's elder brother. She'd seen him briefly before, of course: this was the man with the military plans, the one with a fondness for airships and Charlotte. What a silly girl, you only had to hear two words from him in a foreign language to know he was a bad sort.

"Is father ready?"

"Doctor Death is attending to him now and then he's to meet the Princess."

"These mechanisms, these scientific devices, are wasted keeping one man in the semblance of life," said Pieter using English, and Earnestine realised that he was partly speaking for her benefit. "Nature should be allowed to take its course."

"You wish me to be Crown Prince already."

"Nein, I mean, Ja; of course, it is your right."

"But that would mean an end to the Great Plan."

"I don't see how marrying that young girl to father... it's wrong."

"No-one cares if a royal is mad, diseased or simple, just that he is alive."

"Alive?" Pieter choked back a cry.

"I have an alternative, if only Mordant would give us the secret," the Graf replied. "Think of this knowledge applied like a cotton mill, life brought about on an industrial scale. My ambition is not to wait a few generations to marry into the right circles, but to take what we want with warfare. It will be a conflict on a scale never before imagined. We will become like the Spartans of old, a society dedicated to warfare, but whereas those ancient

Greeks were foot soldiers, we will be the officer class - a race born to lead from high above in the heavens and our troops will be the very fiends brought back from hell."

"The British Empire must not allow-"

"The British Empire is effete. Its people play with a straight bat, isn't that the expression? The British won't know what hit them."

Pieter had used the word '*must*', Earnestine realised: it was an order, a mission and it coincided with her own. Except, the tapestry was dusty and she was going to sneeze. Could she risk moving her hand to nose or would that cause the covering to ripple?

"Your toys are nearly ready then?"

"Ja... why are you telling me something I already know... and in English."

With a flourish, Earnestine was revealed. The tapestry tumbled to the ground. Earnestine tried to remain aloof as if she was supposed to be there, but the dust made her splutter and wave her hands.

"What's this?" the Graf said, approaching.

"Leave her alone!"

The Graf laughed: "You shouldn't get too fond of your playthings. Is she good?"

"I am not!" Earnestine objected, and then she felt foolish.

"Why brother, you have not broken her in."

Pieter flushed with shame or anger - Earnestine wasn't sure.

"Do you want me to do it for you?" the Graf joked.

"Nein, lassen Sie sie allein, sie ist meine!"

The Graf guffawed: "Perhaps, brother, we should fight a duel."

"Pistols at dawn?"

"Sabres, here, now."

The Count made a magnanimous gesture to indicate the walls of the ante-chamber. The ornamentation, signs of history, consisted of shields, emblems and weapons, so that what had been mere decoration changed in Earnestine's mind to become the sharp instruments of combat that they had been before they were put on display.

"These are old."

"As is the night, brother, choose - or accept my authority."

Prince Pieter scanned the swords, grambouchaums and pikes, picked out a pair of crossed sabres and fetched one down.

"Pieter!" Earnestine cried out and immediately felt cowed by Graf Zala's angry gaze. "Your Royal Highness, Pieter, I believe that duelling is forbidden within your regiment."

That was a guess, but she had heard that dictate before. There had been a story in *The Times* about two officers disgraced by duelling over a bet.

"Are you going to hide behind your dollymop's skirts," the Graf taunted as he selected his weapon, a similar rapier to Pieter's own.

"Excuse me!" Earnestine was not going to stand for that and she gave him her Prefect's stare.

Zala's eyes held Earnestine's and then he very deliberately licked his lips.

Pieter leapt forward, slashing wildly to be parried by Zala.

"Good, good," the Graf joked, "I see she has given you spirit."

They circled: Prince Pieter nervous and backing off. Clearly the elder brother was the superior swordsman, bigger in frame with a longer reach, and he had a relaxed, arrogant stance.

"I will give you a scar, brother, something to brag about in the officers' mess," Zala taunted, "and when you are in the infirmary being treated, I shall take another weapon and see to your dolly-mop's scar."

Pieter struck quickly, a stab, a parry and a cut: Earnestine was furious too although she wasn't entirely sure she knew the Graf's meaning.

"Stoppen Sie sofort!" It was the Vögte bursting in.

The clanging swords silenced, their echoes still reverberating through the stone chamber.

"Vögte, Vögte, mein Freund," the Graf said.

"Zweikampf ist verboten!" said the Vögte, his thin frame somehow filling the doorway.

"Pardon me," said Earnestine.

"Duelling is verboten," the Vögte said.

"Don't order me," the Graf replied, towering over the servile man, but the Vögte held his ground.

"We are practising," the Graf continued. "I am teaching my brother as any good brother would. See, the... Secretary, was it? I am showing her how much of a man Prince Pieter is."

"Your father awaits you," the Vögte announced.

The Graf laughed as he left: "Lock her in your room."

"Ja," the Vögte answered.

"I'll do it," said Pieter.

The Vögte stared at him.

"You are holding up the ceremony," said Pieter. "You don't want the Gräfin to know that, do you?"

The Vögte bowed and then hurried after the Graf leaving Pieter and Earnestine alone.

"So I'm your prisoner again?" Earnestine said.

The Prince went over to the desk taking a small key from his pocket. He unlocked a drawer and removed a folded sheet of paper.

"You were looking for this," he said. He slipped it into an envelope and held it out for Earnestine to take. She took it with her left hand, unthinkingly, and realised that he had offered it with his left: it meant acceptance, but surely only of the letter and not some proposition.

Earnestine went to open it, but Pieter stopped her.

"It is in German and you don't have the time," he said, "although perhaps you do for a kiss."

"Oh, very well," Earnestine said, as she slipped the envelope into her shoulder bag and offered her hand. These foreign Gentlemen had such strange customs, but when in Rome do-

The man pulled her towards him and planted his lips on hers: Earnestine struggled and then it was over.

"Now I have something to remember you by," said Pieter. "Here is something in return - think of me."

He slipped a ring off his right hand and slipped it over the middle finger of Earnestine's left hand.

"I'm free to go?"

"You are free of me, if you wish," Pieter replied. "But the others will try to stop you."

He clicked his heels together, bowed smartly, turned and walked out.

Earnestine put her fingers to her lips, touching where his mouth had been to try and elicit the sensation again.

And then she ran.

## Miss Georgina

"Ladies first," said Merryweather.

"You first, Merry. I think the experienced climber should go first to discover any obstacles to our ascent," said Georgina, very much aware that she was wearing a dress and not wanting to be vulnerably placed above this man. He might see an ankle or... perish the thought.

"Georgina, my dear, if you go first then I can catch you if you fall."

"But I don't want to be responsible for knocking you off, so you should go first."

"We'll be tied together to be safe."

Georgina tilted her head to one side like a governess until Merryweather realised he wasn't going to win. The officer stretched out the end of a rope and tied it expertly around his waist. He handed the other end to Georgina, who looped it around herself and then fiddled as she made a few abortive attempts to attach it.

"Here," said Merryweather, taking it off her, "let me tie the knot."

He looped it back around her waist, reaching around her with his strong arms, and for some unknown reason Georgina felt quite breathless. And they hadn't even started climbing yet. Merryweather's expert fingers inveigled the rope and a quick jerk checked it was secure.

"We're attached now," he said.

"Until death do us part."

Georgina regretted the joke immediately: there was the perilous drop as well as the shaming embarrassment of suggestion.

"I- I-"

Without another word, Merryweather turned to the rock face, selected a good starting position and then began climbing. Carefully and methodically, he made rapid progress tugging the rope as he went. The loops of rope at Georgina's feet uncoiled until the final one rose from the ground, straightened and gently tugged Georgina towards the mountain.

"Miss, if you can keep some slack in the rope," he called down, "and don't look down."

"I will directly," Georgina shouted back.

Here goes, she thought, taking grip of the cold stone. The sharp edges bit into her hands, loose dirt caused her fingers to slip, and her boots felt awkward, but she too was making progress. Concentrating on each step took all her faculties until climbing became everything.

The mountain was steep, but not vertical and the rock itself was split and shattered by the elements, so although it looked difficult, some sections were almost as easy as climbing a ladder. This gave her a false confidence until a chunk of rock came away under the pull of her hand in a shower of gravel. She closed her eyes and hung on, hearing the falling rubble bounce and careen below her. The debris bounced off the path, a ledge really, and continued its descent down the cliff.

"Georgina, are you all right? Georgina? Georgina?"

"I'm-" she had to spit the grit from her mouth in a most unladylike fashion. "I'm well."

"Do take care."

Oh, why didn't I think of that, she thought. Charlotte had died on this mountain and she had nearly done the same.

Georgina started up again, carefully, but something grabbed her, pulled her down savagely: her dress was caught. It would be ruined. Once she felt secure, she reached down and ripped it off a jagged outcrop.

Upward again, moving to the left, guided by the rope that went up to Merryweather, which perplexed her until she saw how much easier the going was on that side.

Looking up, she saw that there was enough slack, so she paused to regain her breath and recruit herself. Behind her, the view was spectacular with magnificent snow-capped mountains, it was awe inspiring, and below her was-

Every limb gripped harder, the knuckles on her hands went white and her toes pinched into the crevice with force. She pushed her face against the cold stone, held her body as close as it would go and breathed, rapidly, her lungs expanding uncontrollably, and each intake threatened to fling her from the cliff face and plunge her into the ravine.

"Bally hell!"

She couldn't move, frozen as she was to the spot, and the cold stone leached out more of her resolve with every desperate second.

The rope tugged, the yank making her look up and the jolt making her climb, it was instinctive, calming even, but it was a very long way to fall and Georgina made a point of not looking down again.

# Miss Charlotte

"I have something for you," the Gräfin announced.

"Ooh," squealed Charlotte.

They were in her suite in the castle, where the Gräfin had taken her to change before meeting the Crown Prince. The dowager showed her a small box, the sort that hinged open to reveal a piece of jewellery. "This was my great grandmother's ring, it's a ruby."

Charlotte picked up the box and opened it to reveal the big, chunky ring: "Ooh."

"Put it on."

Charlotte did so, feeling its weight and the way the light shone through the red stone. Tiny slivers of light, like blades, shivered up the far walls cast there by the gem as it took charge of the candlelight.

"You have it on the wrong finger, my dear."

Charlotte looked at the old woman with a quizzical expression. The Gräfin raised her own left hand, her fingers splayed, and counted along with her right index finger.

"A ring on your first finger means you are available, your middle finger means you are engaged, third finger is when you are married and the little finger..."

"The little finger?"

"When you are an old maid."

Charlotte could not stop herself glancing down: the Gräfin's little finger contained a huge blue stone rammed on in such a way that it looked like it would never be removed.

"Yes, my lot has been to see that my family are all married."

Charlotte nodded, not knowing what else to do. Despite finding officers to be fascinating, soldiers to be interesting and cadets to be fun, she found other boys to be rather boring; however, she didn't want to be an old maid as old maids smelt of sherry and did nothing but play bridge. She'd heard Georgina crying once that Earnestine was a monster for not marrying and that she, Georgina, would end up on the shelf as an old maid. Ness, Georgina had complained, you are nearly twenty-one, people are going to wonder what's wrong with you.

Charlotte moved the ring to her middle finger and it went on easily, loose, but she thought it would stay on.

"There," the Gräfin croaked, "now change."

"I'd prefer my uniform," Charlotte said, gesturing to the aerial officer's tunic and trousers hanging on the wardrobe handle.

"A dress for your wedding, my dear."

"The men get to wear uniforms."

Charlotte waited, but the old woman didn't move. The dress was there, a light blue staid thing.

"Now!"

Under the gaze of the harridan, Charlotte took her beloved uniform and placed it back in the wardrobe and then, her back turned, stripped naked before dressing in a fresh shift. A maid appeared to tighten the bindings of her corset, a jerk forcing all the air from Charlotte's lungs just as she was about to ask for it to be tied loose.

"Tighter!" the Gräfin commanded.

Suddenly there were tears in Charlotte's eyes.

"Short breaths," the maid whispered.

"Quiet!"

Charlotte panted like a dog as the blue creation was deposited over her, done up and fussed over. Soon, she was the picture of perfection and paraded before a standing mirror.

"You'll do," said the Gräfin, not unkindly.

Charlotte smiled.

The Gräfin clapped her hands: "Come!"

Charlotte was led in procession along the corridors of the castle. As they passed, servants and underlings bowed or curtsied as the Gräfin passed, deference shown at every stage, and then Charlotte, out of the corner of her eye, noticed their reaction to her own passing: they bowed and scraped too, but they looked away and some - too many - crossed themselves as Catholics do.

They were afraid!

Of her?

Surely they could not be frightened by a small girl like herself. It would be the Gräfin, but their fear of that old crone was manifest in their bowing. For Charlotte it was different... they were afraid *for her*.

When they reached a pair of large wooden doors, the Gräfin halted.

"I will see that everything is in order," she said. "Wait here."

Charlotte waited.

Left with her was a senior maid. Charlotte glared at her, moved slightly, forcing the woman to take more and more extreme measures to avoid eye contact, until finally it was impossible. The woman looked: she had brown, almost black eyes, wide, with the whites visible all the way around. She crossed herself, quickly, an impulsive protective gesture.

"Do you speak English?"

The woman nodded, desperately, twisting to avoid her.

"What is it?" she whispered.

The woman shook her head.

"What?"

"Poor child," the maid whispered, "for you is a fate worse than death."

The big doors opened.

The Gräfin clapped.

Charlotte went in to a small chapel, a wonderfully familiar sight with wooden pews, a font, pulpit and far ahead, an altar below a shining stained glass window depicting the last supper.

Everyone stood for her.

She walked down the aisle: she was so important, the centre of attention with servants and people bowing as she passed. If only her sisters could be there to see her, she thought, then they'd realise how mean and horrid they had been.

Ahead, on her right and facing the congregation, the Crown Prince - her Crown Prince - sat upon a throne on a raised dais surrounded by rings of functionaries. The outer circle consisted of uniformed military, then came the officials and finally the inner ring of family. Charlotte was led forward and, as she got closer to the great man, he seemed to shrink, his finery took on the air of costume and pretence, his bones were clear through his stretched skin and his eyes were yellow and watery. His head lolled to one side and he drooled.

"He's really not well," said Charlotte. "He needs medical help."

"He has the best medical help in all of Europe," said the Graf. "Can you not see the leeches all around?"

On both sides of the room, men in white coats stood waiting, their pockets bulging with stethoscopes and steel instruments. Doctor Mordant was there too.

Charlotte's shoe caught on the top of the dais, her toe striking the stone and she nearly stumbled. The Graf caught her arm and lifted her onto the platform.

"I'm all right," she said.

"May I present His Royal Highness, the Crown Prince," the Vögte announced. "The King!"

Everyone dropped to one knee except Charlotte.

This was the man she was supposed to marry? He was at least a hundred and fifty, she thought, and...

She nearly gagged, the smell was vile.

"Come closer," the Vögte whispered as oily as his slicked back hair.

The Graf, keeping Charlotte between him and his father, pushed her forward. She put her hand out to steady herself and brushed across the Crown Prince's hand. He was cold, icy cold, absorbing the heat from her like metal on a winter's night.

The Vögte gestured with his long, bony fingers and Charlotte leaned forward, turning her face away from the foul abomination when she saw things crawling through his scalp.

"This is the Princess," the Vögte crowed. "Isn't she lovely, a beauty, strong of limb and healthy? She will bear you many sons and daughters."

Charlotte thought she was going to throw up.

"See, see," the Vögte twittered excitedly, "His Royal Highness speaks."

The old man's mouth moved and spittle spilled forth to dampen the crusting that stained collar.

"The Crown Prince asks for your hand in marriage," translated the Vögte for all. He gazed around the room to pass on this wonderful news and dare anyone to contradict.

Charlotte's flesh seemed to shrink back, almost as if her vital organs were huddling together to create a space between her body and her corset.

The Vögte sneered: "Your Royal Highness, what is your gracious answer?"

Bile rose in Charlotte's throat.

"Yes?" he asked again.

Charlotte voice seemed to come from nowhere: "Yes?"

The sigh of relief around the room was louder than the half-hearted cheer.

"Good, good," said the Vögte. "We will have a quick wedding now, a service before God, and then you will consummate the marriage."

"Wedding now?"

"Ja," the dowager replied.

Charlotte pulled away and put the back of her hand against her mouth swallowing the taste of her recent meal back into her gullet. The 'does anyone know just cause' couldn't come soon enough, she thought, and then she'd just tell them.

The priest spoke in German addressing the crowd and then paused: there was an agony of silence and then he carried on. He seemed to be deliberately stretching it out as a form of torture.

The Graf stepped forward with a gold ring, he gestured in front of the jerking form of his father and then grabbed Charlotte's left hand. She pulled away as he twisted and screwed the band onto her third finger.

Oh Lord, she thought, I've missed the 'just cause'. It was then, when the Priest had paused, when the dust had frozen in the pale light from the tall stained glass window. She was lost.

The Gräfin jabbed her in the small of her back: "Now!"

Charlotte cried out.

"I do," said the Gräfin.

"I do?" said Charlotte.

"She does," the crone cackled.

The Priest faced the congregation and announced something, words that flowed quickly and each syllable edged with relief. When he finished, he looked at the squirming bride.

"What?" Charlotte said.

"You may kiss your husband," the Gräfin said, her spindly fingers gripped Charlotte's hair as she yanked her head around and forced the young girl to bend towards the corruption of flesh that twitched in front of her. Charlotte's hair was pulled at the roots drawing back her skin and her lips were forced into a rictus. The Crown Prince's body below her went into spasms and still Charlotte was pushed closer.

A yard, a foot, an inch...

The Crown Prince spewed a mass of yellow bile, a splatter striking Charlotte in the face. She wrenched back, retching herself, as the monster contorted.

An orderly tried to hold him down, but the writhing creature found strength: it snapped up with its teeth and took a bite out of the man's neck. Blood spurted, washing the vile puke from the ruined uniform. The man fell back, his hand over the gushing wound and he called for help, coughing blood across the stone floor.

More technicians entered the fray to hold their Crown Prince down. The struggle increased, full of kicks and jerks. Charlotte looked away: saw the horror on everyone's faces, the shadows struggling and fighting on the wall, her own shaking hands.

Suddenly it stopped.

The technicians stepped away to reveal the Crown Prince: a corpse, ashen and grey, and the smell of death was upon the cadaver already.

Charlotte's gasping drew in enough air and she opened her mouth to-

The dowager Gräfin struck her across the face, a sharp unbelievably sudden shock. Charlotte's jaw was numb, her eyeballs felt loose in their sockets. By the time Charlotte recovered enough to look back, Doctor Mordant, complete with magnifying goggles swooped down to put her fingers to the corpse's throat.

"The King is dead," she said.

Charlotte's surge of relief was so great and, in contrast to her former revulsion and horror, it felt like joy.

"The King is dead!" the Graf shouted. "The King is dead!!!"

The orderlies sprang into action and unceremoniously lifted the body as others brought a gurney forward. They dumped the dead King down and wheeled him away.

Charlotte went over to the Princes standing forlorn by the tapestry.

"I'm so sorry," she began, "but-"

The Graf gripped her arm vice-like and pulled her away.

"Excuse me," Charlotte managed.

"Ignore them," the Graf said. "They are nothing."

"Are you the new Crown Prince now?"

"Nein," Zala replied.

"Your brother... surely younger."

"Your wedding night is only delayed."

"To whom am I to be married now?" Charlotte asked. "You or your brother, Pieter?"

"You are married already."

"Only until death do us part."

"Nein."

The Graf marched out, his stride barely affected by the English girl he dragged in his wake. They went down a corridor with mirrored doors on all sides and then into a dungeon. That's what it looked to Charlotte until her eyes became accustomed to the dark. The Crown Prince's body had already been placed upon an altar at the far end and above, in some strange parody of a crucifix, a brass shape like a giant 'V' overshadowed everything.

A noise, unlike anything Charlotte had ever heard, sparked into being as lightning played between the two arms of the brass mechanism. This was a laboratory similar to Doctor Mordant's high up in the tower. An iron taste dried Charlotte's mouth and the hairs on her forearms tried to crawl.

The Graf came to a stop, far too close to this horror for Charlotte, but although she twisted and struggled, she couldn't get free.

"Mordant!"

The Doctor didn't move: "Turn away."

"This is no time for secrets."

"Graf."

The Graf seethed, but he turned away, pulling Charlotte around as he did so. It was frightening, not knowing what was happening, and Charlotte could hear Doctor Mordant mixing chemicals behind them.

"You may look," said the Doctor.

Everything seemed to be the same as before they turned away.

"Now," said Doctor Mordant.

An operative by the side of the room adjusted a dial and then threw a huge switch. It sparked as it made the connection and then the lightning arced across the room blasting the colour from the scene.

The Crown Prince's body, strapped to the table, convulsed, his entire form jerking in a parody of the life: once, twice and then again.

"Lights, lights," Doctor Mordant instructed. Strange electric lights on cables were brought forward.

"Again," Doctor Mordant shouted.

By the side of the table, Charlotte saw the Crown Prince's dead hand twitch and move.

Doctor Mordant turned triumphantly to the assembly: "It's alive!"

"Ja," said the Graf.

The Crown Prince screamed: an awful noise conjured from some circle of hell. It was as if his human soul had a whole lifetime compressed into a single heartbeat, a brief knowledge before its gibbering, drooling mockery of existence took hold again.

"Long live the King," said the Graf.

"Long live the King," came a reply.

"Long live the King!"

"Long live the King," came the response.

"Long live the King!!"

The chant was picked up by all: "Long live the King."

The Graf let go and Charlotte, suddenly bereft of support, stumbled away to fall on the floor. In the flickering light, the Princes gazed upon their father, gibbering amongst the technicians, with expressions of disgust and anger, and with a terrible resigned despair. Charlotte crawled away on her knees, her hands to her ears trying to blot out the appalling, almost religious fervour.

"Long live the King!!!"

"Long live the King!!!"

"Long live the King!!!"

# CHAPTER X

## Miss Deering-Dolittle

Earnestine ran down a long path that zig-zagged to descend the steep gradient of the mountainside. At the end was a battery built from stone on a flat area and beyond the cliff dropped away. The buildings appeared deserted and the cannons were unmanned. The guns were old, there to fire warning shots to any incoming airships in case of fog as if this was some aerial lighthouse. Hurriedly, she completed a circuit of the two main buildings, which was enough for her to examine the circumference of the enclosure. It was a dead end. The path led to the battery and nowhere else, so she was trapped. The long back-and-forth walk, uphill this time, awaited her.

Still she was not a young lady to flinch at that.

She jumped - a noise came from the largest building, a clatter, something knocked over perhaps.

Flattened against the wall, she saw the castle towering above her, huge and impressive with numerous windows all of which gave an excellent view of her movements. If anyone had seen her, then soon enough soldiers would be descending, back and forth, back and forth, down the long path.

She realised she was fiddling with something: a ring... from Pieter, a red ruby in a silver clasp setting. She didn't have time for nonsense.

Inside there were a few rooms, basic amenities for the gunners who manned the battery in bad weather. There were boxes of supplies, barrels, presumably of gun powder, covered in tarpaulins. Earnestine had a sense that she wasn't alone, something piqued her senses, a sound perhaps. Glancing round she saw a ramrod leaning against the wall, which struck her as a useful weapon, but when she picked it up, a variety of other detritus tumbled and clattered to the hard stone floor. The racket ended with a definitive '*eek*' from the far side of the room.

Earnestine raised the rod, flipped it round so that she led with the heavy end and carefully crossed the floor.

Hang on a moment, she thought, she was the one who was decamping, so she should be hiding.

There was a clear '*shhh*'.

The shape in the folds of a tarpaulin ahead seemed to change. Perhaps they actually moved or perhaps it was simply that her perspective changed, but, like one of those picture puzzles that refuses to be anything other than a vase throughout an entire rainy afternoon suddenly becomes two faces in the evening, Earnestine could see the shape of a figure: a leg, the bend of a knee, a torso... that seemed to go on and on making the hidden person at least ten feet tall - a giant!

With rapid steps, Earnestine went around the shape. The tarpaulin reacted, shifted, contorted and then split into two. The foot end revealed a well turned ankle, then a ragged dress until finally it disgorged a round, beautiful and shocked face.

It was Georgina.

"Ness!"

Earnestine lowered her ramrod.

"Gina?"

"You're alive."

"Evidently."

"Oh thank God, you're alive."

Tears welled in the middle sister's eyes, a quite detestable display of emotion. Something had to be done.

"Georgina, don't be such a baby."

"Sorry Ness."

Earnestine waited until her sister had wiped her eyes.

"And pray tell," Earnestine said, "why aren't you in school?"

Georgina opened her mouth to protest, but at that moment the rest of the tarpaulin moved to reveal a man of some sort. Earnestine considered him disapprovingly.

"Who's this?" she asked.

"I'm-"

"I didn't ask you!" Earnestine told him. "We haven't been introduced."

"This is Arthur," Georgina said.

"Arthur!!!"

"Sorry, I mean, Earnestine may I introduce Captain Merryweather," Georgina said, and she signalled back and forth between them with an open palm. "Arthur, this is my sister, Earnestine."

It appeared that Georgina was on first name terms with some army type.

"Glad to meet you, Earnestine," he said, with the added temerity of holding out his hand to shake.

Earnestine stepped back as if struck: "Miss Deering-Dolittle!"

"My apologies," the man said. "Glad to meet you, Miss D- D- Deering-Dolittle."

Earnestine ignored his proffered hand and gave him instead a tiny angry smile to put him in his place. She tugged Georgina to her feet and then pulled her to one side to converse privately, although the room was not big enough to avoid being overheard. However, this Captain Merry*whatever* took the hint and pretended to examine the barrels of gunpowder.

"Georgina, what were you doing under that blanket with a man?"

"We were only hiding."

"Hiding? What vile practices have you been up to that you need to hide from your own sister?"

"It's not like that?"

"What is it like?"

"Arthur and I have-"

"Arthur!? You're on first name terms with some..." Earnestine looked over her shoulder at the man whistling silently to himself. He did look tall and handsome in some rugged outdoor fashion with a fine blonde moustache, but he was still a man, and she'd found alone with her sister hiding under some tarpaulin, so clearly he had to be some sort of bounder.

"Merry and I-"

"Merry!?"

"Captain Merryweather and I came to rescue you."

Earnestine didn't know where to start: "Rescue me? I am clearly escaping without any assistance and now - oh, do think, Gina - and now I have to chaperone you as well."

"But..."

"Don't whine." It was truly exasperating. "Why didn't you just wait for me by the train station?"

"Ness?"

"Oh, give it to me?"

"Give what to you?"

"The timetable."

"What timetable?"

"What sort of rescue have you been organising, if you haven't even come equipped with the timetable of the trains from here to Calais?"

"Calais?"

"For the ferry." This was impossible. "Gina, you have a plan to get us out of here, don't you?"

"No, we didn't really think-"

"No, you didn't really think, did you? That's your trouble, isn't it? You never think."

"We had a plan."

Earnestine was aghast: "A plan? What was this great plan? You thought you'd stroll in here, find the first man you came across and canoodle under some dirty covers getting your dress all filthy and-"

"I say, steady on!" said Merryweather, stepping forward.

Earnestine raised her finger to threaten.

"I have," she said, "enough on my plate, what with Austro-Hungarian plots to overthrow the British Empire without you and your..." She looked at Georgina: "Floosie! Getting in the way."

"We're hardly getting in the way," Merryweather said.

Earnestine ignored him: "Did you do your homework?"

"What?" Georgina squeaked.

"Your homework: Latin and that poem you had to learn."

"The school was attacked and everyone was killed."

"Yes," said Earnestine, putting on her long suffering calm voice. "But did you do your homework."

"The college was attacked and everyone was killed!"

Earnestine was incandescent with rage: "Yes, but did you do your homework *before the college was attacked and everyone was killed?*"

## Miss Georgina

Georgina was crying and she didn't care, Earnestine was a monster. Georgina sat on some hard box with her tiny lacy handkerchief in her lap, so white against her besmirched skirt, and sniffled.

Away from her, Arthur - and she didn't care that she thought of him as Arthur now - was explaining everything: how he'd found the school, the bodies of the girls and the staff, the village, the train ride, the... something about a mad scientist and unnatural science. The three 'Gentlemen Adventurers' hadn't thought to mention that to her, oh no, but one glance at the regal beauty of the oh-so-wonderful Miss Deering-Dolittle and they were as thick as thieves.

Another snivel escaped; her nose was so full of unladylike gloop.

The awful thing was that, in addition to all the horrors that she had experienced, Earnestine had made her feel guilty about not doing her Latin homework: amazo, Amazon, I'm-a-spot, am-as-gone, am-as-lost, as-an-ant.

Her lip quivered.

She stood and the act was one of defiance, which silenced both her sister and her Captain.

"We found a body at the base of the cliff," Georgina said. "It was dressed in an Eden College uniform and... Arthur examined the body. It was... the name tag was 'C. Deering-Dolittle'. Charlotte's dead."

Earnestine looked at her kindly, a proper caring expression, but said: "Don't be ridiculous! Charlotte is up in the castle probably in a wedding dress by now."

"Wedding dress?"

"Yes," said Earnestine. "She's getting married. I tried talking to her, but you know Charlotte. She never listens! Such a silly girl. She's got them all thinking she's royalty. In fact, I imagine that the girl you found was probably the equally silly girl who Charlotte swapped clothes with. You know what Charlotte's like with her belongings, she doesn't look after them at all. It's not Charlotte you found, but Her Royal Highness, Princess Whomever."

Georgina looked at her empty palm where the remains of a mountain flower had been blown away. It seemed so long ago.

"She's alive! We must save her," Georgina exclaimed, rushing to the doorway.

"No!"

Georgina was incredulous: "No!?"

Of all the daft things to suggest, of course they must save their little sister. It was their lot, their family responsibility, to look after her: Earnestine, as acting head of the family, must surely realise that.

Earnestine spoke, her harsh words grating: "She's made her bed. We have our obligations to the British Empire."

Georgina couldn't believe what she was hearing: "Mother said-"

"Mother didn't anticipate the greater responsibility."

"Ness, I'll-"

"Tell Nanny if you want."

Georgina's face burnt.

Earnestine turned to Arthur, which was a relief because he would put her right.

"You're a Captain?"

"Yes, M- Miss?"

"Then you must do your duty."

"Yes, Miss."

Earnestine tugged something out of her pocket, it was an envelope: "Then get this to England with all haste."

Merryweather took it: he didn't even raise a single objection.

No, no! Never, Georgina thought. How could that witch of a sister leave little Lottie behind? She rushed away to the door, out of the door and started up the path, a path that zig-zagged up the mountain towards the castle, a path full of soldiers, soldiers unslinging their rifles and aiming... they moved slowly as if they were in a dream...

Merryweather grabbed her from behind physically picking her up and manhandling her back into the battery house. Bullets whined and ricocheted.

"How long?" Earnestine demanded.

"Minutes," said Merryweather.

"How did-"

"Climbed, ropes."

"Get her down," Earnestine ordered, her words muffled as she wrenched an axe from the wall. "I'll follow."

"You can't fight them off with that."

"I don't intend to."

Earnestine swung the axe and split one of the barrels. Black powder split across the floor.

"Flint!" Merryweather threw a metal object across the space which Earnestine deftly caught. He then pulled Georgina across the building and out the far side. A glance back: Earnestine splitting barrels and then spreading gunpowder.

At the edge of the precipice, Georgina looked down and froze. Merryweather tied the rope around her waist and slipped it across his shoulders.

"Use your feet to keep away from the cliff!"

"What!? I can't-"

Merryweather pushed her: she dropped, swinging out into the void, flailing her arms to grab the rope as Merryweather took the strain. She plummeted in sudden jerks as the man above let the rope play out. Georgina's feet bashed against the granite, shattering loose rocks away that tumbled, as she tumbled, down to be smashed to pieces below.

She tried to scream, but there was no air in her lungs, and then she was an untidy heap on the path, a ledge barely any distance down the cliff.

Somehow Earnestine's shout reached her below: "Go!"

Merryweather swung out on the rope, his legs kicking only air! Who was holding the other end? Surely not her sister!? As he went down hand over hand, gut wrenchingly falling and catching himself again, Georgina realised that he'd tied the far end to something. As he got bigger and bigger, Georgina grovelled across the path and then he reached the ground with a thud and a grunt.

Shots came from above: sharp cracks.

Merryweather picked himself off the floor and looked up.

Above, Earnestine stood silhouetted against the darkening sky, such a small figure so high up, as she struck the flint. A spark, vivid bright... another, and then a flare of light like fireworks and was gone as soon as it had started. Her sister stood on the edge and, as a fiery explosion rent the sky, she jumped!

Jumped?!

A rope caught, she'd held the other end, and she swung at the mighty cliff like a conker on a string.

Dark, massive shapes swirled and filled the burning, fiery explosion. The noise hit Georgina like a hammer.

Merryweather grabbed her and they ducked into the cliff wall as boulders, stones, cannons and soldier's bodies thumped all around.

Georgina heard a scream, loud and appalling, and doubly frightening when she realised it was her own. The rope tied to her waist snatched tight and threatened to drag her out and down. Whatever she was tied to had been blown over the cliff.

Rocks, pebbles, bits of shrapnel fell in a deadly hailstorm.

Georgina pulled back; the rope tugged and then went slack as the landslide buried the end.

Merryweather stepped out into the maelstrom to pluck Earnestine out of the chaos. Earnestine let go of the rope, her black patent leather gloves were scarred and torn across her palms, and her face was cut and bleeding, but also flushed and alive. She was in her element. She was on an adventure.

"Shall we run?" Merryweather suggested.

"I should bally well think so," said Earnestine.

They ran.

Ten yards on Georgina was grabbed from behind, lifted off her feet and thrown to the ground.

Merryweather came at her with a knife, cutting the taut rope around her waist before pulling her to her feet and hauling her along after Earnestine, who darted, surefooted, ahead. With a shock, Georgina realised that Earnestine might have actually used the 'b' word!

"Your sister's quite something," that man Merryweather said.

Georgina had no breath to reply.

Further along the path opened up: shots were fired and bullets pinged into the ground.

They raced on, rushing past the unmarked grave as they ran for their lives.

## Miss Charlotte

It wasn't until the dowager left that Charlotte felt herself start breathing again. She was pressed hard against the wall of the laboratory wanting to be absorbed into the comforting solidity.

Doctor Mordant busied herself with her equipment and then went to check on the Crown Prince... the thing's bonds. As she checked the straps, the creature lurched, snapping like a wild dog as it tried to attack the Doctor.

Charlotte jumped.

Doctor Mordant was impassive: "It's safe. These leather straps are quite adequate."

It took a moment for Charlotte to realise that the Doctor was talking to her, but they were the only two present who were truly alive.

"Nah... ah," Charlotte managed.

"Yes, it can be quite a shock the first time." The Doctor's Scottish brogue sounded amused. "You'll get used to it."

"I'll never... used to it? No. It's... no."

Now Doctor Mordant turned to face her, her green eyes catching the light and shining through the gloom.

"You'll have to, Your Majesty. You heard the Gräfin."

Charlotte hadn't.

"The Gräfin is a strict Catholic," Doctor Mordant explained. "She wants the marriage consummated immediately."

Everything had been a daze: she felt cold, so cold, and yet she was covered in a wet sheen. Horses sweat, men perspire and women... yes, she'd been glowing badly and now she was shaking.

"I... what?"

Mordant hastened over in quick strides, pulled Charlotte's head back before she could respond and examined her eyes.

"Acute traumatic response... quite expected."

"Can you... I... help me."

"A brandy perhaps?"

"Please."

"But I don't have any, so-"

Doctor Mordant slapped Charlotte across the face with such force that her head was wrenched to one side. Charlotte opened her mouth, her eyes wide, and the vague stone slabs beneath her suddenly became sharp: their relief as obvious as any mountain range and their cracks as clear as chasms. The moment was brief and then blurred as her eyes filled with tears.

Charlotte struck back: Mordant caught her wrist easily.

"Excellent, you seem much better."

"That hurt."

Charlotte touched her cheek tenderly and then thought better of the idea.

Doctor Mordant led the way: "Come!"

Charlotte followed, but kept the Doctor between her and the thing writhing on the examination table. It jerked as it responded to their approach.

"There, there," said Doctor Mordant gently and to no effect.

"He was... dead."

"In German they are called 'Die Untoten', the undead."

"Then it's..."

"Very much alive, of course. There are only two states in biological philosophy: alive and dead. For thousands of years man, mostly the male of our species, has been quite capable of converting a living homo sapiens into a dead homo sapiens. Every nation has organisations dedicated to the task: armies, navies... now aerial forces. But, for the first time, death is commutative: I can bring the dead back."

"You're playing God."

Mordant turned on her: "I am not playing!" she hollered.

Even the monster was cowed.

"My dear," Doctor Mordant began in a reasonable and utterly unnerving tone. "I am a medical doctor. Here to save life, create life, I have taken an oath, the ancient Hippocratic oath. I am here to heal, nurture, give succour..."

Doctor Mordant picked up a syringe.

"Now, my dear, we must consummate the marriage."

"I don't know what that means."

Mordant tut-tutted: "The education of women in modern society is woeful."

Charlotte waited as a kidney bowl, cotton wool and a bottle of alcohol joined the syringe. Mordant put them on a tray and took them over to the examination table. The thing kicked and struggled, but the table was wide enough to accommodate it and the tray.

"A marriage requires many things: a priest, witnesses..."

"A dress," Charlotte said. She was still wearing her wedding dress, although the besmirched virginal outfit that had so delighted her had long lost its appeal.

"Yes, and it must be consummated: a man must lie with a woman. For children."

Charlotte looked back and forth between the Crown Prince and Mordant: the patient and its Doctor, the creature and the Natural Philosopher, the man and the woman...

"I am not getting on there next to that," Charlotte said.

"Oh, but it involves much more than that, but you are right. If we tried it the natural way, then this experiment... patient, with his shackles removed, would tear you apart.

They are crazed. I have not perfected the technique. It's something to do with the size of the skull. My predecessor used a specimen of unusual dimensions, significantly larger than the norm, whereas I have to raise individuals who are chosen for the colour of their blue blood or their work potential rather than for their cranial capacity. Oberst Kroll is the only one I've seen who might be big enough for the process. But I can control these experiments with galvanic charge across the cerebral cortex: even in this state, they soon learn."

"It's wrong."

"Knowledge is always right."

"We're responsible for our actions."

"Take off your undergarments."

"What? Never!"

"I can call the guards - they'd enjoy undressing you."

"I refuse. I'm a Queen!"

"You're not royalty, your accent betrays you. I knew from the first moment. It amused me to see you putting on airs and graces. You're from Essex."

"Kent."

"The Home Counties, so arrogant."

"I'm married to a King, therefore, whatever my background, I'm a Queen... and I command you to-"

"You are a breeding engine! Don't fool yourself into thinking you are anything more."

The Queen, the previous Queen, had given her a bottle of poison telling her that she'd know when to use it. It was now, but the bottle was... wherever Charlotte had put it down.

"Don't worry, this is an easy process. They do it all the time for cattle."

Doctor Mordant bent over the thrashing object on the examination table with the syringe. Charlotte took her chance, hitched up her ruined wedding dress and ran for the door.

It was locked.

She crossed over to the far door, raised the latch and pulled.

It opened.

"Guards!" Mordant shouted. "Bring her back!"

A huge military chest was blocking Charlotte's escape. She balled her fist and struck with all her might only to be casually moved aside. It was the Graf.

"Doctor Mordant."

"Yes, what is it?"

"We have been attacked. Agents were seen leaving. Spies."

"What is that to me?"

The Graf stepped into the room, the gap between him and the door widened with every stride.

"The battery was destroyed by explosive."

"That is your remit, not mine."

"It was blown up, completely."

Charlotte hesitated: blown up, destroyed... and she'd missed it.

"It is an act of war, you know our agreement: I need my army."

"I've raised workers for you."

"Callow, weak creatures and too few," the Graf roared. "I have command of the skies, weapons aplenty and regiments stored in readiness, but how am I to conquer without the secret?"

"How indeed?"

"You will show me the correct combination of your potions."

Doctor Mordant snorted.

"Show me!"

"I have work to do."

Charlotte didn't know exactly what that work was, but she did not want to find out. If she could somehow fan the flames of the Graf's disagreement, then perhaps she could avoid the fate the Doctor had in mind.

"Make her show you," Charlotte urged.

"I will not show you, her or anyone," Doctor Mordant said, her anger and determination making her Gaelic vowels all the stronger. "I am responsible for these developments, responsible for my actions, and I will not be responsible one iota for the death you intend."

Zala showed her the pistol in his hand.

Doctor Mordant shook her head: "Never. Anyway, you can't kill me without losing the secret forever."

"I think you will show me," he replied.

"Oh really? Shall I perform the operation on you? Your big head might easily cope with the process."

"I was thinking of someone else, Frau Doctor."

The explosive noise came far earlier than Charlotte had been expecting. He'd missed, she thought, and shot the bench or some piece of equipment, but there was no sound of tinkling glass or any sign of fallen debris.

Doctor Mordant gripped her abdomen and then brought her hands up in a strange pleading gesture. Her palms were covered in blood and a dark stain began to spread across her stomach.

"Physician, heal thyself," the Graf commanded.

Doctor Mordant put her hand out to steady herself against the bench, but her palm slipped along and she stumbled. She coughed, spittle dribbling down her mouth and her face faded of any pink colour as if she was becoming a daguerreotype picture.

And then something extraordinary: her face contorted, resolve fixed her features and she lunged across the room, arms flailing to support herself on anything that came to hand, knocking over stools like skittles and cascading glassware to the floor. She was moving on her hands and knees when she reached the far workbench and pulled herself upright onto shaking legs. There was the fancy box there and she pulled the lid open, carelessly taking out the bottles within and yanking the stoppers out. She drank, pouring the liquid into her coughing mouth and letting it spill down her face and blouse. The second went the same way, but the third she poured over her stomach, howling like some banshee at the pain.

As she went, the Graf followed with a sheaf of papers in his hand. With each action the Doctor made, he jotted down a note, carefully recording each phase of the woman's struggle.

Mordant weakened, slipping and sliding, her footsteps either splashing in the spilt chemicals or crunching the broken glass. As she went, taking a tortuous path, she threw switches and connected levers. The galvanic equipment sparked and glowed as the apparatus came to life.

The Doctor, fading by the moment, hauled herself onto the examination table and fumbled with the connectors. She clamped one on her hand, her foot and then, tugging skin to collect enough flesh for the crocodile clip's teeth to bite, her neck. She fell back, almost spent, and reached for the lever. Her fingers touched it, the last joint just hooking around it and she gasped as she made a Herculean effort to pull the metal down.

The Graf's hand was holding it in place.

He watched as the woman struggled beneath him, dying slowly, her blood flowing out to mix with the other chemicals.

Charlotte turned away.

"Your secret is mine now," the Graf said. "Such a pity you will not live, or even live again, to see the new world."

Doctor Mordant was gone: ready to live again, but dead.

"Gustav... Graf," Charlotte said.

"Your Majesty?"

Charlotte ran across to him and threw herself into his arms: "Thank you, thank you."

"Liebchen."

He stroked her blonde hair gently.

"Take me away from here, take me with you," Charlotte pleaded.

"I cannot," he said. "I must away into the skies to hunt down these spies."

"I still have my uniform. I can be an aerial officer and join you in the air."

"You cannot, you are the Queen here."

"Yes, I am your Queen: I command you!"

"I am a Graf, an Air General, and you do not have any authority over the military."

"I am your..." Charlotte tried to work out her relationship with the man who towered over her. "I am your step-mother."

Behind her, the remains of his father thrashed and moaned.

He laughed: "My new step-mother! Am I to be your Oedipus?"

"Taking me could be your wedding gift to me."

"Ja, even a condemned man is allowed a last request."

"Thank you."

"Chaining a young girl with spirit to this festering corpse is immoral. This farce of a Great Plan has gone on long enough. We should take what we want by force. Yes, come with me, and when this weak and small man moves no more, you shall be my Crown Princess, my Gräfin. More than that, you shall be my Empress."

# CHAPTER XI

## Miss Deering-Dolittle

Captain Merryweather led them to a bothy by the side of the mountain. The small hut consisted of a single room and an outhouse for ablutions. Once they were inside, Merryweather made up a fire in the stove and this gave Earnestine a chance to take in the table, desk, bunk beds and sink: it seemed that each side of the square represented a different type of room present in a proper house.

"Ah!" Merryweather exclaimed. He was patting his pockets.

Earnestine fished out his flint and reflexively switched it to her right hand before passing it to him.

"You gave me the letter with your left hand," he teased.

Despite the difficult introduction, entirely Georgina's fault, Earnestine was beginning to like this man, he was just the right sort. She resolved to keep him away from Georgina, who was far too impressionable and needed protecting. It would be best if she kept her sister busy. She guided Merryweather over to one side.

"It was an emergency," she said, and then she remembered that Pieter had given it to her with his left hand and she had unthinkingly taken it with her left hand.

He smiled: "I see-"

"Nothing," said Earnestine and she slipped the ruby ring off her finger and hid it in a pocket. She glanced across at Georgina, but thankfully she had not seen.

"Ness," Georgina interrupted. "I've got something for you."

Earnestine saw her treasured flashlight cradled in Georgina's hands.

"Oh, I thought I'd lost it."

"Yes, it's yours. And Captain Merryweather..." Georgina said, putting her hand lightly on the Captain's arm, "...and I found it together."

Earnestine took it back and pressed the button to satisfy herself that that Georgina hadn't drained the battery. It gave the familiar glow. "Wherever did you find it?"

"It was on the floor in the East Wing, you must have dropped it when you went exploring."

"Gina, I did not go exploring!"

"Well, you have it back now, Ness. It's important that you *don't take* anything from other people."

What was she talking about, Earnestine wondered; it wasn't like Georgina to place undue emphasis on certain words in her sentences - what had got into her?

"Captain Merryweather," Earnestine said, "may I have the envelope back please?"

Merryweather took the letter from his pocket and passed it over, right handed.

"Georgina, would you be a dear and copy out the letter please."

"Earnestine, I-"

"I'm sure there will be some writing implements at the desk."

Georgina snatched the letter off her sister and stomped over to a small desk, where she took out what she needed from the drawer making the maximum amount of noise possible. She was such a child, but at least she wasn't whining.

Earnestine sat at the table. The wooden chair was hard, but bliss as her feet throbbed from the running.

Merryweather busied himself with metal cups and a coffee pot.

"This is in German!" Georgina said.

"It uses the Latin alphabet, all you need to do is copy it," Earnestine said. "And don't whine."

"I wasn't..."

Georgina started writing carefully.

Earnestine started to think about everything that had happened, trying to fathom it all out.

"How would you like your coffee?" Merryweather asked.

"Coffee is a degenerate drink," Earnestine said. "We'll all have tea."

"I'm afraid emergency rations on the continent don't offer much choice."

"I see."

"I'll make it medium with plenty of sugar."

He paused at the pot with the coffee and a spoon.

"Five," said Earnestine.

"Thank you," he said, ladling five heaped spoonfuls in. "And one for the pot?"

"I think best, yes."

The pot went on the stove, the heat finally thawing the cold room. Earnestine tilted her head back and closed her eyes. It was so seductive: she could fall asleep here or better still on one of the rude beds. She snapped awake - there was too much to do.

Merryweather was in front of her, kneeling before her, and for a moment she thought.... but he had cotton wool and a bottle.

"Antiseptic," he said. "You've been..."

Earnestine nodded.

"It'll sting."

"I'm not a baby."

He dabbed around her forehead, gently, but even so there was a shock. She kept her lip straight and it must have been the fumes from the antiseptic that caused her vision to blur. The man was thorough, wiping her left side carefully and checking her hairline.

"There," he said, when he'd finished.

"Thank you."

"I'll check it later, just to be sure."

"Didn't one of you say that the school was attacked?"

Merryweather looked to her right; Earnestine realised that he and Georgina had exchanged a look.

"I'm afraid we found the school... everyone had been killed."

"It was awful," said Georgina.

"I'm sure," Earnestine said, without looking round: "Everyone?"

"Except Gina," Merryweather replied pointing behind Earnestine, "yourself and Charlotte, isn't it?"

"Yes."

"You were lucky."

"We can't stay here."

"No."

Georgina interrupted: "But, I thought we'd prepared this as the base camp for the others."

"Don't whine." Earnestine glanced back: "Sit up straight."

"The plan didn't include being chased about the mountains by half the Austro-Hungarian army," Merryweather added.

"You exaggerate. We are outnumbered though. What 'others'?"

"Caruthers and Mac, my colleagues."

"Officers?"

"We're mountaineers looking at possible climbs in the area."

Earnestine raised her eyebrow: that was nonsense.

"And we thought we'd have a shufti at certain goings on with the Austro-Hungarians."

"You were right too."

"What do you know?"

Earnestine didn't want to admit that she didn't know much, so she changed the conversation: "Georgina, have you finished that?"

"Not yet," Georgina said.

The coffee pot sighed and then began hissing angrily.

"Hurry up, will you."

"There are dots and things."

"Umlauts."

"Nearly there."

Earnestine scalded the roof of her mouth with the coffee, but she kept drinking such was the wonderful warming effect.

Coffee - jolly bohemian really.

Georgina finally finished and Earnestine handed the original to Captain Merryweather. While he was reading, Earnestine checked Georgina's copy over, the umlauts and accents were heavy, but diligently present. She hid it away in her shoulder bag.

"I can make some of it out, it sounds serious," Merryweather said. "Lacks details. An attack on the British, I'm sure. What else did you discover?"

"Not much," Earnestine finally admitted. "A lot of areas in the castle were out of bounds."

"When did that ever stop you?" Georgina said.

"Gina!"

She was going to have to take that girl to one side because clearly a good talking to was long overdue. It was self-evident that spending a lot of time with this man - officer or no officer, he was still a man - and alone together too, had clearly had a debilitating effect on the poor girl.

"There's also this," Earnestine said, taking out the small envelope that she'd filled with the strange chemical and handing it to Merryweather. "Careful!"

He examined the contents, picking up a few of the yellowish-grey granules to inspect them more closely. He sniffed them, felt the substance in his fingertips and finally, gingerly, he tasted it.

"What is it?" he asked finally.

"I don't know, but they had crates of the material and were filling canisters with nozzles to load it onto their airships."

Georgina pushed closer. "Let me see?"

"Gina, please, you're not going to know."

"It's silver iodide," Georgina said, and, when they looked at her as if she was mad, she added: "It's used in making daguerreotypes, the natural philosophy of making automatic pictures."

Earnestine realised that Georgina had been spending too much time in museums.

"It's as we feared," Merryweather said as he considered the information much as he weighed the sample in his hand. "They must plan to fly their airships up and down the country photographing. They'll know everything about us: our defences, deployments, railway lines, everything... they'll know more about us than we do."

"For photography, they'd mix the silver iodide with egg white or some fixing agent on the paper," Georgina said. "They wouldn't have it in canisters."

"Perhaps it's a new process," speculated Merryweather.

"How much silver iodide was there?" Georgina asked.

"Canisters," Earnestine made a shape in front of her with her hands about a yard long and perhaps a foot in diameter. "I'd say five by five in a crate, twenty five, times at least three dozen crates that I saw. There was a variety of designs to the canisters."

"That would be enough silver iodide to supply all the photographic experts in the whole of Great Britain for ten years."

"Gina, you must be mistaken," Earnestine said.

Georgina shook her head.

"Then something else?" Merryweather wondered. He sprinkled the chemical back into the envelope and brushed his hands absently on his trousers to remove any residue. "The letter talks about military manoeuvres in London?"

"You can read German?" Georgina asked.

"A little," said Merryweather. He shook his head. "It suggests that they are amassing an army in London. They have regiments already there and the last divisions will be en route soon."

"With all respect, that seems impossible," Earnestine said.

"They could move whole regiments in those Zeppelins," Georgina suggested. "They're huge."

"It's mostly gas, hydrogen, for buoyancy," Merryweather said. "According to our reports, there are cabins in the gondola underneath, and the actual body of the airship is hollow; there are softer balloons for the hydrogen inside, so you can store things and the crew live there, but most of the space is taken up with balloons and fuel in the form of what's called 'blugas' for the engines."

"And there's the weight," Earnestine added.

"Yes, you couldn't move an army by air."

Earnestine grimaced: "I agree, but they were very confident, particularly that Graf Gustav Zala - a nasty foreign piece of work."

Merryweather stowed the original letter and the packet of silver iodide away, and took out a map. He brought it round to show Earnestine, pointing out Innsbruck and Geneva. He traced the rail lines back towards the college and then on into France.

"They'll expect us all to go that route," Earnestine said, thinking aloud. "If I go this way, Vienna, then I can catch the much faster Orient Express."

"Deeper into the Germanic countries."

"A risk I'll have to take."

"And our route?"

"Our?"

"Georgina and myself."

"I think not: I would have to travel alone and a woman travelling alone is... and Georgina would need protection as well."

"I hardly think that I'm much of a threat."

Earnestine gave him one of her tight smiles: "Georgina and I will take the train, you will take the other letter and find another route."

"Ness, it would be better to have a few of the officers with us," said Georgina.

"Gina! I've spoken."

"Perhaps if we stayed together," Merryweather suggested. "I could post this letter to Caruthers and McKendry, with instructions, and that way our forces will increase."

"Very well."

And that, thankfully, was that.


## Miss Georgina

Vienna was a gorgeous city by all accounts. Georgina had been asleep in the carriage by the time they arrived and she'd seen nothing of it. She was so sore when they climbed out: her limbs ached, everywhere, from walking, climbing, falling and running, and then sleeping awkwardly. She wanted a hot bath and then some hot Cadbury's cocoa essence, preferably with a dash of rum. And sweets.

The smells around the station were mouth-watering: stalls with pretzels, chestnuts and...

"Come along, Gina!"

Clearly, her sister never ate and probably survived by drinking the blood of virgins.

"What are you sniggering about, Gina? Honestly."

Merryweather had gone ahead to the postal service and to organise their tickets. He'd also nipped into the telegraph office to contact Caruthers and McKendry. In other words, he'd done everything that her big sister had wanted. Georgina pictured them together: Merryweather kneeling in front of Earnestine back in the mountain bothy, touching and caressing her face with antiseptic, agreeing with her every word and forgetting that Georgina even existed. Not that Georgina minded: what was he to her, after all; they'd only just met and never actually been introduced properly and it was so unfair.

"Don't sniff!"

"Sorry Ness."

"Use your handkerchief."

"Sorry."

"Don't whine, you're such a baby - ah, there he is now!"

The Orient Express was an elegant triumph of the railways with its blue livery and its embellished gold coat of arms of the Compagnie Internationale des Wagons-Lits. Fine ladies and smart gentlemen walked along the platform looking for their particular coach. Uniformed porters weaved their way through the throng as they expertly wheeled fancy luggage, including their own hastily bought belongings, to and fro. In contrast to all this splendour, the three of them looked bedraggled, tired and hardly the right sort. Conversations and shouts in many languages filled the air pierced by a periodic shrill whistle. The steam engines themselves were like sleeping dragons awakening.

Captain Merryweather arrived and took Earnestine's arm to guide her through the maelstrom. Georgina was left to hurry behind. Smoke hissed from the engines across the platform as they passed.

"I managed to book a cabin," Merryweather explained.

"*A* cabin?" Earnestine stressed the indefinite article.

"Yes, in the last coach."

Earnestine looked at the tickets: "I see."

When they reached the last sleeping coach before the baggage car, Merryweather swung the door open and helped them both on board. The Captain had to squeeze past Georgina to reach Earnestine, who had found the right cabin first.

Earnestine looked the facilities up and down, turned around and looked them up and down again. Georgina was still stuck in the corridor unable to see what her elder sister was double checking. People pushed past, a porter, some ladies and a man with his wife.

"There are four bunks," Merryweather pointed out.

"I'm sure Georgina and I will find it adequate."

"I was thinking..."

Earnestine pointedly raised an eyebrow in his direction. She was a tease; that was it: she'd got him eating out of her hand, attending to her hand and foot, rubbing her face with ointment - which had not hurt that cold harridan - and just generally ignoring Georgina.

"Wouldn't it be safer if Arthur..." Georgina paused deciding what to say: "I mean Captain Merryweather is here to protect us."

"Protect us!? We are two young ladies travelling alone in a foreign country. We need protection from his sort... no offence."

"None taken," Merryweather said.

"What will people say?"

"It is an emergency," Georgina said.

"How will people know it's an emergency? Will you go and announce to everyone that we are being pursued by hostile forces?"

"I didn't think that-"

"We are travelling incognito, which is all the more reason to observe proper decorum."

"Yes, but-"

"We will sleep here and I'm sure the Captain has slept in worse places than somewhere else on the train."

"I'm sure there's a suitable easy chair in the restaurant carriage that'll do as a billet," said Merryweather.

"There, see," said Earnestine, "do you see, Gina?"

"Yes, but-"

"I specifically told you not to go on an adventure."

"It wasn't an adventure."

"What do you call running out from school and tagging along with various army types? I mean who are they? What regiment do they come from? Have there been proper introductions?"

"It wasn't a bally adventure."

"Georgina! I will thank you not to use such language!"

"It's not a swear word."

"It is a euphemism for the 'B' word and we do not use the 'B' word."

"You're horrible!"

"Right, I see you have clearly been associating with the military and have forgotten yourself."

"Ness," Georgina howled as Earnestine grabbed her by the scruff of the neck, bent her over and frog-marched to the corner of the cabin. Earnestine wrenched open the cupboard to reveal the tiny sink and mirror.

"I say," said Merryweather. "You're not her colour sergeant."

"I would thank you to mind your own business," Earnestine said to his reflection.

"Yes, but I think-"

"No, you do not."

"Perhaps-"

"This is a ladies' bedroom!"

So it was, and Merryweather went red: "M- m- my apologies, sorry, so..." and he beat a hasty retreat.

"Right," said Earnestine, when she and her sister were alone.

"Ness, please..."

Earnestine took Georgina to the sink, pushed her head over the bowl and then scooped up a few slivers of soap.

"Open!"

"Nn.. nn..."

Earnestine yanked her sister's hair.

"Arr! Guk... neuurghh..."

Earnestine rubbed it back and forth until finally the old soap lathered. She forced her hand back and forth along Georgina's gums and teeth.

"There," she said, not unkindly. "Rinse. Spit. Again."

Georgina ran the tap and cupped water up with her hand to try and remove the carbolic taste. Her hair was wrenched to one side and her eyes watered from the shock.

"And, Gina, don't blub."

Georgina held the bowl and did blub; she let it all out: not the shame of being punished or the vile taste in her mouth, but the horror that Arthur had seen this happen to her and anger that he'd done nothing to stop the hideous harpy treat her in such a... yes, bally rotten fashion.

Earnestine was unpacking.

"We cabled ahead for supplies," Earnestine said. "After all, we don't want to stand out."

Georgina fought the impulse to sniff: "When?"

"You were asleep."

"Is there something nice to wear?"

"You'll wear what you're given."

They washed and dressed in silence. Hair brushing was particularly painful after their experiences and Georgina found the new corset would take getting used to. After it had been tied at the back, Georgina tried to loosen the cords, but she couldn't and she absolutely was not going to ask Earnestine.

Once everything of theirs was stowed away, the remaining and ignored luggage became embarrassing.

"These..." Georgina began, but it was obvious whose they were.

"They are for your Captain."

"He's not my Captain."

"I'll have a porter take them to him."

"Ness, he can't wash and change in the restaurant."

"He should have booked two cabins."

"There probably weren't two left."

Because they were in the last passenger coach, they had to manoeuvre along the corridor for two coaches and cross the rattling divide twice, which was rather frightening, to reach the restaurant car. Captain Merryweather was standing at the bar looking very rough, but chipper with a whiskey in his hand. Earnestine gave him the key.

"Ah yes, I must give this a trim," he said brushing his finger along his moustache. "And a shave."

"Don't be too long," Earnestine simpered, much to Georgina's irritation.

Merryweather gave a little nod and then squeezed past Georgina, his body forced to push against hers and so close that Georgina could smell the whiskey. She looked away, feeling it well within her rights to ignore him completely and yet, even craning her neck far to one side, she suddenly found herself looking into his blue eyes.

"Georgina," he said, and then he went on his way.

"Arthur..." she murmured, but he was gone.

They had iced tea while they waited.

The Maître d'Hotel saw them to a table and held their chairs out for them to sit. Merryweather waited until they were settled. After a term of gruel at the Eden College for Young Ladies and hardtack rations on the mountain, Georgina found the menu utterly mouth-watering. Her attention darted around the many options, the French words a blur of promises. She adored choosing.

"Would you?" Earnestine asked Merryweather handing her menu over to him.

"Certainly."

He called the Maître d'Hotel over and ordered in French, so Georgina had no idea what was coming.

The first course was oysters.

Merryweather and Earnestine relished them, cracking the shells with the sharp implements and slurping them down the gluttonous pleasure. Georgina tried as best she could, inserting the shucking knife near the hinge, but it just wouldn't.

"Oh, give it to me," said Earnestine. She leant over, snatched the cutlery off Georgina, and split a couple of shells for her.

"Expertly done," said Merryweather.

Georgina hated them both: and she hated the look of the oyster and the way it slithered down her throat.

The soup came with Italian pasta, which was much better, as was the fish course, which was a turbot in green sauce. After that Georgina tucked into the chicken 'à la chasseur', but struggled when the fillet of beef with 'château' potatoes arrived, and could only pick at the 'chaud-froid' of game animals in a lettuce base. They'd started with white wine and by the time they switched to red, Earnestine relented and let Georgina have a glass. By the end of the evening, she'd had three!

When the waiter removed their plates, Georgina was simply engorged, the whalebones gripping her waist cut into her expanded stomach, and she felt that, even without the corset, she wouldn't be able to bend. That was it, she'd finished until she realised that the dessert trolley had chocolate pudding amongst its buffet of delights.

Merryweather saw them back along the coaches to their cabin.

Again, when she went demurely past him, Georgina was very aware of his presence, now garnished with cologne.

"Good night," he said. "Sleep well."

Once the two sisters were back inside, it was a relay race to get their corsets off. Despite everything, they were soon giggling just like old times. There were no arguments about who would have the top bunk as they both elected for the lower bunk on either side.

"I couldn't climb..."

"Neither could I."

Georgina couldn't stay mad at Earnestine or even sweet Arthur. If they wanted to step out together, then she'd approve. She would. They were right for each other. She also couldn't stay awake even if she'd wanted to, despite Earnestine snoring.

The train rattled on to Munich and they both slept.

# Miss Charlotte

Alarms sounded: great blaring horns.

Charlotte was torn: risk missing the airship to get her uniform or not.

She ran against the flow of men to her room, undoing her clothes like some harlot as she went. She pulled off everything as fast as possible and gathered the airman's uniform, clipped it together with impatient fingers. The damned boots wouldn't come up at first.

She paused to examine herself in the mirror: she looked smart.

She was still wearing the ruby ring. She took it off and flung the hateful thing down on the dresser. There, she wasn't going to play.

She strode along the corridor and then sprinted up the spiralling stairs.

Outside the wind whipped her hair loose; she saw the mighty behemoth dominate the sky. It roared like a beast, its rotors whining as it strained against its moorings to be free.

A guard stopped Charlotte at the gangway.

"Nein."

"I am your Crown Princess," she told him: "Stand aside!"

He didn't move.

Above, Graf Zala was passing the entrance. He saw her, their eyes met. They looked at each other over the distance from ground to air, and he laughed.

"Come, come!" he shouted.

With five strides she was aboard.

"Welcome aboard, Your Highness," he said. "We shall be airborne in a moment."

There were shouts, desperate activity below, and then Charlotte looked out of the front windows at the sky ahead.

There was a lurch and the ground no longer held them in its sway. The airship pitched, the gusts of wind pushing it dangerously close to the tower. The Graf gave an order, sharp and direct, and the pilot pulled the wheel around fighting the rudder, which did not want to turn against the wind. Charlotte leaned across, grabbed a handle and gave the last push required. The mighty vehicle turned and rose sharply, everyone leaning forward as the floor became a slope.

It rose, cleared the castle and picked up speed as it entered the valley proper where the air funnelled into a rapid stream. The ravine walls rushed past at an exhilarating pace.

Charlotte was laughing. She dragged her attention away from the flight to exchange a glance with the Graf. He too was excited, thrilled for her. Every foot climbed took her further away from the unholy actions below and closer to heaven. She would be like a bird of paradise and never land.

"Faster," she implored.

"We are at maximum revolutions," the pilot said.

"Faster!"

"Ja," said the Graf. "Faster."

The airship soared over the mountains and Charlotte felt so alive.

In the map room, the Graf had shown her the intricacies of navigation. It was not as simple as drawing a line between their start and destination, in this case Eagle's Claw and Strasburg, as the wind's direction and strength needed to be taken into account. Their height was a factor too as the air did not all flow in the same direction, but apparently varied at different altitudes. Once these calculations were made, the final heading was passed to the pilot either by shouting down a voice pipe or by written note. The pilot steered the airship on this heading and the wind blew them into the correct direction.

There had been reports that the spies were heading to Munich and the airship could intercept them at Strasburg.

Under the Graf's approving gaze, Charlotte herself had plotted the heading to Strasburg.

"The advantage of airships is that they can go in a straight line," the Graf explained. "Everything else has to follow a set route. Trains in this terrain must follow the contour lines, but we soar as the eagle flies over mountains, fields, lakes and English Channels."

Their heading was North-Northwest, 340 degrees, but the easterly wind was dragging them further west. Charlotte continued marking their progress on the map, sighting every so often or taking a reading given to her by another air officer. Their progress became a series of jumps marked in pencil rather than a continuous straight line: the wind direction and strength was not consistent and it did shift as they changed altitude. They reached 250 metres, which, Charlotte thought, must be nearly the moon in miles.

It was so thrilling and before long she was so tired.

The Graf insisted that she rest and on his third attempt, Charlotte relented. There were fine rooms, small cabins, which she remembered from when she first sneaked aboard the Zeppelin. She was shown the same room in which she'd met the real Princess, and yet it was different. This was another Zeppelin, identical in design and manufacture, but fitted out with subtle differences.

"How many Zeppelins do you have?" she asked.

"A fleet... four, fitted with different ordinance: bombs, incendiaries and this one, the fastest my Liebchen, is one of three fitted with chemical dispersion units."

"Chemical?"

"Ja, all in good time: navigation today, warfare tomorrow."

When he left her, she slipped out of her uniform and went to sleep in the bunk wearing only her chemise. With the occasional creak, the gentle shifting of the whole world as the Zeppelin manoeuvred was utterly relaxing.

Charlotte thought about... she was tired and...

The airship tilted again, this time downwards, and there was a knock at the door.

"Liebchen?"

"Yes!"

"We are arriving in Strasburg."

"I'll get my uniform."

# Chapter XII

## Miss Deering-Dolittle

The train hissed to a stop: Strasburg.

Merryweather came back, finally: "They are searching the train."

Strasburg wasn't France, it was still in Germany, so they hadn't escaped. They weren't due to cross the border until dusk. It was only about 25 kilometres away, which sounded close, and it would seem even nearer in miles.

It wasn't dark yet, but the evening was approaching. They'd be safe in an hour, if only the train would start rolling again.

Merryweather rocked back and forth in the cabin, clearly wanting to pace, and he rubbed his chin in that 'what to do' manner.

Earnestine pushed her face against the window pane. Outside there were men running about, the spikes on their helmets catching the light even if their insignia weren't visible through the begrimed glass. Far ahead, towering above the others, Graf Zala directed the search.

"They started at the front," said Merryweather. "We'll stick together and try and bluff it out."

"We don't have any papers," said Earnestine.

"I'll say... I'll come up with something."

"I'm sure you will, Merry," Georgina said.

Of course, Georgina was too busy simpering to the Captain to realise the gravity of their situation.

Earnestine coughed to command their attention.

"They don't know you, Merryweather, or Georgina, but I'm a liability."

"Well, M- Miss, I'd hardly-"

"Quiet! The Graf will recognise me. There's more at stake than us, any of us. The message is more important. You go on. You've got papers. My letter. Here, have the silver io-wotnot," she fished out the envelope and passed it over.

"I really think-"

"Luggage!"

"There's no time to move luggage, Ness," Georgina said.

Earnestine ignored her: "Did you book this cabin under your own name?"

"Captain Merryweather, yes."

"But not ours?"

"No."

"Then we move our luggage and you sit tight."

Earnestine grabbed both their bags, manhandled them round in the cramped cabin and out of the door into the corridor.

Whistles blew outside, shouts, and there was some disturbance. The soldiers were flushing out various wrong-doers in their search. That would give them a few more moments. Earnestine clicked her fingers and pointed. Georgina quickly gathered their belongings. Luckily Merryweather hadn't known what to purchase for two young ladies, so there wasn't the usual mountain of paraphernalia strewn about.

They were in the last sleeping coach, and they couldn't go forward because of the soldiers, so the only option was the baggage coach at the very rear of the train. Earnestine stowed their bags and looked about. The carriage was filled with trunks, expensive items of luggage, and a huge number of hat boxes. Further down, there were bags for mail and supplies.

Standing on tiptoe, Earnestine could just see through the tiny, barred windows. The line of activity seemed closer. Merryweather was standing on the platform casually smoking a cigar. There were other passengers: one portly woman in blue was berating a soldier. Merryweather glanced at the carriage, looked along and then stared at the baggage coach. Earnestine pulled back and then looked again. He couldn't see her, the window was too small and dark, but he must know that Georgina and she were hiding there. He frowned, worried, and nodded towards the carriage. He must mean, Earnestine thought, that there were soldiers on the train moving along.

"Hide!"

Georgina immediately started searching for a place. Earnestine found a gap between the mailbags and the wall. No, this wasn't going to work.

The door burst open, clattering, and Earnestine heard men bursting in.

"Achtung!"

"Ah, there it is," Georgina said sweetly.

The soldier started barking orders at her.

"That's all very well, but I'm afraid I don't understand German."

"Platform! Everyone!"

"Yes, I know."

"Platform!"

"But I needed my hat. It's such a sunny day and the sunlight affects my skin terribly."

"Now! Now!"

"Of course," said Georgina. Earnestine hunkered down as she heard Georgina's footsteps move away and hobnailed boots clomp closer as the soldier started to search the coach.

"Door please!" Georgina commanded.

A soldier swore in German.

"If you would hold the door open for a lady: manners maketh man."

There were some choice grumblings and Earnestine heard the door catch again.

"Thank you, most kind."

The door closed: everything was quiet in the baggage coach.

Earnestine waited, convinced that a soldier was standing silently, waiting to ambush, but when she finally crawled out, she saw she was alone. The view through the small window was tantalising and uninformative.

Earnestine sat on a hat box, splitting it beneath her, and wondered what to do. She should hide, logically, and the baggage coach door made such a clatter when she went through, but she wanted to see what was going on: curiosity wasn't a crime.

She quickly scooted into the rear passenger coach and tried the first cabin... the second along was unlocked. She thought it best not to go to their own cabin. Bent double, she shuffled to the window. When she looked out, she was careful to keep the lace curtain in front of her.

On the platform, Graf Zala pushed through the throng, barging Merryweather himself out of the way. The Captain's fist clenched.

"Miss Deering-Dolittle," the Graf exclaimed triumphantly.

Georgina kept her face away from him.

Captain Merryweather stepped out of the throng: "I say."

There was a scuffle as Merryweather was bundled away and... the window didn't afford an adequate view particularly when the Graf came right up to Georgina. Earnestine ducked down. Georgina was facing the window, looking straight at Earnestine, as the Graf blotted out the light above her.

"Fräulein?"

Georgina turned: what choice did she have?

The Graf faltered: "You are not Fräulein Deering-Dolittle."

"No," she said, "I'm... Merryweather."

The Graf screeched at his men: Earnestine doubted even a German speaker would have been able to follow the actual words, but the meaning was clear. The soldiers actually cowered, slouching their shoulders and looking away. The Graf snapped off a few German phrases. The soldiers went about at the double.

"Fräulein Merryweather," he said, "ich bitte um Entschuldigung."

"I beg your pardon," said Georgina.

"My apologies, Fräulein."

"I should think so too."

They bowed to each other and then the Graf clicked his heels and marched away.

A station porter began shouting in German, French and then, finally, English: "Back on the train, back on the train."

They'd got away with it. Earnestine couldn't believe it.

She crawled out from the cabin, jumped up and pretended she was supposed to be inside already. She'd simply be one of the first to get back on the train. She straightened a loose wisp of hair, realised that she probably looked dreadful and made her way to their cabin. Sooner or later, Georgina would appear, Captain Merryweather would kindly come to check they were all right and Earnestine would be sharp with him and tell him to wait in the restaurant. They could have tiffin, afternoon tea or... she had no idea of the time. They were travelling west, so they were moving through the various European time zones, which was... oh dear. Jules Verne's *Around the World in Eighty Days* had Phileas Fogg going east and he gained a day, so they must be losing hours. So starting at breakfast, Tiffin would be an hour early and afternoon tea, assuming the train made good progress to Paris, would be another hour earlier still. Her stomach seemed to suggest the opposite, but perhaps the recent excitement had given her indigestion.

She giggled: her hands were shaking.

Must get a grip before Georgina returns, she thought.

Where was she?

She'd have to go and look for her.

No - impossible.

The Graf hadn't recognised Georgina, but his use of their surname meant he was looking for Earnestine herself. The Graf had seen her at the castle; he must know now that she'd escaped and come to the conclusion - correctly - that she knew something.

Georgina arrived: "Ness!"

"Don't make a fuss," Earnestine chided.

Earnestine sat down, held her traitorous hands together on her lap and pecked her head slightly to indicate that Georgina should take the seat opposite. Georgina sat, fidgeted and stood again.

Georgina opened her mouth: "Arthur-"

"Calm down," Earnestine snapped.

"Captain Merryweather isn't in the restaurant."

"You went to the restaurant first?"

"Of course. He's not there."

"Then he'll be in his cabin."

"This is his cabin."

"Oh yes."

Georgina glanced out of the window: "Where is he?"

"He'll be along shortly, I'm sure."

The train clattered, doors banged shut, a shrill whistle filled the air and there were shouts.

"Arthur!"

"Gina! Sit down! We can't do anything," Earnestine said, putting her hand on her sister's arm and gently, but firmly, pressing her back into her seat. "We would jeopardise our safety, our mission. And his safety."

The steam engine hissed loudly, tugged, the carriages jerked back and forth before settling. Strasburg station began to creep away behind them.

Georgina looked out of the window, looked and looked, craning her neck from one side to another.

"He'll be on the train," Earnestine said.

"There was some commotion, some... The soldiers took him away!"

"He'll be on-"

"They've got him!"

"Nonsense."

Earnestine shifted over and looked out herself: suddenly, she was staring at the Graf and he stared back, his face a picture of surprise superimposed over the reflection in the glass of her own shock. Try as she might, she couldn't break eye contact as the train pulled away, picked up speed, then his face was obscured by the lace curtain and the spell was broken. Through a delicate hole, Earnestine saw him shouting and pointing at the train. Men moved, jumping towards the train. Earnestine pressed her cheek against the glass, pushing as hard as she could to see the rear of the train, men running down the platform and a few reaching the door of the baggage train, pulling it open, jumping on: one, two, three, he stumbled and fell. A fourth made it and then the station was too far behind and the train too fast.

"They're on the train!" she said. "Three. We're out numbered."

"There's Arthur."

"Yes."

Earnestine opened the door, sliding it as quietly as possible. Despite the iron foundry racket of the wheels on rails and the roaring wind, the door's slight squeak seemed to screech above the clamour. She stuck her head out, glanced right and left, and then right and left again: all clear.

Georgina went ahead, shuffling through those patrons who were still settling in their cabins.

Glancing back, Earnestine saw the soldiers coming into the coach at the far end, ducked away and then sneaked another glance. They were checking each cabin in turn and, Earnestine was relieved to realise, this would slow them down.

Moving from one coach to the next gave Earnestine pause. The gap between the metal footplates showed the ground whizzing underneath. Everything clattered and the coaches moved in relation to each other, so the step across was nerve wracking.

Georgina was coming back, when Earnestine met her halfway along the next coach.

"He's not there," Georgina said.

"I see," Earnestine said.

"Where is he?"

If they stopped here, then the soldiers would find them. Earnestine shooed Georgina back towards the restaurant. Once they'd crossed the frightening divide, they were surrounded by genteel customers from all the nations of Europe: a fat Frenchman here, a moustached Belgian perhaps, a tall Englishman, an elegant lady from Vienna and so on, as well as the porters and waiters. Captain Merryweather was not amongst them.

"Ness, where is he?"

"I'm thinking."

They were in German territory, so the soldiers would have some jurisdiction. What was she thinking? They had guns.

"Ness?"

"Don't whine."

There were three options: return to the cabin, stay here in the restaurant or go on. At the door to the restaurant coach, a soldier jostled with a patron.

Earnestine took Georgina's hand and they went forward between the tables and through a menu of aromas.

There was another terrifying gap to negotiate before the next sleeping coach. The going was easier now that everyone had settled, so they reached the next frightening gap and the forward, longer coach, quickly. The one after that brought them into the forward baggage coach. Earnestine knew that they were just running without a plan.

This coach had luggage like the rear baggage coach, trunks, cases and even a set of golf clubs, but it also seemed to be full of chickens in cages and there was even a pig snorting around in a pen.

"This is hopeless," Georgina said.

Earnestine thought so too, but it was her responsibility to put a brave face on it all, so she told Georgina off and jostled her forward. They reached the next gap and stopped. It was a dead end.

"Now what!?" Georgina shouted above the clatter.

In front of them was a black steel wall, the back of the tender, so there was nothing ahead, except tons of coal and then the engine. Glancing around: a ladder up to the tender, sky, the landscape rushing past at fifty miles an hour on either side, the rails whizzing past alarmingly below the coupling, and behind her seven coaches. Somewhere inside the carriages were three soldiers working forward towards them. She leant against another metal ladder on this coach and realised that there was nothing else for it.

"We jump," she said.

"Jump!?!"

"We must get off the train."

"You're gulling me!" Georgina shrieked. "We're travelling at a simply astonishing speed. We'll be smashed to pieces by the air rushing past the train, never mind what would happen to us when we hit the ground. Have you any idea how much faster this is compared to a horse and carriage?"

"We must try."

"Can we slow the train down first?"

"I doubt pulling the cord would do much," said Earnestine. She was becoming rather fed up with Georgina's constant complaining.

"We could surrender?"

"Oh for heaven's sake," Earnestine chided. "They killed that Princess because they thought she was a stowaway. What do you think they'll do to young ladies who are spies - offer us tea and muffins? And besides, we're British."

"They can't be far behind."

"We climb up here and go along the roof."

Georgina's expression made it clear what she thought of that idea.

"Don't be a baby," Earnestine said. She gripped the rung at her head and pulled herself up. The wedge-shaped gap between the toes and heel of her boots fitted neatly almost locking her feet into position, so it was easy to ascend.

Above the edge of the roof, the setting sun was in her eyes, but she could still see well enough. The carriages gently curved to her right as the train navigated a gentle bend, and-

The blast of air threw her against the lip of the coach. Steam and sparks cascading on either side of her. She nearly fell.

"Come on!" she yelled to Georgina, and she hauled herself through the fiery gale and onto the top of the coach.

She began to crawl along but the wind caught the hem of her skirts, lifted them and inflated them like a balloon. She took off into the air, her fingers desperately scrabbled for purchase and she just managed to clasp the strengthening metal strut that spanned the length of the coach. She rose, upside down, and then the wind struck her from the side, squashed the balloon of her dress and dashed her against the roof.

"Gina, be careful!" she shouted, but the same wind that had blown her head-over-heels caught her words and swooshed them down the length of the train.

Georgina rose above the edge of the roof: her face white with fear and her brown hair swirling around her like waves churned by a white froth of smoke and fire from the engine. She crawled up.

"Gina! Your dress!"

Georgina risked a glance at Earnestine.

"Gina!"

"I - - -don?"

Just then, Georgina's dress blew up into a huge bell shape too. She took off, flying right away from the roof. Earnestine knelt up and caught hold, wrenching her arms in their sockets as she herself was pulled up and over, and then, inevitably, the wind caught her own skirts and up she went again. Georgina somersaulted and then the force of the air flattened her skirts: she turned from a balloon into a stone instantly, and a moment later Earnestine also lost her aerial abilities.

They landed in an undignified heap. Anyone in the cabin below would have heard the impact.

Earnestine pushed her head right up against Georgina's: "Be careful."

Georgina reply was punctuated by her jerking breaths and the rushing gale seemed to snatch most of it away: "I was -ing care-, so - - and - - up!"

"Don't swear."

"_"

"I'll get soap."

Earnestine slithered backwards until her foot reached the edge. She glanced behind her: the gap between the coaches was only about three feet.

"We'll have to jump across."

Georgina mouthed words at her, shouting: it could have been "pardon" or "excuse me" or indeed anything at all.

Earnestine pushed herself onto all fours and then got her feet under her: she stood upright, her arms out for balance.

"-u're -plete- mad!" Georgina yelled, unhelpfully.

Earnestine turned until she was standing with her feet apart facing the rear of the speeding train. She had a run up of three good paces. Now she was much closer, she could see that the train roof wasn't smooth and the coach she was aiming for pitched alarmingly. The gap looked wider than three foot.

She took a half step back and then went for it: one, two, three, flying.

The wind caught her skirts, so she sailed - literally - through the air, which made it an extraordinarily long jump. She cleared the gap by three or four yards and then skittered along trying to keep her feet under her. Finally she fell and slid to a halt.

Looking back, she saw Georgina shaking her head very, very slowly.

Oh for heaven's sake, Earnestine thought, and motioned angrily: come on, come on.

Georgina gripped the hem of her skirt with her right hand, which was actually a good thought, and then jumped. The wind caught the free material of her outfit spinning her as she travelled. She landed on her feet, seemed to skate along and then fell into Earnestine's waiting arms.

The second carriage gap was the same, but with a greater degree of jitteriness. Somehow, the further from the engine, the more the chain of stepping stones jiggered and shifted.

Earnestine jumped, fell again and realised that she wasn't really jumping at all. It was the wind catching her and the train moved forward beneath her as she flew.

She got to her feet and walked along the centre.

On the third jump, she enjoyed it.

"I didn't fall over!" she said aloud.

Georgina hit her in the back of her legs bowling her over. She bounced and rolled along the top of the roof. Georgina's hand grabbed hers and they see-sawed, Earnestine coming up and Georgina falling, until Earnestine's other hand grabbed the strut and her feet scrabbled to find some purchase.

Georgina went over the edge!

Earnestine just about held onto her sister above a dizzying drop as trees and telegraph poles zipped past.

"Open your legs!" Earnestine shouted.

"Wh-!"

"Legs!"

Georgina splayed out beneath her waist and her skirts caught the buffeting wind like a billowing sail, it was enough lift to swing her up onto the train roof.

"We're on the restaurant car," Earnestine said.

Georgina was still jerking breaths into her lungs and her eyes were wide and unfocused.

"We're on the restaur-"

"I heard you! We- Oh, oh, oh, please."

"Go in?"

"Yes, oh yes, yes, yes."

They crawled along and gingerly descended on the ladder to the footplates between coaches to stand holding each other shivering but relieved.

"The soldiers?"

Earnestine pointed forward into the restaurant coach and towards the forward coaches, where the soldiers were no doubt searching.

"When the wind blew, I showed some ankle," Georgina sniffed loudly, trying to get a grip on the situation.

"I think I showed some thigh," said Earnestine, and they were both laughing.

It was dangerous, not as dangerous as walking on top of a train travelling at an inconceivable speed of fifty miles an hour, but nonetheless two young ladies holding on to each other, while standing on an unstable metal platform laughing uncontrollably, wasn't safe. And there were three soldiers on board searching for them.

Earnestine pulled herself out of her sister's embrace and checked the window into the restaurant car. Travellers were sitting at tables eating their meals, waiters were serving and... she thought she could detect the wake of a disturbance. Without being able to put her finger on why, she was sure the soldiers had moved forward. They'd had plenty of time during the excursion on top of the train.

The note of the engine changed, less chugging and more whirring.

"We just need to delay until we're in France, then they've no jurisdiction."

Georgina nodded her understanding.

"Perhaps having searched the train they'll give up?" Earnestine said, thinking aloud. Graf Zala knew she was on the train and he didn't strike her as a man who would give up. No doubt he'd instilled that same zeal into his men.

What was that whirring noise?

Earnestine climbed the ladder. She hooked her arm around the top rung before sticking her head above the roof. Despite being buffeted about and deafened by the roar of the wind, she could hear a distinct mechanical noise. She'd heard it before.

A light blinked at the front of the train. It was dusk now, so it was clear in the failing light: on/off... dot/dash/dash... Morse code: that was a 'D' and an 'E', 'U' - a jolt of the train caused her to lose focus for a moment - 'T'... Who were they signalling to? No-one lived in the sky.

Above!

The dark sky was blotted with a massive lozenge shape. Why hadn't she looked up?

"Zeppelin," she shouted down.

"We could signal and tell them to go away," Georgina shouted back.

"Georgina!"

"You've got your flashlight and you know Morse."

"Yes, but I don't know German."

"Oh."

"Do try and think, Gina."

The Zeppelin flared into activity as searchlights came on, cast about and then fixed on the train. One scanned along and Earnestine was dazzled. She had to feel her way down. Georgina appeared smudged by an orange blur.

"They saw me," Earnestine said, blinking.

"You'd be too far away."

"They'll have binoculars."

"Oh my."

Above the noise of steam, airship and wind, there was a loud bang.

"What was that?" Georgina asked.

The percussion from the carriage's wheels changed in pitch and tempo, and the weak light shifted. The train rushed past a section of trees suddenly billowing smoke, thick and yellow, which they had plenty of time to examine because-

Earnestine realised: "We're slowing down!"

"Oh my."

"Gina, we have to get to the engine."

"I guess we're still in Germany."

"Yes."

"What about the soldiers?"

"We'll have to gamble that they are coming back this way."

"But that'll mean we'll meet them... no, no... we'll never make it over the roof going into the wind."

"Gina, don't be a baby, the train is slowing down so it'll be much easier."

"But we've only just-"

Earnestine hoisted her sister up the ladder and pushed, following her as quickly as she could. The Zeppelin manoeuvred to straddle the railway line ahead, and then the giant airship tacked with its engines against the wind, losing altitude, to fly directly above the train.

Even with the train slowing, the predominant air flow, highlighted with tiny sparks from the boiler, blew straight into their faces.

Leading, Georgina lurched up onto her feet and, with a very strange gait, made her way forward. Earnestine pulled herself up too. Ahead there was another explosion. Earnestine shielded her eyes from the glare of the searchlights and could make out the gondola beneath the huge frame of the Zeppelin. She could almost see figures silhouetted in the windows. One of them appeared in a door frame and held something like a model of an airship.

He dropped it.

The object seemed to hesitate in the air staying horizontal, and then its fins came up, or rather the bulbous head dropped. It zinged, striking the head of the train somewhere between the dining carriage and the engine, and disappeared inside. Georgina threw herself flat giving Earnestine an uninterrupted view. When the expected explosion came, it was a damp squib: loud and full of smoke. The crump was followed by a hissing as it threw up a billow of yellow smoke spreading out of the windows ahead as if the front carriage was exhaling after a long draw on a good cigar.

"It's all right. It hit the train and didn't damage anything," Georgina yelled, the rushing air buffeting her words. "It's just smoke."

Earnestine could see that: "Gina, don't be so foolish! Why would they mark the train with smoke?"

"It smells like... beef sandwiches."

"I beg your pardon?"

"That yellow paste."

Earnestine could smell it too: "Mustard."

Georgina giggled.

The train stopped, flinging Earnestine forward, and as she fell, the Zeppelin zoomed overhead. The airship's propellers churned the smoke from the steam engine's chimney. Winking lights appeared in the gondola and the train was raked with bullets. The top of the roof pinged and beams of light appeared shining up from the bullet holes in the roof.

Earnestine screamed: "Go!"

They shuffled along the roof going forward towards the nearest end as another volley went wide. The Zeppelin was closing again, dominating the view. Ropes fell from the gondola and figures readied themselves to abseil down. As Earnestine went down over the edge of the roof, a few bullets ricocheted around metalwork. They'd switched to snipers.

Down on the metal platform at the other end of the restaurant coach, they were completely hidden by the yellow smoke billowing on either side and above.

"It's... strange," said Georgina, coughing.

"It's just smoke."

A man appeared from the sleeping coach in front, his eyes streaming, and he barged into them before jumping from the stationary train.

"Wait!" but Earnestine was too late and a couple of sniper shots cut him down.

"Come on!" she said.

In the corridor inside, there was another man who had fallen to the floor. He reached up to them, his face blistering as they watched; he screamed in French, writhing as he did so.

"We don't breathe the smoke," Earnestine said.

"We must help him," Georgina pleaded.

"In here!"

Earnestine pulled her sister into the nearby cabin.

Through the windows, the searchlights shifted as the Zeppelin came overhead.

"He's dying," Georgina said.

"If we can get the train moving, it'll clear the smoke and they won't be able to board us. We must get the train moving..."

Earnestine grabbed her sister by her arm and shook her, trying to rattle some sense into her, and also to make her own brain work. She grabbed some material off a bunk bed, a nightdress, and ripped it, flinging the pieces into the washing bowl to soak them. She flung the first piece over Georgina and then did the same for herself. The cold shock sharpened her senses.

"Don't breathe or let it touch you!"

"Absolutely."

She went to the door: "Ready."

"You look like a ghost," Georgina said.

Earnestine looked at her sister: "You look like a bride in a veil."

"Deep breaths, then run as fast as you can."

"One... two..."

"Three."

Earnestine opened the door.

## Miss Georgina

Georgina followed Earnestine and they ran headlong into the yellow smog, jumping over the fat, and now dead, Frenchman. They should have saved him, tried at least. The damp linen against her face was suffocating, Georgina wanted to rip it off: she was drowning, falling deeper than ever into the cold waters of the Styx, and then she breathed, taking the air, moist from the damp cotton fabric, into her lungs.

The gap between the coaches was far easier to cross now that the train was stationary.

The smoke was worse, streaming out from a wrecked cabin half way along, and utterly terrifying. Earnestine stumbled, and Georgina was horrified to realise that her sister had stepped on someone. It was a solder in an Austro-Hungarian uniform: they'd killed their own people. Those plans they thought Earnestine had stolen must be important.

"What killed them? Plague?" Georgina asked.

"Or something. What disease would act that quickly?" Earnestine answered and her linen mask went in and out with every breath highlighting her face like a shroud.

"Influenza takes hours, doesn't it?" Georgina was scared.

"We must get to the engine."

"Do you know how to drive a train?"

"The steam engine is a British invention, so we ought to be naturals."

"You can't just browbeat a machine into working."

"I'm sure with a little application we can manage."

Georgina and Earnestine, keeping low, moved out into the corridor. Wisps of yellow smoke swirled as their passing disturbed it.

"It smells of garlic or Dijon," said Georgina.

"Don't smell it," Earnestine replied.

They moved on, holding the material to their faces. The porter still moved, twitching and Georgina leant down to check his pulse, but Earnestine put her hand on her sister's shoulder and shook her head. The man looked mottled, his face breaking out in blisters. His eyes snapped open, wide and unseeing, and he opened his mouth.

Georgina jerked backwards, retching: "Urrgh."

Earnestine knew what it was: "Putrefaction," she said. "They've used some chemical agent, either the substances that bring life with electricity or some reverse compound that brings about death."

"Do you think..." but Georgina couldn't bring herself to articulate what they were both thinking.

"The sooner we get to the engine and breath air that's filled with honest dirt and soot the happier I'll be."

"Me too."

First, they had to negotiate the poor unfortunate on the floor, which they did by waiting for his movements to create a space and jumping over him. They were very glad to reach the far connecting door. In the glass, Georgina saw her reflection and Death loomed over her shoulder. She turned, horrified, and saw an approaching demon, enveloped in a black mackintosh with a face distorted by giant, blank eyes and a snout bulged at the front. His breathing rasped as the monster pulled the poisoned air through the mask.

Georgina recognised them: "Those masks, the... beaks? Like plague doctors wore."

"It has bug eyes... go!"

"Pardon?" said Georgina.

"Go! Go! Fly!"

They went through into the next carriage. There was death and dying everywhere, a charnel house of moving corpses. Earnestine and Georgina ran, not stopping to find a safe way to jump over the decaying flesh, but simply trusting to fortune for sure footedness. Earnestine grabbed Georgina's bustle to hold her up and to stop herself from stumbling. Bones cracked underfoot and their boots splashed in oozing gore.

The next carriage was for baggage. Assigned to each side were crates and luggage while on the floor was a cage filled with rotting chickens, dead but flapping their wings in mindless distress, and the pig was finished too. Earnestine went to a rack to try and find some weapon. There was a set of golf clubs. Earnestine gave one to Georgina.

Behind them gunshots sounded, each single and precise, as their pursuers dealt with the dying.

"We're done for," said Georgina as she compared her No.8 iron with the approaching 8 mms.

"Not yet."

Outside, the sheer blast of air was both clean after the horrors of the train's interior and overpoweringly cold. A few feet in front of them there was the black wall of steel that was the tender.

"We'll have to climb the coal store," said Earnestine, taking off the white covering. Georgina did the same and noticed the yellow stain where she'd been breathing through it. Earnestine had spied a metal ladder and grasped a rung to ascend. Georgina joined her, waiting for

Earnestine's boots to step clear of the rungs. She took hold too and climbed. Above her, Earnestine disappeared over the metal rim and when her own head rose above the edge, she expected to be blasted by black specks and fireflies of burning cinder from the engine, but there was only cold air. Ahead, on her hands and knees, Earnestine crawled towards a geyser of smoke which rose vertically.

A beam of light cut through the darkness causing Georgina to glance at its source. Above them, its rotors labouring to stay steady, was the massive whale-like shape of a Zeppelin. From underneath, blinding when it found her, a searchlight scanned the train. Men dropped on the two ropes, one from either side of the gondola, to land on the train roof further back. The restaurant coach, Georgina reckoned. The first to land, standing stock still, was dressed in black: a black coat, black gloves, black boots, black spiked helmet and a black mask that glistened and it had a snout, while its wide glassy eyes stared along the carriages.

Earnestine was shouting at her, her face distorted and her mouth screaming open: whatever she was yelling was whipped away by the noise and fury of the steam engine. Georgina started forward, crawling across the chaos of coal, her hands and precious skirt ruined by the black muck. When she reached the far end and shuffled round to descend down the far ladder into the cab, she saw the big sad eyes of the masked man gazing across the rocky landscape of the fuel tender.

"There's a bug eyed man," she said.

Earnestine was already examining the levers: "Where's the gee-up control?"

"I don't know. It needs coal." Georgina picked up a shovel from the floor. A thought struck her. "Where's the driver and the stoker?"

"They made a run for it when they train stopped," said Earnestine. She pointed. Georgina saw two bodies lying some distance away cut down by sniper fire from above.

That would be their fate: it would take time for the first masked man to cross to the engine, but their approach was inexorable. And then what? If they jumped off surely they would turn an ankle at the very least and the men, the soldiers, would be upon them even if they dodged the snipers from above. Being chased in some foreign countryside was no safer than being pursued in the train. On foot, the behemoth of the sky would be able to follow them, pointing them out with its searchlight and allowing the nightmare squad to chase them at their leisure.

The controls were brass and steel, and complicated looking.

"Do something?" Earnestine said to her. "You said there's a Bug Eye coming."

"Do what? With what? I'm not armed."

"You had a golf club!"

"I must have put it down," Georgina said, looking around.

"You're holding a shovel."

"Yes," said Georgina, "and he has a gun. I'm not armed."

"Oh, for goodness sake, give it to me," said Earnestine, and she took the shovel off Georgina. "You get the train moving."

Georgina turned her attention to the steam engine's controls. See if she cared if Earnestine wanted to take on the whole Austro-Hungarian army with a shovel.

The dials were in a foreign language that wasn't French or Latin, so Georgina had no chance of deciphering them. All the writing used that strange German lettering that seemed deliberately designed to be impossible to read. Speaking loudly and clearly in English seemed to work on foreigners, so Georgina thought it rude that they didn't return the favour by labelling things in English with big letters. One of the dials was in the red and another's needle jerked around wildly. Didn't Boys' Schools do Engineering? She preferred the study of fauna and flora, finding her butterfly collection so much more natural: she made a face at the whole mess of plumbing and metalwork.

She'd have to ask Earnestine.

Her sister was making her way across the tender, wobbling on the uneven surface of the coal. A black shape squared up to her, it huge eyes reflected the firelight from the engine and seemed to blaze like a devil's.

Earnestine turned sideways, tapped the shovel on the coal as if she was taking a hockey slapshot, except she raised the shovel well above her shoulders, which was not allowed on the playing field. The clang when the shovel connected was satisfying and the bug-eyed creature disappeared as Earnestine struggled to maintain her footing. She moved on, well out of earshot given the racket from the engine.

Georgina went back to controls.

"Coal in here, gets hot..." she mumbled to herself. There was another gauge that was labelled 'Celsius', which she knew was something to do with 'Fahrenheit': it was high. "Heats up water to create steam like a kettle."

Although there was no-one to hear her lecture, it started to make sense. Her index finger wiggled this way and that over the maze, until she was fairly sure that one particular brass wheel was important. She turned it.

Oh, and that was a brake! Squeeze and release!

The engine hissed like an angry snake and she stumbled backwards as the serpent struck forward. She fell over the body on the floor and screamed when she saw an inhuman face.

"It's only a mask," Earnestine said.

The fight between Earnestine and the soldier must have worked its way back to the cab while she was concentrating.

Earnestine handed Georgina the shovel and picked up the dropped rifle.

"Do you know how to use that?"

"Of course," Earnestine said, immediately shooting a ricocheting bullet around the cab. "Maybe not."

"Charlotte would know."

"I wouldn't trust her with a gun," said Earnestine shaking the rifle. "How do you get this thing to reload?"

Above, more figures were sliding down ropes. Although the train was now moving, it wasn't at a speed fast enough to hinder the boarding party.

"They're coming," Georgina said.

They needed more speed. Georgina went and fiddled with controls. The train did gain some momentum and so, above, the Zeppelin appeared to pull away as they moved away beneath it.

"Pressure's down," Georgina said.

"How do you know?"

"This gauge, it shows the pressure and it goes up to here, but the arrow's down here."

"I see."

"We're going ten, just over... dropping I think."

"Ten sounds fast."

"It's in kilometres per hour... so, it's walking pace."

"Oh, that's just dandy."

Earnestine glanced up and over towards the Zeppelin, and her brow furrowed. She was making the calculation, guessing at the airship's top speed, the steam train's, and the distance between them. Her lips tightened in her distinctive way.

"We shovel coal," said Earnestine.

"This is my best petti..." Georgina began, but then she saw her ruined skirts, blackened and ripped. "Fine."

The two sisters grabbed the shovels and collected the coal that bounced and jumped on the vibrating metal floor. Earnestine gripped the boiler door with her hand wrapped in a petticoat. There was a blast of hot air from within. Georgina carefully sprinkled the coal into the maw of the machine.

"This isn't going to work," she said.

Earnestine glanced up at the receding whirring noise overhead, and said: "It has to."

"Aren't we supposed to stack the coal with wood?"

"Just shovel."

Earnestine left the door open, scooped across the floor and flung the coal into the machine. She repeated this, and then switched to the coal store behind them. Georgina followed suit. They shovelled, each working out a rhythm as they went, and more coal from the tender spilled down the chute to replace the fuel they'd spirited away. Soon they were taking it in turns, Georgina desperately trying to keep up with Earnestine and get her swing between her sister's, so they'd be like two arms beating a drum. She would swear that the fire was getting hotter, but maybe it was the... woah, the fire leapt forth and flames spilled around the metalwork.

"Pressure, boiler," she said.

Earnestine understood: "I'll keep shovelling."

Georgina went to the gauges and dials, levers and machinery. She fiddled, tapped the gauges with her knuckle as if they were barometers, and something hissed loudly and urgently. Earnestine shovelled, her palms being ripped and rubbed into a mimic of a domestic's hands. The train was jostling side to side and going much faster, the dark shapes of trees and posts whipping past.

The rail line was making a slow turn to the left, a long arc as it followed the contour of the turning valley. The Zeppelin wasn't anywhere near. It had turned away, its long shape truncated into that of a black oval against the sky, the last rays of the setting sun catching it.

"They're moving away," Georgina said. "Ness, they're giving up."

"The railway curves to the left." Earnestine said thrusting her hand out to show the direction of travel. "They're cutting the corner."

Georgina saw that this was true, that the slower Zeppelin was going as the crow flies while their vehicle was taking a more leisurely, almost scenic, route. The airship would reach the far end of the valley before they did, that was obvious, and then they could simply hover over the track until the train passed beneath them.

"Perhaps we could turn round," Georgina said. "This must have a backwards lever?"

"Do you really want to go back to Austro-Hungary?"

"No."

"Do think, Gina."

When they had been powering along the straight, the fire and smoke had been wrenched backwards, sparks bouncing off the carriages as if they were bullets fired from the funnel, but now they were moving around a curve and the billowing smoke flung a line across the valley away from the train. The wind, which the engine had hurtled towards pell-mell, had been like uphill work for the Zeppelin. But now it tacked across the wind and was gaining speed.

"We'd go faster if we had fewer carriages," Georgina said.

"There must be a connecting clasp or something."

They scrambled up onto the tender and worked along the coal again. The Zeppelin had turned and was giving chase. Men on the end of the ropes waited for the train to come underneath so they could drop down.

The coupling that connected the tender to the first coach was like two iron claws attached with a pin in a hole. Georgina leaned over dangerously and grabbed it, pulled with all her might, but it didn't move. There wasn't room for both of them to do it together, so Earnestine jumped to the coach, leaned in and pulled too. The pin was too big for their cold and dirty hands. It came up and then fell back as a safety chain caught. Georgina churned the links through her fingers looking for the catch as a maelstrom of black pebbles showered across the metal walkway. It was never ending, like a chain of rosary beads.

A masked man, his eyes seemingly larger than ever possible, loomed at the end of the corridor behind Earnestine. His fixed eyes showed no surprise, they did not widen with realisation, but he moved with a renewed vigour towards them.

The chain came apart in Georgina's hand and the pin came up, jagging as the engine tugged and jostled the fuel tender.

The coupling came apart.

A gap of rushing ground opened.

Without its heavy load, the engine jerked forward and Georgina toppled forward into the widening void. Earnestine pushed her away with punching fists and Georgina fell back on the tiny metal platform.

On the other side of the widening space, the masked man grabbed Earnestine. The wind caught his oiled mackintosh, so that it spread like the wings of a monstrous bat.

Georgina was helpless: her sister was just out of reach.

"Ness!"

Mere feet away, a yard, two yards, three...

The engine began to speed away. Earnestine struggled with the bug-eyed monster, getting smaller and more insignificant, shrinking with every moment as the coaches were left behind, swallowed by the swirling yellow fog belching from the tiny train.

And then... there was nothing she could do.

Georgina pulled herself up onto the tender, struggled across the coal and then back into the engine. She grabbed the fallen shovel, a useless weapon, and she screamed. Whining as much as she wanted, she let her tears flow as she shovelled and shovelled and shovelled.

And then everything went black.

# Miss Charlotte

It had been like a merry-go-round ride, and stuffing your face with ice cream, and running about in the hall of mirrors, and brandy butter from the bowl, and Uncle Jeremiah reading adventure stories and Christmas all rolled into one. They'd flown over the Graf's enemies and dropped bombs, fired the Gatling guns that roared and spat tracer. Charlotte had been able to see the bullets hitting the train: *pop, pop, pop.*

All the time, the searchlights had tracked back and forth like the spotlights in a theatre show. Charlotte had once seen a pantomime at the Theatre Royal, Drury Lane, with Uncle Jeremiah. With a shock, she realised that what she'd seen performed there was her own life, complete with Ugly Sisters, who tormented her, until finally she'd married a Prince and become a Princess.

The excitement had continued with the steam engine getting faster, but the railway line curved, so that the wind helped the Zeppelin. They'd caught up and soldiers, air marines, had leapt from the gondola to abseil onto the moving train. Charlotte had not been allowed to try that, for which she was both disappointed and grateful.

And then the train had come apart and the steam engine had sped away.

They gave chase.

Suddenly: "Achtung! Achtung!"

The forward view contained nothing but mountainside.

"UP!" Charlotte shouted, and she grabbed the controls from the terrified pilot. Up the airship went, a savage climb as everything fell, clattering and crashing against the back wall. The airship hit the rock, grinding and screeching, as they scraped up the cliff. Just when it seemed that they would be torn to pieces, they were floating free.

When they levelled and moved away, the steam engine had disappeared into the black maw of a tunnel through the mountains.

The spies had escaped and the Graf fell into a foul mood.

The Zeppelin came to a hover in an open field some distance from the train track and upwind. This was an important consideration, although no-one explained why to Charlotte, and it had involved some tricky steering. The carriages had taken a long time to slow and so the target field was changed.

Finally, ropes were dropped to tie the airship down and metal stakes, like large tent pegs, were hammered into the ground. The soldiers spread out, rifles at the ready as they approached the slowing remains to the train.

And no-one even thanked Charlotte for saving them all.

# CHAPTER XIII

## Miss Deering-Dolittle

The train carriages were still moving forward at speed despite the absence of any motive force. The engine had rocketed away, the angry huffing and belching smoke receding, and then it had vanished, swallowed by the tunnel. The rest of the train was heading that way and might even enter the tunnel too. Perhaps it would become becalmed underground?

Snakes of yellow smoke gathered, the slightest tendril made Earnestine cough and splutter, which was why she stayed on the access plate. The inside of the train was full of the nasty vapour.

Luck had been on her side: in the struggle as they'd both fallen, the soldier had struck his head against the metal footplate.

The unconscious man wore a strange mask, black with huge bug eyes and a snout of strange and deliberate construction. It seemed logical that any new weapon, like the yellow smoke, would have a counter device. So Earnestine leant over, undid the clasps and ripped the rubbery object off. It felt clammy, unpleasant and the idea of it enveloping her face did not appeal. She steeled herself and put it on.

It was claustrophobic: her breathing rasped and echoed, amplified in the enclosing chamber, the world took on an eerie hue, warped at the sides, but the stinging subsided.

The man's coat and boots came off with some difficulty, because when she bent over, she felt sick and wrong footed. The lens in the bug-eye made objects move in waves contradicting her sense of balance. The coat, she realised just before putting it on, would look ludicrous with her bustle sticking out behind her. Earnestine decided to go the whole hog. It was disconcerting to take his trousers off though, wrong, and to leave him in his long johns was undignified. When she removed her dress, she felt a hard object hidden in a pocket: her ring, which she slipped onto her finger. Then she wrenched her dress off and flung it aside, the wind snatched it away and it danced by the side of the train. The bustle she just dropped. Speed was of the essence, other Bug Eyes would be coming. Through the window, with the lens distortion and the yellow smoke, it was hard to see along the corridor, but there seemed to be dark evil shapes moving towards her and-

The glass became the floor, or seemed to, as it came up and hit her forcefully. Hands grabbed around her throat grasping her. She hit out and her assailant stumbled back. The man had come round.

Stupid girl, she thought.

They fought, her camisole ripped under his grip as he held her with one hand, the other drawn back to punch.

She wrenched her neck as she dodged and the man's hand went through the glass panel. Earnestine slipped and fell beneath the man as he roared with pain. He loomed above her, both terrifying and ludicrous with his shirt tails, but Earnestine was at his mercy. A thick enveloping morass of yellow vapour streamed from the broken glass: the man swatted it aside like a bothersome insect and then spluttered and coughed. His eyes bulged wide as he recognised the danger. He focused on Earnestine and came down to grasp the bug-eye with both hands, to tear it from her and to put it on himself.

Earnestine threw her arms around the head and tried to twist into a foetal position to stop him unfastening the mask. They struggled, tearing and fighting and clawing. The man's face was right up against her, his breath casting a mist on her alien spectacles, and all the while he coughed, spat and choked, his spittle flecking her vision as if he was dragging her beneath the waves.

A cough: her vision was splattered with red blood, globules of it, thick and vile. The man became desperate, overpowering her, but it was a last fling. Earnestine pushed him off, but the man's fight was directed towards himself now as he clawed at his face in agony. His skin blistered before her artificially wide eyes and the surface of his face broke as pustules formed and burst. He died, convulsing to his last wheezing gasp.

Hurrying, almost panicking, Earnestine scrabbled for the clothes, the trousers were baggy, the belt didn't have enough holes, so she tied it, the boots were loose and went on easily and finally, with utter revulsion, she rolled the man's body to the edge. It hesitated on the metal lip, the man jerked, brought to a parody of life by the wind, before he tumbled into the air, hit the rails racing below and then disappeared, a splattering cracking as the carriage thundered on inexorably.

Earnestine entered the train, wading through the pea-souper that had invaded every nook and cranny of the carriages. A dark shadow at the far end raised its arm and Earnestine responded in kind. The thing tilted, bowing towards her, and she did the same: it was a nod, exaggerated because the bug-eye prevented the neck from moving properly. She squeezed past him and moved on, wanting to be as far away as possible from the scene of her crime. A fleeting thought of his remains staining the underside of the carriage made her shudder. The vile breath of her victim still reeked inside the bug-eye making her retch. She needed fresh air and fought the desire to pluck the black mask off.

The Bug Eyes had gathered in the restaurant car.

The chief amongst them, his black leather coat open slightly to reveal a spangle of medals, shouted and berated his underlings: his German words sharp, guttural and distorted by the snout of his mask.

The *rat-a-tat-tat, rat-a-tat-tat* of the wheels on the track had become a *chuck-chunk-chunk.... chunk*. Just when

Earnestine thought it was over, there was another, and then an agonising wait for the next, until the wait stretched forever. The carriage had stopped.

When the Bug Eyes filed towards the back of the train, Earnestine joined them. They moved from carriage to carriage passing the corpses of the innocent passengers frozen in their death throes. Earnestine couldn't look and focused on the black shape in front, falling into the marching step when space allowed.

There wasn't another carriage, and the line of soldiers turned to clamber down to the ground. All around a pall of yellow smoke drifted out and settled on the surrounding fields, a stain of death and desolation indelibly infecting the countryside.

The men marched off, down a long winding path through the woods and out into an open space. Tethered to a tree, the massive airship strained at the cables as a ground crew struggled to keep the beast down. The men formed an orderly queue and Earnestine found herself in their midst. The front man went forward under the airship and waved his arms above him, and then he climbed the air upwards towards the gondola.

A second man ascended.

When Earnestine was closer, she saw that they were really climbing a rope ladder, a thin fragile set of rungs strung between black wires. Instinctively, she backed away and the man behind her swore when they collided. Left and right there were fields, open and offering no protection from rifle fire.

She did not want to climb into the belly of that whale above, but she realised she'd have no choice in four... now, three climbers' time.

Her assignment was to reach London and warn them, not join the Aerial Corps of the enemy.

She was under the airship now.

She'd have to risk it.

She was at the front.

A Hauptmann signalled her forward and she ran across the uneven grass and grasped the flailing rungs.

The men ahead climbed the ladder at the end rather than straight on, so Earnestine copied them. It can't be that difficult, she thought, just a case of one leg, then the other. The ruby ring felt solid in her palm as she grasped the metal tube that formed the rung. Luckily, the bug-eyed mask prevented her from really seeing down. In fact to look down, she had to turn her head to one side and stare sideways-

She stumbled.

One leg after the other meant that she was now very high.

She found her footing and concentrated on each hand and leg movement until she was grabbed from above and hauled into the gondola. She wasn't sure where to go as the man ahead of her had climbed with far more expertise and speed, but the next man barged past her, ripping off his rubber mask as he went. Earnestine followed him and he went to a stairway which led up above the gondola. This made no sense to Earnestine, but then she found herself coming up into a huge metal structure. It was like she was in the depths of a ship walking along the keel with struts sweeping up and around. This was the inside of the airship's main body. She'd assumed that this was filled with hydrogen to lift the vehicle, but now she saw that there were balloons inside the airship hanging from above... no, these balloons were lifting the whole airship aloft: it was the metal frame that dangled from the balloons.

Air sailors were quartered here in a strange reversal of normal naval tradition: the officers were below in the luxurious cabins, whereas the crew were above living in the mechanisms of the Zeppelin itself, sleeping in hammocks slung between the metal gantries.

The floor shifted and the air sailors grabbed handholds and leant into the slope. Earnestine tumbled over to much hilarity before edging her way to an unoccupied area. There were a few empty berths, those Bug Eyes that Earnestine herself had seen off perhaps, and she hunkered down in one and removed the smothering mask.

The other airmen were also removing their garments - the stale smell of sweat... no, perspiration - horses sweat, men perspire and women glow. Earnestine didn't feel much glow: she felt cold and rancid. She couldn't stay here, she knew that, so she slipped the mask back on and eased her way back along the walkways.

As she went a few choice remarks in German were thrown her way. She waved and smiled, realised that any facial expression under the mask was pointless, and hurried on.

Down the steps and into the gondola was easy enough and the rope was still dangling from the exit. No-one was around, so all she had to do was shimmy down and disappear into the dark French countryside until they took off and-

"Achtung! Passen Sie auf!"

"Ja!" Earnestine replied, muffled somewhat by her mask.

Earnestine jerked in shock when she heard the Graf speaking.

"So, mein Liebchen, let us have some schnapps."

Earnestine turned away, keeping her back to him as he moved past. Charlotte, dressed in some ridiculous military uniform, followed in his wake: silly girl - silly, silly girl.

Below Earnestine, where the rope dangled, the ground rippled in the distortion of the bug eyes, magnified, closer, then suddenly plummeting down. Giddy, Earnestine grasped a handrail and the ground resolved into a strange model-like landscape moving gently underneath.

They were airborne already.

"That would be lovely," said Charlotte, using that giddy, silly voice that she reserved for times when chocolates and sweets were on offer. Thankfully the Graf and Charlotte went past and into one of the cabins further back along the gondola.

Going down the rope was suicide: she was trapped.

She was going to have to find somewhere to hide.

Upstairs were the quarters for the Aerial Ratings. Sooner or later someone would ask why she was wearing a bug-eye, or they'd ask her to join them in a hand of cards, or for a meal, or almost anything, and it would be in German.

Towards the bow was the control room.

This left only the cabins.

She listened at the door and was relieved to hear silence.

She went in.

"Dummkopf! Schnell, schnell."

Earnestine rushed through, understanding the Graf's yells only too well.

She caught a glimpse of a luxurious room, plush, with four round dining tables big enough to accommodate four chairs easily. It took up the entire width of the gondola section. Charlotte was sitting looking wide eyed and expectantly as the Graf poured some vile concoction from an overly elaborate bottle.

"Ach, Dieses ist untragbar!"

Earnestine raced through the room as quickly as she could. In the brief moment and the narrowing gap as she closed the door, she saw the Graf storming towards her.

"Graf, Graf," Charlotte called after him.

Why hadn't Earnestine heard him speaking?

All she could hear was her own breathing, loud and clear.

She took off the bug-eye mask.

That feeling of claustrophobia and heat left her immediately. The rubber mask was slick with... horses, men... the residue of her glow.

Earnestine found the cabins numbered '1/2' to '19/20', in pairs, and the two at the bow end were larger. One had clearly been used recently, but the others appeared empty. She picked one: her age 20. It had bunks and the white linen looked so inviting. She almost sat down, but realised that she'd mark the sheets.

However, Earnestine realised that she couldn't hide here. Whatever her personal feelings, she was responsible for her sisters. Back along the corridor, she looked around in the next cabin and it showed signs of occupation. She knew she couldn't just sit there either; she'd have to hide as Charlotte might come in at any moment with someone else. There was a gap under the bunks, so Earnestine lay on the floor, shuffled underneath and squeezed herself against the wall as tight as she could.

Plan: she'd stay awake and wait. Charlotte would come to bed and that would give her a chance to have words - sharp words - with the silly girl. Sooner or later they'd have to land and she'd nip down the ladder when the Aerial Ratings disembarked. Good plan, she thought, although she had a terrible feeling they were simply going back to the castle.

She touched the ruby ring.

Perhaps she could close her eyes for a brief moment...

No, she mustn't.

Perhaps just until the stinging stopped completely.

## Miss Georgina

There had been a moment when the Zeppelin had been upon her and then, with a plunging roar, the train had fallen into the depths of a seemingly endless tunnel shuddering in a cacophony of steam and sparks. Georgina had been born again, screaming, on the other side. The engine hurtled on.

Georgina fell to her knees and the dawn light split across the sky. Her energies were spent, the shovel fell from her hands and coal tumbled across the juddering metal floor to skitter and dance in time to the clattering.

She was alone now: father was gone, mother too, uncle, Charlotte lost and Earnestine dead.

"Arthur," she murmured.

No-one replied.

Presently, the steam subsided, the screaming fell silent and the stations sliding by slowed. Soon the speed dropped to walking pace and below. Georgina lifted herself up and flopped over the edge, hanging briefly and choosing a grassy bank to drop onto. She hit it and rolled down coming to a blissful rest below.

The engine, pockmarked with bullet holes, went on without her, past signals that were up or down, and meant nothing to Georgina. It rained, she raised her head and drank the water as it stung her face. Onwards, away from the train line, or sideways: Amazon, Amazo... Am as lost...

There was a French village not far off, guarded by a farmer moving cows from one field to another. They were spooked by a shadow moving across the sun and coming under the arch of a magnificent rainbow, the dark shape of an airship circled.

"S'il vous please, please..." she begged.

Dumped on a cart, she bounced along with an old Frenchman guiding an old horse to a town. Her money was no good, they had no Queen here in their Republic, but he was a kind man.

There were troops from the Gendarmerie gathered on a street corner. Georgina was half-way across and she would reached them had not the direction of the horses and other traffic being on the wrong side of the road confused her, when she heard them speaking German. There were other men in their midst. She backed away, a tram nearly struck her, and every face she saw seemed to be watching her, chasing her, informing on her - there were spies everywhere.

She ran down a side street and into an alleyway, dodging past the piles of litter and mess. The next street was full of shops, patisseries and cafés. Georgina was hungry, but every face hid a glance and every corner had a person to ambush her. She moved with the crowd, then against the flow, working around the town until she came to the main road leading north. There was a road sign: Paris was included, and at a hump backed bridge a four horse carriage was stalled waiting for the bridge to clear.

She ran up to it: "Paris?"

"Oui."

"Will you take me to Paris?"

"Non. Plus de place."

"Please, s'il vous please... for pity's sake."

"Non."

They wouldn't take her. It was so unfair.

She felt utterly lost, am-as-lost, and ineffectual, as-an-ant.

To have got as far and to have failed: Earnestine would be cross - no worse, Earnestine would be disappointed. She'd let the side down, badly, and added to the bad name of Deering-Dolittle (Kent). The worst part of many worst parts was that Earnestine would have known what to do.

"Excuse me! I'm British. Take me to Paris!"

The carriage stopped and Georgina, raising her head imperiously, marched up to the door, waited for someone to open it, and for the other passengers to shift across, before she climbed the steps and sat down.

With a jerk, she was off towards what she hoped was the French capital. The other passengers looked at her suspiciously, full of resentment as if she had been personally responsible for Agincourt, Trafalgar and Waterloo. She decided that she would simply sit there, aloof, and not close her eyes at all once.

Maybe...

A man attacked her, prodding her with a small whip.

She fought back: "What?"

"Paris, vous êtes à Paris."

The coach was empty and stationary, and it was dark outside.

She struggled out, her neck seemed permanently twisted.

"Thank you, oh merci, merci, thank you."

Paris seemed huge, quite on the scale of London, and the strangeness of the signs was enough to thoroughly disorient her. She needed to eat and drink, she knew that: adventures required one to keep one's strength up. She wanted to sleep, a proper sleep in a bed with clean sheets and-

She stumbled.

A man came up to her.

"British Consulate?" Georgina said.

He shook his head.

Georgina tried the next person and the next, and was finally rewarded with a pointing gesture and a lot of French. So, street by street, corner by corner, French or accented English, she was guided to an imposing building. She went up the stairs and banged on the door. Inside, a porter waved her away.

"I'm British."

"Passport?"

"No, I... please."

"Go away!"

"I'm Georgina Deering-Dolittle."

"From Surrey?"

"No, Kent."

"Pah."

"Please."

"Passport?"

"Please, please..."

"Go away."

"Please..."

"I will get men to throw you out."

She slipped down the glass; the Paris cold bit into her and the warmth of technically British soil felt forever from her reach. Below, skulking in the shadows were dark shapes wrapped in scarves and black woollen hats. They

*239*

spoke German and edged up the steps towards the light to carry Georgina off into the night. Other men arrived from inside, strong well-dressed men to throw her back like a small fish that didn't come up to the mark.

They surrounded her.

"I say," said Merryweather, bending down and plucking her up from the paving.

"Arthur?"

"Come in before you catch your death."

She was saved, utterly and completely swept-off-her-feet saved. The door opened and Arthur carried her over the threshold.

The Porter intercepted them: "You can't-"

"Don't be an arse," Arthur said.

And there was Caruthers and McKendry too, and quite soon there was also sweet tea and cake.


## Miss Charlotte

"I apologise for before," the Graf said. "When the culprit is found, he will be severely punished. My airmen are trained to obey, instantly and without question."

"The interruption didn't bother me," Charlotte replied, standing and smoothing down her uniform.

"The schnapps now, mein Liebchen?"

"That would be lovely. Why not in my cabin, then we won't be disturbed."

"Would that be allowable?"

"We are related after all," said Charlotte. "Let me check everything is all right."

"I will get the schnapps and perhaps something warming."

"Lovely."

Charlotte went from the lounge section to her cabin to give it a quick check. Everything was stowed and in order, as she had known it would be. She was about to return and call the Graf through, when she heard a strange noise, a wheezing as if the engines were labouring with a... Charlotte knew that noise and knew it well. She took a couple of steps and turned her head and located the source under her bunk. She knelt down and looked: Earnestine, dressed as a soldier, was tucked underneath, sound asleep.

So it was her sister who had rushed through the lounge: typical of her to try and ruin everything. Well, Charlotte would just follow Earnestine's own advice to always tell your elders and betters everything - she'd inform the Graf and-

There was a knock at the door.

Charlotte stood, kicked sharply under the bunk, and said, loudly, "Graf, just a moment, just a moment, Graf."

There was a mumbled complaint brewing from under the bunk.

"Graf! Do come in, come in Graf, good to see you Graf!"

"Liebchen, are you all right."

"Yes, Graf," she said, and then she had to cough, loudly and continuously until the noise coming from under the bed piped down. "Everything is fine, Graf."

"I brought you a nightcap: hot chocolate."

"Lovely," Charlotte leapt forward and looked, wrinkling her nose: "It's not Cadbury's?"

"Nein, Belgian dark chocolate."

Charlotte took a sip: it was rich, thick and bitter.

"I suggest a measure of schnapps."

Charlotte nodded and the Graf poured a generous helping from a bottle.

"Please," Charlotte said, indicating a chair by the table, but the man came around and held the chair out for her. Charlotte settled herself and the Graf chose the place next to her just around the corner.

They sat for a moment, three sips of hot chocolate each.

"Tell me about your plans," said Charlotte.

"They will be tedious and technical to you."

"Not at all," she laid her hand on his. "I'm interested."

The Graf frowned.

"I spoke with Doctor Mordant," Charlotte continued. "She told me some of it, but she did not have the same... vision as you."

"Nein, she was unambitious."

"She wanted the discovery for herself."

"Ja, and I solved the major technical issue."

"Do tell," Charlotte simpered.

"The problem that this Mordant Process has - or had - is its reliance upon Nature's galvanic processes."

"Lightning."

"Ja, exactly!"

"To bring someone back you require a storm."

"We have engines that can create galvanic energy for one or two Lazarian events, but, alas, to perform the process on a large scale would require more power than all the factories in Britain's Lancashire, Yorkshire and their Black Country combined."

"So?"

"It is our little secret and it will make us the Masters of the World."

"How exciting," said Charlotte. "But won't the British Empire resist?"

"How? With what? They don't even have a Sky Navy. Let them fire their mighty guns into the air and you will find their shells falling back to Earth long before they reach us. They lack the range, whereas we can drop bombs from any height. Military strategy has always dictated that whoever holds the high ground, wins the battle and we hold the very highest ground possible, the sky itself."

"Brilliant."

"It is the classic military strategy to catch the enemy in a pincer movement, but not from the sides: death from above and death from below."

"They'll attack your men too."

"Nonsense, we have these little devices courtesy of Marconi and Tesla. They generate a pulse in the ether, which travels to the detectors attached to the unfortunates: a little shock, more than enough to persuade their cannibalistic tendencies to go elsewhere."

"Oh yes, Doctor Mordant showed me."

"Think of it," he said, "in military terms. We create an army that does not suffer attrition. We fight, and so long as we take the battlefield, then our army is the same for the next battle. We have ten thousand untoten against a thousand enemy, we outnumber them ten to one. We fight and, yes, they kill more of our troops, two thousand, maybe even half our number, five thousand, but then we bring our troops back to life *and theirs!*"

He pointed his finger and then stabbed it down on the table. The cups jumped and the hot chocolate shook.

"So, for the next battle, we have eleven thousand troops. Think of it - every city, every town, every village has a graveyard, recruits at every turn, the whole of Europe's dead rising from the ground at our beck and call, a whole empire."

"Surely the British Empire, the greatest empire the world has ever seen would stop you?"

"How? Each of their men wounded takes ten from the battle in terms of stretcher bearers, medics, nurses and if you are lucky the injured man can be back in the war within a few months; whereas with our army, we stretcher off the dead, reanimate them and then we can return them to the front in the same engagement. Our enemy has to kill us over and over again, we kill them once and then they are dead - kaput. Worse than dead for, with our little electrical box, they are on our side."

"Sounds painful."

"They are dead, they feel nothing, and the last regiment of our troops will be en route soon."

They finished their hot chocolate.

"Mein Liebchen, do you have any more questions?"

"Oh yes," said Charlotte. "Can I get to fly the Zeppelin again?"

"Of course, you would be in charge of a fleet of Zeppelins. Princess, my Liebchen, I have such plans."

There it was: Her Royal Highness, Admiral of the Air; she'd have a uniform and wear trousers and be someone other than the youngest of three.

"Yes," she said.

The Graf stood, clicked his heels and bowed: "I must check on progress. We are coming in to land."

The deck had shifted, the schnapps flowing up the side of the bottle showing the true angle of the deck. They had been descending for a while.

"Of course, can I..." and then Charlotte remembered her sister hiding under the bunk. "I shall rest here if I may."

"Of course, until later then."

He bowed again, ever the officer and gentleman, and left.

Charlotte considered him: his handsome features, the aquiline nose, his pointed beard, his piercing eyes and his funny, but charming, accent. Most of all, she thought about his uniform with its black epaulettes and-

"Ow!"

Earnestine hit her heel again and struggled out from under the bunk.

"Charlotte! Charlotte! Words utterly fail me."

"He was nice and we are related."

"He's planning to conquer the British Empire."

"Oh that."

"Yes, that."

"I'm sure not... I didn't really... do you like my uniform?"

"You are a silly girl, a stupid, silly girl."

"You can't talk to me like that, I'm royalty."

"Do you know what happened to the Princess?"

"I'm the Princess."

"The real Princess."

"I'm a real Princess, I'm married to a Prince."

"The real Princess with whom you exchanged places."

"No... yes, she went back to elope with her Hauptmann."

"She was thrown off the battlements of the Eagle's Claw castle. In your coat, your best coat. Georgina thought it was you. You really upset her. And that's what will happen to you. And you'll deserve it. They'll throw you out and it's a lot further down to the ground from a Zeppelin."

Earnestine was angry, blinking and tightening her lips.

"Did you listen to what that dreadful man said?" Earnestine demanded.

Always about the listening, Charlotte thought: "Of course I listened."

"And?"

"I get to wear a uniform and fly a Zeppelin."

"And the rest of it, the military strategy and his tactical plans."

"Oh, that. It sounded like a History lesson. Do you remember Miss Green and her interminable-"

"Charlotte!"

"Did he really kill the Princess?"

"Yes, and everyone at the college."

"What college?"

"The Eden College for Young Ladies."

"Oh."

Earnestine checked her strange rubber mask, fussing and angry. Charlotte thought about her own uniform, the tight cut and the wonderful trousers and suddenly realised what it represented. The badges weren't mere brooches and jewellery, they had meaning: the Sky Navy had real bombs, real guns, real...

"We shot at people on a train."

"I know."

"It was... far away."

"It wasn't far away for me."

"They were like dolls. It didn't seem to count. It was like a game. I didn't think-"

"No, Charlotte, you didn't think. You were shooting at Georgina and me, and people died, quite horribly."

"Oh, bally hell."

"Don't swear!"

"Sorry."

Earnestine looked out of the window: trees tops were visible: "It's bad enough with you being on the wrong side," she said, "a traitor no less-"

"I am not."

Earnestine turned on her: "Don't lie! You're a traitor."

Charlotte felt tears welling in her eyes. Earnestine never valued her and always had an angry word. It wasn't fair: "I'm not, I'm just... playing the double game like... this is an adventure, isn't it?"

"Charlotte Deering-Dolittle, this is not an adventure."

"It's not?"

"No," said Earnestine, emphatically. "Now, I'm going to disguise myself as a soldier and escape, and you will find a way to escape too. We have to warn Whitehall and the War Office and save the British Empire."

"If you say so."

"Yes, I do say so."

Earnestine pulled on her rubber mask, straightened her coat and marched out.

Charlotte followed, utterly cowed. A soldier stopped Earnestine after they'd gone through the dining room. They struggled for a moment by the exit with the open air behind them, both dangerously close to the edge.

"She's... He's with me," Charlotte shouted.

The soldier saluted.

Without looking back, Earnestine swung herself out into the open air and disappeared.

Other soldiers came past too.

The airship had docked and the rope ladder descended to an open field. The soldiers hesitated at the end before they dropped the last few feet and rolled in the grass. Soon there were enough men deployed to handle the ropes and tie the massive vehicle to the ground.

"Liebchen?" the Graf asked.

Charlotte jumped in shock.

The Graf put a concerned hand upon her shoulder. His touch was heavy.

With the dexterity of long practice, the men off-loaded their equipment and then the ropes were released again. The Zeppelin took to the air, the ground below dropped away leaving her in this metal and canvas prison in the sky.

"Mein Liebchen, are you all right?"

"The wind in my eyes, that's all."

"Ja, of course."

Below, one of the soldiers, masked, stared up at the rising Zeppelin with big, blank, but nonetheless accusing eyes.

# CHAPTER XIV

## Miss Deering-Dolittle

Earnestine's plan had failed at the first hurdle. There was far too much security and the fences were formidable. She was also still dressed as a Bug Eye, so she ended up helping with large canvas bags that required two people to carry. They sagged awkwardly in the middle, making them tricky to move. The man opposite had shouted some instructions in German, so Earnestine had replied with "Jawohl" and then added some deep grunts.

The bags went into wooden crates clearly marked in German, French and English for delivery to an address in London via the West India Docks. This immediately suggested another plan: she'd simply stow away in the crate and wait until she heard cockney voices unloading the crates upon arrival.

She carried three bags in all. They arrived by horse drawn cart and the crates were being loaded into cattle trucks on a train. The rail line terminated here and went out through some woods beyond going presumably to a port. Thankfully the whole operation was performed with great efficiency, the carts being reversed as close to the train as possible, so that it could all be completed quickly.

When the moment came, when the men were looking away, Earnestine put her leg over the crate and hopped in, quickly lying down and shuffling the last bag over herself. Another weight landed on top of her, before the crate lid was placed over and nailed down with awful finality.

Panic!

If the crate would be airtight, then she'd suffocate, but moving the bag aside she saw light streaming in from various knot holes and the gaps between the planks. The crates were well made, but from cheap materials.

The crate was hoisted onto the train; she felt the giddy moment of flight and the unceremonious landing.

She waited.

Her bed, such as it was, was comfortable once she'd shifted it around. Whatever was in the bags was sharp and soft in varying degrees.

Finally, she heard the carriages door clattered shut. It was dark now.

After what seemed like an eternity, while they loaded the other cattle trucks, there came whistles, shouts and the familiar hiss of a steam engine. The crate jerked and then, in fits and starts at first, the train went on its way.

Should she fall asleep?

The clattering start of the journey had shifted her position, so she shuffled and jiggled until she was comfortable again... except for this sharp... what was this? It was awkward to reach her pocket, but eventually she eased out her flashlight and moved it up her body to her face.

She couldn't turn it on for too long.

Flash: the bags were still sealed.

Flash: the stitching could be pulled. She did this in the dark, feeling the rough cord with her fingers, finally she yanked it open.

Flash: there was something dark, difficult to make out. She pulled the canvas apart again and it ripped coming open.

Flash: it was some round object, dark and made of fur. She turned it.

Flash: oh, it was a man's face and *I must not explore, I must not...* Earnestine dropped the flashlight and retched. It was a body, a man's body, and all the bags contained cadavers. She was trapped in a crate of corpses. Panic rose, utter terror, and she flailed about to escape, but all she did was cause the bodies to shift and so she sank between them.

It was a train of the dead.

# Miss Georgina

She asked only how Arthur had escaped; it seemed incredible that he was just here.

"Don't worry, I'll always keep you safe," he said.

"But how?"

"I caught the next train," he said, sipping his whiskey. They'd all gathered in the smoking room once Georgina had freshened up. "Although there was something of a delay due to some problem on the line."

"The next train?"

"It is the steam age, they have timetables on the continent too."

Gently, by tiny degrees, the trio extracted as much information as they could. Georgina wanted to help: she described the Zeppelin attack, the bomb that released the yellow smoke, the soldiers in their frightening masks with snouts like those doctors in plague times.

Caruthers and Merryweather exchanged a worried glance: "Gas?" they said together.

Georgina corrected them: "Smoke. It killed, choking death and their skin blistered, it smelt like cooking or mustard or beef: it was... horrible."

Arthur put his hand on hers.

"We separated the engine from the coaches to get more speed and to keep - they boarded the train from the air - and Earnestine... she was on the other side when it came apart."

Arthur squeezed her hand: "Perhaps she survived."

"No, I saw her fall, fighting one of those Bug Eyes, and there was smoke everywhere. It's all right, she would want me to be brave."

McKendry and Caruthers stepped aside to talk privately. It was so quiet that Georgina could hear every word.

"Pyro?" McKendry asked.

"Sulphur mustard from Zeppelins, it's an horrific thought."

"And the silver iodide?"

"I don't think that reacts usefully."

"Perhaps it's another weapon?"

"It's used to make daguerreotypes, Merry said."

"I said," Georgina interrupted. "But they have far, far too much of it according to what Earnestine saw."

"Perhaps she was mistaken?" Caruthers suggested.

"Earnestine, mistaken? No, never."

"Daguerreotypes? Galvanic processes? They are up to something. Mac, I think you should take the first train to England. Now. Don't pack, go. The sooner you get word to the Club, the Admiralty and St John Brodrick, the better."

"Yes, Sir."

McKendry turned on his heel and his long strides took him quickly away.

"And I have arrangements to make too - Merry, Miss Deering-Dolittle," Caruthers said, turning to take his leave.

Georgina wanted to correct him. She was only Miss Georgina. The eldest sister was Miss Deering-Dolittle, Earnestine, who was... so now she was the eldest, and perhaps even the only one of them left. Arthur held out a handkerchief, which seemed a very strange gesture.

"You are a remarkable girl," he said.

"I don't feel so, but thank you."

"Georgina?"

"Yes?"

"I was w- w- wondering..."

"Yes?"

"Nothing, n- never mind, it'll wait."

Caruthers, Merryweather and Georgina caught a cab to Gard du Nord station and then they boarded an express to Calais. Suddenly, speed was of the essence. There had been reports of Zeppelins manoeuvring north and Caruthers complained about the low cloud. Whole fleets of airships could be crossing the Channel utterly unseen. What could the Royal Navy do? There was nothing in

Plymouth to stop this armada. Considering Caruthers and Merryweather's fears, Georgina despaired: what could they do?

The bustle of French gentlemen and Parisian ladies was too much for Georgina and the sight of the trains was a nightmare, but she steeled herself and climbed aboard: get back on the horse, she thought.

The train was a step down from the Orient Express, but, after they'd settled, they made their way to the restaurant coach to find the menu quite tolerable, once it was translated from French. Georgina ordered coffee with croissants and then stared out of the window letting the blur of scenery defocus her eyes and empty her head.

The journey seemed interminable and then Calais came all too quickly.

Caruthers saw them through border control with their passports and a ten franc note. The *Mary* was already boarding, so they went straight up the narrow gangways and onto the black and white vessel, which had been decked out in colourful bunting.

"I'm sure we were seen," Merryweather said.

"Yes, I saw them too," Caruthers said.

"Where? I didn't see anyone," Georgina said.

"We've been observed at Gard du Nord and here at Calais," said Merryweather. "Spies."

"Where?"

Georgina looked round: suddenly all the men looked sinister, dressed as they were in black.

"It's all right," said Merry. "We're on the ferry now, there's little they can do. They'll hardly get an ironclad down the Channel in time."

They went to the restaurant to consider lunch or dinner with menus that couldn't decide whether they were French or English, and fell between two shores. They ordered fish: plaice in lemon sauce with potatoes fried in the French manner, which turned out to be thin chips. Caruthers and Merryweather had bottled beer, whereas

Georgina ordered lemonade so strong it stung her eyes from the inside.

With loud hoots and horns, the *Mary* set sail. On the quay everyone was waving, sweethearts painfully separated, families bidding farewell, friends parting. Even Caruthers and Merryweather turned to look, and then they went on deck.

Georgina was alone: she had longed to be back in England and now that she was crossing the Channel, it was all empty and hollow. Their house in Kensington would be there, but it would be dusty and quiet; there would be no more laughter and pranks, no more stories and excited discussions over maps.

"Calm," said Merryweather, when they returned.

"Rough later," Caruthers added: "You can see the clouds gathering north already."

"A little rain never hurt anyone," said Merryweather.

Merryweather drank his beer smudging the froth across his moustache. Georgina leant over and wiped it off with her napkin.

"Oh Merry," she chided.

"Gina?"

"I'll pop along to the radio room again," said Caruthers. "See if there's a telegram reply."

Off he went.

Georgina finished her lemonade, Merry found some dregs left in Caruthers's bottle of best.

"Georgina."

"Yes."

"I was w- wondering... we'll be in England soon."

"Yes."

"I expect I'll have a lot to do."

"Yes."

Outside the swell rose, white horses pranced on the breaking waves. Sunlight struck sharply highlighting the ebb and flow until the dark clouds gathered and the pitch and toss swung the lamps violently.

"The thing is," Merry said eventually, "we've been through a lot, you and I, and we work well together, so I w- wondered if perhaps you might agree to extend that arrangement and basically what I'm trying to say is-"

"I feel sick."

"Oh."

Georgina could taste lemonade and lemon sauce and fish. She stood, lurched and sat down again.

"Always best to look at the horizon, old girl."

The queasy sensation increased, particularly as she tried to navigate the treacherous tables and chairs to the exit, and the metal staircase was a test, but even so, at the back of her mind, she objected to being called 'old girl'. She was young, the middle sister, and it was Earnestine at twenty who was the spinster on the shelf. Had been, she reminded herself. Even that aching loss was nothing next to the urgency in her stomach.

The desk was awash with spray. Drizzle fell from the heavens, and Georgina slipped across the wooden planks to the hand rail. She held it, her hands going instantly cold against the slick wood, and she stared at the lurching horizon as if she was demented. The clouds gathered, rolling grey balls packed with rain and dark shapes; she could hear them grinding together.

Spray showered her: salty, reminding her of the fried potatoes in the French style. Her hair, splattered with sea water and blown around, must be in such a state.

Old girl indeed.

Merryweather was there: ha! Ridiculous: 'merry' 'weather'.

She felt his presence behind her, knowing instinctively that he had followed her, so she turned, making sure that one hand gripped the rail. Captain Arthur Merryweather looked at her aghast.

"Captain Merry... oh, weather-"

Anger swamped the dreadful nausea: he wasn't even looking at her.

"Cap-"

"Zeppelin!"

She turned round, scanned the sky, but there was nothing except oncoming storms and-

"Oh Lord."

As the dark clouds obscured the sun turning the day into dusk, so the pinpricks of light in the Zeppelin became sharper. It was a tiny constellation moving against the firmament of the sky.

"I'll get Caruthers."

Merryweather turned and lurched across the desk, leaving Georgina-

He left her!

Left her... and 'old girl', and drivels on about wondering this and wondering that and doesn't get to the point.

It was a truly awful day.

The bunting trailed across the ship, flapped pathetically, wet and dark and limp. Georgina hated bad weather.

The deep whirring of the Zeppelin's engines cut through the noises of the gale and the *Mary's* engines. It was overhead, travelling straight across them, and turned to a parallel course. The ferry pitched alarmingly.

It was very dark now: a dark ship on a dark sea under dark clouds with a dark shape brooding over them - a moment later the bright beams stabbing down from the Zeppelin. The light flailed about, losing its target. Georgina realised that the flying vessel must be having as much trouble in this weather as they were. The beams of light strode away like some sort of gigantic three legged war machine made of light.

A wave struck the bow of the troubled *Mary*. The ship didn't heave, but the wash flew across the deck, stinging Georgina when the curtain of salt and spray struck her. Although she fought the impulse, her hand still went to wipe her face and at that moment her feet slipped from under her. She fell awkwardly, striking her elbow: the pain was searing, funny despite the situation, and then the boat seemed to explode.

Light was everywhere, the three beams from the hovering Zeppelin converged, straight down. The beast was above them, directly above them. The flash was just the dazzling illumination.

"Miss!"

One of the men was shouting. Georgina blinked: it was a sailor: young, honest, good natured, salt of the sea... and then the boat really did explode.

Something, a black mark, had hit the bow and then, in a moment of fire, the deck seemed to rip apart. Planks of wood and other shrapnel went up, caught in the search lights as they spun and ricocheted off the metal walkways. The lad jumped in the air, caught for a moment with his arms wide, and then the blast caught Georgina, pinning her to the deck.

She'd been lucky, she'd already been on the deck and so the force of the explosion had travelled over her to strike back the wind in one brief, fiery moment. But the crewman no longer existed.

A second bomb missed, sending a column of water like a geyser heavenwards.

The *Mary* juddered before the rolling sea caught up and began to roll her hither and thither. The sea reared up again, higher, and Georgina thought that the storm had intensified. Surely this metal tub could withstand the pounding weather better than that stretched fabric balloon?

A cry: "Water! We're taking in water!"

Georgina clambered to her feet and tried to see who was shouting. Above her, the black lozenge of the Zeppelin blotted out the angry black sky. It was manoeuvring, coming back for another attack run.

"Abandon ship!"

"Arthur!" Georgina yelled, but even she couldn't hear her own cries.

There was a clang, like a low bell, followed by a series of further chimes: Georgina laughed; it sounded just like bell ringing as if a village campanology group was practising in the Channel. To her right, starboard, one of the lifeboats pitched and tossed, dropping alarmingly as it was released into the waters. It splashed as it struck the surface.

The deck was no longer level and everything sloped towards the front of the ship. Georgina's shoes started to lose purchase on the slick polished timbers. She struggled her way uphill knowing that she had to get into one of the lifeboats.

Another cry: "Women and children first!"

Once she'd reached the starboard gangway, she could see the sailors helping people off the ferry.

A gentleman waved his cane and barged to the front: "Get out of my way!"

The world went silent.

Georgina could no longer hear the storm, the waves, even the strange siren bells were quiet. The bombs, if they continued dropping, exploded without a murmur. A sailor, caught by a gunshot from above, fell away, bounced once on the deck and then slid away to disappear into the churning white foam that engulfed the bow.

Georgina threw herself sideways through the door and under cover. She went away from the murder and away from the lifeboat. She had, with that act, chosen death. Her hearing returned with the bumping noise of wooden lifeboats and a strange staccato thumping. She was alone, soaked and frozen on a sinking ship, abandoned by her comrades and sister-less in this godless sea.

"Gina! Gina!"

Stepping into the canting restaurant came Captain Merryweather. From nowhere! He'd not forgotten her, although Georgina forgot herself and fell into his arms: "Arthur."

"I told you I'd keep you safe."

"Yes."

"Shall we leave?"

"Leave?"

His question seemed quite preposterous. She must be drowning already and he was some messenger from another world.

"Yes, leave," said Merryweather, "and with some alacrity, if you don't mind."

Georgina was already on the move, caught up in Merryweather's grasp. He manhandled her onto the port side towards a hail of bullets. Flashes and bangs produced trails of fire from above that pinged and zinged about the dying metalwork of the sinking *Mary*. The Zeppelin, close enough to blot out most of the setting sun, was spitting sparks along its full length: the airmen were using small arms against them, trying to pick off Merryweather and herself.

"Oh Lord," she said.

"Over you go."

"Over where?"

Merryweather picked her up and threw her straight over the side.

Georgina screamed.

## Miss Charlotte

Charlotte felt the lurch again and she was thrown across her cabin. She'd been sick, suffering from the mal de mer... no, mal du ciel. She felt wretched, but it was not the storm that caused her the most grief for it was every gunshot and every bomb explosion that stabbed into her soul.

She was crying, tears streaming down her face in a most un-English manner, but then she wasn't English.

She was something like Belgian by pretence and Austro-Hungarian by marriage: she was the enemy, she was the monster.

There was another set of flashes from above and then from below. The dreadful crump of the bomb going off followed quickly and then... one, two, three... the roar of thunder.

Strike us down, Charlotte screamed inside, let God hurl a thunderbolt and burn us all to hell.

But it didn't happen.

The Zeppelin belonged to the new age: industrial, powerful, defiant and utterly unstoppable.

She'd stop them.

Drunkenly, Charlotte fumbled with the door catch, plunged out across the corridor and through the dining room. In the space beyond, a soldier manned the horrifying American gun, its multiple barrels spun and spat fire, racketing percussive detonations continuously. The endless firing lit the faces of these slaughter technicians as they killed from afar. There was no glory here, no shining uniforms and no medals; just killing that went on and on.

On the bridge, the Graf threw back his head and roared.

"Das Schiff sinkt!" he shouted and then he saw her: "Liebchen, she's going down!"

Charlotte went to the window and saw through her tears the lashing of the rain against the glass, the downpour and the churning sea. There was no boat, nothing - it had gone to the bottom.

More innocent lives on her hands.

"Does it not excite you, Liebchen?"

She thought before she spoke for what seemed like the first time ever. She thought of many things, but she said, "Yes, mein Graf."

"When we get to England, we shall have this weather again and nothing will stop us."

"Jawohl!"

# CHAPTER XV

## Miss Deering-Dolittle

Earnestine had fought against the grave until exhausted and now existed in a place beyond panic. The crates had been manhandled and then lifted through the air onto some vessel's open deck. She'd seen glimpses of the merchantman through the knotholes and gaps before her box was surrounded and imprisoned by the rest of the evil cargo and the stygian gloom became impenetrable.

Now, the ship lurched in a storm and waves overflowed the deck. The crates were soaked, the water spilling through the precious air-holes and cracks before flowing out as the ship rose again.

Earnestine's stomach had nothing more to give; she retched still, and drowned in the mix of vomit, salt water and putrefaction.

The dead continued their voyage as if across an endless Styx.

## Miss Georgina

Georgina had fallen, plunged into the wet spray and the cold depths, except that hands had grabbed her, manhandled her and passed her like a baton. Other men, naval sailors, all of whom seemed to be held by others, had taken hold of her in turn. Others leant with all their might striking the hull of the floundering ferry with long poles as they tried to keep the two vessels apart. Each time the sea swelled, the poles connected making bell-like sounds. This new boat appeared to be languishing on its side already half sunk, and as Georgina reached out and held the cold metal rungs, the *Mary* went down so that she reached upwards. Other hands had grabbed hers, pulled her up and then down through a metal hatch.

"Miss Deering-Dolittle," Caruthers said: a familiar face, ruddy and alive.

"Caruthers."

"Mac's ill - sea sick."

"Oh dear," Georgina said. She pushed her dress down into position, soaked and bedraggled though it was. "That's such a shame."

"Indeed. Mac was the one who had the foresight to intercept and follow you."

Caruthers took her by the shoulders and conducted her out of the way. Sailors fell into the ship that was more pipework than superstructure and finally her Arthur joined her. A sailor sprinted up the metal ladder and clanged the hatch closed, spinning the wheel to seal it.

"All in!" Merryweather shouted.

"Dive!"

"Arthur, w-"

A klaxon deafened her and the ship lurched violently: like the *Mary* it went down nose first, buffeted by the waves and then, magically, the rough churning that had become so much part of her life stopped.

It was calm.

The metal deck beneath her levelled and remained level, the tossing, rolling and yawing simply finished.

"*HMS Holland*," McKendry said by way of explanation. He was another familiar face, although pale and green. "I volunteered as the vessel's Able Seaman - or not so Able Seaman as it turned out - and we thought we'd shadow you underwater."

"It uses a petrol engine on the surface, but batteries beneath the waves," Caruthers added. "The French have the *Gymnote* and the Spanish the *Peral*, so we thought we ought to get into the game. We may not be able to get at those blighters in their airships, but they can't get us underwater."

"They have more air though," McKendry said.

"Yes, we'll probably suffocate," said Merryweather happily. His face consisted of one huge smile with his other features forced aside by his obvious joy as he regarded Georgina.

The penny finally dropped: "It's a Nautilus," Georgina said.

"Bruce-Partington finally got the thing working," said Caruthers, "so we thought we'd come and rescue you."

"Although we'll regret it now," McKendry added, "as we're now all breathing the same limited air supply."

"Can't we get more?" Georgina asked.

"We can't risk being bombed by their air power. Now rest, save your strength, do as little as possible," said Caruthers and then he raised his voice: "And that goes for the rest of us."

Georgina sat on the cold damp metal floor as did the crew, squeezing between the pipes and machinery.

"The less we do, the less air we use up," said Merryweather with a gentle squeeze of her hand.

Georgina nodded, shuffled over and lent against him. After a hesitation, he put his arm round her and she closed her eyes.

"That it, sleep," he said. "Best thing."

The noises of the deep, the throb of the engines and the whirr of the propeller were soon Georgina's whole world. The air became stale and as the minutes stretched, a sharp pain developed in her forehead.

Georgina jerked awake; she couldn't get her eyes to open at first. Her head throbbed, worse than ever.

The Nautilus started to rock from side to side, tubes and apparatus began to swing as pendulums. The bow of the vessel rose and it seemed to Georgina that the metal walkway had apparently been built up a mountain. A Naval Rating stumbled at the ladder and fell, Caruthers took his place climbing the stairs. Metal noises clanged above, noises like far, far away voices; a reminder of the world she'd left, of happier times, when she had been alive, for surely this was Hell, and she was one of the dead, tormented by the heat and the dripping foul stench of acid.

A light shone ahead, drawing her closer, but she couldn't move; and then the hatch seemed to shine as tendrils of clarity fell like ink in water, spreading and diffusing. Dirt seemed to rise, sucked up through the hatch, as the hot rank atmosphere of the Nautilus was drawn up and colder air was sucked down to replace it. As the air exchanged, it seemed that a dark lens was removed as the lights better penetrated the fumes.

A cold shock coursed through Georgina as the first of this ventilation reached her. She'd expected something wonderful, cool, like lemonade on a hot summer day, but it stung, full of brine and the rank odour of fish: it was glorious. On her hands and knees, Georgina went forward going up the flow of air like a salmon travelling upstream.

"Get her above!"

Hands and arms came around her body, and she was hoisted aloft. They pushed and pulled her up the metal pipe to the deck. There the last squalls of the storm lashed her, drenched her clothes and froze her skin. Standing on a stone quay, a crowd had gathered: men in their Sunday best, women in the latest fashion and children dressed as sailors with ice creams. They all stared and Georgina raised her leaden arm to wave.

She was alive.

## Miss Charlotte

A crowd had gathered by the edge of the field as the airship glided in to moor. They waved madly, a flickering of movement like a breaking wave. When Charlotte descended, struggling to get her old-fashioned crinoline pushed between the rails of the staircase-on-wheels, she smelt roasting chestnuts. It was like a fair had come into town, except that the airship was the only exhibit in the field and the rest of the stalls were assembled beyond the fence by the road.

They were north of London, somewhere - Charlotte didn't know, but she had recognised the shape of the Thames from maps, the loop by Greenwich and the West India Docks on the Isle of Dogs as they had floated over. The dark shadow of the Zeppelin had rippled over the streets like a shark moving under water.

Functionaries bowed as she stepped down onto British soil.

"Your carriage awaits, mein Graf, and Your Royal Highness."

The horses and the carriage were black. Once she was aboard, a lone woman in a closed carriage with a single man, the Graf drew the window blinds denying her a chance to see her home city. It would have seemed alien, she knew, after being so long away, but it was behind her eyes that the changes had occurred.

"We will ride in an open carriage to our coronation, Liebchen," the Graf said.

"Ja."

It was a short walk from the carriage across the pavement to the Embassy and then she was back on Austro-Hungarian soil. As she crossed, there was an explosion as a man operated a daguerreotype camera, the magnesium burning brightly on the flash lamp held aloft. For a brief moment it was a broadside of light, then she was inside and back in the gloom.

An officer clicked his heels and bowed: "Graf!"

"Our cargo?" Graf Zala replied.

"English, mein Graf?"

"Lieb- Her Royal Highness knows no German."

"Of course, Excellency," he bowed again, this time to Charlotte, and when he turned back to the Graf, he said. "The last delivery is expected directly."

The hallway was large, imposing, with an eagle motif in the hangings. It was marble, built to impress and subjugate. It seemed to Charlotte to tower over her. The weight pressed down, and, as she looked around, she saw the servants standing in a line by the wall cowed, each hoping not to be noticed. She had power, an ability to overawe others, not because of who she was, or anything that she had done, but by right of birth - in her case borrowed. Her eyes came to rest upon a maid at the end, a girl no older than herself. She wished she could exchange places and trade this life to regain her former existence. She understood why that frightened girl had agreed to swap clothes in the Zeppelin so long ago.

Charlotte didn't want to be Princess Whoever anymore, she wanted to be little Lottie Deering-Dolittle again.

# CHAPTER XVI

## Miss Deering-Dolittle

"Did yew 'ear sommat?"

"No... an' neither did yew."

"There, I swear."

"Swear all yew like mate-"

"Sommat's alive."

"No."

"'Ear it?"

"Tha' not payin' us enuff."

Another thud sounded and the lid came off the coffin. From the mouldering innards a hand thrust up, clawing the air and then a face appeared. There was a sudden inhalation of breath, followed by a choking rasp and a flailing of limbs as the creature pulled itself from the grave.

"Oh Lord... run fer it."

Earnestine fell over the edge of the crate, slithering in the muck as she tried to stand, but all she could do was crawl away. She coughed, great black globs of vile mucus. She was... where? The floor was hard, stone, and her fingernails dragged and scratched against it as she struggled away from the mortuary. She found a door and used the handle to pull herself upright.

Beyond was a yard, horses to one side, people in the distance.

A woman screamed, loud and piercing, a full shriek that ended when she ran out of air and fainted.

Earnestine ran a few steps, realised that she wasn't going to escape and so doubled back into the warehouse again. It was the West India Docks, London, but she needed to get away from this warehouse, controlled as it was by the Austro-Hungarians. Perhaps the wide open gates in front of her would lead somewhere.

She stumbled to one side.

Kroll and some other men came in, silhouettes against the sunlight beyond.

The Oberst would help her - surely?

But Earnestine instinctively drew back and she threw herself into a pile of muck and turned her head away.

It was a dock-hand who spoke first: "Tha' was sommat."

"Nonsense. Your imagination." Kroll's voice.

"I swear."

"Gin?"

"Never! Taken the pledge I 'ave."

"Be away."

"'Ere!"

"It's broken from the inside, and look a trail going towards..."

The door creaked open and the men stepped through. Kroll shouted some orders, loud enough to penetrate the wooden wall. After a moment or two, the door opened again.

"So one was still alive." Kroll again.

"Can't get far, surely?" Another voice: someone Earnestine didn't know.

"P'raps."

"Crawled into the sewer to die, no doubt."

"We take no chances. Get these crates into the tunnels as quickly as possible."

"I shall see to it at once, Oberst, there won't be anything for the Peelers to find, if they do come looking."

"Excellent."

A click of the heels, boots marching away, and then the door to the yard creaked again.

Earnestine risked a peek. They hadn't seen her. She was as misshapen and filthy as the muck pile she had fallen onto. She took her chance and ran for the light. It dazzled, brighter than she imagined heaven would be like, and everything was bleached of its colour and form. Gulls cried out in the air and there were distant voices like angels.

She fell off the jetty and landed on the shoreline amongst the pebbles.

Her eyes becoming accustomed, she set off along the bank, clattering as she went. Her one glance back was enough to see a huge warehouse with a ship unloading and the general activity. The crates were going down into the sewers.

Presently, she came across some old women bent double as they picked at the detritus for cockles, whelks and periwinkles.

Earnestine saw the water then, the lovely Thames rippling and shining as it reflected the sunlight. She threw herself down into it, felt the shiver of cold run through her body and she let the water wash away the residue of death. When she emerged, she felt cleaner and alive.

"Awright dearie! Yew don't wan' ter do that. Water's dirty. Full o' muck. Yew catch yaar death."

Earnestine felt bemused.

"Sewer come aht there."

The women pointed to a great outflow tunnel that led to the Thames. It was huge, like a railway tunnel that led into the bowels of the Earth.

"Unless, duck, sailors wan' their dolly mops ter be mermaids smellin' like da sea." She cackled and the other harridans joined in.

"I beg your pardon?" Earnestine demanded.

"Ooh, airs an' graces."

Earnestine stomped up the shore ignoring them and found the stone steps that led up to the road. There she was, suddenly, back in the London she knew. She'd get a cab. Looking down at her clothes, which consisted of the military uniform she'd stolen a lifetime ago, she realised that she was drenched and still as black as pitch.

She was still trying to decide what to do, when a man dressed in rough clothes with a leather apron on came up to her.

"Mornin' Darlin'."

"Good morning."

"What your name then?"

"If you must know, Earnestine."

"I understand the importance of being Earnest."

"Very witty, I'm sure."

"How much lad?"

Earnestine blinked: "How much... lad?"

"You're a woman."

"Of course... what did you think I was!?"

"Well, I don't mind, it's all the same to me."

"What's all the same?"

Earnestine walked away and then realised that she was going east and Kensington was possibly ten miles the other way.

"Do you know anything about the sewers?" she asked a labourer as she passed him.

"Marvels of the age," he said. "If not we'd have cholera and the stinks. Remember the Great Stink of '58?"

"Of course not, I wasn't born then."

"Suit yourself."

"I doubt you were either."

She looked at the entrance again and wondered: "Where does it go?"

"Go? All over London of course, underground. They say there are a hundred miles of tunnels and that be the truth of it."

Earnestine nodded, taking it in.

"I'd have thought you'd have come from the sewers."

"I beg your pardon."

"You pong and that's the truth, but Fred don't mind that."

"I beg your pardon?"

"You pong-"

"I heard."

Earnestine walked along the embankment at first, but then decided to head north to avoid going past the rest of the docks. As she went, she moved into better parts of the city and the glances and pointing increased as she went.

It was shaming.

## Miss Georgina

It was a fine crisp morning along the promenade as Captain Merryweather and Miss Deering-Dolittle took the air. Georgina walked by the iron railings and looked out at a sea that seemed to belong to another realm from the raging depths that had assailed her the previous day. Arthur walked by her side with a discreet distance between them, but even so it seemed unseemly, naughty, to be out alone with a man. Last night she had stayed in a seaside boarding house. It was, of course, the only course of action they could take. After the voyage, the culmination of such a chase across Europe, they had needed to rest and no trains were running to London at that time.

Telegrams had been sent. There was nothing to do, nothing that could be done, and so everything had taken on a holiday flavour. As she'd entered the dining room in the new clothes that had been sent out for, the men had stood and fussed over her: standing, holding a chair out and so forth. She hadn't wanted breakfast, but once the food had arrived she had tucked in with aplomb. Tea, Darjeeling, had been served with devilled kidneys, followed by smoked kippers and ham. The courses then became confused, with Caruthers having his poached eggs before his rolls and butter, and everyone else vice versa. Georgina hadn't had the services of a maid when dressing, and she was grateful for this, because she hadn't been able to tighten her corset properly.

As they walked on, seagulls yawked overhead and the pier came into view. It was such a bright day; she'd have to buy a parasol.

"Georgina?"

"Yes?"

"I was w- wondering... life is short, we must seize our opportunities when they present themselves, so I was thinking, if it is all right with yourself, if you would agree to my asking you a question."

"Yes."

Captain Merryweather's face lit up: "Why thank you, Georgina."

"Yes?"

"Yes?"

"You wanted to ask me a question."

Captain Merryweather's face fell: "Ah, thing is... I wondered, that is to say, w- w- would you consent to be my... if we could..."

"Yes?"

"Get married."

She'd done it.

And she'd bagged a Captain. He hadn't even asked about a dowry (although to be fair she'd not checked whether he could support her in her accustomed lifestyle). All that talk in the dormitory after lights out, all that giggling practice with paper folded to act as a fan: in front of face with right hand, come here; swinging lightly, take me home...

What's more, she was going to enjoy it: "You aren't on one knee," she said.

"Sorry, excuse me, of course," said Captain Merryweather. However, he did not go down on one knee. "I should, of course, ask your father."

"Well, he's exploring... up a river."

"Oh, I see, then perhaps your m- m- mother?"

"She's also exploring... up a river."

The penny dropped for Merryweather: "Oh, you're the Kent Deering-Dolittle family."

"Yes."

"I just assumed you were from the Surrey Deering-Dolittle family."

"No, I'm afraid not. Is that a problem?"

"Well... er... no, of course not."

"I don't know anything about your family."

"Ah, Merryweathers, right. We hail from Dartmoor, where the family seat is. Father, Major Philip Merryweather, was killed at Amoeful, and mother, Agnes... well, it w- w- was an awful shock."

"I'm so sorry."

"It was twenty five years ago, I was young. There was a governess, and Mrs Jago, of course, and good old Fitz."

"You must have admired your father to follow in his footsteps."

"Into the army? Yes. He was a great man. When I have a son I'm going to name him Philip Merryweather after my father."

"That seems most estimable."

"So, I do rather need to ask the acting head of your family."

"That would be Earnestine..." Georgina swallowed: her life was being filled up by this Captain as it was being emptied by the realisation that her sister was gone. "I am the acting head of the family now."

"Yes, of course."

Earnestine had waited, Earnestine had put her sisters first and, upon reflection, that had been a mistake. It was Georgina's turn now and she too would put the Deering-Dolittles first.

"In that case, I will have to ask myself for permission."

Arthur face was filled with such elation.

"I haven't decided to give myself permission: you may ask me?" Georgina nodded towards the ground: once, twice...

"Ah, of course."

Finally Captain Merryweather went down on one knee: "Will you, Georgina, marry me?"

"Hmm, let me consider..."

Arthur looked so crushed and-

"Yes, yes, I will," she said. She did not have the heart to tease him anymore.

"In London, there's a chapel connected to the Club. Caruthers and Mac can be witnesses, so I thought-"

"Now!!?"

His suggestion was shocking, utterly notorious: engagements were supposed to be for six months to three years, and not a single afternoon. No-one got married instantly, not even if they were in the pudding club.

"We should seize our opportunities," Merryweather said.

He was squinting up at her, his face shining in the late morning sun.

"Yes, yes," she said. "Why not?"

In the mad whirl on the way back to the hotel, she bought a new umbrella, an expensive Fox's Paragon 'never inside out', which was much more sensible than a parasol, and it did look like rain.

## Miss Charlotte

Charlotte's plan was simple: swap clothes with the maid and exit via the servant's entrance. She'd got into this by changing clothes, so she could get out of it by changing clothes.

Unfortunately, the servants didn't come and go; they lived in the Embassy and they were all Germanic: English, even at a loud and shrill tone, wasn't understood. So, the maid, who had answered "Olga" to three different phrasings of "can I borrow your clothes?", had left still in her black-and-white uniform.

So, in the end, Charlotte put on her Aerial Corps uniform and marched through all the military preparations as if she was supposed to be there. There were so many soldiers, air corps and officers that she seemed to fit in, and she'd have been in heaven had it not been for the nature of these manoeuvres.

She knew the guards at any exit wouldn't let her just leave, but at the rear of the building, she found an empty room with a sliding window leading to a ledge that she could crawl along. So, risking it, and finding climbing so much easier in trousers, she shimmied down a drainpipe as if the entire Austro-Hungarian Embassy were a tree for scrumping, and then she'd run off down the road. Luckily Kensington wasn't far.

Strangely, there was a carriage waiting outside number 12b, Zebediah Row, and climbing in was a gorgeous woman dressed in white.

"Gina!"

Georgina went pale when she saw Charlotte as if she had seen a ghost.

"Gina... it's me, Charlotte."

"Lottie?"

"Yes."

"Oh thank the Lord, you're alive."

They embraced, holding on to each other for a long moment.

"I have such news... why are you dressed like a man?" Georgina asked.

"I'm an aerial officer. It's got trousers and-"

"Are you wearing your corset?"

"No," said Charlotte. "It didn't go with the uniform."

"A man's uniform - honestly Charlotte, you'll look frumpy. Go and change at once."

Charlotte didn't like that idea, so she changed the subject: "Why are you dressed like that?"

"Charlotte, prepare yourself for a shock."

Charlotte stepped back dubiously.

"Our sister, Earnestine, is... has passed away."

"No, no, she's-"

"And I am getting married."

"Married?"

"Yes."

"Before Earnestine?"

"She's... not with us anymore, so-"

"But she is, she's-"

"So - Charlotte listen - so I'm now the eldest sister and acting head of the family."

"Yes, but-"

"Here."

Georgina passed Charlotte a small package. Charlotte opened it to reveal two sticks of seaside rock.

"Can I eat them now?"

"No, we're going to my wedding."

"But-"

"There'll be cake afterwards," Georgina chided. "Now, go and get changed... oh, the carriage is here already."

"I suppose I'll have to wear my uniform, after all."

Georgina pulled her veil over her face: "Lottie, please don't ruin my wedding."

"I won't, but-"

"There's no buts, Charlotte. We have to seize our opportunities. Arthur says so and I agree with him. This is the calm before the storm and we want to be married while there's still time. If Earnestine were alive, then things would be different, but she's not, and so there it is."

"If Earnestine was alive, then you wouldn't marry?"

"Of course not."

"In that case, congratulations."

# CHAPTER XVII

## Miss Deering-Dolittle

Earnestine was very aware that she looked like a drowned rat. She felt like a drowned rat. She was sore and exhausted. She rang the doorbell twice before Cook answered and she had to say her name three times before she was recognised.

"Been on an adventure, dearie?"

"No, I have not!" Earnestine said emphatically. She was in no mood for frivolity. "A bath please."

"We're in the middle of laundry, Miss, and the maid-"

"A bath!"

"You've just missed Miss Geog-"

"NOW!"

Earnestine was already peeling off her clothes and dropping them like dead animals on the hallway tiles.

"Oh, Miss, I..." The maid ran to start boiling water and filling the tin bath.

"Do you want me to wash these?" said the maid, doubt tingeing every syllable as she touched the filthy garments gingerly with her toe.

"Burn them," said Earnestine. "And don't touch them, I know where they've been. Use the fire tongs."

"Yes, Miss," she curtseyed. "I'll start a fire."

"Not in the house, outside!"

"Yes, Miss."

"But first bring me the brandy."

"Miss, the brandy's been put aside for a special occasion."

"Bring the bal- brandy!"

The maid scurried off.

The hallway was just as she remembered it: the walls and tiled floor tinged with red and blue light as the sun streamed through the stained glass windows of the porch.

The small table was awash with post, including two copies of *The Strand Magazine* (she'd have to hide those from Charlotte), and the hallstand with father's hat still hanging there. She caught sight of herself in the mirror and didn't recognise herself either.

While the bath was filled, Earnestine had, quite sensibly, washed standing up in an attempt to remove most of the stains. Three flannels lay in a heap, dirty and probably destined for the fire once they'd dried out. It was a hardship she endured in order to fully appreciate the hot bath.

Quite soon, Earnestine was soaking in the family tin bath, it was hot, wonderful, frothy from various concoctions she'd dumped in, and she knocked back the brandy from the bottle. When she reached for a second swig, her hand clinked loudly against the bottle. Something black filled her hand.

In sudden desperation, she cleaned, and the ruby shone in its silver setting once more. Not that she was bothered, of course; it was just a silly trinket forced on her by a foolish young man and actually quite ostentatious. Turned around on the third finger of her left hand, it looked more tasteful and like a wedding ring... No. Ridiculous.

She put it back on the middle finger of her left hand, where it felt most comfortable. Wait... just because he'd put it on that finger didn't mean she had agreed. There was no understanding between them.

She took it off again and slid it over her index finger. There! No longer engaged, she was now looking for a husband. In fact, no she wasn't. She wanted nothing to do with men, so she took the ring again and placed it around her little finger. Now she displayed to the world that she intended to die a maid. Unfortunately, the ring did not fit well upon that finger being too loose.

Having tried every finger, she took it off for a fourth time to study it. The ruby was warm and red, which she supposed signified... absolutely not! She felt nothing for him and she ought to just give it back.

She placed it carefully on the floor and then lay back to enjoy the warm water.

What to do?

That was the question...

Dead, bodies, drowning!

She spluttered to the surface and realised that, glorious though this was, she was in no fit state to stay in the bath. To have survived that perilous journey and then to drown in a bath would not do at all, so she got out. She started shivering: the cold, not anything to do with fear, of course, and the brandy on a very empty stomach made her light headed and woozy. She called for the maid to bring her something to eat and scoffed down a ham with pickle sandwich in her room. Her room! It was surreal to be back in Kensington as if... but things had happened, terrible things and there were worse things coming. There was an army hidden in London. There was not a moment to lose.

But she was so tired and she ached, and the sheets were clean: forty winks perhaps.

Earnestine did not fall asleep as soon as her head hit the proverbial pillow. Instead, she held onto the hard object she'd secreted under her pillow and she didn't think of him at all - obviously - and quite soon she was fast asleep.


## Miss Georgina

In the chapel's antechamber the two sisters fussed over each other.

"Do I look beautiful?" Georgina asked. She was very aware of Charlotte's sudden examination.

"Yes, you do and... I'm proud to be your Maid of Honour."

"Thank you."

"Are you nervous?"

"Terrified."

Charlotte gripped her sister's hand and squeezed: "You'll be fine."

"Thank you," she said, but it wasn't enough. "Go and see."

Charlotte snuck off to look into the chapel, which gave Georgina another chance to check herself in the small mirror on the wall. Yes, she thought, trying to be objective and view herself as a stranger would for the first time: she had a trim figure, and her bustle gave her a shapely womanly figure, her dark hair in ringlets framed her round open face.

"Gina!?"

Georgina turned back, panicked: "What is it?"

Charlotte's face beamed and she was almost jumping up and down with excitement: "They're all in uniform!"

"And they ready for us?"

Charlotte nodded.

Georgina knew it was all too quick, too rushed and she was seized by a feeling of dread. This was a mistake: surely she knew that, and she so wanted Earnestine's wise and forthright counsel. Should she? Shouldn't she? Earnestine would have known at once. But then, of course, her very presence would have made it impossible.

"Who are you marrying?" Charlotte asked.

Georgina beamed, happy, feeling suddenly and utterly ready: "Arthur."

"Is he a good man?"

"Oh yes."

"Then I approve."

"Thank you."

Charlotte turned her sister towards the door and gave her the tiniest of pushes.

Georgina took her first step towards the threshold of a new life. The hush was almost overpowering and then the organ started up. She walked slowly, trying not to tremble. All the officers to her right looked so strong and upright as they stood to attention, whereas the left hand side was empty: all her relatives, the Kent Deering-Dolittles were in their own procession to the source of a river or like Earnestine... best not to think about that now.

There was only Uncle Jeremiah, dear befuddled Uncle Jeremiah with his white sideburns and whiskers and his hair askew. He eased himself around, smiled up at her over his half-moon glasses and put his hands together in prayer and praise.

'Oh, oh, Gina,' he silently mouthed, utterly entranced.

When Georgina reached the front she couldn't see the empty pews. By then, she only had eyes for her Captain.

The Chaplain spoke, a disembodied voice almost, as Georgina could only really see her veil and vague ghostly shadows beyond. Only Arthur was close enough to be real.

"Dearly beloved, we are gathered together here in the sight of God, and in the face of this congregation, to join together this Man and this Woman in holy Matrimony..."

It's really happening, Georgina thought.

"...unadvisedly, lightly, or wantonly, to satisfy men's carnal lusts and appetites, like brute beasts that have no understanding..."

Georgina wondered about the words 'wantonly', 'carnal' and 'lusts'.

"First," the Chaplain continued: "It was ordained for the procreation..."

'Procreation' was another such word.

"Secondly, It was ordained for a remedy against sin, and to avoid fornication..."

And 'fornication'.

"Thirdly…"

It was all a whirl, passing too quickly!

"…Therefore if any man can shew any just cause, why they may not lawfully be joined together, let him now speak, or else hereafter for ever hold his peace."

The silence was palpable, a heaviness that settled over everyone and for Georgina it went on for a geological age. Finally, the Chaplain looked down from his step, his face very serious.

"I require and charge you both, as ye will answer at the dreadful day of judgement when the secrets of all hearts shall be disclosed, that if either of you know any impediment..."

She wasn't the eldest, she thought: it should have been Earnestine's turn. It wasn't fair! While she worried, the Chaplain turned to Arthur and asked him a lot of questions.

"I will," Arthur answered clearly.

"Georgina Victoria Alexandrina Deering-Dolittle," said the Chaplain, and it snapped her back into the present, "wilt thou have this man to thy wedded husband, to live together after God's ordinance in the holy estate of Matrimony? Wilt thou obey him, and serve him, love, honour, and keep him in sickness and in health; and, forsaking all other, keep thee only unto him, so long as ye both shall live?"

Georgina couldn't seem to get her throat to work.

She felt Charlotte's nudge from her left.

"I will."

"Who giveth this woman to be married to this man?"

There was another silence, this one filled with scrapes and shuffles.

"My father is..." Georgina began, but she couldn't think of the words.

"I will," Charlotte piped in.

"Oh!" said the Chaplain, looking down his nose.

"She is dressed for it," said Caruthers and a titter went around the congregation. "Bloomerism clearly has its uses."

"Yes, yes, of course, why not," said Georgina, all of a fluster. She put her right hand in Charlotte's right hand, who passed it to the Chaplain, who placed it in turn into

Arthur's safekeeping, who had already promised to always keep her safe.

Charlotte stepped back smartly and joined the ranks of soldiers as if she was some brand of junior rating.

Facing each other, hand in hand with Georgina, Arthur repeated each phrase after the Chaplain as if somehow she was marrying both of them, and so, despite the repetition, Georgina didn't follow any of the echoed words.

Arthur let go.

Georgina was confused and then realised that it was her turn to take his right hand in her right hand.

"I, Georgina Victoria Alexandrina," said the Chaplain.

Funny, she thought, that he had the same name as she did.

"I, Georgina Victoria Alexandrina," he repeated.

"I, Georgina Victoria Alexandrina," she said, and then it all came tumbling out. All those peeks ahead in the prayer book during boring sermons and all the late night rehearsals that had taken place in her mind since before she could remember took over and the rush was exhilarating: "Yes... I take thee Arthur Philip Merryweather to my wedded husband, to have and to hold from this day forward, for better for worse, for richer for poorer, in sickness and in health, to love, cherish, and to obey, till death us do part, according to God's holy ordinance; and thereto I give thee my troth."

Arthur took his hand back and turned away from her.

"Caruthers," he murmured.

"Ah," said Caruthers, stepping smartly up: "Right you are."

Caruthers put their rings on the bible that the Chaplain held open. The Chaplain blessed it and handed it back to Arthur like a waiter delivering with a tray. Arthur took it, took her left hand and gently encircled her fourth finger. Her heart trembled as he did so.

"With this ring-" the Chaplain said.

"With this ring I thee wed," Arthur began and then he too took over to speak it all as she had done, "with my body I thee worship, and with all my... worldly goods I thee endow."

The Chaplain took over: "In the Name of the Father, and of the Son, and of the Holy Ghost. Amen,"

"Amen," murmured with increasing volume around the chapel.

"Let us pray," said the Chaplain.

Everyone knelt, although the happy couple struggled because of Georgina's dress until Charlotte came to the rescue to straighten it out. By the time Georgina was settled, the Chaplain had finished the prayer.

"Amen," everyone said.

"Those whom God hath joined together let no man put asunder," he said, before standing tall and facing the whole congregation. "Forasmuch as Arthur Philip Merryweather and Georgina - excuse me - Georgina Victoria Alexandrina Deering-Dolittle have consented together in holy wedlock, and have witnessed the same before God and this company, and thereto have given and pledged their troth either to other, and have declared the same by giving and receiving of a Ring, and by joining of hands; I pronounce that they be Man and Wife together, In the Name of the Father, and of the Son, and of the Holy Ghost. Amen."

"Amen."

Charlotte came forward and lifted Georgina's veil back. Magically colour came into the world for Georgina as the Chaplain spoke about life everlasting.

"Amen."

"Psalm sixty seven: Deus Misereatur, God be merciful unto us."

Everyone stood, fumbled with their hymn books and sang: God be merciful unto us.

After the standing, it was kneeling again as the Chaplain read from the Book of Common Prayer and the congregation gave the responses. Georgina and Arthur exchanged a smirk. She was happy, he was happy, so she was happy twice.

"...by whose gracious gift mankind is increased: We beseech thee, assist with thy blessing these two persons, that they may both be fruitful in procreation of children..."

That was a good idea, Georgina thought, children, although how precisely that worked she was unsure.

Everyone said "Amen", so Georgina did too, and then there was another "Amen".

She must concentrate, she thought, to remember it all, so that she and her Arthur could talk about it in the years to come, but the Chaplain's words were a buzz: Adam and Eve, the touching duty of a wife to her husband. Arthur had to love her, the two of them shall be one flesh, he was to honour her as unto the weaker vessel.

And Saint Paul had advice for her: she was to submit herself to her husband. She wanted to, but she wasn't precisely sure what was meant. They could hold hands now, she knew that, and walk side-by-side in the park *without a chaperone*. Indeed, they didn't need to be separated at night, which was simply an astonishing thought.

"...and are not afraid with any amazement," the Chaplain said: "And, to finish, may I be the first to say: you did it without a single stutter - well done, Merry."

He held out his hand, which Arthur shook, and the congregation with their deep voices, all said: "Well done, Merry."

"Yee ha!" McKendry whooped, which suited the mood perfectly.

# Miss Charlotte

Charlotte had been allowed champagne, which was fizzy but nothing like lemonade at all. The officers at the reception had been tall and smart with wonderful uniforms, and she'd caught the hiccups.

All too soon all the cake was gone, and everyone was waving the happy couple off. They were only going to a hotel, but it was the Savoy.

"I'll be fine," said Georgina as she held Charlotte's hand. "I know what to do."

"Hmm," Charlotte mumbled.

Uncle Jeremiah bade her farewell, holding her hand in both of his.

"My dear," he said. "You know about the birds and the bees?"

"Oh yes," Georgina replied. "I've studied: ornithology, entomology and lepidoptera - I have an excellent butterfly collection."

"Excellent, excellent," said Uncle Jeremiah, who, as usual, was not really listening.

Merryweather joined them having escaped from his colleagues. He held the carriage's door open and helped his new wife, Mrs Arthur Merryweather - just imagine, her sister married - up the steps. With a last wave, they were away clattering down the street.

Caruthers hailed a hansom cab for Charlotte and another for Uncle Jeremiah. The old man had insisted she take the first.

Charlotte was happy and content as she turned into Zebediah Row and saw the sycamore trees that she remembered so well. The road had been named after Samson Zebediah, who was famous for having a road named after him and nothing else. It would be remembered now for the road on which the Deering-Dolittle Sisters lived. Omnibuses would bring nosey visitors to the street who would point and buy souvenirs from street hawkers. Their house was on the odd side of the street: 12b, and the gate creaked open to welcome her home.

Charlotte pulled the cord to ring the doorbell. Through the mottled glass, she saw a shadow loom towards the door. Cook would let her in, and after she'd refused more cake from the woman, she'd have a lie down. The strange shape opened the door and became Earnestine.

"Ness!"

"Charlotte, what time do you call this?"

"Ness! You're here."

"Evidently I'm going to get no sense out of you. Where's your chaperone, I'd like a word with her. Lottie, out of the way!"

Earnestine pushed past into the empty pathway, tut-tutted and then opened the little gate with its angry creak and went onto the pavement. She looked right and left, right and left again, and then came back.

"Where is your chaperone?"

"I didn't have one," said Charlotte.

Earnestine did that startled tic with her eyes, blinking, and then her lips narrowed: "I see," she said.

Earnestine went inside leaving Charlotte in the porch. Charlotte followed and saw that Earnestine had gone into the drawing room, the room that was sealed from the dust for special occasions. When she went in, Earnestine was standing by the fireplace, her hands held together in front of her and a stern expression on her face.

Charlotte waited: she knew there was no point in saying anything.

"Well," said Earnestine. "I'm waiting for an explanation."

"I caught a cab home from the Regimental Club-"

"Regimental Club?!"

"We had ham with little... and then cake, wedding cake, and-"

"Wedding cake?!"

"Fruit cake with marzipan and icing with-"

"I know what wedding cake is."

She wants an explanation, but she won't let me finish a sentence, Charlotte thought.

"Go on," said Earnestine.

"I had champagne and it made me burp."

"Charlotte Deering-Dolittle, you are-"

"Gina let me."

"I will have to have words with Georgina Deering-Dolittle as well."

"Well, you can't, she's married."

"We'll see about that... Charlotte! It's bad enough that you've been gallivanting without having to make up lies about it."

"She is married."

"Don't be absurd: Georgina is the middle sister, she simply wouldn't get married before her elder sister. I am the eldest, I am not married, ergo: she is not married."

"She is."

"Why would she do that? Pray tell me. Although why I humour you, I don't know."

"She's in love."

Earnestine blinked, her lips practically disappeared: "I see."

"She thought you were dead, so... that made her the elder sister, so it's all right really."

"All right really!? I'm here, aren't I?" Earnestine put her hand on her bosom as if Charlotte didn't know who Earnestine was. "I'm alive, therefore she is not the elder sister, therefore she has no right to get married."

"Georgina was lovely and the service was lovely and everyone was so nice and you are so horrid... just because you're an old maid."

"I am not an old maid."

"You're twenty!"

"Listen-"

But Charlotte didn't listen: she talked: "Georgina was the eldest for a couple of days and she got married, whereas you've been the eldest for simply years and years and years and haven't got married once. And there are girls who are grandmothers at your age."

"Don't exaggerate," Earnestine said. "Where is Georgina now?"

Charlotte kept quiet.

Earnestine stepped forward, grabbed Charlotte by her ear and twisted. Charlotte yelped.

"Where?"

"I'm not telling - ah, ah - the Savoy."

Earnestine let go.

Charlotte refused to rub her ear: she wasn't going to give Earnestine the satisfaction, but it hurt so much.

Earnestine went back to her pose by the fireplace, blinked and her lips tightened: "The Savoy, you say."

"Yes."

"Right!" Earnestine announced and she went for the door.

Charlotte tried to get in her way, but nothing could stop Earnestine once her mind was made up and she marched down the path to the road. The gate squeaked in protest as it closed.

Earnestine shouted, her hand aloft: "Cab!"

When people wanted a cab, there never was one, but now that Charlotte wanted them to stay away, one was passing. It turned and sidled back to the pavement.

Charlotte intercepted Earnestine.

"You can't go there!" Charlotte threw her arms wide, physically barring the way to the hansom. Earnestine took a step forward forcing Charlotte back until the youngest reached the door itself, her hands gripping the frame on either side

"You can't!"

"Why not?"

"Because... I don't know... it's her special night."

"Special night? What are you prattling about?"

"She thought you were dead."

"So, she'll want to know I'm alive straight away."

"I think she'd prefer to know in the morning."

"Nonsense." Earnestine prised Charlotte's fingers from the frame and wrenched her away. "And, Lottie, we'll have to have words about your attitude."

"On your head be it," Charlotte whined.

"On my head be what?"

Earnestine grabbed the door handle, pulled and-

"I told you, I keep telling you, but you don't listen."

Earnestine stepped back: "I beg your pardon?"

"She got married in a chapel and everything, and now she's gone to the Savoy with her new husband."

For a moment, Earnestine was speechless, but only for a moment: "I see."

"Yes, she thought you were dead and-"

"She thought I was dead and so the first thing she did was fling herself at the nearest man."

Charlotte beamed: "He's a Captain."

"I might have known," said Earnestine. "I caught her hanging around with one on the Continent and now... she's far too forward. She'll get a reputation."

"He's a Gentleman Adventurer."

"An adventurer? What sort of profession is that to look after Georgina?"

"He's a good man and-"

"Charlotte - go to your room!"

That was that: Charlotte went to her room.

# CHAPTER XVIII

## Miss Deering-Dolittle

The doorman of the Savoy didn't want ladies of her sort, he said, so Earnestine tore him down a strip. She assured him that she was not a lady of any sort! Once he was on the back foot and in his place, she stormed up to the front desk.

"Tell me at once which room Mister and Mrs..."

There was a long pause.

"Miss?"

"The newlyweds?"

"Captain and Mrs Merryweather-"

"Merryweather!"

She might have guessed. It was the man she'd caught her sister with under that tarpaulin before anything happened. And now, anything could have happened or *be happening*.

"They are in Room 802, which has a private bathroom and, like the rest of the hotel, is fully lit by electricity."

"I see."

"You can take the all-electric lift to the eighth floor," the clerk explained, and he pointed.

The all-electric lift soon deposited Earnestine on the eighth floor. Room 802 was very nearby and Earnestine marched to the door, turned the knob and went straight in.

The cosy bedroom had a huge bed, a few other pieces of furniture beside the bed, and there were flowers on the bedside cabinet and the bed was made up with fresh, white bed-linen along with bedding, and a man's pyjamas on one side of the bed and a woman's night attire on the other side of the bed. What was her sister thinking: being alone in a room with a man *and a bed*?

It was indeed lit by electricity and the lights were on, but there was no-one home.

Perhaps, she thought, they might be-

The latch opened on another door and a deep male voice preceded a figure.

Earnestine did the only thing she could do and hid in the wardrobe.

"So, erm..."

It was Captain Merryweather: clearly he had survived capture in Strasburg and managed to reach England.

"Yes, dearest," Georgina replied. Dearest indeed, Earnestine thought.

"Darling, I could... do you want..."

Earnestine was incensed: now a 'darling' from him.

"Whatever you think is best, dearest."

"Oh. Right. Erm..."

"Dearest?"

"I'll... erm... wait outside for a short while."

"Don't be too long."

Earnestine heard the main door open and Merryweather leave, followed by that irritating humming that Georgina did when she was happy. Now was the time to emerge and tell Georgina exactly what Earnestine thought of this outrageous... only Earnestine wasn't at all sure what she thought, exactly.

There was a rustle of bedclothes.

Silence.

Well, she wasn't going to stay in the wardrobe all night. She'd spent far too much time in confining wooden boxes recently and... best not think about that.

A knock at the door: *rat-a-tat-tat*.

"Come in, dearest."

The door creaked, much as Earnestine's curled-up knees threatened to echo.

"Ah yes, erm..." Merryweather said. "Darling."

There was some... what was that?

The famous electric illumination of the Savoy went out. It was dark at first, but then Earnestine saw that the slice of light from the gap between the doors had simply changed colour: no longer the bright and unearthly orange but a softer bluish tone caused by light from the window.

"Dearest, may I look?" Georgina said gently.

"Darling... erm... of course."

"Oh, my word."

There was something sharp sticking up in Earnestine's back: an umbrella or a parasol.

"Good heavens, is it supposed to do that?" Georgina asked.

"Perhaps we should start with a kiss, darling."

"Of course!"

"I meant on your lips rather than your hand."

"Oh, sorry, dearest."

That was it! Earnestine was going to - ow, that was sharp - if she could get up and... because they weren't even engaged. They were married.

"You can take your hand down, dear."

"Sorry, dearest, there."

They probably were allowed to kiss on the lips. But they hardly knew each other, which made little difference, but even so... perhaps she could offer to be their chaperone?

"Darling, I'll just..."

"Of course, oh!"

The issue, perhaps - and Earnestine felt guilty about this - was that she'd kissed Pieter on the lips. Well, he'd kissed her, but she'd let him. Or rather she hadn't stopped him, but then she hadn't known what he was going to do so, until it was too late, and he had. So, in effect she'd missed it, which was doubly cruel of him.

"Dearest," Georgina simpered. "Could you perhaps stop being so gentle and do... whatever it is you are supposed to do?"

"Sorry, darling."

"Surrey."

Her sister was slurring her words now. She'd probably drunk a lot of wine thinking she was a proper adult now she was married, but she was only seventeen.

Georgina started again: "Kent, Surrey."

"Sorry?"

"No, Surrey."

"I beg your pardon?"

"Kent, Surrey, Dorset, Essex, Sus - ah - sex, Middle - oh - sex..."

"What are you doing?"

"The Home Counties."

"Pardon?"

"I thought I'd start with the Home Counties... why have you stopped?"

"It's a little distracting."

"Really?"

"A little... darling."

"I thought... well, dearest, I mean to say."

"I don't suppose you could explain why?"

"We were told to... lie back and think of England."

"I see."

"So I thought I'd start with the Home Counties."

"Ah. Darling, do you have to do it aloud?"

"No, I don't suppose so."

Earnestine decided she'd have nothing to do with gentlemen: they were nothing but trouble. She saw no purpose in turning out the lights to play *I, Spy* or *Geography* games... or whatever. Georgina had married the first man she'd come across and was currently doing whatever it was that she was doing, and silly Charlotte... well, the less said about her predilection for cadets the better. No, Earnestine had fallen in love with Pieter and-

Earnestine sat bolt upright.

"Arthur! What was that?"

"Nothing darling."

"Oh dearest."

"I thought I heard something too."

"Please, Arthur, I'm working up the Pennines."

She'd gone and fallen in love with Pieter. It was stunningly obvious. Of all the stupid things for her to have gone and done.

"Nor- folk, Suf- f- folk. Folk."

"You're doing it again, darling."

"Staffordshire... Rut - rut - land."

"Ah!"

"Riding! Riding!"

"Yes, yes."

"*Cum*... bria!"

What she needed to do was-

What on Earth had those two just done?

What had she just missed?

The two on the bed let out long sighs and there was the ruffling of bedclothes. Perhaps, thought Earnestine, she could wait until they'd fallen asleep and then sneak out quietly.

"Arthur dearest."

"Yes, my darling."

"I've just thought of some more counties, mostly in the Midlands, so would you mind, my love."

"Of course, dear, if you'd give me a few moments to recruit myself."


## Mrs Arthur Merryweather

In the morning, Georgina found herself thinking of Earnestine, which was understandable as she missed her sister, and dreaming about her dear Arthur. She found it hard not to compare the two. Usually newly married brides - she smiled - who had looked up to their fathers, now looked up to their husbands. They were their new guardians after all. This change of regime obviously brought new freedoms and curtailed others. However, as her own father had never really been present and

Earnestine had so powerfully filled that dominant niche in her life, it was therefore Earnestine she compared to Arthur. Her sister was like a low pitched grating sound: whereas whenever she thought of Arthur it was with a sigh. He was a very handsome husband, and caring too. He'd gone down to breakfast early to leave her time to get ready, and... but there was this growling sensation, a constant reminder somehow of Earnestine. Perhaps it was the new-fangled electric light? Did they snort? She'd no idea, but, by stopping to look at the strange bulb in the centre of the room, she herself was no longer bustling around the room, and, as she was silent, the noise seemed louder. It was a buzz and a snort as if the gas phutted and popped? She expected the Savoy to have thicker walls. She went back to sorting out her clothes, folding some in the chest of drawers, which was by the window, and the longer dresses, which she turned to the wardrobe to deposit-

"Bally Hell!"

The figure slumped with the shoes and her new umbrella jerked upright: "Pieter... Gina! Don't swear!"

Earnestine half-fell out and half-staggered to her feet, bent and old looking like some Horrible Helga come back to haunt her. Already Georgina could taste soap in her mouth.

"What! Wardrobe... alive... in my... what?"

"Georgina, do try and use proper sentences when you speak."

"Sorry, Ness," Georgina mumbled. She hung her head down. This was awful. She should be pleased to see her sister; she was, but she also felt like a naughty girl caught with her hand in the biscuit tin. And in a man's bedroom too.

"Charlotte tells me... well, I want to hear it from your own lips."

"Hear what?"

Earnestine's own lips tightened and her arm shot out to point at the bed.

"I'm married," said Georgina.

"That may be, but it is a matter for discussion. Clearly I need to see this gentleman's financial records, before I could possibly consider consenting to such a match."

"It's too late, I'm married."

"It's not too late to have it annulled."

"I consider it far too late."

"That's for me to decide."

"It isn't."

"Don't be childish."

"Am not, and you can't tell me not to be childish."

"Of course I can."

"You cannot."

"Can."

"Cannot."

"Can... why ever not?"

"I outrank you."

"I beg your pardon?"

"I am a married woman," said Georgina, "whereas you are just a spinster."

Earnestine blinked: "I see."

And Georgina stood upright: shoulders back, chest out, head up, because she realised that, for the first time ever, she could do anything, anything at all (with Arthur's permission naturally) she wanted, and so she was finally free of the eldest sister's dominion.

Georgina reached into the wardrobe and took out an umbrella.

"Here," she said. "A present from the seaside."

"Yes."

"It's a Fox's Paragon, never inside out."

"Thank you."

"You're welcome."

"Did you get anything for Charlotte?"

"Of course. But she's eaten it already."

"I see."

"My husband," Georgina declared, "will be waiting. Come along, sister."

And with that Georgina swept out allowing herself a big smile once she passed Earnestine, who followed in her wake.

## Miss Charlotte

Charlotte didn't see why they had to wait for Earnestine and Georgina, but they did. She tried not to fidget. Finally, the two made their entrance, Georgina looking radiant followed by a rather bedraggled Earnestine. The men stood: Captain Merryweather held the chair out for Georgina and McKendry for Earnestine. Caruthers had held the chair out for her earlier and he was the senior officer, so Charlotte felt she was ahead on points.

They all sat.

Earnestine mouthed 'what are you wearing?' at Charlotte, who pretended not to understand.

"Sorry to barge in on you all before breakfast," Caruthers said, "but there are matters to discuss. Tea?"

Charlotte had had tea already with her toast and marmalade.

A pot was finally brought and the small milk jug topped up.

"We need a plan of action," said Caruthers.

It seemed obvious to Charlotte: "Get the army and shoot the lot of 'em."

"Charlotte, language" Earnestine snapped.

Georgina coughed.

Earnestine blinked rapidly and sat back.

"Thank you," said Georgina. "And Charlotte, please watch what you say."

They were both telling her off now. Wasn't she the prodigal daughter returned to the British side, even if she was still wearing the enemy uniform? Surely, that entitled her to a fatted calf with pickle and trifle for dessert?

Caruthers summed up the situation: "The Austro-Hungarians, the faction headed by Graf Zala at least, are preparing for war. Or that's the suspicion."

"It's not a suspicion," Charlotte said.

"How can you possibly know that?" Georgina asked.

"He told me."

"We know about their airships and the ordinance they've been stockpiling, but perhaps if each of you would tell us what you know," Caruthers suggested. "Miss Deering-Dolittle?"

Earnestine said nothing.

"Earnestine, please," Georgina prompted.

"The enemy have been transporting corpses across Europe-"

That was horrible: "Corpses!?"

"Yes, Charlotte, please be quiet."

"Yes, Charlotte, quiet," Georgina repeated: "Please."

Earnestine continued: "Corpses, which they have been unloading at the West India Docks. These they have hidden somewhere within the London sewers."

"There's probably a hidden entrance to the sewers from their embassy," said Caruthers. "But why transport corpses?"

"I know," said Charlotte.

Earnestine said nothing.

"Go on," said Georgina.

"Well," said Charlotte. "It's called the Mordant process after Doctor Elizabeth Mordant. I met her in the castle and she was nice at first, and then really unpleasant. But the point is, and I saw this happen, they have this apparatus, which uses galvanic energy, sparks and everything, jolly scary, to erm... bring back from the dead people who have died. And then they control them with a little brass box that makes sparks and gets them to do whatever they want."

"I've seen that," Earnestine said.

"So have I," Georgina added.

"Galvanic power can be used for many things," said Merryweather. "This hotel for example is lit by electric light and the lift is powered with it. The theatre next door is, I believe, the first building to be lit entirely by galvanic engineering."

"Frogs legs can be made to twitch with it," said McKendry. "And so it's not a huge leap to imagine bringing a whole creature, even a human being, back to life and make a Vodou Zombi for real."

Charlotte giggled: "Huge leap... frog... sorry."

"You'd need a lot of power," said Merryweather.

"The machines in the castle were simply huge," Charlotte added, trying to make up for her silliness. "And they only raised one person."

"Could it be something to do with that silver iodide?" Earnestine suggested.

"The sample that Miss Deering-Dolittle brought back," Merryweather added.

"I studied daguerreotypes and it's part of the developing process," Georgina said.

"Perhaps, dear, they mean to take pictures to plan an attack."

"There is too much for that, dearest."

"It is the final piece of this puzzle and I'm sure we'll fathom it out," said Caruthers, "and we would never have got this far without the gallant help of you Deering-Dolittle sisters. Oh... my apologies, Mrs Merryweather."

"Once a Deering-Dolittle, always a Deering-Dolittle," said Georgina.

"We're a club!" said Charlotte.

"I think it would be best to be a Society," Earnestine said. "The Society of the Deering-Dolittle Sisters of Kent."

"We're the Derring-Do Club," Charlotte insisted.

"Charlotte please," said Earnestine.

"Let her have her fun," Georgina said.

"She needs to-" Earnestine stopped, almost bit her lip. "Very well, Mrs Merryweather."

"Well, the Derring-Do Club has our profound thanks," said Caruthers. He stood, and the other men stood too. "Now, if you'll excuse us, it's time for you young ladies to leave it to us men."

# CHAPTER XIX

## Miss Deering-Dolittle

They ordered more toast.

It was so infuriating: they were just sitting around while the Austro-Hungarian carried out their machinations.

But the men would deal with it, Earnestine knew, and they should stay at home even though a terrible conflict was approaching. They'd win through; of course they would, they were British. She should do something, but that smacked of a lack of faith in the men and it would be an adventure. And Pieter was on the other side and she didn't want to act against him.

"What's that?" Georgina asked.

"Nothing!"

Earnestine took her hand away from the ruby ring, now dangling from a silver chain around her neck and hidden beneath her clothing. She was only wearing it in case the opportunity arose to return it, and for no other reason whatsoever. In fact, she decided she'd take it off as soon as she could and to remove all other reminders of Austro-Hungarians.

"When we get home, you'll take that ridiculous uniform off," Earnestine said to Charlotte.

"What's it like being married?" Charlotte asked.

"It's..." Georgina looked at Earnestine and went red, "nice."

"I've been engaged three times now," said Charlotte, "but only married once."

Earnestine dropped the butter knife: "Three times!?"

Charlotte counted them off on her fingers: "Prince Pieter, Graf Zala and the Crown Prince."

"And married?" Georgina asked.

"Well, technically he was dead, so it probably doesn't count."

"Was he alive when you married?"

"Yes, but then he died."

"So you should be in mourning clothes."

"Oh no, he's alive again."

"This galvanic process?"

"Yes."

They buttered toast and spooned marmalade.

"And you, Ness?" Charlotte asked.

Earnestine felt like she'd been miles away: "And me?"

"Have you had a proposal yet?"

"Absolutely not!" Earnestine realised she was fiddling with the lump on her chest. "Can we change the subject please?"

They ate in silence. None of them fancied the kippers.

After breakfast they caught a hansom cab back to Zebediah Row.

"You should change now," Earnestine said, absently. She thought of the men going to save them all and wondered if they'd mind if she went to watch - just to watch, nothing more. Adventures were behind her, of course, but watching would be acceptable, surely?

"Can I wear it indoors?" Charlotte announced. "No-one will see."

Earnestine gave her a look: "We're not having rampant bloomerism in this house. You will change at once."

They all climbed the stairs to Charlotte's bedroom.

"Do I really need to change?"

"You need to wear a dress, Lottie," said Georgina.

"You need a clip round the ear," said Earnestine.

Charlotte turned to Georgina: "Gina! Tell her she can't talk to me like that."

She was annoying, Earnestine thought, particularly when one was trying to think: "Don't whine."

"Ness, be nice," Georgina said.

"Georgina, spare the rod, spoil-"

"This one!" said Charlotte, holding aloft her pretty party dress. She hung it on the wardrobe door and began to unbutton her flying tunic.

"Perhaps this dress instead," Georgina suggested, picking out something more sensible.

"Wash!" said Earnestine.

Charlotte stuck out her tongue, dropped her trousers on the floor and went off to find some water for her wash bowl.

"Charlotte!" Earnestine admonished: "Who's going to pick that up?"

"My maid," said Charlotte as a Parthian shot.

"Your maid!?"

Charlotte was no longer in the room, but her voice carried: "I'm a Princess."

"Right!" said Earnestine, but Georgina stopped her.

"Be nice."

"I'm going to wash her mouth out with soap."

"You are not."

"I am."

"Are not."

"Gina, don't be childish, we have to be the adults here. You are too soft."

"I am not."

"You-"

"You are too harsh."

"You have to be looked after."

"I am married. Arthur looks after me."

"Then move in with your husband and leave the rest of the family to get along without your interference."

Charlotte came back: "Help me with my dress."

"Corset," said Earnestine.

"Oh, noooo!"

"Yes, corset," said Georgina.

They found a suitable whalebone and flipped it around Charlotte.

"Breathe in," Georgina suggested.

"I am breathing in," Charlotte insisted.

The two elder sisters came around the back of the younger once she was clipped in and each took a lace cord.

"She needs to be put straight," said Earnestine.

"I know, but she doesn't need to be yanked into place, a gentle pull can be more effective."

Earnestine pulled sharply, tightening her side: "Cruel to be kind."

Charlotte gasped.

Georgina took a stance and pulled gradually: "There, there, see."

"But you run the risk of leaving her to become loose."

"I think you'll find that-"

"You need to be strong," said Earnestine and she yanked hard on the lace on her side.

"Ow!"

"Firmness, but not brute force, is needed," said Georgina and she pulled too.

"That's... oh- ah!"

Earnestine brought her knee up to brace against Charlotte's back: "A short leash."

She pulled.

"Arrghhh!"

"Don't be a baby, Char-"

"Ness! Here!" said Georgina, pushed Earnestine aside and bringing her knee up. "Gradual control is what's needed."

"Aaah."

Earnestine stepped in and hoicked again.

Charlotte tottered where she stood: "-n't bre-."

Georgina loosened the laces slightly: "Some give and take."

"Aaaaaa..."

"She might become undone," said Earnestine.

"A little care and she'll be fine," Georgina said, finishing off with a tidy bow.

"What are you two talking about?" Charlotte demanded. "No, no, I'll put my own dress on, thank you."

Earnestine sighed and wondered what was happening at the Austro-Hungarian Embassy. Men were most likely risking their lives.

"Why do you keep touching the top of your bodice like that?" Georgina asked.

"I do not," said Earnestine, jerking her hand down.

## Mrs Arthur Merryweather

Georgina prepared their lunch, a cold collation, as it was Cook's day off.

Earnestine picked at it, her sharp face revealing that her sharp mind was wandering.

"I shouldn't be here," Georgina said. "I'm married. I should be in my husband's household."

"Yes," said Earnestine, "you should."

The doorbell rang and Captain Merryweather was announced.

"Darling?" he said.

Georgina suddenly felt so utterly happy. It was almost as if she'd called for him and there he was. She ushered them into the Drawing Room.

"They aren't going for it," he said.

"Going for what?" Earnestine asked.

"Major Dan says we can't just burst in there unannounced. The letter is evidence, and our testimony about the college and the ferry, but it all has to go through committee. Apparently the Austro-Hungarian Embassy is part of Austro-Hungary despite being in Belgravia. I'm going over his head. I have an appointment this afternoon, but it'll be the same story."

"I'm sorry, darling," Georgina said.

Merryweather relented: "It's not your fault. They just won't take your word for it. If Caruthers, Mac and I had seen it with our own eyes, but, unfortunately, we didn't. I'm afraid your word doesn't carry enough weight. If only we could find a way to obtain proof that they have smuggled in war materials, then they'd have to let us act."

"But what about the letter?"

"The War Office is trying to find someone who can speak German to translate it," Merryweather said, "but that'll take time and plans do not mean action."

"I'm sure I could get in," said Charlotte. "They think I'm a Princess."

"Do they?" said Georgina.

"I *am* a Princess," said Charlotte.

"Lottie," said Georgina patiently, "it's far too dangerous to go on your own."

"I don't have to go on my own."

"I suppose she could take a maid," said Georgina.

"And who might that be?" Merryweather said.

"Well..."

"Two maids," interrupted Earnestine.

"No, I forbid it, darling," said Merryweather. "I promised to keep you safe, and I'm not letting you stroll into that den of iniquity."

"We could take the men," said Charlotte, brightly.

"Charlotte," said Earnestine, "they are hardly going to accept you back if you turn up with two maids and three... what? Butlers?"

Georgina was distracted by the daguerreotypes arranged in their frames on the pianoforte and on the wall. There was the expedition picture with her Father and Uncle surrounded by native guides on the banks of the river. There were other pictures of the Deering-Dolittle family ranged in mismatched frames with one of the three sisters as little girls taken before their Mother went off on the rescue mission.

She supposed that she would be leaving to, going to live in Arthur's residence...

"Arthur, where do you... I mean, we, live?"

"Well-"

"There's the Zeppelin," said Charlotte.

"Yes, dear," Georgina replied, not really listening. "Please don't interrupt."

"Surely if we got one of their bombs, then Major Wotnot would have to believe us."

"By Jove," said Merryweather. "Would they let you in just because you're in their Aerial Corp?"

"That and I'm married to the Crown Prince."

"No," said Merryweather, although his eyes betrayed excitement at the idea. "They wouldn't let me through with you and it's too dangerous for you girls."

"It's in a field, miles away," said Charlotte. "I just go in and say I've forgotten my... umbrella."

"That might work... no."

"Arthur, you can keep watch," said Georgina. "Either we get what we want or we don't. Nothing can happen."

"What if they don't let you leave afterwards?"

"Then you have the excuse you need to come and rescue us," said Georgina. "There's no other way, dearest."

Merryweather sat back and folded his arms in front of him, a sure sign that he wasn't happy: they had won the argument.

"I think perhaps," said Earnestine, "that you men might have need of us women after all."

## Miss Charlotte

Tiffin was jolly exciting because they'd been invited to dine in the Regimental Club. Not the stuffy main area, but the side wing that allowed women too. After tea and Battenberg, the men went to see some old soldier who kept an office in the Club. And there was sherry, but sadly only in the smallest of glasses.

Merryweather explained to Georgina: "If you don't mind waiting outside while we see M-"

"I'm fine, darling," said Georgina, "don't fret."

She smiled sweetly at Arthur and put her hand on his arm. He nodded and went in, the large oak door closing behind him.

It was dull, Charlotte thought, sitting in the corridor with her sisters as they were both being silent and boring.

There was a shout from inside the room.

"Thunder and lightning, Merryweather!" The voice of was husky, the sign of a heavy smoker. "This report reads like one of Wells's concoctions. This is all very Doctor Moreau."

"I think, Sir, it's more Shell-"

"Sherry?"

The sisters didn't hear the next exchange. There was mumbling, but it was a chance to take in the opulent surroundings, the oak panels and dusty paintings with various mismatched chairs lined up against the walls at intervals. It was an expensive waiting room.

"Balderdash!"

"Sir, sir... please."

"We cannot raid a foreign embassy. It's tantamount to an invasion, an act of war!"

"Sir, it's not the embassy, it's a field, practically in Hertfordshire and-"

"It's just not done. We have to play by the rules otherwise we'll be as bad as Johnny Foreigner."

Charlotte couldn't really tell who was speaking any more, the shouting and the distance made the voices all sound the same.

Another rumble sounded from inside: "Who? Dash it, man, out with it."

"She has a uniform."

"See," said Charlotte, "I'll have to change into my uniform."

Her sisters reacted as one: "Shhh..."

The volume dropped again and it seemed almost as if the two men were circling each other as the General's bass rumbles oscillated with Captain Merryweather's level baritone.

"You're going to send these gals into that hellhole?"

"It's the only way."

"The only way? Are you telling me that all that stands between the British Empire and disaster are three young ladies?"

"My Lord, they are jolly plucky young ladies."

The door opened, all the sisters jerked back having unconsciously leant forward.

"Well, on your own head be it."

"Sir."

Merryweather closed the door: "Darling, I think... I'm afraid."

"He agreed?" Georgina said.

"Yes, I'm afraid he did."

# CHAPTER XX

## Miss Deering-Dolittle

Back at the house as Charlotte changed, Earnestine checked she had everything. She'd have to travel light, she knew, so she chose the small kit: umbrella, flash-

"This will be such an adventure," said Charlotte.

Earnestine tightened her lips: "No, it won't!"

Where was she? Umbrella, flashlight, shillings and a pound note, penknife and Pieter's ruby ring on a chain tucked in her bosom.

"Charlotte, take some gloves," said Georgina.

"Those don't go with the uniform."

"Lottie, put them in your pocket in case it turns cold."

It was like old times, bickering like this, and so bizarre that they were about to take a terrible risk.

They waited in the drawing room, not saying anything, and then gathered outside in Zebediah Row once the carriages arrived. There were six, full of men: soldiers, soldiers in civilian clothing and Peelers with their helmets, handcuffs and truncheons. Major Dan had tried to cover every contingency, so that he could move once there was proof. Some of them were going to the airship field and others were heading off to watch the Austro-Hungarian embassy.

Captain Merryweather was in charge of the contingent going with the sisters to the Zeppelin, Captain Caruthers was destined for observation and Lieutenant McKendry was disguised as a cab driver. Charlotte had been excited - silly girl - and had leant over the maps as everything was discussed. They went on about some girl, Emilia or Emily, who was going to be here... and here... and there, but Earnestine had paid no attention. She found her thoughts wandering to the Austro-Hungarians and the possibility of meeting... no-one in particular.

Charlotte spoke first: "We showed them, didn't we?"

"We- you first- we did," said Georgina and Earnestine together.

They all laughed.

"What's the joke?" Merryweather asked.

"Oh, Arthur," said Georgina.

"It's the Derring-Do Club against the world!" said Charlotte.

The giggling hansom journey seemed to go on forever and then they came to a halt all too soon. No-one seemed to want to say anything even after the vehicle had stopped rocking on its suspension. Outside the horses snorted.

It was exciting: a little adven- no: *no trouble, no exploring and no adventures*. They were on an errand, that was it.

Captain Merryweather coughed as a prelude to speaking, but Georgina, Earnestine noted, put her hand on his knee.

"We'll be careful," she said. "We won't take any risks and we'll demonstrate caution at all times."

"I'd be happier if you'd take this," he said, and then added: "Darling."

Georgina blushed.

"It's my service revolver," he said. "A Webley, Mk 1."

"The British Peacemaker," said McKendry, indicating the big black object.

"I can't carry that," said Georgina. "It's huge."

"I'll have it," said Charlotte.

"Shhh, Lottie!" said Earnestine.

"I know, darling," said Merryweather. "But how about this, the Bull Dog Revolver, the civilian pocket revolver, and it'll go in your sock garter. I usually keep it in my sock garter on these... climbing expeditions."

"As you well know, my garters are up here," said Georgina.

"You could put it in your purse, darling."

"Honestly, I wouldn't know how to use it," said Georgina.

"I-"

"Lottie!"

"You keep it," said Georgina.

With obvious reluctance Merryweather raised his trousers and put the silver gun back in its place.

As they came to a halt, Earnestine realised that this was it, but it wasn't. Merryweather disembarked to transfer and organise the rescue party. Once he'd done that, Earnestine had to look away across the green fields towards Essex as Merryweather leaned in to touch and canoodle with his wife. It was typical of Georgina to flaunt her good fortune.

And then the sisters were alone with McKendry at the reins.

The cab jerked on and rounded to the entrance to the Zeppelin field.

There was some shouting, heavily accented, and then Charlotte stuck her head out of the window.

"I'm Princess... oh, er..."

With a snap to attention: "Your Royal Highness."

"I left something in the Zeppelin," she explained.

The guard shouted in German and the hansom moved forwards before coming to a stop again.

The sisters disembarked.

There were three Zeppelins, clearly being readied for launch, with their motors idling and a multitude of men pulling ropes and manoeuvring the huge behemoths from the air quay.

"Which was mine?" Charlotte asked. "They are my maids. Come, come!"

She strode across the field to one of the Zeppelins. Earnestine and Georgina followed in her wake, each trying to see everything and keep their heads down.

There were distant shouts: "Seile los sofort!"

One of the Zeppelins took to the air, rising in a remarkably graceful manner for something so huge. They had appeared large before, but now Earnestine was underneath one the sheer magnitude of the airship struck her again. She shielded her eyes from the sun to observe the rising and turning.

"It's starting," said Georgina.

"Yes," said Earnestine and then she realised what Georgina meant. While they'd been having tiffin and waiting for the men to endlessly discuss action in their Clubs, the Austro-Hungarians had been moving ahead. Indeed, as if to emphasis Earnestine's thought, the second Zeppelin was being cleared for launch. By chance, they were under the third.

"Come on!" Charlotte shouted from the gondola. She'd climbed the steps while the others had watched the spectacle.

"What do we do?" said Georgina.

"We stick to the plan: we get a bomb and then report back," Earnestine said.

They went up the stairs and into the gondola beneath the huge rigid balloon. No-one appeared to be on board, probably because they were concentrating on launching the other Zeppelins.

Next to a vicious looking gun, there were canisters in crates arranged by the door, but none of them were bombs.

"What's this?" Earnestine asked.

"Ooh," said Charlotte. "That's an American gun: the Gatling. It can do a thousand rounds a minute and-"

"No this," said Earnestine. She read the label: "Silberjodid."

"Silver iodide," said Georgina. "This isn't going to take off with us on board, is it?"

"Don't be silly," Earnestine said.

"This is all new, I didn't see this before," Charlotte said, examining a machine feeding into pipes that stuck out of the gondola at angles. "There's a place here for the canisters."

Earnestine took over: "Goes in here... and... funnels outside - why?"

"It's used for photography," said Georgina, "that's all I know. It says 'Regenmacher' on the side."

"Isn't 'macher' 'maker'?" Earnestine said. "What was a 'Regen' then? A type of daguerreotype perhaps?"

On the side of the machine was a sign with instructions, frustratingly in German, as well as numbers, possibly heights in metres, which Earnestine knew were about a yard, and symbols like clouds.

"You use this above the clouds," said Earnestine, mostly to herself.

"Is it poisonous?" Charlotte asked.

"Not particularly, I wouldn't want to eat it, but they have far worse yellow smoke weapons," Georgina said and she shuddered. "They were dreadful, really awful..."

Earnestine knew why as she remembered the horrors on the train all too well: "Don't be a baby, Gina."

Earnestine poked at the machine with her umbrella: what could it be?

"Perhaps they spray it on the clouds to stop it raining," said Charlotte.

"That seems unlikely," said Earnestine. "Why come all this way to make it sunny? I could believe it of the MCC."

"Maybe it's to make it rain," Georgina said.

"Oh Gina! Do think. It rains all the time in Britain, why would anyone want to make it rain more?"

"Maybe they want to ruin our cricket, maybe they want it to be stormy, maybe... I don't know."

"Gina, turning drizzle into rain or rain into a thunderstorm might have utility in the desert, where you need irrigation, but-"

Suddenly, it was obvious, utterly obvious.

"Ness, you're worrying Charlotte and me."

"Thunderstorm *and lightning!*"

And they'd launched one Zeppelin already, the other was ready too.

Get to McKendry and the hansom, ten minutes, drive like the wind back to London, forty minutes, and then argue with Major Dan for a month of Sundays... they were too late. Their time had run out. Graf Zala's Great War plan had succeeded.

"We have to try!" she said. What else could they do? "Come on!"

She led the way to the staircase, her foot touching the top step, when she saw Kroll directing the men holding the ropes.

They looked at each other, recognition in their expressions. She shouldn't have come; her very presence had betrayed them.

The heavy Oberst started to move: "Achtung!"

"Cast off!" shouted Earnestine at Charlotte.

"They do it outside," she replied.

What had they shouted before?

Earnestine turned: "Leaning loss!"

Kroll reached the bottom of the stairs.

"Ziler. Los. Zofart!"

Some of the men reacted and let go, but not enough. The Zeppelin skewed around. Kroll stepped across the widening gap and was, for a moment, standing on the stairs and the access ledge. Earnestine pushed him, lightly, enough though for him to slip.

The Zeppelin was solid, firm and sound; whereas the ground with all the people seemed to jitter and pitch about.

Kroll hung on to the lip, looked up and snarled.

More men, fearful of being drawn into the sky, let go and that was enough: the Zeppelin rose.

Kroll's feet slipped off the top step and he dangled in the air.

Earnestine and Georgina each stepped on a hand; the man cried out and then dropped onto the grass below.

The ground fell away at an alarming rate.

Kroll stood up, unhurt, and began to order the men towards the other Zeppelin.

The men became like dolls and there was McKendry on the hansom cab and beyond, somewhere, was Merryweather and their potential rescue party. They'd assumed that the Austro-Hungarians couldn't take them from the field without being intercepted, but the enemy had flying machines and could take them anywhere.

"There's no-one on the bridge," said Charlotte, "but we'll need to barricade the rear door as there will be airmen in the main fuselage."

"We're flying!" said Georgina.

"Yes," said Charlotte, "rear door."

"We're in the air," Georgina whined.

"Leave it to me," said Earnestine.

"Oh lummy..."

The rear door turned out to have a bolt, so it was very straight forward. She also found a few chairs in the cabins and put those in the way. Unfortunately everything was flimsy as it was made from light wood, but it might slow them down. Earnestine wondered when they'd realise.

Back at the bridge, Charlotte operated the controls like an expert. She let go of a lever and the engine note changed abruptly. The floor tilted alarmingly as the airship rose. Earnestine found her stomach lurched.

Georgina was there too, bent double with her hands gripping the ropes that acted as rails on both sides of the gangway: "We're flying... oh help."

"It's jolly exciting," said Charlotte.

"We're going to crash," Georgina whined.

"Don't be ridiculous," Earnestine said. "Who's ever heard of an airship crashing? It's lighter than air, so it can't crash."

"It'll explode!"

"An airship is lifted by the negative weight of hydrogen. Hydrogen burns with oxygen to produce... come on... Gina, you know chemicals - hydrogen dioxide, which is water. Any fire on a Zeppelin would automatically put itself out. Do think, Gina."

"We're coming up to 850 metres," Charlotte announced, reading off a dial.

"What's that?"

"Er... about two and a half thousand feet, maybe more."

"We'll fall," Georgina said.

"Don't whine, Gina, you're a married woman."

"Turning to 180," Charlotte said.

"What's that?" Georgina asked.

"South!"

It would take them half an hour at least to land, assuming they could, and they were miles away from McKendry and the hansom. Perhaps they should go straight to London. Was there anywhere to land in London?

"Follow the other Zeppelin!" Earnestine shouted.

Charlotte started manoeuvring.

Georgina cried out: "What?"

"We have to stop that Zeppelin before it starts regen maching."

"There are soldiers and peelers and gentleman mountaineers to do this," Georgina shouted: "Down there!"

"Yes and we're up here, so it's up to us."

"This is an adventure," said Charlotte.

"No, it isn't," said Earnestine. "And keep your eye on the... sky."

"I'm levelling."

"Charlotte, we're still below the clouds."

"Eight fifty metres is the operational ceiling."

"One can't spray silver iodide on clouds that are above one."

"It would be dangerous."

"I think they'd take the risk considering what with the stakes being so high."

Charlotte grinned: "All right, I'll try for a thousand metres."

At Charlotte's bidding, the Zeppelin rose and a mist seemed to descend. It was quieter, the windows spotted with moisture, and then, like a Nautilus rising from the depths, they broke free and were greeted by the most brilliant sunshine. It was breathtaking, even Georgina came to stare.

"One thousand metres," Charlotte said. "Steady at one eighty, speed thirty eight... nine kilometres an hour."

"Look sharp," Earnestine said. She noticed pairs of binoculars clipped into wall brackets and she handed them to Georgina before selecting a pair of her own. It took a few moments to adjust and find the best position to avoid seeing her own eyelashes, but then the clouds below jumped into focus. They looked the same despite being magnified, there was nothing to give them any sense of scale in this strange cotton wool landscape. There were no trees, houses or animals to act as a yardstick.

"There!" Georgina said.

"Where?"

"Down... sort of left a bit by that fluffy pointy one just down from that."

Earnestine scanned left and up and down: fluffy wasn't really specific enough and she was just about to remonstrate with Georgina when she saw it. A black shape like a whale swimming in a sea, it undulated, rippling as it moved and appeared very unlike the rigid superstructure of an airship. It can't bend like that, so...

"Shadow!" Earnestine said. "It's... the sun is there, so..."

She nearly blinded herself and had to take the binoculars down to blink away the orange spots. When she put them back, she moved with more care and direction and found the source of the shadow. There, the evil shape of the Zeppelin glided above them. She could make out the cruciform shape made by the airship's fins, the motors on their spindly arms flicking as they cut through the sunlight, and the tiny gondola beneath.

"We're getting closer," Georgina said.

They were and Charlotte was turning the wheel to move them into position behind the other airship, rising to their level slowly like a hunter closing in on its prey.

Dust spattered the front window.

Georgina spoke for all of them: "Silver iodide, they've started."

Earnestine wondered how long they had been spraying the chemical and how much was required to start a storm. They must have done tests, flying Zeppelins over Europe and drenching the ground: they'd know - it wouldn't be guess work.

"Now what?" Georgina asked.

"Well, this is a ship of the sky," Earnestine said, "so forward guns or torpedoes or... height charges."

"There are bombs and a Gatling gun," Charlotte said.

They didn't need binoculars now to see their opponent. The other airship was clearly travelling slowly, possibly to optimise the density of silver iodide striking the clouds.

"Right," Earnestine said. "Charlotte, get us above the other Zeppelin. Georgina, you man the Gatling gun and I'll find some bombs."

"I don't know how to use a Gatling gun."

"Gina, you've driven a steam train, how hard can it be?"

"You've driven a steam train?" Charlotte said, excited.

"Yes, I have," said Georgina.

"Wow... oh, Ness, can I? Can I?"

"Charlotte, you are flying a Zeppelin," Earnestine replied. "You'll just have to be satisfied with that."

"Why does Gina get all the fun?"

"This is not a game."

"No, it's an adventure."

"It most certainly is not."

# Mrs Arthur Merryweather

Georgina was too frightened to be really cross. Earnestine was being bossy again and then Charlotte, the younger sister, had taken over. She seemed to know how to fly a Zeppelin and how to fire a Gatling gun and... it must be something to do with wearing trousers. Why couldn't saving the British Empire involve embroidery?

Earnestine and Georgina fussed over the Gatling gun. Charlotte manoeuvred their airship above the target. The enemy in their gondola were below the rigid dirigible envelope and so their approach was hidden.

They came close, very close.

Earnestine aimed and... nothing.

"Get Charlotte!" Earnestine shouted.

"Can you not get it to work?"

"Get... oh, I'll do it."

Earnestine ran off and moments later Charlotte appeared.

"Sit here," she said.

"I can't kill anyone," said Georgina.

"We just shoot the tail off and then they'll have to land."

"Right."

"Pull this."

Georgina didn't see what Charlotte did, but she heard a metal sound like a bolt moving.

"Now... aim... and just a gentle squeeze..."

Georgina aimed at the eagles on the tail fin, squeezed ever so gently and-

Sound! Kick! Fire! Screaming... her own screaming as the thing came alive and spat angry sparks that traced a fiery path to the other airship. The fins exploded, and then because the monstrous machine had a life of its own, it sprayed bullets everywhere. Holes appeared in the side of the Zeppelin, lines of dots like unpicked sewing. The canvas covering ripped as the wind tore at the panels.

It stopped: Georgina had her mouth open, but nothing came out.

"That was spiffing," Charlotte said: "Move over, my turn."

Georgina moved away feeling sick.

Charlotte blazed away for a while, the *ratta-tat-tat-TAT-TAT-TAT-*

"Stop it, stop it!" Georgina had her hands over her ears.

It stopped, but the noise rang on in Georgina's head.

"That was horrible," said Georgina, "we're never doing that again... I can still hear it."

"That's..."

Charlotte stuck her head out of the open doorway, craning up.

"Careful!"

"We're being shot at," said Charlotte. "Another Zeppelin. I'll tell-"

There was a crashing noise, wood splintering, and they both knew that the barricade at the back of the gondola section was being attacked.

Charlotte dragged the Gatling gun into the middle of the corridor and fired a burst of from the appalling gun.

"Don't!" said Georgina, but it was too late.

"I'll tell Earnestine," said Charlotte. "You keep them out."

Georgina took hold of the gun and prayed no-one would try and break through the flimsy door.


## Miss Charlotte

When Charlotte reached the bridge, she saw that the first Zeppelin, the one they'd shot at, was going down, pushing the clouds aside in its descent.

"Well done," said Earnestine.

"We're being shot at."

"Are we?"

"Yes, from above, the other Zeppelin."

"Kroll."

Charlotte grabbed the controls and yanked a lever back.

Georgina arrived: "They're in."

"Why didn't you shoot them?" Charlotte shouted back.

"I can't..."

Something pinged around the bridge, a bullet.

Out of the starboard side, Kroll's Zeppelin loomed, a dark shadow in the bright sunlight.

"Achtung!"

The sisters stopped: an Austro-Hungarian soldier stood in the doorway.

Charlotte winked at Earnestine: "Hold on."

She pulled again: the engines whined and the floor tilted from a gentle upward slope and turned into a wooden cliff. Objects fell backwards, cups, maps, Georgina, the approaching soldiers...

"Not up! Down!" Georgina shouted.

"Up!" said Charlotte.

"Down," said Georgina, who was half-way up the wall by the door. "Sooner or later one of those lunatics is going to puncture the airbag and we don't want to fall too far."

"Up," said Charlotte, "because the higher we are, the more likely those lunatics will see sense and stop firing."

"Down!"

"Up!"

"Will you two stop arguing?" Earnestine yelled.

"Zeppelins fire downwards, so if we are above them they can't hit us."

"We have to destroy that Zeppelin."

"How? The Gatling is... back there."

An engine stuttered, but kept turning.

"The air's getting thin," Charlotte explained. Her breathing was laboured as if she was wearing a particularly tight corset, but she was in her aerial uniform.

"Then we have to go down," Georgina pleaded.

As their forward momentum waned, the airship began to settle back to the horizontal.

"We need to go up," Charlotte cried out as she desperately tried to get more out of the controls.

"Down."

"We need to lose weight."

"Shall we kick a few Austro-Hungarians overboard?" Earnestine joked.

They looked at her, knowing that it was her decision between up and down, between Georgina and Charlotte.

"Up or down?" Charlotte asked, hopeful that Earnestine would pick her suggestion.

"Forward!" Earnestine said. "Ram this Zeppelin into that Zeppelin."

"That's... decisive," said Charlotte. Oh, her big sister had some wonderful ideas sometimes. "Jolly good."

"You're insane!" Georgina wailed.

The engines whined and complained as the massive Zeppelin slalomed around the sky. The other Zeppelin loomed in the front windows, turning to give them a broadside. Tiny lights winked from the windows, clearly they were being shot at, and then the pilot of the other air vessel realised the danger and tried to dive.

Both Zeppelins, ponderous beasts that they were, reacted tardily, so they had plenty of time to see the collision developing.

There was a loud hollow sound at the moment of contact, the tension in the canvas skins enough to absorb the impact as they jostled and bumped along, then their port propeller struck the side, ripping and shredding until it connected with a metal strut and then the rotor tore itself to pieces.

Everything pitched.

There was a hideous grinding sound as the two airships, pushed together by the starboard engine, slid along and then stopped.

Charlotte turned the ship's wheel, but only achieved a sickening motion back and forth.

"We're caught," said Charlotte.

Earnestine looked: "It's the ropes, they've tangled in the metal framework."

Charlotte risked a quick glance. Sure enough the ropes from the bow had caught on the exposed frame of the dirigible. The two airships were locked together.

"We can board it," Earnestine shouted. "Come on!"

"What!?"

"Someone is going to have to climb down the cable and stab the other Zeppelin's airbag."

"Are you going to bedlam!?" Georgina yelled: "It'll drop like a stone."

"The bag will deflate and the airship will float safely to the ground," said Earnestine. "You've had mountaineering experience."

"What! No, no, no..." Georgina begged.

"Not you, Gina, you're married, you have to keep the Deering-Dolittle line going, whereas I'm expendable, but I could do with some advice."

"What about me?" said Charlotte.

"I think Lottie, you should just keep out of trouble."

Oh, Charlotte thought, she was going to miss out again. Ness never let her do anything.

"Ness, please, think," Georgina implored.

"Once I'm across," said Earnestine, busy collecting a pair of goggles and a Verey Pistol from the rack at the side of the bridge. "I'll set a fire or some sort of sabotage."

"It will explode!"

"Don't be silly, Gina, no Zeppelin has ever exploded."

# CHAPTER XXI

## Miss Deering-Dolittle

Everything in the gondola was smashed to pieces and packed against the far end. The feeble barricade had now been reinforced by every piece of furniture. At the exit ramp, open to the elements, the other Zeppelin filled the view, a wall of canvas, ripped and holed in places.

Earnestine put the Verey Pistol into her bodice and put on the goggles, which needed tightening, and then she leant out reaching for the rope.

The other airship was lower and only 20 yards away, give or take, and the interior was holed, so she'd be able to clamber inside. It would then be easy to use the criss-crossing struts as a ladder to reach the deck. But first she had to reach the mooring rope.

She couldn't.

"I can't reach it," she said.

"This is insane," said Georgina.

Earnestine thought it was crazy too, madness beyond belief.

No adventures, Earnestine thought, avoiding her calling. Oh to hell with this, we're Deering-Dolittles. Not Surrey, but Kent, known for disappearing up rivers and mad schemes and - yes, for adventures.

"Give me my umbrella," she said.

"Here," said Gina, "but we're above the clouds, so it won't be of any use."

She reached out with it... a bit further and yes, it hooked over the rope.

"Ness!"

Firm grip, she kicked off and her skirts caught the wind and she flew out, blown horizontal by the slipstream around the two airships. For a moment she dangled between the two great walls of canvas, and then she slid down to bounce against the outer skin of the other Zeppelin.

For one dreadful moment, she thought she'd fallen off and hit the ground, but she'd thumped into the hard surface of the outer skin of the other Zeppelin.

Now she had to open her eyes and actually find handholds, but she found she couldn't move.

The wind whipped around her, stinging her face. There was a ladder, set against the outside, clearly designed for someone to clamber about risking their lives, probably to trim the mainsail or whatever this damned stupid aerial boat required. It was too far away, yards and yards - too far. The wind was blowing her towards it, sideways, backwards along the vessel, so it would just be a case of letting go.

She'd fly, briefly, and then grab hold. All she had to do was let go. Let go.

"Let go," she said aloud, the wind grasping her words and flinging them into the bluster and buffet of the slipstream. "Let go!"

She unhooked the umbrella and let go.

The wind did exactly what it had been doing, so she flew back, missed the ladder and struck the exposed metalwork that had been ripped into jagged struts by the collision. She struggled through the opening and into the main fuselage itself.

Suddenly, after the roaring gale outside, it was a quiet, reverberating space. She was again stunned by the sheer size of the vessel, like a hangar containing the round balloons that kept the airship aloft.

She worked her way down gingerly. The last time her knees had been this scraped and gashed was when they'd all played *Source of the Nile* down in the woods as little girls. That seemed a long time ago.

Crew appeared, disgorged from the gondola below, as orders were shouted in German.

Earnestine sank to the deck, conscious of how ludicrous it was to try and bring down the ultimate war machine single-handed.

A crewman ran past her with an axe and clambered nimbly up the superstructure to hack away at the rope. It zinged when it split and whipped away like a venomous snake.

"Deering-Dolittle!"

It was Kroll, the huge man standing over her.

"I can see why Pieter finds you attractive, you are such a spitfire."

Earnestine pulled herself upright and stumbled away over the metal deck.

Kroll was laughing: "Where can you run, we are kilometres away from the ground."

He pressed a button on a machine and a figure lurched towards Earnestine. She shied away, changed direction. Coming towards her was the ruined visage of a man with buck teeth and she recognised him as the March Hare.

"Schneider!"

The dead man reacted to the noise but not to his name. The brass fitting in this skull fizzed and his groping arms came up to grab her.

"We kept him here because we didn't want the Prince finding out," said Kroll. "He is one of the Untotenfallschirmspringer."

"I beg your pardon."

"The Undead Parachute Corp."

Earnestine doubled back, nimbler than the monster, but running out of options: "I'm none the wiser."

"These," said Kroll, turning round to show her his backpack. "They are inventions to allow one to descend to the ground."

"Really, how lovely."

"This is a new age, the age of air war, when we, a landlocked country, can go over any defences, any blockades, any fortifications to attack the very heart of an empire. This war of air and untoten, we call it *Blitzkrieg*."

"I don't know German."

"Blitzkrieg means 'Lightning War'," the Oberst said, laughing. "When the lightning comes there will be war."

"But why?" Earnestine shouted, dodging away from the pursuing creature. "Why all this killing?"

"I'm a soldier," said Kroll. "What else would I do?"

She was back where she started at the port side, the open sky in front of her marked by the blot of the other Zeppelin, now an expanding distance away.

The walking corpse closed in, stumbling and lurching on the pitching walkway.

At Earnestine's feet was her umbrella. She flipped it up and brandished it like a sword, poking at the Schneider's approach. They circled each other until the blue spark ordered the creature to attack.

Leading with her right foot, Earnestine stabbed forward. The point of her improvised weapon pierced the creature's flesh, cracked a rib and was sucked forward through its body as its attack continued. Earnestine pushed. The monster jerked and toppled backwards, hovering for a moment on the edge of the precipice before being ripped out into the void.

Earnestine herself was dragged forward until the handle of the umbrella wrenched free of her grip. She tottered on the edge before grabbing a handhold and her knees slammed against the deck by the opening. Schneider was a flailing shape and then a receding dot.

She heard Oberst Kroll stumble, his polished boots slipping on the walkway.

"Fräulein, such courage."

She'd die now, she knew it, and that meant she'd never see Pieter again. Instinctively, she reached for his ring and felt the bulk of the Verey Pistol. She pulled it out, turned and aimed at the big man.

"I can't miss you at this range," she said.

"You can't fire that in here," said Kroll. "Blugas, hydrogen."

"It's not 'can't'," said Earnestine. "It's 'shouldn't'."

She fired.

She missed.

The fiery projectile soared upwards across the vast cathedral-like space to penetrate a distant gas bag. For a moment the balloon shone brightly like a gas lamp, beautiful and bewitching, and then it exploded.

A blue radiance, painful to see, trembled along the inner skin of the dirigible like bubbling water flowing along the ceiling above her. There was heat and it gave off water enough to make a rainbow flicker over the gantries and ropes. When the effect reached the far end, the pure burning of the escaping gas ignited the canvas and gas of the motors, the blue rising flames suddenly turned fiery and angry, a roaring combustion that raced back along the walkway.

"Mein Gott!"

A second balloon burst into flame and a third, and then, like dominoes, the combustion exploded each one in turn. The light was blue, a blue beyond blue, and then red flames rippled like angry clouds raining fire.

There was a roar as the air was sucked in. The whole Zeppelin acted like a chimney, and then there was yet another burst of flame as a blugas balloon went up. The shockwave of flames hit Kroll, picked him up, and blasted him through the ruptured skin of the airship and into the void.

Earnestine ducked, burying her face in her hands as the heat washed over her. She'd been protected by Kroll, he in turn by the pack of his parachute.

She ran.

Where was there to go?

Where were the lifeboats?

Behind her, the bow of the Zeppelin split open like a peeling fruit or an opening flower, blooming with rage and fire. Metal split and melted and sprang loose. The Zeppelin was finished: she could either burn or jump, and so she threw herself through an opening and into the atmosphere beyond.

The cold air took her breath away before a wall of heat hit Earnestine hard, punching her forwards and dishevelling her hair and clothing. She grabbed at nothing because there was nothing. The huge domineering airship became tiny so jolly, jolly quickly, a bursting fireball that went up as the metal skeleton of the Zeppelin, its skin in flames, began the long fall to the ground below.

Earnestine tumbled, over and over, waving her arms desperately as she tried to swim in the thin, cold air. Arms out and spread, she was suddenly flying, stable, and looking down. It was a long dive towards London's hard paving.

Kroll was like a comet trailing smoke to mark his incandescent trajectory, a Chinese firework going straight down. He was on fire.

Earnestine put her arms back and in against her body, her petticoats fluttered and flapped in the increased airflow and then, as the air was sucked out, they stuck to her legs and she plummeted. She found she could turn, tiny alterations to her palms having a decided effect. The streets below looked so far away, but the sudden slapping of mist told her that her velocity was extraordinary. Droplets formed on the outside of her goggles were blown away.

She flew; it felt powerful and incredible as she spiralled around the trail of smoke.

As she whizzed down, she saw Kroll struggling with his parachute, the burning pack generating the smoke trail she followed.

Earnestine made herself into an arrow and flew, closer, closer...

She hit him, sparks erupted from his singed clothing and she almost failed... no! Caught hold, her fingers wrapped around one of the parachute's straps.

With her other hand, she yanked the clasp open before the shocked Oberst realised what was happening. His face was blackened on one side where he'd caught the explosion and his eyes were bloodshot.

He fought back, tried to hit her, while Earnestine concentrated on the harness. When it came free, the two opponents hung for a moment connected by their tenuous hold on the thin straps.

Earnestine pulled and she had the pack in her hands. She yanked the ripcord.

Nothing happened.

Kroll punched her in the face and she span away.

She saw him wrench the pack on...

Ground.

...click it into place...

Ground.

...pull the ripcord....

Ground.

...the silk parachute burst open, a white rose bloom that burst into red. Like tissue in a fireplace, the thin material, ignited by Kroll's burning clothes, shone and then blackened instantly into ash.

Her last chance - gone.

No!

Not Earnestine, not a Deering-Dolittle.

She brought her knees up to make herself into a ball and the desperate Oberst seemed to fly upwards.

The sky was awash with clouds and bright, blue expanses of brilliant sky, pierced by falling shapes, burning canvas and fire. She squinted when the sun passed across her vision followed by the flare of vivid red flames of the doomed Zeppelin before her tumbling brought the huge expanse of the Earth into view. It was a massive panorama of grey streets and the sunlight glinting off the snaking Thames. There, somewhere, was the House of Commons, the loop around the Isle of Dogs and-

There!

Yes.

A small falling dot!

She straightened again, her skirts flapped briefly and then tucked back like the wings of a diving hawk.

She struck Schneider's corpse hard, her fingers torn backwards as she hurtled past, and she dropped below him, even flapped her arms, and then threw herself into a star shape, the air resistance pummelling her and slowing her. The wind caught her skirts, braking her descent enough to fly her back up. She caught him, clambered up his legs, just as the creature turned its murderous intentions on her.

She held his jacket with one hand as she searched for the clasp to the harness.

There was no clasp, no straps, no parachute - they hadn't put one on him.

The corpse, still very much animate, opened its slobbering mouth to bite and snap, its spittle flecking the air. Hand-over-hand she crawled around him until they were face-to-face. She grabbed the handle of the umbrella, and shoved her elbow joint into the hook of the handle.

Her foot was seized in a vice!

Kroll grasped her ankle.

His momentum caused the three of them to cartwheel.

The ground was suddenly there below, full of hard roofs and pointed towers.

She pulled, the umbrella came away and-

She cried out!

It opened explosively, the thin metal ribs pulling on the stretchers, the whole curved shape threatening to invert. She seemed to leap up into the air as the corpse and the Oberst plummeted towards the model buildings. They struck an angled roof punching two distinct holes through the slates to reveal the rafters beneath.

The black canopy distorted, bowling the wrong way, and then she hit the roof herself, spine-jarringly, and slates clattered loose. The canopy righted itself with a beat as she slid down the slope. Slates, knocked free, cascaded into the street below to explode, hurling sharp fragments everywhere.

Earnestine was in the air again, twirling like a spinning dandelion seed to settle on the pavement over the road with a heavy crunching impact.

She rolled.

Her head connected with the pavement and for a moment she saw swirling specks. She did see lights: a myriad of fiery shards like shooting stars falling to earth. It was a glorious sight, the doomed airship disintegrating high above.

She picked herself up, feeling embarrassed as all the passers-by looking at her in amazement. Then, in a panic she checked her arms, legs, face and chest, a flurry of pattings up and down: she was still in one piece.

"Oh, golly gosh!"

Above the flaming Zeppelin still fell like a rapidly setting sun.

They'd won!

There had been three airships: one hadn't used its Regenmacher for long, theirs hadn't at all and Kroll's was a flaming wreck. Without a thunderstorm their army was nothing - just so many old bones and so much rotting flesh. Earnestine gazed up, elated, and almost felt like crying out for joy (not that she would, of course) such was her euphoria.

A droplet of rain splattered on the lens of her goggles.

Then another.

And another.

The pavement began to mottle as a dark pattern appeared and these tiny lakes spread and joined to create a sea, the rain now ricocheting off the flagstones. Passers-by unfurled umbrellas or ran for cover. The pelting water washed away hope, but it was only rain, just rain. There was a flash and... one, two, three... from twelve miles away a deep ominous rumble.

Earnestine howled.

"Steady on, miss," said a passing gent, "it's only a spot of rain and you have a brolly."

The fight was far from over.


## Mrs Arthur Merryweather

The storm was operatic, great swirling heaving waves of dark grey clouds lit by savage flashes of light, a maelstrom of thunder and lightning as if angels and demons fought for the sky itself. The Austro-Hungarian crew, now back in control of their Zeppelin, guided the damaged craft down into the dark pit of hell.

Georgina and Charlotte stood together at gunpoint.

"Don't worry," Georgina whispered. "Arthur will save us."

The damaged Zeppelin shook and vibrated as it continued its downward movement. When they landed, the internal hydrogen balloons being vented to reduce buoyancy, the craft settled, creaking and forlorn like an industrial whale beached on the land.

It was in another field and so Captain Merryweather was not there to rescue them. They were on their own.


## Miss Charlotte

"What is the meaning of this?" Charlotte demanded. "I will to be treated like-"

"A precocious British schoolgirl."

Charlotte was quiet and held on to Georgina's hand; they were both drenched and shivering.

The Graf was dry, handsome, with his neatly trimmed saturnine beard as sharp as his words. His features were a mix of those stern and remote faces painted on the enormous canvasses in solid gold frames that blocked every inch of the walls. Scattered across these long dead people was his aquiline nose, his piercing eyes, his heroic chin, his intelligent brow; but this man was real, blue blood coursed in his veins and his uniform had not faded in the light.

They were in the Austro-Hungarian embassy.

"That's what you are, really? Ja?"

Charlotte said nothing.

Georgina spoke out: "He killed the girls in the boarding school!"

The Graf was taken by surprise: "How did you... you are clever as well as beautiful."

"Thank you- No!"

"Why did you kill them?" Charlotte asked.

"It was necessary," said the Graf. He stepped away from her and waved his hand as if to encompass the room, but Charlotte knew that his meaning lay further afield. "We have a duty to our nations and to history. Think of... I'm sorry I can only put this in military terms."

Charlotte knew she'd understand: "Then put it in military terms."

"If a nation invades your lands, then it rapes and pillages, it destroys everything. Your army fights back, your people flock to the cause, and, with God's blessing and a good general, you force them back and win the day. But you cannot stop there, you must push on to destroy the aggressors in their own land, so that they never threaten you again. If that army, cowardly, hides within a city, then you have no choice but to lay siege. You know that there are people within the city, innocents, perhaps even subjects of your own, but you must push ahead for the greater good. Do you see? It is the same. It is glory."

"Murdering innocent girls in a school?" Charlotte said.

"There was a... competitor hiding within that school's walls. There was an opportunity. We had little time. It was worth trying."

"You mean to kill Prince Pieter, your brother."

"Ja, without him the Great Plan would be nothing and my plan would be inevitable."

His breeding and lifetime's training could not hold back his emotions, so Charlotte could see the pain etched on his face. She wanted to believe him. She wanted this strong man to live up to his uniform. She wanted...

"But the girls as well, women *and children*?"

"I am not proud of what I have done. I did not order them to kill the girls, I gave explicit orders to the contrary, the soldiers exceeded their commission," - the Graf paused to hold up his hand to quell Charlotte's objection before continuing - "but even so, I, and I alone, am responsible. That is what it means to be imperial."

"It's still wrong."

"Yes, yes, so you must help me put it right. Stand by my side, together, be my conscience, so that I may spend the rest of my days atoning. My backward country is a medieval land, it must be dragged into the new century. We must have industry and commerce and education, schools, yes. A hundred schools for our brave boys and our vital girls."

Charlotte wavered under his spell: "Yes."

"But no, you are nothing to me, there is no blue blood in your veins."

"I'm British."

"When they finished at the school, we gathered them all together, afterwards."

"I saw," said Georgina.

The Graff began a wide circle of the room: "They were checked against the register. We are nothing if not thorough. The school kept accurate records, something to be admired."

Georgina again, angry, her word twisted by bottled emotions: "And?"

"There were three missing. All sisters." There was a rustle of paper before the man murdered the vowels: "Deering-Dolittle: Earnestine, Georgina and Charlotte."

He stopped and stared at them: "I met an Earnestine at the castle and you! Yes, you are familiar from... Strasburg. You said you were... Merryweather."

"I am."

"But before then, you were a Deering-Dolittle. I have heard of you, a family from England... Surrey."

Charlotte couldn't help herself: "Kent!"

"We found a stowaway on the Zed Oh Three."

"Really?"

"A girl. We assumed from the school. One of the Deering-Dolittles, but I think that was a mistake. I think that you are not the Princess and she was not the school girl."

"I guess you'll have to marry her now," said Charlotte.

Georgina stifled a sob.

"Nein," the Graf answered. "We shot her and threw her body over the parapet for the eagles."

Charlotte remembered the terrified but determined princess: "No!"

"My grandmother, the Gräfin, will be so upset."

"You cad," said Georgina.

Charlotte remembered that Earnestine had told her about the Princess, blamed her even, and Earnestine had been in the other Zeppelin when it had turned into fire.

A flash lit up the high windows.

"You will have to excuse me," the Graf said, clicking his heels and bowing formally. "The capacitors must be charged by now and I am needed. England is a dreary country, no mountains, but it is known for its-"

There was a flash.

"Rain, its wonderful rain."

Thunder rumbled on distantly.

# CHAPTER XXII

## Miss Deering-Dolittle

"You've done your bit now, Miss Deering-Dolittle, you can leave it with Major Dan and ourselves."

"Thank you, Captain Caruthers."

The men stood.

Earnestine remained seated. She was very conscious of the rain water seeping out of her skirts and bustle, and soaking the chair.

The men left, active and certain of their commission

Earnestine sat primly, breathing in and out as much as her corset allowed, and gradually calmed down. Her job was done and it was a relief. The men would, of course, do the best they could, and they were Gentlemen Adventurers, so clearly far more able than herself; however, she could be proud: she had fulfilled her responsibility admirably.

The carriage clock on the mantelpiece ticked.

When this was over, when Major Dan, Captain Caruthers, Captain Merryweather and Lieutenant McKendry had solved this, there might well be an article in the Times and, if there was any justice, it would mention in passing the gallant assistance that three sisters had afforded the British Empire in a time of crisis. It might even mention their names and go some way to redressing the balance in the reporting that the Kent family tended to suffer.

The ticking continued: a flash lit the sky briefly.

Of course the odds were against them, but they were men and better used to handling these matters than a young lady like herself, even a Derring-Do... She corrected herself: Deering-Dolittle.

The clock ticked on. Outside the rain pattered on the window and a rumble of thunder sounded in the distance.

"Oh to hell with this!" Earnestine said aloud.

Back at Zebediah Row, Earnestine dumped her wet clothes on her bedroom floor and then, dressed only in her undergarments, she pulled the battered suitcase from on top of the wardrobe.

There was a cough.

A woman stood in the doorway in a prim, black dress with starched white lace trim. She looked over her glasses at Earnestine.

"I heard you were back," she said.

"Yes, Nanny."

"And you've been partaking in some very unladylike activities by the look of things."

"I don't have time, Nanny," said Earnestine.

"Of course you have time!"

"I'm sorry, but I can't sit around fanning myself while the British Empire falls."

"It's up to the men to sort that out."

Earnestine dressed, sensible red Worsted and a small bustle.

"Your underclothes are damp," said Nanny, "you'll catch your death."

"Then I'll catch my death."

Earnestine took everything out of her canvas bag and laid them out on her bed.

Just the essentials and a few other items, she thought, so the medium kit. She weighed the canvas bag in her hand before checking everything was in place: penknife, compass, flashlight, spare batteries, binoculars, matches, tinder, sewing kit, spare button, handkerchief, whistle, map of London, pencil and notebook, water bottle, dark lantern, extra socks, a bandage and both packs of Kendal mint cake.

"You should stay here," Nanny insisted.

"I'm a Deering-Dolittle and I must go."

"I believe your mother gave you strict instructions."

"She did," said Earnestine: *no exploring, no trouble, no adventures.*

"I thought you, at least, had listened."

"I have to go."

"Up the river?"

"Not that."

"You might not come back."

"Then I won't come back."

She ran down the stairs past Nanny, past the daguerreotypes of her grandfather, uncle, father and mother and slammed the door behind her.

A moment later she let herself back in to fetch her precious umbrella.

She caught a Hansom cab to the deserted docks and found the passageway that led down into the sewers. She lit her dark lantern, opened the shutter to allow just enough light to see by and made her way into the marvel of the age.

Peg for her nose, that's what she'd forgotten.

## Mrs Arthur Merryweather

"Arthur will save us," Georgina said.

"We could grab one of those cavalry swords," Charlotte suggested.

Georgina glanced up at the rosette of blades and hilts set on the wall. There were many military souvenirs on display, sharp evil things, and suits of armour guarding either side of the grand fireplace. It seemed a foolish room to keep enemy prisoners, for that's what they were, she realised, but then there were plenty of soldiers coming to-and-fro with messages and they were the weaker sex.

"They're not fixed, just held in loops."

"Charlotte, sit still."

Georgina sat with her hands on her lap, carefully arranged. The unfamiliar ring on her finger was comforting.

"We should do something."

"I'm sure the matter is in hand."

"The Graf is our enemy, isn't he?"

"Yes."

"He looked so smart in his uniform," said Charlotte.

"Oh for goodness sake, you silly girl," said Georgina. "Lottie, the man is a... he's some sort of foreigner."

"You can still admire his uniform."

"Lottie!"

"We must do something," Charlotte insisted.

"Arthur will have everything in hand, I'm sure."

"But it's one for all."

"It'll be dangerous," said Georgina.

"Not for us, the Deering-Dolittle Sisters," said Charlotte holding up her hand to prevent Georgina interrupting: "Even if you are a Merryweather now, you are still one of us."

"One of us?"

Charlotte summed it up: "The Derring-Do Club."

"You've had that idea in your head for a while, haven't you?"

"Yes, and I did a coat-of-arms for us in my French exercise book."

"Instead of doing French?"

"You're as bad as Ness!"

"Thank you."

The electric lights flickered: surged in brightness. One above the fireplace exploded and the room was plunged into darkness.

The Graf roared: "Ha, ha! Es beginnt!"

Candles were lit.

"What are you doing, Liebchen?"

Charlotte was standing on tiptoe on a chair and reaching for a sword.

"It looked pretty," Charlotte said. "I was going to have a closer look."

"Sit with your sister."

"I wouldn't have broken it."

Charlotte came down and sat with Georgina again.

The Graf considered them for a moment: "Watch them," he ordered. A soldier snapped to attention and then stood on guard.

"I wouldn't have broken it!" Charlotte repeated. "I was only going to look."

"Honestly, Charlotte," Georgina said.

"We have to do something."

"Arthur will save us."

"How?"

"Even now, he, Captain Caruthers and Lieutenant McKendry, along with a detachment of Peelers, are no doubt presenting a warrant at the embassy door."

"They won't accept a warrant. There's diplomatic immunity."

"Nonetheless, they will insist and brush aside all objections. If not, they will force an entry. Peelers will go left and right, up and down, and they'll search the whole building rooting out these villains. But my Merry will storm ahead-"

"Revolver at the ready."

"If you like," Georgina agreed. "And then he'll barge in here, give the Graf a piece of his mind and... there'll be fisticuffs. But Arthur boxed for his regiment... probably. They'll fight back and forth, knocking over candlesticks and suits of armour until finally Arthur will just biff him on the nose."

Unconsciously, Georgina punched with her own hand, a sharp uppercut in miniature.

She raised her voice: "These cowards who murder innocent girls will show their true colours and run all the way back to that cold, horrible castle, while we put out bunting and bake cakes. See if we don't!"

There was a commotion at the door.

"I say," said Merryweather, as two burly soldiers hauled him in.

"Arthur!"

Merryweather looked across, relief on his face: "Georgina! Are you safe?"

The guard stepped forward menacingly; Georgina stayed seated.

"Not really, dearest," Georgina said.

"But you are unhurt?"

"I'm unhurt."

His captors threw him to the marbled floor, but Merryweather ignored them: "And these bounders have treated you reasonably?"

"Yes dear."

"Bring him!" The Graf ordered as he swept out.

Merryweather struggled and other soldiers came to subdue him. They picked him up and dragged him along the floor pulling his red regimental dinner jacket askew and ripping some of the braid loose.

"Arthur!"

"I'm afraid, darling, things haven't gone according to plan."

And then he was gone.


## Miss Charlotte

Charlotte looked around the grand room: "Their uniforms are different."

"Charlotte," Georgina replied. "I think-"

"All the guards who were here at first went with the Graf, so these are all new ones."

"I suppose."

"I've got an idea."

"Idea?" said Georgina. "You're not going to fight your way out."

Charlotte stood up, turned and waved her finger at Georgina.

"Let that be a lesson to you!" she shouted, loudly.

"I beg-"

Charlotte stepped back: "You! Yes, you."

"Jawohl."

"Guard her."

"Fräulein, you must-"

Charlotte shrieked: "Her Royal Highness to you!"

The man quailed, then clicked his heels and snapped to attention.

"Better. And make sure she doesn't escape. She's one of those troublesome Derring-Dos," said Charlotte, and she swept out imperiously, with a slight shrug to Georgina as she left.

The trick, Charlotte knew, was to have a reason to be wherever she was: collecting the late slips from the second form, putting up a notice for the chess club or running an errand for Miss Hardcastle. These worked for the corridors, the main hallway and anywhere in the College for Young Ladies. Here, in the Austro-Hungarian Embassy, they were all useless strategies. Worse than useless.

Outside the Grand Room in the corridor were two guards. She'd managed three yards before being captured. Perhaps she could persuade them to delay taking her back, so that her sister wouldn't be too disapproving.

The officer clicked his heels smartly and bowed from the waist. His waxed moustache stuck out as rigidly as his attention.

"Excuse me, Fräulein."

"I'm lost," Charlotte said.

"I'm sorry, Your Royal Highness, I did not recognise you," he bowed. "Please allow me to escort you back to the Royal Party," he said.

"Thank you."

The officer led the way and two other guards boxed her in at the rear as her escort. So, she was going to go down the corridor to be re-introduced to the Graf only to be marched back again.

Charlotte was shown in to the billiard room, which had wooden cues as well as the ubiquitous armoury of swords and spears attached to the walls. A younger, clean shaven version of the Graf stood with a drink.

"Prince Peter," she said.

"Pieter," he said, clicking his heels. "At your service."

"I would like, very much, for you to release an Englishman, who is being held captive here."

"You would?"

"It is a Royal command."

"From a school girl?"

"Ah... you know too."

"You are still technically a Princess, if not by blood but by marriage."

Charlotte shuddered.

"I am impressed," he toasted her with his glass. "It is not everyone who can climb the social ladder so quickly."

"Or can cast off those responsibilities so quickly."

Prince Pieter grew sombre: "Sadly no."

"The officer is very dear to my sister."

"Indeed."

"So if you could help."

"Alas, this English officer, you and even myself are prisoners here."

"You?"

"Ja."

"But perhaps he could be a prisoner here rather than in some smelly dungeon?"

"It would please your sister, you say."

"Yes, she and the officer are one," said Charlotte. "I'm the youngest Deering-Dolittle and-"

"Deering-Dolittle!"

"Yes."

The Prince dashed his glass down and strode over to the door. He hammered loudly and shouted in German, before turning back to Charlotte.

"This officer, his name?"

"Merryweather."

The Prince began shouting and the word 'Merryweather' included amongst the German like an island in a stormy sea.

Presently, a large number of men appeared. Captain Merryweather in red was the exception to all the black material and brass buttons. The guards kept their heads down to avoid the gaze of the angry Prince.

"You!" the Prince demanded: "Explain yourself! Why are you here?"

"I'm here to find my bride," Merryweather said.

"Miss Deering-Dolittle?"

"That's her."

"Deering-Dolittle!" Pieter interrupted. "Your bride? But that's impossible. Miss Deering-Dolittle and I have an understanding."

"An understanding - what utter nonsense!"

"I assure you that it is true."

"What about marriage vows?"

"I was going to take her as a mistress," said Pieter.

"No! I challenge you!" Merryweather shouted. He turned to one of the guards: "Caruthers, give me your glove."

There was a sudden shuffling of men by the door, a pushing and shoving, rather like a change of partners in a dance, and guns were levelled. Charlotte recognized two of them: Caruthers and McKendry.

"Drop it!" McKendry warned. He and Caruthers had been in disguise: they'd come in with Merryweather using the old 'prisoner-and-escort' trick from the Penny Dreadfuls. They had the jump on the two real Austro-Hungarian soldiers and there was nothing those two could do but surrender; so guns clattered to the floor and were kicked away to skitter across the marble. Charlotte claimed one.

"Miss?" Caruthers warned.

"Souvenir," Charlotte said.

"What is the meaning of this?" Prince Pieter demanded.

"We're just here for a little reconnoitre," Caruthers explained. "If you don't mind, old boy."

"Caruthers, your glove!" Merryweather insisted.

"Steady on, Merry."

"Your glove."

"What for?"

"I'm going to call this bounder out."

"Merry, duelling is strictly forbidden in England."

"We're not in England, technically we're in Austro-Hungary."

"Which you have invaded by force," Prince Pieter added. "And the wearing our uniforms means you are spies, rather than soldiers."

Merry turned his rage on the calm Austro-Hungarian: "What, precisely, pray, are your designs upon Miss Deering-Dolittle?"

"Honourable."

"With an 'understanding to have her as a mistress' - you cad."

"Steady on Merry," said Caruthers, as he tried to take over from the guards and hold his comrade back. Captain Merryweather shrugged him off just as easily as they had the Austro-Hungarians.

"I am happy to put my steel to the test," Prince Pieter said.

"Ooh, this is so exciting," said Charlotte.

Prince Pieter took note of Charlotte's presence: "Perhaps the Princess should retire."

"And miss the fun," Charlotte objected.

"Princess!" said Caruthers.

"Oh, I forgot to mention that," Charlotte admitted.

"Sabres?" Merryweather said.

"I believe form requires you to challenge me first?" said Prince Pieter.

"Fine!" Merryweather tapped his pockets. "Anyone got a glove?"

There was a general show of checking pockets, but to no avail.

"Caruthers?" said Merryweather, his hot temper turning to embarrassment.

"Chap at the cloakroom collected hat, coat, gloves, the lot."

"I've got this lacy pair," said Charlotte helpfully.

Merryweather came over: "Thank you."

He took the pair, paused with a pained expression as he saw how light blue and feminine they were, and then handed one back: "I only need the one."

Merryweather strode into the centre of the room.

"I call you out, Sir," he said with muster. He flung the glove to the ground, an effect lessened in impact when it fluttered down like a wounded butterfly.

"It's hardly a gauntlet," Caruthers said.

Prince Pieter clicked his heels, bowed and with extraordinary dignity picked up the lacy object.

"Right-" Merryweather began, but events paused as the Prince returned the glove to Charlotte.

"Thank you," she said, beaming.

"Your weapons, Prince?"

"I choose sabres."

"Right... do you have any sabres?"

Prince Pieter pondered for a moment: "I think there are some on the wall in the display room... Hauptmann!"

A captured officer snapped to attention: "Ja!"

"Fetch some sabres."

"Jawohl."

"He can't go, he's our prisoner," McKendry said.

"I give you his parole," Pieter said. "Hauptmann, you will obtain two matching sabres from the Display Room and return. You will not raise the alarm."

"Jawohl."

McKendry kept hold of the man's collar: "I don't think so."

Merryweather, Caruthers and McKendry huddled together as much as they could while keeping an eye on their two prisoners and the Prince.

"We could fight with foils..." Pieter suggested signifying the weaponry, "... or spears... or billiard cues."

"I can't fight with foils," said Merryweather, "he's aristocracy, they use foils all the time. And they practise!"

"Fair point," said Caruthers. "All right, you, straight there and straight back."

"Ja," said the Hauptmann.

The man departed for the display room.

The rest of the men stood around for a while, admired the paintings as if fascinated by the illustrious Austro-Hungarians on show.

Suddenly, the mantelpiece clock chimed, its tinging announcement of midday taking an age.

"Nasty weather," said McKendry.

"Ja," said the Prince. "Is it usual for this time of year?"

"We have a lot of rain here," said Merryweather.

"Ach, so my brother has been boasting."

"It's something to do with low pressure from the Atlantic."

"British science and industry rising to the greatest challenge of the age, predicting the weather."

"Yes, ha, you could say that. Jolly tricky..." Merryweather stopped himself from laughing aloud and steeled his expression: "...and all that."

"Ja."

"Yes-sss."

"Yass."

"There is the matter of the seconds," the Prince said.

"Right," said Merryweather. "Caruthers?"

"Preferred being your best man, but delighted, old boy."

"And you?"

"I choose the sister as my second," the Prince said. Charlotte took a few paces into the assembly.

"Thank you."

"You can't choose a woman as a second, she's not even supposed to be here," McKendry said.

"I believe my step-mother has every right to be here."

"Step-mother?!" said Caruthers.

"Yes," said Charlotte, "I was going to mention that as well."

"But you're old enough to be her... older brother."

Everyone pointed their guns at the door as it opened!

It was the Hauptmann laden with cutlasses and various other swords. He placed them down on the baize of the billiard table.

"This is a farce, Merry, let's just call it off and have a brandy."

"Rubbish," said Merryweather, his gander up. He picked out a cutlass and swept it back and forth experimentally to get a feel for the weapon.

"You are not trained in the cavalry cutlass," observed the Prince.

"No, I suppose not."

"How about pistols?"

"Why not just punch the living daylights out of each other and be done?" said Caruthers. "And then we can get on fighting the rest of them."

Charlotte, completely beside herself with the idea of it all, jumped up and down and the men squared up.

"There's a lady present," McKendry pointed out. "Miss, I think it best if you retire to the... somewhere else?"

"I will not," said Charlotte. "I'm not going to miss two men fighting over me for anything."

"Your Royal Highness, with all due respect, I am not betrothed to you," said Pieter.

"But you sent Ness to talk to me."

"Yes, but then you married my father."

"Look," said Merryweather, "let's just get on with it, shall we? We are pushed for time as it is."

"Very well," said Pieter, swishing his blade again. "To the first blood."

Merryweather was having none of it: "To the death."

# CHAPTER XXIII

## Miss Deering-Dolittle

When Theseus navigated the labyrinth to face the Minotaur, Ariadne had given him a ball of thread to find his way out. Why couldn't they, Earnestine thought, have simply made a map? She made a pencil mark in her notebook: 75 paces further in to this turning. Not that she'd needed to keep such a careful record, because the Austro-Hungarians with their typical efficiency had placed duckboards over some of the channels making the trail particularly easy to follow.

Deeper in, she had heard a roaring, not unlike some mythical monster, and the clatter of machinery, joined as she crept closer by deep guttural voices.

She hid in an alcove between two study brick columns, shutting her dark lantern.

Guards came and went, like a line of ants in activity and in appearance: they were black Macintoshed and complete with their fearful looking breathing apparatus.

They'd created a new tunnel connecting the sewers to another set of tunnels beyond. As Earnestine worked her way around, she realised that this was the main route linking the Austro-Hungarian's underground base to the rest of the system.

Above was a sign: a flick of flashlight and she noted down its legend: 'Junction XXIV'.

A group of soldiers passed by and Earnestine hung back in the shadows again. Once they had gone, Earnestine wondered if she should find their source or their destination, but no-one won prizes at the Geographical Society for finding the delta of the Nile.

She nearly tripped over some rubber-coated cables that trailed down the passageway. These were clearly some sort of flexible pipes for the galvanic energies.

At the end of a tunnel, she found a set of clothing.

She put a coat on, buttoned it and then selected a bug-eye, repelled as she pulled the pliant seal over her face.

She climbed a ladder and came out in a brightly lit chamber with fine wooden doors.

She picked one.

This was a changing room similar to the underground one and Earnestine went on into a carpeted corridor. The sudden change was disorientating as she moved from the underworld of dank brickwork and into another world of plush, wallpapered decadence.

"Achtung!" It was the Vögte, the Graf's underling: she was caught. He shouted: "Achten Sie auf den Teppich!"

Why didn't they speak English?

If the Vögte was here, then perhaps Pieter... but he was in Austro-Hungary and she didn't care either.

The Vögte was rudely pointing his finger at her, stabbing downwards at her feet. Earnestine frowned inside her mask and looked down. Framed in the round distorting lenses, she saw her stolen boots and where they had tracked mud across the deep pile carpet. That was muck from the sewers and it would be near impossible for the maid to scrub it out.

The Vögte was regarding her, a gaze trying to penetrate her disguise.

She should run. She knew the way back through the sewers and it would take time for him to summon help.

An officer ran up breathlessly.

The man thrust a revolver into her hand and called her to follow.

She did so, stomping down the corridor.

Behind her, the Vögte let out a cry of exasperated despair.

## Mrs Arthur Merryweather

Georgina sat primly, feeling forgotten.

An officer and a soldier dressed in that appallingly frightening mask burst into the room and rushed across. The Bug Eye one stopped to stare at her for a moment before moving on.

The other officers moved over to the door to see what was happening.

No-one was looking at her.

There were swords and spikes and other sharp implements attached to the wall. The chair Charlotte had put under them was still there, but it really wasn't Georgina's style at all.

She stood, brushed her dress down and calmly walked to the other exit.

In the corridor beyond there was a contingent of military men.

"Afternoon, Graf," said Georgina. She kept her head down and maintained her pace. The top of the main stairs leading down to the exit was only ten yards away: nine, eight... there was a lot of mud tramped into the carpet.

"Miss Deering-Dolittle."

Georgina partly turned: "Mrs Merryweather," she corrected, and she kept going.

Seven.

"Stay!"

Six.

A gun was cocked with a loud click.

Georgina could see down the stairs, across the entrance hall lit by the light of the street. There was a flash of lightning as if someone had taken a daguerreotype using flash powder.

She turned and faced them.

"You only had to ask," she said. "Please."

The Graf's face tightened: "Please."

"That's better. Manners maketh-"

The Graf turned to one of his men: "Where's the other one!"

The officer looked nonplussed.

"Don't you understand English?" the Graf yelled.

"Nein, mein Graf."

"Wo ist der andere?" The Graf barged past and strode down the corridor. "Bringen Sie sie hier."

The officer came up to Georgina. "Kommen Sie mit mir," he said.

"I'm so sorry," she said. "I don't understand German."

"Kommen! Sie! Mit! Mir!"

"Shouting isn't going to make it any clearer. Good day."

She had her foot on the top step before he grabbed her by her collar and manhandled her down the corridor.

"I can see you've not been properly - *ouch* - educated."

She was soon back in the Grand Room.

The Graf was staring at the chair under the swords as if he was counting the family silverware to make sure nothing had been stolen.

"Kommen Sie!"

## Miss Charlotte

Charlotte was entranced. The two men circled each other, their eyes focused on their opponent and their determination-

"Can we move the billiard table?"

"Ja, it is in the way."

They put their sabres down on the massive table and each took one end to heave.

"This is heavy."

"Ja!"

Caruthers waved his gun impatiently: "Merry, for goodne-"

The door burst open.

They grabbed their guns and sabres, but the two soldiers who broke in had the jump on Caruthers and McKendry. Just as the two Gentlemen Adventurers had their weapons trained on the Austro-Hungarians, so the newcomers had their weapons pointed at the two British.

"This changes nothing," said Pieter. "The English were willing to act as... referees so we could fight for Miss Deering-Dolittle. I'm sure we will show the same sportsmanship and fair play."

Captain Merryweather assumed a fighting posture: "Right!"

Prince Pieter followed suit: "En garde!"

They circled, wider now that the billiard table was no longer central in the room, and then slashed at each other, their blades clashing. Merryweather was a wild flash of scarlet to the Prince's more measured dark movements.

There was another raucous interruption at the doorway.

One of the Austro-Hungarian soldiers, the one in the strange mask, pushed another forward. Caruthers and McKendry seized their chance and regained their weapons.

"We're the referees now," said Caruthers.

"You fight for Miss Deering-Dolittle?!" the masked soldier demanded in a voice muffled by the bug-eye mask.

"Ja," said Prince Pieter. "We have an understanding."

"Well, she must have meant to break it off, because Miss Deering-Dolittle and I are married," said Merryweather.

"Is this true?" Prince Pieter demanded.

"I was his best man, old boy," said Caruthers.

"And I was Georgina's Maid of Honour and I gave her away," Charlotte piped in.

Prince Pieter looked confused: "You're married to Miss Deering-Dolittle?"

"I'm married to Mrs Arthur Merryweather," Merryweather insisted.

"Let's not confuse things," said Caruthers. "She was Miss Deering-Dolittle."

"Earnestine?" Prince Pieter asked.

"No," said Charlotte, "Earnestine's the eldest, I'm the youngest and Georgina, Mrs Merryweather, is the middle sister."

Pieter look to Merryweather.

"I married Georgina," said Merryweather.

"For me, it is Earnestine," Pieter replied. He lowered his sword: "It appears we've been duelling under a misconception, please accept my apologies and my congratulations."

"Yes," said Merryweather. "All rather embarrassing."

Caruthers began to laugh and McKendry joined in, which made the two combatants look all the more foolish. Soon the mirth was added to by the Austro-Hungarian guards until everyone, except the bug-eyed one, was laughing.

"I don't think you need to fight a duel," McKendry concluded.

"Let's have a drink," said Caruthers, taking the cutlass off Merryweather. "You two might even end up as sort of brothers-in-law."

"This is so disappointing," said Charlotte.

Merryweather put out his hand and Prince Pieter shook it.

The masked soldier stepped forward levelling a revolver at the Prince: "That is not true."

"I assure you it is true," said Pieter.

The door burst open again and into the room came the Graf flanked by some soldiers. The situation was reversed yet again.

"So, brother, consorting with the enemy," said the Graf.

Oblivious to everything, the Bug Eye soldier stepped right up to the Prince.

"We do not..." Earnestine ripped the mask off, "...have an understanding."

# Chapter XXIV

## Miss Deering-Dolittle

Pieter was surprised to see her. Earnestine could see it in the way his blue eyes seemed to widen. She was pleased to see him and so angry.

"Gentlemen," the Graf said, "I think I have the upper hand now."

Caruthers, McKendry and Charlotte passed their revolvers over to the Austro-Hungarians and then went over to join Merryweather by the Billiard table. Caruthers surreptitiously picked up a red ball. The Graf himself took the revolver from Earnestine's unresisting hand.

Merryweather leapt forward: "Georgina!"

His colleagues held him back.

Earnestine turned to the door to see Georgina escorted in by yet another soldier. He pushed his captive over to Charlotte.

"I tried," Charlotte said.

"Me too," said Georgina.

The Graf turned his attention to the three British men: "If I am not mistaken you are three of Major Dan's finest."

Caruthers opened his mouth to quip, but the Graf turned to the young ladies.

"And all three sisters together, a full set," he said. "Even we in Austro-Hungary have heard of the infamous Deering-Dolittles from Kent. You are all mad."

"We're not mad," Earnestine retorted, "we're explorers."

"You're troublemakers," he replied.

She pulled off the black mackintosh to show her sensible tweed dress beneath and her medium kit bag. The Graf snatched it off her.

"Fräulein," the Graf said, "this is no adventure."

"I know."

"Brother," said Prince Pieter, his place in the room betraying that he was neither with the Austro-Hungarians or the prisoners. Or by her side, Earnestine noted.

"Pieter?"

"Release the young ladies. They have nothing to do with this."

"Nothing to do with this!" the Graf said. "I chased this one half way across Europe and together they destroyed one of my Zeppelins, seriously damaging another. What are they doing here on Austro-Hungarian soil? Practising the pianoforte? Embroidery? Bearing sons?"

"Gustav!"

"Pieter, be careful, the Gräfin's Great Plan needs you, but my Great War does not."

"You mean to go through with this."

"Hear the thunder."

They listened. There was only the rain, but then there was a flash.

"Nichts kann mich jetzt aufhalten!"

Thunder rumbled under the Graf's laughter.

"This is madness," said Pieter.

"Nein, but to keep you on your best behaviour, I will take the women as hostages." The Graf gestured to his soldiers. "Bewachen Sie sie, bringen sie die Frauen. Kommen Sie!"

Three soldiers selected a Deering-Dolittle each to escort.

"I need one of the men, a volunteer."

"No!" Pieter leapt across the room and the Graf struck him across the face so hard that he lifted the Prince off the floor. The younger man fell awkwardly and McKendry went to him.

"A volunteer!" the Graf insisted.

Merryweather stepped forward.

"Good! Kommen Sie!"

The Graf, prisoners and escort marched out leaving a few of the guards with their guns levelled at Caruthers, McKendry and Pieter. At the last moment Earnestine caught Caruthers's eye.

She nodded, he nodded back.


## Mrs Arthur Merryweather

The last thing Georgina saw as she was dragged out was Caruthers rubbing the red billiard ball on his trousers as if he was playing cricket and was about to run up to bowl.

They were dragged along corridors. Along the way, she reached for Arthur and occasionally their hands touched.

Finally, they arrived at what looked like a changing room and from there they went down an awkward ladder into the bowels of the Earth.


## Miss Charlotte

"So what's this understanding?" Charlotte asked Earnestine.

"It's just some nonsense that the Prince developed when we were talking in his bedroom."

"Bedroom?" Charlotte repeated. "You were alone in his bedroom."

"I was not alone, he was there too."

Charlotte opened her mouth wide: "Earnestine Deering-Dolittle!"

"It wasn't like that! I was his secretary."

"Is that what it's called?"

"You are not too old to have a good spanking."

"Are you challenging me? Do you want to borrow my other glove?"

"What!?"

"So you were flirting with the Prince when he was engaged to me?"

"I was not flirting, he was courting."

"Same thing."

"It most certainly is not."

"But-"

"Charlotte, this is not a subject we will discuss - ever!"

"Is that because they're going to kill us?"

"Not just that, there are other reasons too."

# CHAPTER XXV

## Miss Deering-Dolittle

Earnestine found it difficult to think with Charlotte's incessant prattle. Back wherever he was, Caruthers was going to try something and she had to be ready to do her bit.

They reached a small room that had been tiled. It was a laboratory or an operating theatre, full of strange galvanic equipment and flickering lighting. The Graf went to talk to a man in a white coat, dumping her medium kit bag on a side table. They were pushed to one side and then an orderly expertly attached a thick shackle to one of their wrists and a heavy chain was threaded through the loop and connected to solid metal hoops set in the wall. Finally, the end was fixed with a large padlock.

Charlotte sat down and in doing so she tugged at the chain forcing Georgina to sit and then Earnestine had no choice either.

As he was the man, they'd taken no chances with Merryweather: he was secured with two shackles and chained to a loop of his own.

"They're going to kill us, aren't they?" Charlotte said.

"Of course not," Merryweather said.

"Arthur, dearest, please don't patronise Charlotte," Georgina said. "She'll never learn if we don't explain things truthfully. Yes, Lottie, they're going to kill us."

"And then bring us back to that horrible undead state?" Charlotte had gone pale. All her blithering had been a way to avoid thinking about what might happen in this dungeon. She had seen this before, Earnestine realised, and she was rightly terrified of the ungodly process.

Chains, tiles, apparatus, the Graf, the orderly, a Doctor, soldiers, chains... it was hopeless.

## Mrs Arthur Merryweather

Merryweather coughed: "Only the men."

"Oh! Dearest."

"Darling, I'd rather not be... you know."

"Untotened?"

"Yes."

"Dearest, once you escape and get a gun, please save two bullets."

"Three!" Charlotte asked.

"Four," said Earnestine.

The Graf had finished talking to the white coated orderlies and turned to them.

"To calibrate the process fully, I will need a corpse," he said, "ah, but which?"

His revolver tracked back and forth, hesitating first on Earnestine, then Georgina, Arthur and finally Charlotte.

"Which one is the pluckiest?" he asked.

"They're all plucky," said Captain Merryweather.

They were in trouble, Georgina knew that from the way that Earnestine had narrowed her lips and from Arthur's kind look in her direction. She knew that he would save her. He had a gun strapped to his ankle. He was just waiting for the right moment: any second now.

And she felt proud that despite their desperate straits, her husband was made of the right material, and he'd spoken the truth when he'd said they were all plucky.

The Graf fired!

## Miss Charlotte

Charlotte jumped at the shot: she touched her chest and found she was unharmed. Glancing left, she saw that all the others were fine too, looking about like her to see where the bullet had gone.

"Oh my," Merryweather said, "what jolly bad luck."

A thin trail of vivid blood leaked out of his chest to soak invisibly into his scarlet uniform.

Georgina screeched: "Arthur!!?"

Merryweather turned away from his wife and looked directly at Charlotte.

He coughed up some blood as he tried to say something.

"Don't," Charlotte said. "Save your strength."

"Emily," he said. "Em... ily... I... slip... way."

Charlotte reached out, he was just close enough, and put her hands on his shoulders, but his eyes rolled upwards and he flopped forward, gasping. The chain attaching them all together, and to the wall, jerked and strained as Georgina tried desperately to reach her husband.

"Put him on the table," said the Graf. "And connect him up."

"But, Mein Graf," said the Doctor, "he is still alive?"

"Then finish him off."

Georgina's despair rattled in her throat.

The Doctor bent over the fallen Captain, wrenched him away from Charlotte, and then twisted the dying man's neck around. Merryweather's body jerked once and the Doctor, satisfied, signalled to the two orderlies. The white suited men did as they were told, neither looking any of the three sisters in the eye. Once they had removed his chains and dropped poor Merry onto the table, they connected up the wiring and emptied a liberal amount of chemical from the jars over his body. Finally, the surgeon stepped forward and cauterised the bullet hole.

"Leave him alone!" Georgina hollered.

The surgeon added a brass control box to Merryweather's skull making a sharp noise like a brazil nut cracking. He checked his patient and then, satisfied, he nodded to the Graf. Zala waved them him and his orderlies away.

"Do not worry, her husband's departure is but brief," said the Graf. "In a moment the electrical pressure will reach a critical point and its artificial life force will run through the wires themselves. The husband will return to embrace his bride and eat his wedding breakfast."

He chuckled as he left, slamming the door behind them and the lock turned with an awful finality.

Charlotte noticed the blood on her hands.

# CHAPTER XXVI

## Miss Deering-Dolittle

Earnestine considered the table, each wall, the ceiling and the floor, the door, the chains holding them to the pipes, the plumbing itself and finally the door again.

They had to get out, soon, sooner - now!

The strange apparatus fizzed.

The situation was desperate: they were chained up and captured by the Graf, who was in Earnestine's opinion, quite mad. She had to think. And it was raining.

Soon this lunatic would harness the galvanic power of lightning, the charge would course down copper strips to activate thousands of corpses and the army of the dead would rise out of the ground to destroy London.

And they were chained up and captured and it was still raining. No matter how many times she checked everything in the room, nothing came to mind.

"We have to get out," Earnestine said.

Charlotte ignored her: "Gina, Gina..."

For the first time, Earnestine looked at her sister. Georgina was shockingly white as if all the blood had been drained out of her rather than the poor unfortunate Captain. Her mouth was open, slack, and her eyes wide, utterly unfocused.

Earnestine interrupted Charlotte's cooing: "Gina!"

There was no reaction.

"Ness, her..."

Earnestine reached over, clunking the chains as she did so, and struck Georgina across her face, the slap echoing off the cold white tiles.

"Bally hell, Ness!" Charlotte screamed at her.

"Language!"

"She's lost her husband."

"I'm sorry. I'm so sorry, but we have to do something!"

Earnestine pulled her wrists and yanked the chains, dragging the other two down as she shortened the length available to them. Georgina moved for the first time like a lifeless puppet whose string had been jerked.

"If you both got closer to the end," Earnestine said, "then I could reach the door."

"And do what?!"

"I don't know! Something! Anything!"

The apparatus crackled, energy sparking across the exposed wires and a streak of lightning arced across the upright terminals. The might of the thunder god was tamed within those metal rods. It glared, cutting the very air in two, and a taste of rust filled the cell.

Charlotte pushed her chain through the gap between the pipe and the wall, she pulled at Georgina's bonds too and Earnestine could move, stand even, with enough slack to reach the door. She struck it with the palm of her hand, once, twice, and then over and over until it stung.

"Help! Help!" she shouted.

Then she remembered her medium kit bag. There it was on the side table containing its bounty of a penknife, compass, spare batteries for the flashlight, binoculars, spare buttons, spare socks and... Kendal Mint Cake, and none of it any damned use.

The electricity leapt up the wires, burning a line across their eyes, everything was crossed with an orange slash as the image was etched into their eyes. Captain Merryweather's body jerked again, but this time in a strange parody of dying. His features were outlined in blue and white, bright marks, and his buttons glistened and sparked.

"Arthur," Georgina murmured weakly.

Charlotte's sobs became audible: "Oh please, Gina, don't look."

Georgina glared at Earnestine: "Arthur..."

There was a moment between the two sisters, each unable to tear away from the other's accusing look. A moan issued from the corpse, a hollow and inhuman sound, as the hands spasmed and grasped.

Earnestine was all out of ideas.

Georgina spoke: "....has a gun in his sock."

Earnestine estimated the gap between the metal hoop in the wall and the surgical table, measured the chains in her mind and knew that there weren't enough links - nothing like enough - even as she scrambled towards the reanimating corpse. Her free arm thrust forward, her hand outstretched, but his leg was a foot away. She strained, the metal manacle cutting into her wrist: ten, eight inches away. The others yelped and Earnestine leant further, six inches... five.

Too far and too late.

The corpse came back to life.

Its leg hit her hand as the body turned and sat up. Earnestine fell to the floor as she scrabbled with its trouser leg to find the small revolver strapped above its ankle.

The monster turned its head down, its eyes red and inflamed. It looked at the prone girl and bared its teeth.

Her nails broke on the straps, her fingers bleeding as the metal object refused to come out. Merryweather's cadaver reached down, its hands touching her hair, her head and then her throat.

"Arthur!"

The creature responded to the noise of Georgina's cry, its yellow eyes focussing on her.

Earnestine found the gun, wrenched it free and slithered back, tugged along by the others pulling at the chain. She found the padlock, pushed the barrel of the gun right over the keyhole and squeezed-

Blind and deaf.

The blast at that range threw Earnestine into the air. She flopped awkwardly to one side. In the distance, seemingly miles away and underwater, screaming but unheard above a sound like rushing water, Charlotte was mouthing something.

The padlock was scorched, but it was a Yale and Towne and it was still in one piece.

"Only five rounds in the Bull Dog!" Charlotte shouted.

She fired again, braced and ready this time, and hearing the explosion. The lock jumped like a frog and split - thank goodness - and the chain slipped free.

The others must have been ready, for the metal links clattered like train carriages through the tunnel of her manacle and she was free. Earnestine dodged the attacking creature and made for the door, but it caught her.

The gun went off in her hand, smashing the white tiles on the floor as it ricocheted.

The monster stumbled.

Earnestine reached the door and deftly inserted the stubby British Bull Dog into the handle mechanism. It exploded, a single round doing for it completely. The air seemed to rush inwards as the door opened.

"Last round," Charlotte yelled.

Earnestine turned, levelled the firearm at the abomination and-

"NO!"

"Gina, I must!"

Georgina stepped into Earnestine's line of fire, the gun right up against her forehead.

"I must shoot him," Earnestine shouted.

Distantly, trapped in the room, Charlotte screamed.

"He's my husband."

"There's only one bullet."

Georgina put out her hand: "Give it to me."

Earnestine pushed Georgina out of the way, aimed and then changed her mind.

She gave her sister the gun.

## Mrs Arthur Merryweather

"Arthur, I'm so sorry."

## Miss Charlotte

The blood splattered over Charlotte's face.

Georgina dropped the now useless gun to the floor. It clattered on the tiles.

"I loved him," Georgina said.

"Yes," Earnestine said. "He loved you."

"Yes," said Georgina and she looked accusingly at Charlotte. "Who was Emily?"

Emily?

"It's just the three of us now," said Earnestine.

"Yes," said Georgina, as she allowed Earnestine to lead her out into the passageway.

"Get my bag," Earnestine said.

Charlotte collected the canvas bag from the table and then saw the discarded revolver. Of course, Earnestine wouldn't have bought any spare rounds, but there might be some ammunition somewhere to reload it. She picked it up: it was a good gun and she knew a fair amount about weapons from all those cadets and-

"Pass me the map."

As Charlotte looked in the bag, Earnestine passed a lantern to Georgina, who took it automatically, and then Earnestine snatched her notebook. The shackle still on her wrist clanked with Charlotte's. Charlotte checked in the kit bag and found a penknife. The attachment for getting stones out of horses' hooves fitted the basic lock and some jiggling freed her. She moved to Earnestine's.

"Ouch... oh, yes," said Earnestine.

Charlotte got the thing off.

"I think," Earnestine continued, "we're somewhere here. Maybe that way is Junction Thirty-four."

"You've written Ex, Ex, Eye, Vee," said Charlotte, undoing Georgina's shackle

"Yes, Charlotte, it's Latin.  They numbered the junctions, slipways and passages."

"Emily... Em- il- y."

"Not now, so down here-"

"Not Emily!" she said.  "Em, el, ee!"

"I beg your pardon," Earnestine said.

"What did Merry say?"

"Charlotte, I think for Gina's sake-"

"What did he say - exactly!?"

Earnestine was clearly taken aback: "Emily, I slip away."

"No, he said 'I slip way'... the I$^{st}$ slipway."

"I've got the third and fourth, so the first will be..."

"Come on!"

"Where?"

"Emily!"

Charlotte went into the passageway.  It was brick built, part of the sewers, with an arched roof.  Charlotte moved quickly looking at the walls.  High above she saw a sign nailed into the wall: 'Junction XVII'.

"Here!  Junction Seventeen."

"Left," said Earnestine, "no, your other left.  Your other, other left!"

"Ness, there are only two lefts."

"I mean straight on".

Further on, there was 'Junction XVI'.

She found another sign: "Passage Twenty Three."

Earnestine came around to catch up, leading Georgina by the hand.

Charlotte pointed: "Ah!"

It was 'Slipway II'.

"Got to be... yes."

The three sisters went on, deeper it seemed, into the tunnels and passageways.  Georgina held the lantern, its light gleamed off the slick and damp walls and reflected off the dark water to cast ominous shadows. Earnestine flicked her flashlight on and off, its yellow illumination pale and false against the honest fire of the lantern.

"Slipway I," said Charlotte and she began to hunt around.

"There's no-one here," Earnestine stated, obviously. "Who are we looking for?"

Charlotte found a long metal box hidden behind a supporting column. She flicked the metal catch and flung it open.

"Emily: 'M', 'L', 'E'," she said. "The Magazine Lee-Enfield rifle developed by Mister James Paris Lee at the Royal Small Arms Factory, Enfield, ten rounds in the magazine, five shell charger clip, muzzle velocity of two thousand, four hundred and forty one feet per second, effective range up to five hundred and fifty yards."

Charlotte flipped the weapon up and over, expertly, and then her dainty finger moved from the front to the rear as she explained.

"Fixed post front sights, sliding ramp rear sights, bolt action," she clanked the bolt open and then rammed it home before bringing the weapon up to shoulder. "This bit sticks out when it's cocked, then hard into the shoulder, feel it on your bone, and then you line this 'V' in the back sight with the foresight, target, the enemy, so aim for the head... squeeze the trigger, don't jerk it, gently squeeze... and-"

It went click.

"Bang! Dead. See?" Charlotte held it up and continued explaining: "Then bolt back - one - and the empty shell is ejected, then - two - bolt back in. It catches the round and then - three - flip it back into position: ready to fire. It couldn't be simpler."

"One, two, three," Earnestine repeated, her hand miming the action she'd seen.

Charlotte thrust the rifle towards Georgina: "Gina, have a go."

"I'd honestly rather not," said Georgina.

"And it's aim - fire, always aim-fire. Aim-fire. The trick is to hit the target, not use up bullets. And count your rounds: one, two, three, four, five... at ten, you need to change the magazine or manually load bullets in like this."

Charlotte took a bullet and showed them where to insert it and how to ram the bolt home.

"And see," Charlotte explained. "You can shove them into the magazine too. Or the charger over the top."

"How do you know all this?" Earnestine asked.

"I... er.,. read a book," said Charlotte. "Look, there's another revolver and ammunition."

"Lottie, did you talk to those cadets, who you let ogle you at our old school?"

"I might have done," said Charlotte. She began to stuff handfuls of the smaller shells into the pockets of her Aerial Corps uniform. Men's outfits were so much more convenient.

Earnestine tutted: "You should be ashamed."

"They showed me how to fire the rifles."

"What good is firing rifles for a young lady?"

"It's going to be jolly useful in the moment," Georgina interrupted.

"Gina, don't take her side," said Earnestine. "Exactly how... words fail me."

"To show me how to hold the rifle to my shoulder, they took turns to put their arms round me and-"

"Charlotte!"

"It was lovely."

"Charlotte Deering-Dolittle!"

"Ness?"

"Clearly, once we've saved the British Empire, I shall to have words with you about decorum and... pretty much everything."

# CHAPTER **XXVII**

## Miss Deering-Dolittle

Earnestine held the button of the flashlight down using up the battery, but this was a desperate situation. They all clustered around the map.

"This is their headquarters," said Earnestine, needlessly interpreting her perfectly legible and neat script. "All their galvanic cables go there. So they have to go down this tunnel that goes to Junction Thirty Four to reach the sewers."

"We tell Major Dan," said Georgina, her voice still cracking with emotion.

"By the time we get there, Graf Zala's army will be everywhere."

"We're lost then."

"When Caruthers and McKendry escape, they'll-"

"If?"

Earnestine considered for a moment: "No, they'll escape and they'll get help, but... we have to give them time to organise something."

The map in Earnestine's hand blurred in her vision. So many times Uncle Jeremiah had traced her hand down this or that river, following the tributaries and it had all been so exciting and clear. She felt lost: there were knuckles and faint blue veins on the back of her hand, but this was all just pencil scribbles.

"It narrows here," said Charlotte, pointing.

"Yes."

"So, this is our Thermopylae, we hold them here, and then fall back here, which we'll call the Alamo."

"Can't we pick British battles rather than Greek and American defeats? Thermopylae and Alamo weren't exactly victories."

"They were."

"Not for the people involved."

"But they did turn the tide of the war."

"British."

"I'll think of some."

Earnestine folded away the map safely in her bag and then they collected the ammunition box. They emptied it to make it lighter as they only needed three rifles after all. Charlotte had taken the revolver - no-one had questioned this. She loaded Merryweather's small gun too as a spare, each pocket of her enemy uniform assigned to a different revolver's ammunition. Although why they didn't make the guns take the same ammunitions, so Charlotte could use one bag, was beyond Earnestine. And why could Charlotte remember point 455, point 320 and point uncle Tom Cobley, and not remember to tidy her room or do her Latin homework?

There were ropes on either side of the box, so it swung between Earnestine and Charlotte. Georgina quietly brought up the rear.

They sloshed along the passageway, the light from Earnestine's lantern casting its beams about the curved brick ceiling. There were slopes with stairs at the side in places where the unpleasant water cascaded down.

"Is it me or is it getting deeper?" Charlotte asked.

"It has been raining," said Earnestine.

They reached the right spot where two tunnels joined and further down was a raised brick area. They could hear distant mechanical sounds - they were close now - and their voices dropped to urgent whispers. Charlotte pointed and then hefted the ammunition box up onto their final redoubt, a metal covered platform, waist high, bolted into a brick base. At the far end a rectangle of shadow hid an opening. There were any number of passages leading off: they had to hold them here, otherwise they would overrun this underworld and then emerge all over London.

"We can't keep going back and forth for bullets," said Earnestine.

"Let's fill our bags," Charlotte said. She yanked open the top and handed a rifle to Earnestine.

"We better take up position," Earnestine said, "Gina, can you fill the bags for us?"

"Sorry?"

"Fill the bags with bullets."

"Yes."

Earnestine and Charlotte went to select the first line of defence while Georgina began to fill the bags.

"This is too wide for Thermopylae..." said Charlotte. "It's more like Isandlwana."

"That was a British defeat," said Earnestine.

"How about Laing's Nek?"

"The Boers won."

"At the end, our boys' rifle fire allowed a retreat."

"What about-"

Georgina snapped at them: "Stop bickering and pick something!"

"Sorry."

Slowly, as they waited, the distant galvanic noises, sparks and pops began to be joined by growls and wailing. The sounds grew and, as the distance shortened, it became more distinct; there were splashes too, signs that the untoten army was near.

"With all this water," Charlotte whispered, "we ought to choose a naval battle. How about the Battle of Santa Cruz de Tenerife, Nelson's first against the Spanish."

"So this is Tenerife then?"

"Yes."

Earnestine considered the dark, moody passageway, the constant dripping and the stench of foul water, and so unlike a Spanish island in the Atlantic. It was not the only part of Charlotte's scheme that disturbed her.

"Lottie?" she whispered.

"Ness?"

"Why do you choose nothing but British defeats?"

"Oh... I thought you'd have realised," said Charlotte, biting her lip. "It's simply because we don't stand a chance."

"Ah... yes, of course. Perhaps we could call the last redoubt 'Rorke's Drift', it would..." Earnestine thought hard for the right phrase, "...cheer Georgina up."

"Very well," Charlotte turned to shout to Georgina. "Gina! We're calling the final redoubt 'Rorke's Drift'."

Georgina didn't reply.

"Ness, Georgina doesn't look cheered up."

"She's had a trying day."

## Mrs Arthur Merryweather

Georgina felt she'd finished sorting the ammunition. No matter which containers she shifted the brass cylinders into, they didn't multiply. Indeed, some slipped from her shaking hands and dropped into the dirty water.

With each handful dumped in the purses, she said: "Ammo."

"Gina," Earnestine said. "Now, I think."

"Ammo... ammo... ammo..." It reminded her of something.

"Gina!"

Done, she thought, and all divided equally like chocolates at Christmas. She went over to the other two and handed out the bags: "Two boxes in... Rorke's Drift, a purse each and the kit bag."

"Thank you," said Earnestine, putting the medium kit bag over her shoulder.

It came to her and she mumbled it aloud: "Ammo... ammas... ammat... ammarmus... ammartis... ammant."

"I beg your pardon?"

"I was just thinking."

It reminded her of another rhyme too: Amazo, Amazon, I'm-a... and she did feel lost, utterly and completely.

"Amazons are warrior women," Georgina said.

"So are we," Charlotte replied. "We'll get them, won't we?"

"Yes," said Georgina, "they don't deserve to exist. We should wipe them all from the face of the Earth, purge their filthy perverted way of life and be done with them all."

"And then we'll deal with the Austro-Hungarians."

"I was talking about the Austro-Hungarians!"

"There's Pieter," Earnestine said.

"Do you love him?" Georgina asked.

"I beg your pardon!"

"Do you love him?"

"Don't be ridiculous! Our families haven't been introduced."

Charlotte interrupted any further discussion: "Look out!"

The light at the end of the passage flickered, shadows moved, cast down the long tunnel by the creatures.

The light at the corner was almost completely obscured and then the untoten army came into view.

"Fire when you see the whites of their eyes," said Charlotte.

"Their eyes are bloodshot," said Georgina.

"Fire when... I tell you. We must stop them at twenty yards."

"That pipe in the wall?" said Earnestine.

"...yes."

The rifle felt slippery in Georgina's hand, and heavy, suddenly she couldn't hold it up. Unbidden tears welled in her eyes and the approaching monstrosities appeared to blur and vanish. She could feel her heart in her chest beating and, despite her corset, her breathing quickened making her head spin. She took up position to

Earnestine's right and levelled the rifle. It wavered far more than the other two.

"Gina, hold it together," said Earnestine. "Stiff upper lip."

They were as ready as they'd ever be, she knew, and it felt good to be standing shoulder to shoulder with her sisters.

"For Queen and Country," Earnestine said.

"For Arthur," Georgina added.

"Let's nobble some Austro-Hungarian untoten right in their nancy," said Charlotte.

Earnestine was horrified: "Charlotte... language please!"

## Miss Charlotte

Charlotte kept her gun steady, and the head of the central untoten was obscured by the far sight as it nestled in the valley of the near sight.

Earnestine was lecturing quietly, droning on and on like the undead army approaching them: "Lottie, if we don't maintain our standards, then what would be the purpose in winning... or, in this case, the purpose of making a stand? Being British doesn't make us automatically better; instead, we must strive to better ourselves so we can be an example to the peoples of the Empire."

Or something like that, Charlotte didn't listen.

Instead, she concentrated on the dishevelled and lurching approach, an attack that blurred.

She blinked: suddenly the untoten jumped into focus.

"Concentrate on your flank," she said. "If they get around us, we're done for. Their numbers will count against us. And pick your targets... wait for it... wait... wait..."

It became a chant or an off-stage prompt.

I've left it too late, she thought.

But she said: "Wait..."

The books said to do this, but they seemed close, too close, far too close.

"Wait..."

Surely they were done for.

The approaching army reached the pipe, came level, shuffled further and-

"Fire!"

# CHAPTER XXVIII

## Miss Deering-Dolittle

Silence.

The noise of the echo was extraordinary, but Earnestine dropped to her knee and started reloading, counting in her head to follow Charlotte's quick lesson - *one... two...* The bolt came back, the spent round expelled and then she rammed it home, it went in... thank you, thank you.

*Bang-bang-bang... bang-bang... bang!*

That was Charlotte's revolver emptying.

Earnestine was up, aim... *aim*, she forced herself to take her time, Charlotte's drill ringing in her ears along with the gunshots. She picked one, the nearest struggling over the bodies of its compatriots... good heavens, she thought, Charlotte must have clocked one with each of her six rounds. Mustn't let the side down, Earnestine thought, there... squeeze and-

*Bang!*

The monster's head exploded.

Down, reload.

A hail of spent cartridges hailed down as Charlotte emptied the chambers of the revolver. She was quick, her hand reaching into one of her pockets for fresh shells.

*Bang!* Georgina fired quickly above her making Earnestine jump despite the hammering they'd already been subjected to.

Earnestine stood, there was another easy target, so she fired - too quickly and she only winged the creature.

Amazing how elegant the .303 rifle was, the burnished steel bolt and the fine wooden stock with its grain and-

*Bang-bang... zing! Bang-bang-bang... bang.*

Earnestine couldn't get her fingers to work, the stupid dumb bolt thing jammed, caught on the edge of the chamber-

"Ness, take your time," said Charlotte's excited tones cut through the percussion.

Cartridges fanned out in the light like shooting stars, tumbling through space as Charlotte had flipped open the revolver and thrown the smoking brass cylinders free. They bounced off approaching corpses.

The bolt went home.

Charlotte overtook her, standing to fire again, this time with the rifle. She was clearly saving the revolver for emergencies.

Earnestine stood too and fired, a double explosion with her sister: *bBANGg!*

Reloading.

Georgina stood, firing once.

Earnestine brought her rifle up, thumping it against her shoulder. They were bearing down now, the targets looming large and easy.

Down again, chasing Charlotte and feeling a flush as if she was on the lawn knocking the balls around with ease, the mallet singing, the hoops-

A monster was overhead, slavering and its raw eyes searching down. Her rifle went off in her hands, an instinctive reaction, and the bullet found its target more by luck than any skill. The head exploded, spraying brains across the beautifully constructed arched ceiling.

Earnestine half-rose, realised where she was, back in the first part of the reload-aim-fire sequence, and crouched again. The bolt came back and the empty round flashed briefly in the firelight to fall upon the brass-flecked floor, the objects bright and shiny amongst the filth. How many rounds had she fired? The thought leapt into her mind, pushing everything else out: she'd fired... out of ten... she didn't know. There were lashings of spent cartridges on the floor, so if she divided by-

Charlotte's revolver started firing.

Divide by eight... count to three, ten rounds, five in a charging clip... there were too many numbers! Her hands moved automatically, the bolt going in and she rose, aimed, fired!

"Tactical withdraw!" Charlotte screamed; her face ignited like one of those new-fangled photographic flashes with each detonation of fire and thunder from her service revolver. "Rorke's Drift!"


## Mrs Arthur Merryweather

They backed up.

Georgina stumbled as she was trying to reload. There were untoten around them now on both sides trying to outflank them. Bodies twitched impossibly on the floor. Georgina's knee connected with the platform and her rifle sprang free to clatter across the wrought iron metalwork. She yelped and Earnestine's strong hands grabbed her by her blouse, lifted her and flung her across the platform surface. Georgina fell awkwardly on top of her rifle and this, more than anything, shocked her into fighting.

She turned, sitting on the floor, and pulled the trigger.

Nothing!

The trigger was loose and quite useless.

She hadn't reloaded.

Two creatures grabbed Earnestine, pulling her back. Charlotte appeared as if from nowhere, fired at the right hand one and then emptied her revolver downwards to shoot those that were grabbing Earnestine's ankles and legs. The youngster flipped the big black gun open skilfully. Unbelievably, Georgina heard the tinkling bell-like sounds as the six spent cartridges pinged off the hard stone floor.

The monster that held Earnestine bared its teeth; bloody canines came down towards the young lady's bare throat.

There was a metal-on-metal sound and Georgina's rifle reloaded as if by itself, her body now reacting like it was its own clockwork model. She lunged forward, half crawling, and shoved the barrel into the mouth of the undead man. And fired, blowing its head off at less than point blank range.

"Get on!" Georgina yelled, feeling the rasp of air forced across her throat, but hearing only her blood pounding in her skull.

Earnestine came up and over the edge. Her lips opened and she mouthed 'rifle', spittle drizzling across Georgina's face. Earnestine's weapon was loose, rotating almost majestically as it dropped hard against the gantry, its butt vibrating the surface and its barrel belched fire. The roof above exploded, brick shrapnel and mortar dust hailed down. The rifle hovered and then slowly, ever so slowly; it toppled like a felled tree disappearing into the charnel house below.

"Bally thing-"

Earnestine turned and disappeared after it.

"Ness!!!"

Georgina wasn't sure if she'd shouted, or whether it was Charlotte, as she flipped her own rifle, hefted it round and struck an approaching untoten. She hit another, double-handed backhand, then under arm like a croquet mallet. The fake human burst offering no resistance and Georgina tumbled forward, the rifle's heavy momentum carrying her over the edge. She landed on something soft, something disgustingly soft and-

Everything was suddenly slavering corpse, a massive face, teeth and false breath, reddened eyes mad with fury and rage; blood flecked across Georgina as it came down for the kill and-

Earnestine stood briefly in Georgina's vision, rifle in hand as the untoten split apart from the shot. Charlotte was above them, standing on the platform and firing like a demented harpy engaged in her own struggle and yet she was making every shell count.

Georgina fired another round and rolled herself onto the gantry using her momentum to bring herself to her feet. Her gun was to her shoulder and she fired again, the reloading now just part of the action.

Earnestine hurdled onto the platform too, again turning and firing.

Charlotte had reloaded, a blur of fingers popping rounds from the medium kit bag. She fired again, not at those nearest enemies trying to climb aboard, but further away.

Georgina was on the right flank and concentrated from right to left: Earnestine was on the far left working as if across a page. She only hoped that they overlapped, because Charlotte wasn't even looking at the central area but kept firing, the revolver up and aimed with precision.

Except when one vile claw reached across and seized her ankle; she fired down, a single shot.

There was a respite, a blink of an eye.

Georgina risked taking in the wider picture.

Charlotte was firing at Thermopylae. It didn't make sense at first, but then Georgina realised and loosed off a round in that direction when Charlotte was reloading. The untoten were struggling over the wall of bodies that had built up across the Spartan pass and this was slowing them down. The killing ground below the redoubt was cleared by Earnestine's methodical approach and suddenly they were no longer under direct attack.

The blink of an eye became a pause.

Except there were still creatures coming into the area below from...

Georgina looked round, saw and shouted: "Behind us!"

# Miss Charlotte

The enemy closed from both directions, a pincer movement cutting off any retreat. Charlotte didn't know how they'd outflanked them, but it hardly mattered. The fog of war confused everything. If their task was to prevent the enemy reaching the sewers, then they had failed utterly.

"Down!" she shouted.

The others ducked either side and she let rip with both revolvers, flipping her head left and then right to take aim, firing alternately. They retreated backwards, giving ground. The British Bull Dog clicked empty first, but the Webley had another chamber. As they killed their opponents, so the bodies formed a slope and the creatures came higher each time they reached the edge, until finally one stumbled up and onto their redoubt.

Like a tide, the attack breached their defences.

It was over: each shot required them to take a step back. In the narrow brick-lined confines the noise was deafening. Georgina screamed long and hard letting all the air out of her lungs. Charlotte knew it was hopeless.

Left and right, they were boxed in, but strangely, the brick wall behind looked distorted further along, like a turning was appearing when Charlotte fired, the glow of the discharge etching a frame with light.

"Door!" Georgina shouted, pointlessly, and she grabbed Charlotte and dragged her along.

"Gina!" Charlotte yelled, shocked that Georgina had jumped up into her line of fire.

Charlotte reached the indentation in the wall. In the dark it had been invisible, but the sparks from the gunfire had highlighted the alcove.

Earnestine pushed up too, levelled her .303.

"That's not loaded," said Charlotte

"I know," Earnestine said. She jabbed the barrel into the lock and levered down. The lock was fine, good solid Sheffield steel and it bent the barrel out of true, but the rotten, wooden door gave and the entire bracket came away.

"In!"

The others didn't need any prompting and forced the door open.

Charlotte grabbed the lantern as they piled through, and just in time as the untoten hands grasped and clawed at them. The lantern slipped from her grip as she put her hands to the door. It didn't go out. They pushed the door back, pushed and pushed and shoved and heaved. Hands appeared around the frame, above, to the side and even underneath. Charlotte fired through the door and then used the empty revolver as a club, banging the impervious flesh as hard as she could.

Georgina took over, bashed down with the butt of the Lee-Enfield as Charlotte bent to reload. Three rounds between her fingers, and again.

If only she had time to reload the spare revolver. Earnestine heaved, her boots slipping and sliding on the floor. She kicked the lantern, which sparked but stayed lit.

Inch by inch, they coerced the door back into position and no!

It flung open. Untoten fell through the door.

Charlotte stood and fired, six rounds, one after the other at the targets.

"Run!"

Georgina, carrying the crazily swinging lantern, was already moving away.

As they ran, Charlotte yelled out instructions: "We form a British Square and fall back along the passage."

"There are only three of us!" Earnestine shouted. "How can we form a square?"

"No... it's when - *argh* - one, fire, two drop back, three reload, then one stand and fire."

"That's what we've been doing."

They paused, using up their lead to reload, pushing five rounds from a clip into the magazine. She handed out a clip each from the medium kit bag. As her sisters fiddled with the metal and pushed in the bullets, Charlotte reloaded the revolver: three rounds between her fingers, again, swap over, three rounds, again... drop one because it's the British Bull Dog. She took a charger clip too. There was no time for anything else as the creatures were nearly upon them.

"Yes," Charlotte continued, "but... like when we sing a round, then one of us is always-"

"Got it! Come on."

"Count your ammo," Charlotte commanded. "Ness!"

Earnestine fired, the charge blazing at the end where she'd damaged the barrel, and then she ducked and went to the back.

"Gina!"

Georgina fired and followed Earnestine, who was now down on one knee flicking the bolt of her rifle.

"Lottie!" said Charlotte. She aimed - fired, 'one', and then whipped around, back to the end of the line, and down to reload. She opened her mouth to shout Earnestine's nickname, but she heard the gunshot.

And then Georgina's.

And it was her turn again.

They'd moved back three paces and the untoten had advanced perhaps two. She picked off the leading creature - 'two' - and ducked to go around again.

Another two shots rang as she twisted, reloaded and then stood.

Yes, the gap was widening: not fast because the passage allowed them to advance two abreast. They'd be utterly overwhelmed if it hadn't been for the rear ranks stumbling over veritably dead corpses of their comrades.

Aim, fire! 'Three'.

She went round again, suddenly reminded of barn dancing: dosey doe, take your partner by the hand... she shot another. 'Four'.

Earnestine shouted: "Last round!" and she fired.

Then Georgina: "Last round." Her shot ricocheted sounding a high-pitched whine.

On Charlotte's move, she saw the far door: it looked solid and would perhaps hold them for a while.

"Ready to run for it?"

Georgina was running already, having mistaken the command. She had the lantern, thank goodness, but her speed meant that it was increasingly difficult to see the approaching untoten.

"Go, go!" Charlotte shouted. She fired her last round - made it count - and then she pulled out the Webley revolver and fired: one, two, three... aim, four, five... six. She turned and ran, the silhouettes of her sisters jumping as the lantern bounced around, and then a glorious rectangle of wonderful light appeared. Georgina vanished into the frame and then Earnestine. Charlotte jumped through, she heard the door slam behind her, a bolt going across like a Lee-Enfield loading but heavier.

They'd made it.

She blinked, her eyes taking a moment to adjust to the brightness after the gloom of the sewers.

Even the air smelt fresher.

And then she saw: the room was vast, cathedral-like, and full, utterly full, of writhing untoten.

# CHAPTER XXIX

## Miss Deering-Dolittle

Earnestine found herself standing in what looked like the future: bright and shining with manifest machinery.

"It's an underground station... a new one," she said.

They were on a landing, like the circle of a theatre looking down into the auditorium of stalls and stage below. There was a staircase that descended to a strange scene, a Dante's inferno framed by the modern Victorian arches, and another leading up to some kind of upper circle.

Below, with an angry hiss of steam, a train lurched along the rails and then stopped. Like a giant piece of clockwork, a gantry of cabling lurched from one goods wagon and moved back to fix itself onto the next in line.

"They're using it to bring the corpses into London," said Earnestine, the final piece of the puzzle falling into place. "And through the underground system they can reach from Euston to Waterloo and even Kensington."

Under the gantry, there was a brilliant flash, a lightning bolt so much brighter for being contained inside. The curve of the tunnel, covered in white tiles, concentrated the effect like a concave mirror. An acrid smell displaced the stench of death that permeated everything. The young ladies blinked trying to remove the afterglow of the flash.

Moments later, the undead began to spill out of the wagon, more and more, with their control boxes fizzing with life as the monsters shambled along the platform searching for a way out.

"This isn't good," Earnestine said. "All the stations have exits to the surface, if they're here then... we have to stop this."

Charlotte reloaded, shoving the revolvers back into the front of her jacket when she was done, and then she checked her rifle.

Again, the rolling stock shifted, clanked, and then moved on one carriage forward, and the framework of electrodes moved away from the upper gallery to attach to the next boxcar.

"It's all autonomous," Georgina said.

Charlotte passed a charging clip to Earnestine.

"We need to put a spanner in the works," Earnestine insisted.

"We can't go down there!"

"We must."

"No, no, no..."

"Whatever we do, we have to do it soon," Charlotte interrupted: "Those things will be through that door soon, and if those down there spot us, they can just come up those stairs."

"We have to try," Earnestine said. She pushed the ammunition down into the magazine.

"Then let's go!" said Charlotte, but Earnestine put her hand out to stop her.

"That would be suicide," Earnestine said.

"We decided to commit suicide quite a while ago."

Georgina was looking around, her eyes tracking various pipes and cables: "It must be controlled from somewhere... I think... there."

She pointed: the 'upper circle' consisted of a landing over the rail line and halfway along there was a wide opening from which shone bright, galvanic light. The framework of electrodes hovered nearby and then moved back again to create the next squad of untoten.

"Worth a try," Earnestine said, and she bent low to climb the stairs and work her way along the landing to the opening.

There was a low moan, coherent amongst the murmuring.

"Lummy, that's torn it," Charlotte said.

"Achtung!"

A man, dressed in white with dark goggles, appeared as he stepped through the opening to stand on the landing.

Georgina shouldered her rifle.

Charlotte was quicker, dropping the man with a single shot. He was the first 'living' man they'd 'killed'.

"He was a technician," Georgina said.

A voice shouted from below, full of command and confidence: "Ach, my Liebchen, so you all survived. How resourceful of you English, but no matter. You will witness Der Anbruch des Totenreiches - the Dawn of the Empire of the Dead."

Georgina fired!

Her shot was wide.

The Graf, somewhere amongst the mechanisms and machinery down on the station platform below, ducked anyway.

"Naughty!" he chided, his booming voice projecting over the noise to their upper circle.

To kill the Graf, they'd have to cross the station, and to do that they'd have to face the army of untoten growing by the carriage load every few minutes. But that technician must have been doing something. The galvanic energy arced again, the blue light slicing the air and leaving her feeling blind.

"Get along the landing," Earnestine yelled.

"Nein!" the Graf shouted. "Stoppen Sie."

Stoppen? Why? What was so important?

"Ziehen Sie den Netzstecker!"

The wide opening turned into a large room with tiles on the walls between stone corners and a magnificent domed roof constructed in brick. There were pipes, metal wheels with handles and engineering that made it seem like they'd walked into a giant steam engine.

"It's a pumping station," Georgina said. Earnestine didn't understand her at first and then realised: all these tunnels were connected: the sewers, the underground railway, the flood water culverts - all seemed to intersect here in a mishmash of levels and landings.

"I'll cover the stairs," Charlotte hollered. She took the medium kit bag with all its ammunition off Earnestine and ran back to the landing.

There was a growl from one side.

Even though the untoten was dead, and his bulky body crushed and distorted, Earnestine recognised him at once. She felt the blood run cold from her face heralding a faint: "Kroll..."

## Mrs Arthur Merryweather

Earnestine had frozen.

When Georgina entered the pumping room, the huge monster turned towards her for a moment, and then lurched back towards Earnestine.

Georgina waved her arms: "Here! Here!"

The creature turned again, but despite Georgina being closer, the creature returned to its first target.

The reanimated man opened its mouth, spitting and then tried to form words: "Der... ring... do... little."

Earnestine's reply was barely audible: "Kroll... how?"

"You killed... me."

Earnestine's reply was a mere whisper: "You tried to kill me."

The golem's attention was now entirely on Earnestine and she was trapped. Georgina lifted her rifle, rammed the bolt home and... aim, fire!

Click!

No ammunition: she'd wasted her last bullet fruitlessly trying to hit the Graf.

Georgina backed towards the landing.

"Charlotte, ammo, ammo!" she shouted, nearly conjugating the word.

"Here."

Charlotte held out a handful of bullets.

Georgina went over, grabbed them, pushed two into the magazine with shaking hands.

"What is it?" Charlotte asked.

"An untoten's talking," Georgina said.

Charlotte concentrated on the untoten approaching up the stairs and didn't look round.

"Does it have a big skull?"

"Yes! Very big!"

"Doctor Mordant said they might retain brain function if they had a large head."

"Did Doctor Mordant say how to deal with them?"

"She might have done."

"And?"

"I didn't listen."

"You didn't-"

"It was boring!"

"Education is never boring, it's... never mind."

Back in the pumping room, Kroll had stepped towards Earnestine, its great hands reaching forward like claws.

Aim... squeeze.

A tile just above Kroll and Earnestine exploded.

Bolt home: last round.

If she fired now she might hit Earnestine.

As Georgina inched forward, her foot kicked the fallen white-coated technician.

The man had a device in his hand.

Georgina grabbed it and ripped it from the man's black, rubber gloved fingers.

There was a switch: it made a light come on.

Kroll jerked as the contacts in his skull box fizzed and sparked.

Georgina strode closer, the buzz in Kroll's head increased and the creature reared back, distraught.

It screamed.

"This repels them," Georgina said, but no sooner had she finished than Kroll lashed out smashing the device away. The thing skittered across the tiled floor. Kroll grabbed at his head in pain and then wrenched at the brass box attached to his skull. He pulled it out, wires coming from inside his cranium and dripping with thick viscous matter.

"I am... free!" it said.

Earnestine raised her rifle and shot it.

Georgina looked away from her sister, not wanting to see the triumphant expression, and saw something that didn't fit the iron and brick design: "That's not part of the pumping station."

It was a brass and mahogany box, the size and shape of a writing desk and styled much like the hand held device. This was the key, she thought: there were lights, tiny bulbs to indicate various settings, but suddenly they went out. As Georgina started to go over to get a closer look, Earnestine tapped her on the shoulder and pointed.

"Sluice gate controls," Earnestine said. "Open the gate, let the water in."

"It says 'flood control'. There would have to be water in the tunnels."

"They made it rain."

"Yes, they did, didn't they?" Georgina felt a flicker of hope as Earnestine grabbed the handle and began to heave at the wheel.

"It would have a certain irony," Earnestine grunted. "Can't - shift - it."

"Here!"

The handle was cold, steel bolted to the iron wheel that was set into a pipe. She pulled... pushed, jerked it up and down.

It turned a mere fraction of a degree, rust flaked at the axle.

"It's useless," Georgina said.

Earnestine shouted: "Charlotte!"

"I'm busy," came Charlotte's reply, followed by distant firing.

"Now!"

"In a minute."

"NOW!!!"

Charlotte ran over, while Earnestine shook her arms to loosen them.

"I think-" Georgina began.

"We all push together, one mighty effort," Earnestine said.

"Yes."

They took hold, squeezed around with six hands on the handle and spokes of the big iron wheel.

"One for all," Charlotte said.

Earnestine took charge: "Two... Three... NOW!"

The wheel squealed.

Georgina yelled as she pushed, her hand crushed beneath Earnestine's heavy pressure, and then it gave, span, and they were flung to the ground as if they had been thrown from a merry-go-round.

Earnestine took the handle and pulled. With effort, it moved for her alone. The elder sister, so confident, turned the handle all the way round and round, until it came to a stop and then she stepped back, gasping and bent double with her hands on her knees.

Nothing happened.

Maybe it took time, Georgina thought, and wondered if this control really did open a gate somewhere.

Still nothing happened.

Earnestine straightened up suddenly: "Charlotte-"

"Oh Lawks!" Charlotte sprinted back to her guard position, taking up the rifle and slamming the bolt into position as she ran. She fired from the hip. A creature had reached the landing and was thrown back, toppling from sight to the station below. If it was on the landing, Georgina realised, then they'd lost control of the stairs down to the station. They'd be trying to come up to the landing next.

It was hopeless, Georgina knew, but she was drawn to the strange brass control panel that was so clearly European amongst the good honest British engineering.

"This is the master control for the boxes," Georgina said, mostly to herself. "The devices on their skulls... we need to..."

She began to fiddle with the screws that held the cover in place. If only she had a proper tool kit.

Earnestine ran up and used the rifle butt against the edge.

"Hey!" Georgina said, but she stopped herself when she realised that the cover had broken loose. She put her fingers under it, ignored the way it cut into her skin, and yanked it up to reveal the machine's innards. It was all wires and brass fittings.

"Do you know how to work this?" Earnestine asked.

"It's not like a steam engine."

They looked: it was a conglomeration of confusion, and just like a steam engine.

"This makes no sense," said Georgina.

"It's labelled!"

"In German."

Georgina worked her way along the small parcel labels that were attached to the various wires. On them, in neat handwriting, there were words in that infuriating Germanic script. She read them out: "Anhalten, zurückkehren, angreifen, zerstören..."

"Means nothing to me," Earnestine said. "Why couldn't they use Latin or Greek?"

"I think this controls those boxes on their heads," Georgina interrupted. "These cogs are used to select which individual or group to command."

Georgina pushed the cogs around until all of them were displaying.

"Hurry!" came a plaintive cry from behind them.

"Shhh, Charlotte, we're concentrating," Earnestine replied.

"I'll just try one," said Georgina. She picked 'anhalten' and pressed the button: nothing.

"Did you press it?" Earnestine asked.

"Yes! Of course I pressed it. Look! Press! Press!" She stabbed at it again and again. "Why does nothing work?!"

"Gina, calm down."

Galvanic energy would be like steam, and steam engines need coal, so... "Power!"

To reconnect the power, they'd have to go across the landing, down across the underground station and through the army of the untoten to where the Graf must have turned off their galvanic supply.

"Ness!! Gina!" Charlotte shouted. "They've reached the stairs to the landing!"

That was it then, Georgina thought, unless she had a flash of inspiration: flash.

"Flashlight."

"Gina?" Earnestine asked.

"Your flashlight has a battery!"

Earnestine fumbled into her pockets and pulled out her precious flashlight. It showed a dim glow when she depressed the button, then she unscrewed the base and tugged out the brown battery.

Georgina fiddled around the cables and finally found two to connect to each end.

"Help!" Charlotte yelled.

"Hold it," Georgina said. Earnestine did and Georgina threw the switch. Nothing... no wait, an indicator light shone dimly.

They looked over their shoulders to see the untoten standing erect over a fallen Charlotte, their control boxes fizzing with power. Charlotte scrambled backwards.

"Anhalten," Georgina said. "And *halt*... en?"

"And when the battery is flat?"

"I'll try the next setting."

Georgina turned the control to 'zurückkehren' and flicked the master switch again.

Instantly, the moans of the untoten became a roaring, and, as one, the creatures lurched forward.

"They are coming back into the room!" Charlotte informed them.

"Next is 'angreifen'," Georgina said and she operated the device again.

Charlotte screamed.

"Angry! Angry!"

Georgina struggled for the next setting and flicked the switch.

"Nothing!"

"No, they are attacking each other."

Indeed, when they sneaked a look into the underground station, they saw a writhing ocean of monsters tearing each other apart, but in the centre a calm group of men led by the Graf marched through a parting sea of the horrors.

## Miss Charlotte

Charlotte fired: timing was the key she realised. It wasn't a question of using all her bullets or even killing the highest score of untoten, but of slowing their advance. So she waited until an untoten reached the top step and then blew its head off. The body fell, taking some of the others with it, and so the process began again. However, as the pile of bodies at the lower level turned the stairs into a ramp, the effect of the body falling was reduced. The delay between each shot became ever shorter.

The others joined her, firing at the creatures, trying to push back the tide, but even though the advancing force also attacked itself, the inexorable progress forced Charlotte further back and then around into the control room with the others.

Georgina used up her one round.

Earnestine fired four: "I don't have any left," she said.

Charlotte reached for another round, but she couldn't find a bullet amongst the stuff in the medium kit bag. She checked her right pocket, nothing - she cast the Webley aside - and then her left pocket. Her hand encompassed all the remaining ammunition. She flipped open the other revolver, spilled the spent brass onto the floor and then reloaded. Disturbingly, one of the five chambers remained empty.

"I've only got four bullets," Charlotte said.

"We can't let them-"

An untoten.

The explosion took even Charlotte by surprise and the smell of cordite stank. An untoten at the doorway, minus head, toppled to the ground.

"You were saying," Earnestine said.

"I've only got three bullets."

# Chapter XXX

## Miss Deering-Dolittle

"We can't let them take us," said Georgina.

"I agree," Earnestine replied.

"Arthur was horrified by the idea of being untotened. He didn't want to turn on his friends and he said he'd save a bullet for the both of us: he'd... me, and then himself."

"In that case you did him a great service."

"I loved him."

"Which order?" Charlotte asked, turning to the others and bringing the gun between them.

Georgina could see issues: "Age, alphabetical..."

"I should be last," Earnestine said. "It's my responsibility."

"I'm married, so..."

"Widowed."

The two glared at each other.

"Of course," said Earnestine, "you decide."

## Mrs Arthur Merryweather

Georgina glanced between her sisters: the tall authoritative redhead and the shorter, pretty blonde. How could she choose an order, how could she shoot one of them, or be shot by one of them?

"I don't want to decide."

There were groans and howls approaching, sounds of untoten closing in.

"There's not much time," Earnestine said.

"I've got the revolver, so perhaps I should decide," Charlotte said, rather too cheerfully.

It was the same silver gun that Georgina had used against Arthur. It was too horrible.

"We're the Derring-Do Club," she said, "we should... that is... I think..."

"Fight to the end," said Charlotte.

"Damned right," said Earnestine. She grabbed Charlotte's wrist and steered the revolver to point at the opening.

"Make them count," said Georgina.

Charlotte sniggered: "Did Ness use the 'd' word?"

"Concentrate on the opening," Georgina commanded.

"Aye aye."

An untoten appeared. Charlotte waited until it had turned, a full target, before she fired. It dropped over the other corpse.

That was it then, two bullets: they were truly lost.

## Miss Charlotte

Another two appeared.

Maybe, Charlotte thought, there might be some way to get them to line up. What had Caligula, or was it Nero, imagined: that all of Rome could be killed on a single night by a running man with a knife, if they all just lined up properly. Latin - it was never really her strong point.

One of the creatures turned, sensing her, and moved forward.

This one, she thought, then the next... and then what?

It stopped, confused by the bodies at its feet as it tried to work out how to step over the obstacle.

"Shoot it!" Georgina said, but Charlotte ignored her.

It could work.

She waited.

Yes, the next one lined up, turned and started negotiating the bodies as the one in front stepped down. If she just...

She shifted, pushing Earnestine to one side, and... squeeze - *bang!*

It was so exciting, much better than cardboard targets. The head just exploded, the brass control box spun away, sparking blue, and then both bodies dropped to the floor creating a pyramid over the threshold.

"I got two!" she said. "Did you see that?"

Earnestine had, you could tell by her face.

"Wasn't it stupendous?"

"Yes, jolly clever Lottie," Georgina said.

"Do concentrate on the entrance," Earnestine chided.

"But two with one bullet?"

"Yes," Earnestine said, "a pity you didn't think of that when we had boxes of bullets."

Another untoten turned the corner: it had been Schneider, the March Hare, back yet again.

Charlotte shot it.

"That's it," Charlotte said, "no more ammunition."

The next one round the corner was alive.

"Good evening," Graf Zala said. He didn't click his heels or bow.

"Perhaps, Lottie, you shouldn't have announced that we had no more bullets," Earnestine said.

All those rounds she'd dropped like a trail of breadcrumbs marking their journey through the sewers just to make reloading the five chambered Bulldog quicker. Charlotte threw the empty revolver away, picked up Georgina's fallen rifle and held it like a club. It felt hefty.

The Graf smiled: "Ach, so there are the three of you like bad fillérs."

He held a small box loosely in his right hand. It clearly repelled the untoten: the creatures shuffled behind him, trying to get around an invisible barrier to attack the young ladies.

"This isn't fair!" shouted Georgina.

"Fair!" the Graf laughed. "Fair? In war? That's rich from you English. Do you think this is like your English sport, all fair play and not arguing with the referee about whether it's leg before elbow?"

"Umpire and wicket," Earnestine corrected.

The Graf chortled: "Miss Deering-Dolittle, so concerned about the rules. War is not your cricket; play will not be stopped by rain."

"I challenge you to a duel," said Earnestine.

"You! A mere woman? Challenge me to a duel? No, there is no honour in fighting women."

"And there's honour in cold-bloodedly murdering women?"

"Or men chained to the wall," Georgina said.

A light breeze swept through the room.

"One of the men as my champion then?" Earnestine suggested.

"One of the men: that Captain and his Lieutenant... or my brother Pieter. As you know I could defeat them all, you've seen me with a sword, but no, Miss Deering-Dolittle, no. They will be processed and join the ranks of my untoten regiments."

"Like my husband, you monster," Georgina screamed, a sudden squall adding to her gusto.

The Graf noticed and turned: "What is that?"

Something howled through the tunnels.

"We did open the flood gates," Earnestine said. "It just took time."

"That's air," Charlotte pointed out.

"Being pushed by the weight of water."

The Graf started running: "Mein Gott!" He forgot the sisters in his rush, the untoten controller repelled his creatures, parting them in a way that would not work against the onrushing water.

"It'll wash all the untoten out into the Thames," said Georgina.

Charlotte realised what this meant: "Then it's over."

"Yes," said Earnestine, "but I really think we should be somewhere else."

They looked out onto the landing overlooking the train. In front of them, the gantry moved again, ready to activate another wagonload of corpses. The running Graf reached the platform. Already the ranks of monsters were reforming behind him, noticing them, and starting to shamble back towards them.

"It's full of untoten," Georgina said.

"Yes," said Earnestine, "but very soon it'll be full of water."

"Be eaten or drowned?" Charlotte asked.

And then, the deluge came.

# Chapter XXXI

## Miss Deering-Dolittle

The water burst from the tunnel below, swept around the train and gushed along the railway line under them. The wave broke on the staircase, washing the untoten away.

"The Graf went up that staircase," said Charlotte.

Earnestine looked and saw a black opening, the first few steps visible before they disappeared into the darkness. Between the landing and that far staircase was a platform, a train, strange galvanic equipment, flood water and a growing mass of untoten.

"He's got away," said Georgina.

"No," said Earnestine. "He might... Pieter."

Despite the water, the train below them moved forward and the gantry rose, swung up and back to attach to the next carriage. The electrodes buzzed and fizzed, the doors opened a moment later to disgorge the horrific contents, the monsters attacking each other and then seeming to scent the sisters.

Earnestine spoke: "When it comes forward again, we'll jump onto it."

"I beg your pardon," Georgina said.

The machine moved through its cycle once more and Earnestine took two strides back and then ran at the edge, leapt up and sailed through the air to land uncomfortably on the metal gantry.

Charlotte yelled: "Tally ho!" She made the jump easily and kept hold of the rifle.

"Gina, come on!" Earnestine shouted.

"I'll wait for the next carriage," Georgina shouted back as the mechanism moved away.

"Gina! We stay together."

Untoten rose from the waters and slipped up the stairs. They bit and tore at each other, but the mass moved ever closer, pushed by the force of their struggle and the rising waters. One spied Georgina, a sniff upon its ruined face, and then it shambled closer. Another followed.

"Ness," Georgina whined.

The mechanism clunked as it went through its cycle.

Georgina backed into the control room.

The machine clunked over to its near position.

On top of it, Earnestine held out her hand trying to reach across the divide, just as she had when the train carriages had separated in Europe.

Earnestine and Charlotte shouted: "Now!"

Georgina ran, quickly, dodging the untoten, but one caught her dress when she jumped. The monster yanked her back as the material ripped free, so that she twisted in flight. She hit the gantry, and then fell forward towards the frothing flood waters full of writhing creatures.

## Mrs Arthur Merryweather

But her bodice hoicked up as hands grabbed her from behind. Earnestine and Charlotte pulled her up just as other claw-like hands caught her flailing boots to drag her down.

The machinery bounced around, then moved up. As Georgina rose, one of the hideous monsters came with her out of the flood water. They saw the danger: Earnestine held tight and Charlotte slithered down Georgina's dress, grasping the bustle for support, and reached lower with her free hand. The creature bared its teeth as Charlotte tugged at Georgina's laces: once, twice and-

The boot came off and the creature fell away with it. When it struck the surface, it splashed the water aside, briefly revealing a submerged horde of untoten.

They were safe on the gantry as its actuator lurched it away from the landing, but they all had to duck beneath the fizzing and sparking electrodes to avoid being struck by the artificial lightning.

"All together," said Earnestine, "then run for the doorway."

"Wait!" Georgina shouted. She bent down and undid her other boot. "Ready."

Earnestine and Charlotte chanted together: "One, two... jump!"

They launched themselves up, each holding one of Georgina's arms.

They all landed in the water as if they had just leaped out of a bathing machine in Brighton for a dip: it was icy and shockingly cold. They sloshed forward, ineptly, until Georgina's bare feet found purchase on the steps. She fell to her hands and knees, and moved upwards like a toddler, clambering until she was out of the water.

Earnestine and Charlotte kicked and clubbed back some of the drowning untoten and then they too ran up the staircase.

Up they went, round and round, dizzyingly and then along a rough corridor lit by burning torches. It slanted upwards, sharp and cutting underfoot, until they came to a simple door.

Georgina opened it and beyond was darkness, except she saw a band of light shining across her toes. Reaching out, she felt something push back, a heavy material, and as it moved before her, more light appeared on her left. It was a tapestry hiding a secret door.

The corridor beyond was plush, with beautiful wallpaper, and Georgina recognised the décor of the Austro-Hungarian embassy.

They made a strange out-of-place trio in this rich and important building: Earnestine with her flashlight, Georgina barefoot like a pauper and Charlotte with an unloaded rifle. They were dirty and soaked.

"You kept your rifle dry," Earnestine said.

Charlotte beamed.

Somehow they had come full circle. None of them had taken compass readings, Georgina was ashamed to realise.

"Billiard Room," said Earnestine. "This way."

"No this," said Charlotte, "I walked all round here trying to find a window to climb out of."

"They'll have moved them," said Georgina.

"We have to start somewhere," Earnestine replied.

"There'll be soldiers."

"Then we'll deal with them, we must find Pieter and the others."

Georgina felt herself turning cold and dead herself: "There'll be untoten. Like Arthur... they may be untoten already."

"Then we'll deal with them."

"No."

"We must. Do you want them to remain like that?"

"No!" For Georgina that was worse, horrible beyond belief. "Let's get there in time."

"That's the spirit."

"We're the Derring-Do Club," said Charlotte.

They'd used that expression to taunt them at the college, but now it seemed to Georgina like a rallying cry.

Around the corner were bodies, servants caught and attacked by untoten. Clearly the staircase hadn't been the only way from the tunnels to the embassy, and the waters had forced the army of the dead to turn on its own side.

They reached a big mahogany door.

Charlotte paused with her hand on the elegant brass handle: "One for all," she said.

"England, Harry and Saint George," Earnestine replied.

Georgina could think of only one thing: "Revenge."

In they went.

# Miss Charlotte

There was no-one there.

The billiard table was still pushed to one side.

"The Prince and Merryweather's swords haven't been tidied away," said Charlotte.

"I beg your pardon," Georgina said.

"Oh, they fought a duel."

"Who?"

"Prince Pieter and... I'm sorry, Captain Merryweather."

"Why?"

"Over you and Ness."

"They got confused," said Earnestine. "Gentlemen, honestly, they get themselves in such a dither and need us to sort them out."

Earnestine pointed at the billiard table with its motley collection of swords taken down for the duel.

"Gina, get some weapons," she said, and then added: "A sword, not a cue."

"I don't know how to use a sword," said Georgina.

"Do you know how to use a cue?"

"No."

Earnestine came over to help and saw something amongst the paraphernalia. Charlotte looked, but there were only the swords and two white billiard balls.

"How many balls are there in billiards?" Earnestine asked.

"How should I know?" said Georgina.

"The red one's missing," Earnestine continued. "I think Captain Caruthers plays cricket."

What was her sister talking about? Girls weren't allowed to play cricket: their game was hockey.

"Well, of course," Georgina replied. "He's a Captain, so he must have gone to one of the better public schools and he would have played cricket there."

"He was going to attempt to escape."

"With a billiard ball!? Against soldiers with guns?"

"I expect he'd make the attempt, so we need to go and rescue them."

"Ness," said Georgina, "against soldiers with guns."

Charlotte held up her Lee-Enfield with a grin: "We have a gun."

"Ness, she's no bullets left," Georgina reminded.

"We have to make the attempt," Earnestine said.

Georgina didn't reply, but she took a sword off the billiard table.

Charlotte led the way back to the corridor. There was a choice of directions: back the way they had come or onwards. Onwards, she thought, up the river.

Soon, they reached a place where another corridor crossed their path.

"Which way?" Georgina asked.

"This one," said Charlotte.

There were signs of struggle: dropped objects, knocked over furniture and paintings askew on the wall, so on they went, but Earnestine sprang back: "Wait!"

# CHAPTER XXXII

## Miss Deering-Dolittle

On the floor, just along the corridor to the left, and rolled against the skirting, was a small red ball. Earnestine bent down and picked it up: it was heavy, a red billiard ball. Captain Caruthers had pocketed one when they were captured after the duel. She tossed it aloft as if it was a tennis ball and caught it again. It was hard, solid and certain.

"The Captain made his move here," Earnestine mused, "and it didn't work."

"How do you know that?" Charlotte asked.

"No unconscious guards."

"Now what?"

"They went this way."

Earnestine marched along the plush carpet, a stride that turned into a run and then a race. Time was running out and she heard shouting, English voices. But where? There were doors everywhere. She touched the ring dangling at her neck: *Pieter, Pieter...* but she was just doing her duty as a British subject.

"That one!" Charlotte shouted.

Without thinking, Earnestine burst into the room beyond.

It was a drawing room.

Standing by the fireplace were Captain Caruthers, Lieutenant McKendry and... *he was alive, Pieter was alive.* Unfortunately, the Graf was pointing a revolver at them and the Vögte fawned at his shoulder.

Startled by their sudden arrival, the Graf stepped back, covering them, but he kept an eye on his prisoners. They made to move forward, but the Graf flicked his aim back and forth between the two groups until they accepted his supremacy.

"The Deering-Dolittles - extraordinary!" the Graf said. "See, your women have come to rescue you."

"Your secretary, Mein Prince," said the Vögte. "Perhaps you can dictate your last Will and Testament."

How could that hideous weasel be so cruel, Earnestine thought.

Charlotte levelled her rifle and the Vögte flinched.

"It's not loaded," said the Graf.

"Ach, in that case, drop your weapons," said the Vögte, indicating a table. The sisters traipsed over and dumped the swords, the rifle and Earnestine's medium kit bag onto the polished surface. "Now, over there."

They joined the others.

"Are you in one piece?" Caruthers whispered.

"Yes," said Earnestine.

"Where's Merry?" Caruthers said.

It was Georgina who replied: "That man murdered him!"

"Casualty of war," said the Graf, easily. "Let us be going: Vögte, Pieter."

Prince Pieter caught Earnestine's eye and then stepped forward to confront the Graf.

"Nein," he said. "I will stay here."

"You have your duty," said the Graf. "All will be forgiven. You can rule this country, if you like, when we come back and conquer it."

"I will not be part of your Great War."

"You will, mein Bruder, dead or alive."

The Graf clicked back the hammer of his revolver and pointed it at Prince Pieter, moving in to point blank range, an inch, no more, from his forehead.

"Do you have the guts," goaded Pieter.

Earnestine's heart leapt into her throat: *no, please, no; a thousand times: please no.*

Prince Pieter stood his ground without flinching: "You can kill young ladies, girls... no, not even that: you had your lackeys do it for you."

"Careful, Bruder."

"You can't kill your own brother face-to-face, can you?" said Prince Pieter. "And with your Great War in ruins, you need me for the Great Plan."

"The Great War is not in ruins. We have merely suffered a setback. Like Napoleon, we over-reached - too far, too ambitious, too soon. But my plans are only adjusted. I will settle for conquering Europe and when I have swept through France, Belgium, Poland and the Ottomans, and converted all those living enemies into dead allies, I will turn my attention to this small country. My fleet of Zeppelins will drop bombs on their armies, their factories, even their fields and the streets of their cities until they surrender."

"Never," said Caruthers.

"Then I will turn your green and pleasant land into nothing more than craters and mud, full of the dead ready to be harvested for my armies. We will invade Russia and march on Moscow to oust the Romanovs."

"That's been tried."

"The dead don't feel the cold."

Earnestine's fist tightened around the billiard ball ready to fight, but he was right and Earnestine could not see a way out. The British may keep the waves, their ships safe at sea, but this maniac would conquer the lands with his unholy cannon fodder and the skies with his monstrous airships.

Suddenly, a decision made, the Graf stepped away.

"Stay with your woman," he said, and he turned to the Vögte: "Halten Sie sie hier."

"Jahwohl," said the Vögte, accepting the Graf's revolver. "Und Ihr Bruder?"

"Ach er," said the Graf, who then turned back to them: "I am afraid, Gentlemen, Ladies, this innings is over and I must retire to the gazebo."

"Pavilion," said Earnestine.

The Graf left, walking out as if he had all the time in the world, waving his control box in case there were any untoten.

He was escaping: they had lost.

## Mrs Arthur Merryweather

"You English," the Vögte laughed. "How you won such an Empire is beyond me. You suspected we were building up our military power here and yet you did nothing. Mein Graf will conquer the world..."

Caruthers leaned over, whispered: "Once his lecture is over, he'll kill us."

Oh Lord, Georgina thought, no.

Earnestine interrupted: "It's because we play cricket."

The Vögte paused, perturbed by the disruption: "Cricket?"

"What do you play?"

"Chess."

"All that cunning and deviousness," said Earnestine, "McKendry?"

McKendry startled: "Er, base... tennis."

"Serves and *smashes, McKendry,* all power; whereas cricket is a gentlemen's game."

The Vögte was all sneers: "Gentlemen's game?"

"Fancy a game of cricket?" said Earnestine. She showed him the red billiard ball, which was not unlike a cricket ball. She bounced it lightly in her hand: "Here - catch!"

She flung the ball at him, an easy throw and instinctively he went to catch it. McKendry demonstrated his skills at boxing with a quick left hook and the Austro-Hungarian went down.

Charlotte recovered the dropped revolver off the floor and Georgina drew her foot back to kick him.

"Nein, nein - mercy." The man was fawning pathetically, his attitude changed in an instant once he knew they had the upper hand.

McKendry knelt down and took off the man's tie to secure his hands behind his back.

Caruthers fetched their equipment from where it had been dumped on the table. He began to distribute their meagre supplies. Earnestine seemed distracted, looking everywhere but at Pieter, so Georgina took the medium kit bag and glanced inside at the binoculars, batteries, map, spare button and saw, down at the bottom nestling with the Kendal Mint Cake, a single bullet. She took it out: they could have used this to kill the Graf when they were in the underground station. Again her Arthur was denied justice.

"We must get after the Graf," said Earnestine.

"We will," said McKendry.

"Yes," said Earnestine, "we all will."

Caruthers had kept the rifle for himself.

"It's empty," Charlotte said, and she checked the revolver the Vögte had dropped. "So is this."

"That's why my brother and this wretch didn't kill us," said Pieter, looking down at the miserable servant. "I no longer want you in my service."

"When the Graf has conquered the world, I shall make you my servant."

"I think not."

McKendry stood up: "I'll have the revolver, Miss."

"It's empty," said Charlotte.

"Here," said Georgina and she held up the brass cylinder with its polished point.

Charlotte took the round: "That a .303, I need a .455."

"Revolver, Miss," said McKendry.

"I found it," Charlotte replied.

"Lottie!" said Earnestine, "play nicely."

Charlotte frowned and handed the revolver over to the Lieutenant. He flipped open the chamber and checked.

Charlotte made a face as the man realised that the .303 round was useless. She handed it to the Captain instead, who pushed it into the magazine.

"The Graf will be going for the roof," said Prince Pieter, "there's a Zeppelin berthed there."

"You keep an eye on him," said Caruthers, nodding to the captured Vögte.

"Ja," said Pieter, "he is my responsibility."

The others fell into line: Caruthers in front, then Earnestine, Georgina and Charlotte with McKendry to bring up the rear. They were one short, Georgina knew, and the pain was almost overwhelming, but Georgina wanted justice.

"Right," said Caruthers. "Best foot forward."

## Miss Charlotte

They were too late.

When they reached the roof, the Zeppelin had already cleared the small set of steps that had led to the gondola section. Now they went nowhere. The massive Zeppelin dwarfed the flat space and the noise from its rotors was deafening. In the airship's doorway, the Graf saw them, their eyes met. They looked at each other over the distance from ground to air, and he laughed.

"Auf Wiedersehen, mein Liebchen!" he shouted.

Behind him in the gondola, untoten troops, complete with parachutes, lurched and threatened, but they were held at bay by the galvanic device in their master's hand. At the touch of a button the Graf could unleash them anywhere in London, England or the World.

"Only one bullet," Caruthers said. He checked the rifle, brought home the bolt and levelled it.

The Graf spotted the danger and stepped back disappearing from sight.

Caruthers swore: "Damn."

"He'll go to the bridge," said Charlotte. The Zeppelin was turning, coming about into the wind to face them. "You'll get one chance."

Caruthers sighted and then hesitated: "Who's the best shot? McKendry, you've been a trapper."

Earnestine spoke: "Charlotte is the best shot."

Caruthers frowned at her, saw her determined expression, and then, decision made, he brought the Lee-Enfield smartly up to the present arms posture.

"Ma'am," he said.

McKendry started to object: "You-"

"Let her do it," Earnestine insisted.

Charlotte took the weapon from Caruthers, pushed the butt tight into her shoulder and checked the precious round was loaded correctly.

Georgina fished in Earnestine's medium kit bag and pulled out a pair of binoculars. She gave them to Caruthers.

The Captain looked, scanning along the gondola: "He's not there yet."

Charlotte readied herself, taking deep breaths.

"I think... yes, front window, that's him."

Charlotte levelled the Lee-Enfield. Along the barrel, she could see the Graf enter the bridge. Zala gesticulated to the pilot as the Zeppelin rose.

"Take your time," said Caruthers as he focussed through the binoculars.

Charlotte centred the fore sight above the Graf's dark beard and then let what she saw fall snuggly into the 'V' of the back sight. The distant Union Flags on far off buildings blew to the left, but the Eagle of the Austro-Hungarians fluttered with the downdraft of the airship's rotors. She was firing up, an increasing angle, and the cabin containing the target was rotating as airship continued turning clockwise. The Graf was framed in the slanting window, the glass would refract the light, so she needed to compensate for that distortion as well. All these

418

elements she removed instinctively like dismantling a rifle or unpicking yet again another hopeless piece of embroidery.

But it was easier without a cadet reaching around her to show her what to do.

She aimed true.

The Graff stepped to one side.

She could still see him, his braid around his right arm, but not his chest or head. She could hit him, she was sure of it, but it would be a wound only. She needed a chest or head shot to be sure.

"It's not a clear shot," said Caruthers.

Charlotte lowered the rifle.

There was the pilot, she could see him, but killing him would do no good: the Graf knew how to fly a Zeppelin.

"Go for the main section," McKendry said. "There's hydrogen there, it'll explode."

"We fired a repeating gun into it with a whole box of ammunition and it did nothing," Georgina said.

Earnestine agreed: "The superstructure protects it. I had to fire a Verey pistol inside before I got one to explode."

"Crikey," said Caruthers.

"Perhaps-" McKendry began, reaching for the rifle.

"Let her do it," said Earnestine.

Charlotte ignored them.

She brought the gun back up, aimed.

The Zeppelin was turning, it was now or never, but Graf wasn't stepping into view. It was hopeless... unless... yes. She shifted, aimed lower, let the rifle move with the great behemoth.

McKendry spoke: "Perhaps-"

"Shhh," said Earnestine and Georgina together.

Squeeze... so gently, so very gently.

She saw the wood splinter with the shot.

"You missed," said McKendry. "He's still alive."

"No, she didn't," said Caruthers, still holding the binoculars up. "She hit that control box."

"Good shot, Charlotte," Earnestine said.

"Yes, Lottie," said Georgina. "Thank you."

"Oh my word..." said Caruthers. "It's..."

"Can I see?" Charlotte asked. "Can I see? Can I see, please?"

"It's not for a lady," Caruthers replied.

"I'm not a la-"

"Charlotte," said Earnestine, "be quiet."

Above her, Charlotte imagined she heard the Graff shouting as his untoten army turned on him, tearing him limb from limb.

"He's done for," said Caruthers, finally and he lowered the binoculars, "so's the pilot."

The airship rose, caught the wind and slalomed away towards Covent Garden. They stood for a long time watching it until the black shape was swallowed by the dark clouds.

"A ghost Zeppelin," said Caruthers. "It'll wander the skies like the Flying Dutchman."

"Until it crashes to the ground," said Charlotte.

"Perhaps," said Earnestine, "we should go in out of the rain."

# EPILOGUE

## Miss Deering-Dolittle

It rained, which was appropriate for both England and a funeral, and a patch of umbrellas opened like a ring of mushrooms as the men appeared, holding the thin shields above the sisters.

Everyone was all in black and the leafless trees were like skeletal hands reaching from the ground. The overcast sky was grey and forbidding. The small group, led by the three sisters, came from the church and gathered by the graveside.

Earnestine shuddered; Georgina, dressed in bombazine fabric with crepe and a widow's cap, cried, softly, but she was allowed to, and Charlotte looked serious.

When his three Gentlemen Adventurers had not returned, Major Dan had organised a makeshift militia and they had marshalled in time to deal with the few, the very few untoten who had escaped the flood. The Graf's great army had been washed into the Thames and out to sea. There had been no reports of Zala himself or his Zeppelin. The wind had been easterly; he must be floating over Mongolia by now, Earnestine thought. Prince Pieter had ordered Mordant's unnatural science to be destroyed and he had promised to oversee the process himself. All the notes would be burnt.

And Pieter - beautiful Pieter - himself had his duty: Russia beckoned. He was a minor European Royal, but Royalty had their responsibilities. One only had to consider Queen Victoria herself. If he married one of the daughters of Tsar Nicolas II, Olga, Tatiana or Maria, then the Royal bloodlines would be folded back towards the European dynasties. One day, perhaps even a direct issue of Pieter, an Austro-Hungarian-Saxe-Coburg-Romanov child, would inherit the thrones of the British Empire, the

Russian Empire and the German Empire along with thrones in Spain and Brazil: three quarters of the world's land. There would be peace, a wonderful glorious peace that would mark the coming twentieth century out as a golden age unblemished by the taint of war.

What was the happiness of two people compared to that?

They were near each other now.

"You have your duty," she said.

"Ja."

Earnestine stepped forward, wanting to hold him and kiss him, but they moved apart and stood on either side of the yawning gulf of the freshly dug grave.

## Mrs Arthur Merryweather

As her dear Arthur was carried into the church on the shoulders of his colleagues, Caruthers and McKendry at the front, the Vicar had read the traditional announcement.

"I am the resurrection and the life, saith the Lord: he that believeth in me, though he were dead, yet shall he live: and whosoever liveth and believeth in me shall never die."

No-one had appreciated the words, so desperately ironic and terrible.

He'd gone on: "worms destroy this body" until finally "the Lord taketh away".

It had been a lovely service, everyone had said so as they left the church, so it must have been. Georgina had a few handkerchiefs embroidered 'APM' and she'd used most of them already. Caruthers had spoken about Arthur's bravery, his actions and awards, and his love for poor Georgina. Their life together had been cruelly cut short, everyone said - so short, so sad, so sorry.

But she had enjoyed the precious little time they'd shared.

The reading had been from Corinthians: "...risen from the dead, and become the first-fruits of them that slept. For since by man came death, by man came also the resurrection of the dead..."

She saw his ruined face as if it were in front of her, and she had seen that fleeting expression of understanding and forgiveness.

The Vicar droned on: "...what advantageth it me, if the dead rise not?"

But she would not remember that, or if she did it would be in cold, dark moments; instead, in an act of will that Earnestine's example had taught her, she would remember him alive.

"...but some man will say, How are the dead raised up?"

They are raised up, she thought, in our memories and it was her choice whether she should remember his death or his precious, wonderful life. This was more powerful than any monstrous apparatus born of Unnatural Philosophy and Galvanic processes.

"...so also is the resurrection of the dead: It is sown in corruption; it is raised..."

She would live, she thought, a good life, a life dedicated to her lost husband and she would make him proud.

And then they went to the grave, outside in the persistent, dreary rain.

"Man that is born of a woman hath but a short time to live, and is full of misery. He cometh up, and is cut down, like a flower; he fleeth as it were a shadow, and never continueth in one stay."

But he was not full of misery. Certainly not that one night, and there were other moments too when she thought back across London, the seaside, under the sea, on the doomed ship *Mary*, on the train through Europe, on the mountain, in the school, when he stuttered in the hut and when he'd appeared out of the snow to save her. She saw him smiling, always a smile - for her.

The Vicar, his balding head glistening with the rain, read on in a muttering voice: "In the midst of life we are in death..."

She would remember his life and lock it away in her heart.

"...the soul of our dear brother here departed, we therefore commit his body to the ground; earth to earth, ashes to ashes, dust to dust; in sure and certain hope of the Resurrection-"

Georgina flinched at the mention of resurrection. For a moment the sisters were back underground facing the unspeakable horror of it all.

The priest, oblivious, droned on: "...to eternal life, through our Lord Jesus Christ; who shall change our vile body, that it may be like unto his glorious body, according to the mighty working, whereby he is able to subdue all things to himself."

"Present... fire!"

The soldiers of the late Captain Merryweather's regiment raised the weapons and fired a volley, the sound muffled in the wet air. The bolts clanged back and forth. It was as if the burial itself was a re-enactment of the battle they'd fought below.

"Fire!"

In her mind's eye, Georgina saw those terrible creatures lumbering towards them again.

"Fire!"

The third volley jolted her back to the present and she was standing in the graveyard again.

The funeral was done.

The dead lying all around them stayed in their graves and the horrors were only in their minds.

Uncle Jeremiah patted her hand to comfort her, before he shook his head sadly and made his way to his carriage. Some lady in a burgundy dress and a hat with a black veil opened it for him, but Georgina's eyesight had misted over again. The officers came next and mumbled some condolences, words oft-repeated by soldiers used to losing comrades. Georgina heard none of it. Eventually, the troops armed with umbrellas broke formation and made their sorry way down the path.

The rain too had deserted them.

Finally, even her sisters took a few steps back to leave her by the graveside. In that oak box, once bedecked with a Union Flag, but now only spattered with handfuls of mud and earth, was her husband. She knew she should feel something, but it was as if she had been killed and her body merely carried on as a facsimile. Like an untoten.

## Miss Charlotte

"You can cry if you want," said Earnestine.

"No," said Georgina.

Standing at a respectful distance was a contingent of Europeans gathered in a knot around Prince Pieter. As they passed, the Prince bowed to each in turn.

"Fräulein Charlotte."

"Your Royal Highness."

"Frau Merryweather."

"Your Royal Highness."

"Fräulein... Derring-Do?"

"Miss Deering-Dolittle," Earnestine said.

"Miss."

He clicked his heels and moved on, walking slowly towards the open iron gateway.

"Ness?"

"Gina?"

"Go to him."

"Gina, it's-"

"Ness, go to him."

Earnestine picked her way carefully over the graves and as she approached, Pieter came forward until it was just the two of them surrounded by stone angels. The Austro-Hungarian stepped forward and took her in his arms.

"Lawks! She's kissing him," said Charlotte.

"Disgusting," said Georgina, "if anyone sees..."

"What's the harm?"

"Charlotte! He's to be engaged to another woman, so that activity makes our sister a loose woman."

"But... you're as bad as Ness."

Georgina considered for a moment: "Thank you."

Charlotte made a noise and leaned closer to try and catch what the Prince was saying.

"Goodbye, mein... my love."

Crown Prince Pieter held out his hand and Earnestine took it. He held her grip far longer than was seemly, before he clicked his heels and bowed formally, taking her hand higher and kissing it for far longer than was decent.

And then he was gone.

Earnestine seemed only vaguely aware that time was passing as her sisters joined her.

Georgina plucked a small embroidered handkerchief from her handbag and passed it to Earnestine.

"Here," she said.

Earnestine looked down at the white cotton square fluttering like a flag in the breeze.

"What's that for?" Earnestine asked, "there's nothing in my eye."

Georgina's bag snapped shut: "Of course not."

"It's not back to school, is it?" Charlotte asked.

"No," Earnestine said, "it's Georgina's decision, but I think that the Derring-Dos would-"

"Ness," Georgina interrupted, "I'd rather you were in charge."

"Are you sure?"

"Yes."

"In that case, as we've just saved the British Empire, I think the least they can do is finance a little expedition up the river."

Charlotte jumped: "Spiffing!"

"Charlotte, although Mrs Merryweather and I agree with your sentiments, perhaps a little more decorum please."

"One for all," said Charlotte and she put out her hand.

"And all for one?" said Georgina, and she added her own.

The two girls looked expectantly at Earnestine.

"An adventure?" Earnestine said.

Come on, come on, Charlotte prayed, and then her sister, Ness, added her own hand to the clutch and summed it up in a word.

"Abso - bally - lutely!"

*The End*

*will return in the*

**Year of the Chrononauts**

**David Wake** is a writer, director and technical stage-manager and has an MA in Writing from Birmingham City University. He's been part of SF fandom for many years and published this book to mark being a Guest of Honour at ArmadaCon.

Thank you for buying and reading *The Derring-Do Club and the Empire of the Dead*. If you liked this novel, please take a few moments from your own adventures to write a review and help spread the word.

For more information, and to join the mailing list for news of forthcoming releases, see www.davidwake.com.

**Many thanks to:-**

Dawn Abigail, Roy Abigail, Apple, ArmadaCon, Sarah Bartlett, Bridget Bradshaw, Andy Conway, Dave Gullen, Charlie Harry, Pow-wow, Jessica Rydill, Smuzz and Marta Soldevilla.

Cover art by Smuzz: www.smuzz.org.uk.

Evil forces threaten festive season and only Carol Christmas can save the day...

A grim fairy tale told as a children's book, but perhaps not for children at all.

––––––––

*"Genuinely charming..."*

*"You're an odd person."*

*"You've woven all our fears about the commercial side of Xmas into a very compelling Twilight of the Gods drama. Beautiful."*

*"Yes. It's amazing. Click publish before someone gets you to water it down."*

––––––––

**A tonic for the Xmas Spirit**

This novella is available as an ebook and paperback

In a world where phones are more intelligent than humans, but are still treated as mere fashion accessories, one particular piece of plastic lies helpless as its owner is about to be murdered...

The phone tells its own story as events build to a climactic battle that will decide the fate of augmented, virtual and real worlds.

———

*"Excellent novel – by turns strikingly original, laugh-out-loud funny and thought provoking."*

*"Want to read it again soon..."*

*"A thoughtful, tense and funny look at a future that seems to be already upon us."*

———

This novel is available as an ebook and a paperback.

In the near future, no-one's thoughts are their own and privacy is a thing of the past. Everyone shares their lives in the global social media network and pre-meditated crime is no longer possible.

So when Detective Oliver Braddon finds a dead body, the victim of a planned murder, he is plunged into a dangerous investigation, and forced to use unorthodox means, as he tracks down a murderer, who can kill without thinking.

———

*Published Easter 2014*

———

This novel is available as an ebook and a paperback.